BAZAAR

MILES JOYNER

This is a work of fiction. Names, characters, places, and incidents are products of the author's imagination or are used fictitiously and are not to be construed as real. Any resemblance to actual events, locations, organizations, or persons, living or dead, is entirely coincidental.

World Castle Publishing, LLC
Pensacola, Florida
Copyright © 2025 Miles Joyner
Hardback ISBN: 9798305201901
Paperback ISBN: 9798891263369
eBook ISBN: 9798891263178
First Edition World Castle Publishing, LLC, March 25, 2025
http://www.worldcastlepublishing.com

Cover: Krystal Penney
Editor: Karen Fuller

ACKNOWLEDGEMENTS

I first have to acknowledge my parents for fostering an environment for me to pursue creativity at a young age, especially my mother Amri, who convinced me to write novels instead of spending every paycheck on micro-budget films shot guerrilla style in the streets of Montgomery County. I also greatly appreciate my writing mentor, J.M. Clark, screenwriter Tess WS, and all the members of Novels in Progress DC for their constructive feedback in supporting their fellow writer. None of my progress as a storyteller would have been possible without the contributions from my lifelong friends Zach Bitango and Randy Louis. I also have to acknowledge my close friend and tactical consultant, U.S. Navy veteran Bruce Green, a former master-at-arms who did in all real life what I attempted to write in fiction. Finally, I must acknowledge Karen Fuller for editing my book and taking a chance on my debut work.

CHAPTER 1

The only lighting inside the dark room was a couple of red LED lamps. They didn't bother the eyesight of eighteen-year-old Aaron Williams, who was wide-eyed in fascination at his Ultramaker XT 3D printer going to work. The last of the white filament flew out the extruder onto the print bed, and he couldn't have felt any more like a father watching his wife through the glass, holding their newborn baby.

He reached onto the platform and gripped his new plastic handgun that shot real, metal bullets. Like its predecessors, the Mini Talon had been banned from all sites hosting 3-D printing design files. However, Aaron was able to obtain it through torrents online, and now he had the opportunity to add it to his family of firearms that lay around the room, including an assault rifle with a lower receiver printed with the same material. But unlike the rest of its siblings, the MT wouldn't be another one of Aaron's toys to fire off rounds at tree targets deep in the woods. Some of the former models exploded on tests from the videos Aaron watched online, but he was confident the new version would not fail to take out his intended target in a few days with its untraceable ballistics.

Danny would be his escape. The son of a local pho restaurant owner was Aaron's only friend outside the digital realm. Danny Phat took very little in life seriously, but for all the flaws, he knew every back road of the entire DC, Maryland, Virginia area. He could whip his raggedy-ass decade-old Nissan Altima pretty well. Either way, Aaron had no driver's license and he wouldn't risk getting pulled over or traced to a rideshare app.

The young 21st-century gunsmith couldn't take his eyes

off his latest creation. He loaded a magazine, cocked the weapon, and listened satisfyingly to the crisp click. It blew Aaron's mind to think the ammunition clip had fit perfectly into a gun made from the same material as his storage cabinet.

He was ready to test the gun. Would it fire smoothly? He had two days to test it and find out before he had to execute his assigned job.

August 20th, 2024. 1:30 AM.
Washington, D.C.

Liquor-induced shrieks and screams of laughter carried over the bass thumps throughout a bumping Adams Morgan, the corridor of D.C. that served as one of the city's nightlife hot spots. Neon lights shined on the designer-brand, clean-cut, modern-day yuppies who strut out of the nightclubs and the plaid-shirt bearded hipsters who stumbled out of the brewing taverns. A lot were on their nights off from studying, but the cost of drinks was far higher than college town prices so the professional class of everyone from policy aides to software engineers got just as wasted. Regardless of education or socioeconomic background, many women looked for their best friend whom they lost in the partying, and many male counterparts hoped to be that lucky dude they might have run off with.

Isaiah knew that's what his best friend Adamu Attah wanted to be at that moment. But it was past Last Call, and Isaiah had put pressure on him for them to start heading back to their university dorms. He could tell Adamu didn't get it. The youngest patriarch of the politically rich Attah family from Nigeria had no issues getting cheeks back home, but American girls apparently weren't as impressed with his super-forward approach. Isaiah tried to explain this to Adamu outside the Astro Lounge on 18th Street with neither a female around his arm nor a single new contact in his phone, but before he could bother to listen, a tipsy trio of curvy young women strolled out after him and caught his eye. Long braids, luscious shapes formed from their Lycra dresses, flawless different shades of ebony skin. Isaiah just knew Adamu would try again.

"AY!" The belles reluctantly turned toward the source of the attempt at a mating call. "Where we goin' tonight?"

"Nowhere that involves ugly!" The tallest out of the three formed a smirk under her glasses, her two graduate degrees having only enhanced a life's worth of sharp rebuttals to catcalling in her neighborhood. She laughed, and the pack began to leave the scene. No different than a kid eyeing the milk chocolate bar right before checkout, Isaiah knew Adamu just couldn't take no for an answer. The shorter one with the most voluptuous figure became the unlucky winner to have her hand grabbed without permission.

"C'mon mami, ditch these bitches—" Adamu was snatched mid-sentence by a bouncer whose neck rolls formed a poop emoji and got tossed like a rag doll into the hands of Isaiah a few feet away.

"Dumbass!" screamed the short one as the three marched off down the street.

"I'm royalty, hoes! Some other BITCH will get blessed with this big dick tonight!"

"HEY!" The head of Astro Lounge security had enough. So had Isaiah.

"I'm so sorry, sir, he's drunk."

"Get him the fuck outta here before I break his jaw."

"Yes, sir. Again, I'm sorry!"

The situation was all too familiar to Isaiah. Except now, instead of guiding a destroyed Adamu down the Terrapin-flagged residential streets of College Park, Maryland, from one frat house to another, they had graduated to bar hopping in D.C., where the young bachelor had been able to finally drink legally for the past ninety minutes.

"Sometimes you're a freaking embarrassment, Adamu."

"Shut the hell up and get an Uber. We're going to Starline."

"Starline?"

"Strip club." Adamu gulped down a wad of vomit from coming out. Isaiah looked away in disgust, but something else caught his eye as they turned the corner.

A Metrobus stop bench rested thirty yards from their position. He figured that was where they could gather themselves after such a night. He used the remainder of his stamina to finally reach the bench and slap the back of Adamu to the hard rubber as if to try to wake him up. Isaiah checked his phone. 2% battery.

"Dammit...Adamu!"

His eyes opened, barely able to comprehend where he was even at, let alone being able to give Isaiah a response.

"Your phone. Mine's about to die." Body in total slow motion, Adamu managed to tap his pockets.

"Sh-Sh-Sh-Shit" eeked out of Adamu's mouth.

"WHAT?!" Isaiah tapped his friend's pockets. "Where is it?! Or your wallet?" Another tap. Wow. Alcohol and a night of partying caused his buddy to lose track of his valuables. Unbelievable.

"The hell is wrong with you? This isn't Saint Catherines anymore!" Isaiah yelled at him, referencing their boarding school back in Victoria Island.

Vomit rose through his esophagus, except Isaiah could tell from the lump in Adamu's throat that this batch was going full projectile. Isaiah jumped out of the way right in time for only a chunk to get on his shoes. The rest of Adamu's day's intake became a red-yellow puddle at the side of the bench. The gross site, as well as the realization that their options were fading, prompted Isaiah to throw his fist and scream a few "fucks" to himself. He looked up at the bus stop sign and saw that the 92 bus had a destination of SHAW-Howard, a Metro station. Maybe the route was their best bet if the bus got there within fifteen minutes and they made the last train, figured Isaiah as he composed himself.

He looked away, and something else caught his eye. Several blocks down Marion Street walked a hooded figure. Not too brisk, but certainly with purpose right toward their position. Isaiah squinted, and the street lamps revealed a teenager in a dark blue hoodie with jeans. The getup, time of night, and even the location were enough for Isaiah's nerves to merge into his skin. Yeah, they were in the "nice part" of D.C., but Isaiah's classmates had been robbed on campus, so it could happen anywhere. The young male got closer. When he was thirty feet away, Isaiah was still unsure of how to react or whether to react at all. The feeling might have been what his student counselor emphasized as overthinking.

"Com'on now." Shifting from foot to foot, Isaiah sunk his hands deep into his pockets, a reflex move he made whenever he was nervous. At the same time, he heard his parents' judgmental biases about inner-city youth, fighting to stave off his own similar thoughts.

"Hey, bro," the figure said once he reached the bus stop. They traded 'sup' nods. Isaiah's was way more reserved. "My phone's dead. You got the time?"

"Mine's dead, too. Sorry."

"Hate when that happens out of nowhere." Isaiah started to ease up to the source of the voice that seemed extra friendly with a hint of anxiety. The jitters he noticed from the kid were probably from him panicking over his phone being dead, figured Isaiah. Something he clearly could relate to, given his own situation. The original image shaped in his head was starting to look too judgemental. The teenager looked at Adamu who hung over the bench, motionless and barely conscious. "I'd ask him, but he looks done."

"Yeah, he lost his at the club. Long night." Isaiah gandered at his friend draped over the bench, now sharing sympathy with his comrade.

"Ah, so THAT'S why the phone is dead. Had it out the whole time booking them females. Can't even be mad at him."

"Not even," laughed Isaiah, trying to shake off whatever anxiety he had left.

"Word, y'all heading to Howard?"

"Nah. We go to Maryland. Trying to figure out a way back, actually."

"Shit, I'm in the same position. Know where the closest metro is? Wonder if we can make the last train..."

The sign, Isaiah remembered. They had to just keep walking down Marion."Yeah, I think—" POP POP. The friend of the target was not getting up from the two .380 caliber bullets that were just blasted through his skull with the utmost precision and professionalism. Aaron didn't waste a beat as he tactically shifted the open sights of his plastic 3-D printed pistol to a groggy Adamu struggling to get his words out. "Please," he cried. "I-I don't have my wallet, but I can give you anything. I'm rich as fuck I swear—" POP. Three total gunshots. The first one might have caught attention, but the second one was supposed to send any potential eyewitnesses running. At least, that's what he learned from observing the few shootings he witnessed around his way. Aaron stowed the pistol away in his waistband holster. He checked the surroundings for the fifth time that night. There was no sign of anybody. He picked the right spot and predicted Adamu's every move since the club perfectly. But where the hell was Danny? His Altima was supposed to be turning that corner before the first shot. VROOM. SCREECH. There it was. Revved and making too much damn noise as it peeled from an alleyway to scoop Aaron. The passenger door flew open, and Aaron jumped in. They took off before any sirens could be heard.

"Woo!" yelled Danny as he whipped around another corner. The two dressed pretty similar but everything Danny did was exaggerated in an attempt to blend into the projects they were heading back to. Everything from the Commander's fitted hat to his Foamposite pressed against the gas pedal contrasted the plainer attire of Aaron, who didn't care at all about the brands his former classmates worshipped on a daily basis.

"Fool you a BEAST!"

Aaron needed a moment to gather himself. Despite his success so far, taking someone's life for the first time was a difficult realization to settle into. Let alone two lives. His parents never intended to raise a killer. His dyslexia limited the options the school offered. Danny's advice about selling drugs or sketchy affiliate marketing plans wasn't a solution either. He knew what would end up to him down that familiar path. He also took note of how naive Danny's hype was in the latest additions to the district's homicide rate.

"You were late" was the first thing out of Aaron's mouth.

"Chill, fam. Traffic around the corner was O-C. Stop acting like I ain't do my job." Aaron's eyes just rolled in response. Maybe if it was another debate at Danny's spot about Harden Vs. Curry over some french fries drenched in mambo sauce, he'd entertain the bickering. But not after carrying out his first homicide. He wanted silence.

"But yeah, slim, you did the damn thing. How much did those lames have anyways? Real live starving in this bitch." Aaron's eyes widened. Unbeknownst to Danny, Aaron was just supposed to make it only look like a robbery.

"Shit, I forgot to run through their pockets."

"The fuck you mean forgot? Nigga what was the whole point of tonight?"

"I still got you...and I told you not to use that word around me."

"Imma call you a whole lot of other things if you don't get my bread, muh fucka. Fuck type shit you think this is —"

"DANNY! SHUT THE HELL UP! Please." Aaron didn't yell often, but the authentic rage in his voice shut down whatever gangsta persona Danny was going for. By then, Aaron knew Danny finally realized it wasn't another discussion about the NBA playoffs.

"Just get us to P-G," Aaron said. P-G was the county of their home right outside the nation's capital, Prince George's. "Stop somewhere, and I'll cover, but I can't talk right now." Nothing but the sound of road bumps and night traffic until Danny began to piece together a hint as to what the real motivation for that night had been.

"Aaron." Danny had to pause for a moment. "Are you saying this was a hit?" Aaron didn't care to answer Danny's curiosity. He stared at the night-lit city outside the car window. He had just clocked out, and there was no desire to talk about work. The murder of Adamu happened two hours after midnight, meaning his death landed on the date Aaron had bet on the assassination market called the Bazaar.

CHAPTER 2

Yemi arrived at the metro station and was greeted by the same familiar good-morning smell of cannabis and urine that marked his commute every day. The bright spot was that he didn't have to wait long as the Green Line train was already pulling up to the platform. He was still several stops from L'Enfant Plaza, where he would transfer to the Silver when he received an incoming call.

"You get my text?" asked Yemi immediately once he slid the green phone icon.

"File on all four of them will be ready by the time you get off," the voice of a young woman replied to him. Yemi heard a loud slap, like the sound of two kitchen mits slamming together, while he spotted a fast blur of motion from the side of his face. He took notice of an urban professional in headphones tensed up like something had just hit the stomach area of his purple Ralph Lauren polo. Next to him, retracting his arm into his body, was a man with a sloppy white turban complimenting his disheveled, mostly white amalgamation of a robe and loose shirt plus pants combo. The man was in some type of a trance, muttering a language Yemi had never heard before, but Yemi didn't need to make sense of anything he was saying to realize he had just hit the kid wearing headphones.

"Yemi?" asked the woman over the phone.

"Do you know him?" Yemi asked the young man. He shook his head 'no.'

"Know who? What are you talking about?"

"Not you," Yemi said back to his sister. The man in the white rose out of the seat he had just sat in and started a dazed shuffle to Yemi's side of the car. His motion was somewhere between a religious praise dancer and a drunk Usher performance. He took a step toward Yemi and got within a couple of feet of him, his back against the Metro Map. He was in a position quite similar to when he struck the man in headphones.

"One sec, Karen."

"Yemi—." He dropped the call. The Libyan tribal rebel reject was over six foot, and while maybe not athletic, he wasn't crystal meth skinny either. Yemi launched out of his seat.

"Back up. Now." His new adversary immediately took some steps back while he muttered in his inaudible language.

"Sit the fuck down," Yemi continued to order him. The man did as he was told, but Yemi could tell even in his delusional state, he was still full of enough pride to continue antagonizing his more diesel foe. The man removed something from his pocket. It was bright orange, and Yemi thought it could've been anywhere from a bright-colored flashlight to a travel-sized container of detergent. But a blade soon protruded from its end, and Yemi recognized it as a boxcutter from Home Depot.

The man three feet across from him started to slice the air and make threatening gestures toward Yemi. Still talking in his faux foreign language, it looked like a character from a 1970s kung fu flick getting ready to strike his opponent but in a seated position. Yemi kept his eyes glued on the threat. The train suddenly stopped.

"There is a medical emergency on the Hyattsville Crossing Platform," the conductor voiced over the intercom. "We've been told to hold." There was about to be a medical emergency right here, Yemi thought. The only question was who would be leaving this train car on an EMT's gurney. He was always open to his daily routine having an exciting tangent every so often, but being stuck on a Metro car engaged in a standoff with an armed man sick in the head who had already assaulted someone would be the last thing he'd want on his agenda.

The man continued to violently cut the air. Yemi had his eyes on him, but his mind was racing through the different options of action. The intercom button to alert the conductor must have been on the opposite side of the car since he didn't see it anywhere near their automatic double doors. Walking away to find another seat on that end was the smarter decision anyway. However, the savior complex was itching at him to stay put to ensure the rest of his fellow passengers were safe. No matter how much his career went in the direction of gathering intelligence instead of directly protecting the public, those instincts were still present, no matter how much Yemi tried to convince himself that he didn't care anymore.

Yemi's lack of verbal response or actions seemed to entice the man to rise back up. The passengers in rows parallel to Yemi bolted from their seats, but a young Latino family of three behind the knife-wielding man was trapped in the corner of the car. Yemi could tell the father wanted his family safe, but he could tell the man was resorting to a cowering position and wasn't aware of how to respond to active threats. Yemi knew then he had to take action.

The man in white rambled some more in his faux language. Yemi looked for openings in the man's wide, haymaker-like swipes slicing through the air, but he stayed seated. The man then turned 90 degrees and was only a couple of feet from the Latino man's toddler daughter. Yemi had seen enough.

Yemi had never taken a formal martial arts class, but he knew a kick to the back of the knee would force him to collapse. The man had barely turned ninety degrees, but Yemi had his foot planted in the middle of the man's hamstring and had the man's wrist locked in a firm grasp within a few movements. Having control of the man in white's weapon hand, Yemi used his free left to quickly grab his head through his turban and smashed the man's face into the metal bar of the Metro seat, right in front of the entire family.

"Go!" Yemi ordered to the family as he shifted his head in the left direction.

A tooth went flying from the man's mouth at the same time Yemi heard the knife drop to the floor. The loose denture didn't hit any of the family, but the mother and father of the daughter leaped out of the seat, grabbing their little girl with them to escape. Yemi used his arm to hold the top back of the man's neck, to keep him pinned against the bar, and he didn't see her flinch once. Once the family was out of the way, Yemi picked his head up and slammed the man against the bar again.

"P-p-please, brother." Yemi could finally hear English from the man's voice, even with metal pressed into his face. The voice sounded less like surrender and more like a man admitting to being a victim of his demons. "I'm just a crackhead. I'm sorry."

"Do you need help?" asked Yemi. Yemi kept the same grip on him, but he eased up a bit once he kicked away the blade.

"What kind of help?" the man pleaded. "I can't stay in the ward or any of those places, man." The train finally started to move.

"Next station," the intercom announced. "L'Enfant Plaza." Yemi patted down both sides of the man in white. No other object seemed to be on him.

"You and I are getting off at the next stop," Yemi said down to him. He looked down the car to make sure the family had made it to the opposite end of the car. They did. The man and woman faced toward the front car, but the daughter wrapped around her mother's neck stared back at Yemi to the point they even made eye contact. He focused back on the man. "I'm going to call to get you help, but I'll let you go. It's up to you if you stay." He could feel the man in white give a few heaves through his lungs. The silence provided enough of an answer for Yemi to know how to wrap up the situation. He would just text Karen an update from the platform.

It took an additional twenty minutes to get from L'Enfant Plaza to Northern Virginia on the Metro. The Tysons Corner skyline used to impress and motivate Yemi in the early days of the countless times he had taken this trip. He remembered the streets of Lagos on the tail of rapidly moving kidnapping cartels, and it's itched at him to return to the work that made him feel alive. But as he saw downtown Tysons at eight in the morning welcoming his entry, he decided he was going try to enjoy the sight of the closest thing to a mini East Coast Silicon Valley.

Whenever he entered Titus HQ, Yemi would see the same Bahamian security guard, Orlando, almost every morning. Yemi had noticed that Orlando was never the one responsible for watching the baggage scanner.

"Peas n' rice, man. Been trying to tell you," snickered Orlando as he took Yemi's laptop bag from the conveyor belt. "Jollof by itself just doesn't cut it. You gotta put some protein in there to give it any taste." Yemi chuckled as he went through the body scanner. Orlando had dragged on this 'debate' for weeks. And by debate, it was mostly just the security guard trying to assert West Indian cultural superiority over the motherland.

"Not even in the mood today." He grabbed his stuff. "Let's just admit we'd both rather be back home."

"Shit. I hear you on that."

Police were baffled by the double murder on Marion Street. The first twelve hours of it was a robbery gone awry after nothing was found on the second victim. By the following day, it was revealed that Astro Lounge handed over Adamu's iPhone 15 and the wallet found in the bathroom by one of the bouncers. That made two bodies, two wallets, two phones, three bullets, and no motive or leads. Adamu clearly got into trouble that night, yet all trails to any possible suspect were cold. But even though Yemi may not have identified the killer, he knew the fertile ground in which the roots of the murder were planted in. Yemi was 100% certain it was the first major homicide in the United States to be tied to Bazaar.tor, a marketplace on the dark web that listed bids for predicted death dates to various figures ranging from a conservative politician caught in a massage parlor after lobbying against prostitution to liberal pop stars who pissed off the wrong tax bracket. Such concepts were nothing but academic thesis until the Adamu Attah killing.

Yemi's office at Titus didn't differ much at all from his studio apartment. Plain, no attempt to "reflect his personality," just the tools to get his job done. Multiple computer monitors revealed months of intense research. Some carry-out containers littered the desks and a trash bin.

Yemi had seen the first half of Fight Club, but he knew it was a privilege to even be able to clock into a guaranteed income. His father always reminded the two children about how their upper-middle-class upbringing in Rockville, Maryland, was a far cry from the poverty-stricken Niger Delta he had grown up in. Yemi's co-workers were friendly people for the most part. Kenny Simmons, the new junior consultant who had been promoted from intern, pushed the limit sometimes with his Lion King references and other stereotypical African jibes. Kenny and Jacob, the other junior, were the Black/Asian Beavis & Butthead of the Titus Strategic Development wing.

A couple of knocks on the door, and Yemi already knew who it was. The 25-year-old walked into Yemi's space without any permission. Kenny gandered at the computer monitors, seeing the Bazaar lists.

"The Daily Attack, huh?" Some of the opened tabs were somewhat on the sensational side of headlines. As Yemi had come to find, it was only the individual renegade journalists or rogue bloggers who began to connect Adamu's murder to the Bazaar.

From Kenny's attitude, it seemed he had the same assertion about their credibility the mainstream outlets did.

"Fake news like shit." Yemi rolled his eyes at the kid's voluntary ignorance and continued to work. Kenny looked around at the room's decor. "Didn't you say you've been here for almost a year? Why does it feel like a cell block with wifi in here?"

"Can I help you with something, Kenny?" Yemi was not easy to offend and he didn't even bat an eye from gathering his documents together. But he wasn't going to let Kenny get away with throwing zingers freely on a day that important.

"Oh nah, nah. I'm just saying..." Kenny backtracked, knowing he had come close to crossing that line. "I'm just saying we're the same breed, brother. Driven. No days off in this corporate jungle. Feel me?"

In Yemi's eyes, those types of statements with empty ambition didn't warrant a response. He continued to get ready for the presentation. Kenny saw an ID badge with a 'Raptor' logo next to one of the computers. He took notice of the logo, the face of a hawk staring right at him.

"Never understood that."

"What?"

"Raptor. Why didn't your sister call it 'Falcon' or 'Eagle Security' or something if she wanted that logo."

"Raptor also means a bird of prey. You know, the thing velociraptors evolved into."

"Oh, right... Where did she get the capital anyway?"

"Investors." Yemi kept it brief in answering the shallow questions.

"You finally got enough people to believe that you're a prince after all those e-mails?" Kenny smirked as Yemi stopped his work in motion. The joyous smile on the naive kid faded as Yemi looked up, his eyes piercing through Kenny's soul. He crossed the line. Big time. Yemi knew that Kenny knew he wouldn't be able to take on the older Yemi in a mental OR physical battle. "Hey, sorry, I didn't mean—"

"Get your clowning ass out of my office," Yemi scoffed with laughter. A visibly shaken Kenny pretended to laugh along with the returned prank, but Yemi could sense it was hard for Kenny to hide the fear that was generated in him for those few seconds.

"Uhm, uhm. You getting breakfast?"

"Yeah, just give me a second."

———

"It's able to avoid prosecution from law enforcement because, in all legal terms, it's still just a prediction market. Now, given the proximity of so many international V.I.Ps, I predict the Washington, D.C. area to be one of the top 5 global cities that will be impacted by the Bazaar along with cities like New York, Istanbul, Hong Kong, and Dubai," Yemi quipped in the dark room only lit up by the PowerPoint. It switched to the next slide, a heavily zoomed-in graphic of Adamu's Bazaar listing. "I believe the murder of Adamu Attah over the weekend was linked to the marketplace."

A slide of an online news posting from the website Afrileaks.org with the big, bold headline THE ATTAH-POPCO FILES loaded up next.

"According to the popular whistleblower site, Afrileaks, when Chiedu was serving his term as an ambassador, he gave the oil company POPCO a little too much leeway in domestic policy... Initially, this pissed off the Biafra Freedom Movement, who I think put the first bid down as it seems they might not always be trying to gamble on boat raids in the Nigerian Delta. But you see..."

Click. A Venn diagram followed with several different groups that all had an interest in killing Chiedu Attah. One circle was labeled The Anat Network.

"Since two weeks ago, the economic activity of the Bazaar has multiplied twelve times more than it's ever been in its four-year existence. And over seventy percent of the new waves of income I've traced are sources connected to the Anat Network." Everybody in that conference room was familiar with the Anat Network, given that some of their friends were actively waging a covert war against their offshoots in the Middle East. Although a minority religion, Sydykism was a movement that had outpaced Islam, Christianity, and Judaism in its international growth. The followers found themselves marginalized in the nations of the dominant belief systems and what started as a resistance movement soon turned into another excuse warlords used to pacify populations into submission. Of course, the majority of Sydykists opposed the blatant terrorists such as The Anat Network, the most notorious of the fundamentalist factions. The Anat Network was a big global push to have the world run under harsh religious law and pursued an aggressive mass internet promotion strategy. Yet despite all the social media accounts and video channels attached to their name, they proved quite adept at constantly evading capture from counter-terrorist operators.

"I'm positive they are the ones who infused capital into targeting the entire family of Chiedu. The bitcoin value on his head has tripled in just the past week. With the completion of the Attah homicide, I'm sure they see it as a new source of income."

"So this is gonna turn DC into some kind of war zone or something?" The comment came from the young Jacob, who quickly slid his Galaxy back into his pocket, wasting data on another LinkedIn flex. And not a care in the world for the data Yemi was presenting.

"DC's always been a war zone," the follow-up to Yemi's answer was senior consultant Kirk Fitzgerald.

"Just this time it's not in Southeast," remarked Kenny next

to Jacob.

"Or Congress," added Kirk. The last statement spurred some obligatory chuckles from the rest of the group his age. Kirk nodded for his colleague Yemi to continue.

"Local groups with connections overseas may get orders from a superior to ensure that a prediction goes through. This creates an ample opportunity for specially trained private security teams to offer local protection for 24 hours on dates our research point to being the highest value."

Kirk clapped first, and a low-scale applause filled the room of 8. Even if everyone didn't pay full attention, it was the future direction of the company, at least for Kirk's division.

"Lights, Jacob." Kirk caught the nephew of his supervisor on the phone. If only H-R could see the brat whom they gave the position over one of his far more qualified Marine Corps buddies, he wondered... The embarrassed Jacob quickly abided and hit the switch.

"Mind-blowing stuff, Yemi. Really. I think I've heard enough to take this to the next level... Does anybody have any further questions for Mr. Uzunma?"

"Nope."

"No. Great presentation, Yemi."

"Good. I should have something in everyone's inbox by tomorrow morning," stated Kirk. The meeting was adjourned.

Tysons, Virginia. A model for what an "edge city" was supposed to be of skyscrapers, foot traffic, and accessibility. Not even fifty years prior, Tysons Corner was a parking lot added to farmland. The checks from the politically-tied bureaucrats twenty miles away had turned it into the hub of activity that Yemi had belonged to for the past couple of years. He looked out the window onto the downtown business district of the suburb and realized it may be the last time he would have that view from the fourteenth floor if he stuck with his decision. The purified water out of the cone cup had never tasted so good.

An elevator ding from the center of the lobby interrupted his reflection. He heard the voice of Ted, one of the attendees of his presentation.

"I'm telling you, this place will blow your mind. They're opening up another one in Olney. I'm sure you're fucking sick of the Y by now..."

Yemi went to get another refill. He was parched today more than usual. The conversation swung from around the corner of the elevator walls. Ted was talking to Kirk, whose body language suggested he was mostly an unwilling listener throughout their dialogue. Kirk spotted Yemi, the man he probably was much more eager to speak with.

"Basketball courts, Krav maga classes, a cafe with a full keto menu... You get all that with the platinum membership. But look, just come check it out. I can get you a free day pass."

"Ted. Do your own thing, man. Just stick to this one for more than two weeks, for Christ's sake," Yemi watched Kirk shove Ted in his jelly roll beneath the chest. Ted couldn't help but laugh at his constant failure to convince Kirk of any of his lifestyle choices. "I gotta talk with Yemi. I'll Slack you within an hour."

They bumped their fists and split. Kirk nodded his head towards Yemi excitedly. It was time to take the executive protection market to a whole new sophisticated level never before seen on this side of the Western world. Kirk had already gotten a text confirming their possible first client worth millions. This murder had scared some in the high echelons of the D.C. power structure who found themselves or family members on the dark web through their private connections. The Bazaar was no longer just a subject for a Vice documentary. It was the real deal. And it created opportunities for real money on all sides of the law.

"This is what I live for, honestly," Kirk said as he slapped his comrade on the back in solidarity. "We could just be any two guys in the corner of a mall somewhere with some trade school dropouts and still land these kinds of contracts based on your research alone." Yemi smirked and nodded, not saying a word but doing his best to share in his superior's excitement. Kirk has always supported him. That fact and the current mood made the inevitable incoming news harder to deliver than it already was. Yemi needed another gulp of water before he could respond.

"But it's here. At Titus. We're connected, so inside the beltway, I think sometimes we're a subdivision of Homeland Security." A pause between them, but Kirk stayed smiling. Yemi figured his presentation was the best news his superior had heard all week.

"How's Karen?" Kirk asked. "She got a handle on things over there?"

"Yeah," chuckled Yemi. He may have had enough water, finally.

"Was she part of some 30 under 30 thing I saw online recently?"

"Yup," Yemi said. "Forbes."

"That's crazy," Kirk said as he made his way to the same five-gallon fountain. "You, though. You're a busy man yourself. And it's about to get a whole lot busier."

"The team is going to be all yours, brother."

"Huh?" Kirk jerked around from the fountain. "All mine? How is that possible when you're the reason all this is happening? Give yourself a little credit, man." Yemi could tell Kirk was reading that he didn't see the same common groove they had always shared after small victories.

"I'm sorry this is last minute. I'm going full-time at Raptor and due to unforeseen reasons, today has to be my last day." Kirk took a 180-degree turn. He wasn't even able to lift the cup of filtered water to his mouth as he tried to process the new information.

"You're starting your own squad over there, aren't you?"

"We're in totally different markets."

"That's not what I asked." Kirk stopped himself. Both he and Yemi knew taking things too personally could burn a bridge that could always be crossed in the future from either direction. "Sorry, I didn't mean—"

"Perfectly fine. Your frustration is understandable, given my timing." Yemi watched Kirk nod his head to get his focus together and finally take a sip.

"Well, it's hard to believe Titus is going begin this journey without its hardest working consultant. Nonetheless..." Kirk stuck his hand out, and Yemi gladly shook it. "I wish you and your sister the best in your endeavor."

"Thank you. I want you to know this was a very difficult decision to make. I can't imagine being where I am without our efforts." But in reality, Titus had felt like a cage, and Yemi yearned to fly again.

"I'm confident the two of you will succeed, but if anything doesn't go as planned, there will always be a spot here for you. Same with Karen." It was hard to tell whether Kirk was being genuine or if he thought Yemi was going to launch his entrepreneurial parachute only to crash land back in Titus within a year. But out of respect for his former partner, Yemi gave him an assuring head nod. Their friendship was still intact.

"We never hung out outside of this place. I have to introduce you to my family sometime. You know, if it's not too awkward, given that we're going to be competitors and all." The two shared grins. Beneath the smiles was the shared knowledge there was a better chance of balancing the national deficit than that ever happening but once again, no love was lost. "Anyways, time to go entertain some boring ass emails from the board. Take care, Yemi."

"You too, Kirk." Kirk left Yemi to finish his self-reflection at the end of that chapter for his career. He stared one more time back out at the tallest buildings in Northern Virginia. He knew someone like Kenny or Jacob looked at the same things every day, dreaming of owning it all and speeding out of the parking garage to hit I-495 in a Porsche Boxster. Such shallow ambitions, Yemi thought. They would never be a Sun Tzu or a John Boyd. They would never push the boundaries of strategic intelligence in the field of international security, blinded by their material greed. They were going to end up being another two useless cogs in the machine by the time they were his age and that was only if the taxpayer was still clueless enough to be footing their salary. He gulped the water down and tossed the cup into the recycle bin. He hoped the new venture would be able to help pay off Karen's student debt, though.

———

Unbeknownst to Kirk, the actual headquarters of Raptor was close to what he joked about being the "corner of a mall somewhere." The Greenbelt Shopping Plaza had six occupants left when Raptor moved in. There was the check cashing place, which had been the most consistent business there, having operated for twenty years straight. The International Latin market had steady, loyal local customers and managed to stay around for five years. The restaurants, though, were always changing, and another Peruvian chicken spot to add to the dozens in Prince George's County became the tenant beneath Raptor's offices. One space was vacant, having been an Ethiopian coffee shop that failed to attract any of the runoff from the nearby University of Maryland. Raptor rented out the outdated top-floor suite, converted from a tax office whose accountant passed away from a stroke a year prior to getting their first client.

Yemi had never been happier to pull into the desolate parking lot. Karen mentioned in a text that she and Jasper had narrowed the search down to four candidates for the squad positions. Jasper Kidanu was Yemi's closest friend, and it was Jasper who introduced the siblings to the potential of Bazaar.Tor for the security market in the D.C. area. Jasper's background was Ethiopia's intelligence agency, the NISS, and he came to the West side of Africa to assist Yemi in counter-terrorist operations when the Boko Haram situation was out of control. When the Titus opportunity arrived at Yemi's feet, and Karen wanted to launch Raptor, he decided to bring along Jasper to the States. It turned out the 28-year-old Karen wouldn't have even survived the first six months of entrepreneurship without the strategic expertise of Jasper. At the moment, they were just a small firm patrolling garages and warehouse facilities, but their head was above water, according to Yemi. With the new Executive Protection Team, they could finally jump ahead of the DC market with their knowledge of the Bazaar.

While the exterior wasn't dilapidated in the slightest, the inside of Raptor HQ might as well have belonged to private investigator Thomas Magnum from the 1980s. Yemi made his way through the disorganized file cabinets and peeling tables to join Karen and Jasper in the back meeting room, eating Chinese.

"There he is," said Jasper with a mouthful of lo mein. He swallowed before continuing. "The man with the plan to get us rich."

"Define rich," Yemi responded as he sat and motioned for some of the take-out. He then glanced towards Karen. "You know what, I like what your boyfriend Isaac said about money."

"Oh God." Karen shielded her face behind the chopsticks. "Don't do this, Yemi."

Jasper laughed, amused.

"Who's Isaac?"

"Old boyfriend of hers from the Wake Forest days. Rasta man. Babylon dangles the gold in our face he stole from under our feet." Jasper and Yemi laughed at Yemi's exaggerated Jamaican accent when he landed on the word "Babylon."

"Okay, right now, you're forgetting I cut your check. At least part-time," said Karen, even as she couldn't help but smile a bit at her own past.

"Nope." Yemi bit a piece of General Tsos and swallows. "Full-time as of today." The room was in shock for a brief moment at the realization Yemi quit Titus. Jasper had been trying to convince Yemi to follow his intuition for months but didn't know Yemi was going to go through with it. Karen, on the other hand, was hoping Yemi would use his former employer as some kind of middleman for their future clients. The siblings always had differences in this arena. Even though they both were eager for their startup to take off, Karen had dreamed for the past four years of looking out her floor-to-ceiling office windows onto the packed K Street corridor before she clocked out and rode the Red Line to her quaint condo in Columbia Heights. Several of her classmates built the life she envied through their summer internships in D.C. in between semesters while Karen sweltered in Carolina heat, helping her boyfriend plant community gardens to provide food security for low-income communities. Isaac dropped out his sophomore year, though, and his jealousy after her graduation turned toxic. Eventually, Yemi visited Winston-Salem to explain to Isaac that Karen wasn't one of the vegetables in his plant beds, and if he laid a finger on her, Yemi would make sure his corpse served as the next season's fertilizer. Karen left him but ended up with a sociology degree in her parents' basement. Yemi watched her shed whatever rigid lifestyle idealism Isaac planted in her mind and even considered interning at Titus while maybe going to grad school until she saw the subsidies for minority-owned businesses in the county of the house she had grown up in. When she became a blurb in a blog about women of color in the private security industry, it lit another fire under her to explore unchartered territory with her brother leading an executive protection squad.

"I thought you said Kirk was interested in a possible collaboration."

"It's never really a collaboration with behemoths like Titus. Plus, they would never let me command my own squad." Yemi enjoyed his meal as Karen came to the realization stubbornness is a family trait, but Yemi specifically had never liked someone outside of the bloodline taking charge of his future. "Better this way, trust me. It's more ideal to be small and efficient nowadays."

"We'll be more lean," chimed in Jasper.

"Yeah, more broke, too," laughed Karen. The rest chuckled along because it was true. The Executive Protection Team was keeping their profit margins on the line. If this next client pulled out, they would be in the red the next quarter for sure. "Anyways. Here are their files. You'll recognize one of them." She slid a manila folder to her brother. He broke from chowing down and opened it. He gandered down at profiles of the four proposed squad members.

NAME: TERRY BLACKWELL
AGE: 38
SQUAD POSITION RECOMMENDATION: Protective Intelligence Agent, Driver
BACKGROUND: Formerly a medical technician with the USAF Security Forces. Served in Saudi Arabia on the base's Special Reaction Team where he received active-shooter training. After his discharge at 26, he joined the US Park Police and was a member of their SWAT Team for a decade. Last year, he was forced to resign but is currently involved in a legal situation with the USPP under details he is legally barred from disclosing.

REASONS: Is very proficient in squad tactics in addition to being the only candidate with combat first-aid experience. Very high marks on firearms-related skill tests as well. Can be a good buffer when dealing with law enforcement in tricky situations involving our clientele.

NAME: LYLE EVANS
AGE: 29
SQUAD POSITION RECOMMENDATION: Criminal Intelligence Specialist
BACKGROUND SUMMARY: Lyle is one of our highest-performing property guards. We are already familiar with his bounty-hunting career in Georgia. However, apparently, he got his start in residential security in Jamaica. His father's firm, Quick Alarm Response, was shut down by the Jamaica Constabulary Force when his funds were tied to a drug kingpin with ties to a Colombian cartel hence why he left this off his original resume.

      REASONS: He saw a lot of action and has deep knowledge of tracking gang patterns or other criminal behavior we may need on the strategic side. Will not show any law enforcement bias in understanding potential problems tied to the Bazaar.

NAME: VICTOR OSORIO
Age: 51
SQUAD POSITION RECOMMENDATION: Explosives Specialist
BACKGROUND SUMMARY: Victor recently moved to D.C. from Venezuela, where he served in their military before joining the tactical unit of the National Police in 2011. When things got hot for the federal government during the Guaido coup, he left for the States, where he currently works at a controlled demolition firm in Phoenix, Maryland.

      REASONS: Highly skilled along with squad-based experience at a low rate as it seems the HR of local establishments don't take kindly to his former employer. He also demonstrated to us extensive knowledge of improvised explosive devices.

NAME: NICK RICE
Age: 23
SQUAD POSITION RECOMMENDATION: Communications
Specialist
BACKGROUND SUMMARY: A recent Computer Science (minor
in Criminal Justice) graduate from Morgan State University. He
was valedictorian of his class, ran cross country, and served as a
part-time MSUPD officer on campus while still finishing his last
two years as a full-time student.

REASONS: By far the most technically proficient of any
applicant. Has a wide demonstrated knowledge in everywhere
from countering cybercrime to advanced drone infrared
surveillance. His youth and lack of combat experience (but still
firearms certified) give him an affordable rate.

"Kid's young," said a concerned Yemi. He told them
nobody below the age of 25.

"You gotta see what he can do," assured Jasper. "Minutes
into our interview, Mr. Rice had the cameras in all of our locations
on his iPhone."

"Android," corrected Karen. "But yeah, it was wild."

"Why in the world would you give him access to the
portal?"

"We didn't." The two laughed at their response in unison
to reveal how shocking Nick's ability to hack their systems was.
Most places would probably end the interview, and Titus would
certainly notify the authorities, but Raptor needed a maverick to
help stand out early in the game. Plus, Yemi knew he wouldn't
get another opportunity for his squad's technical expert to be this
cheap.

"Well, he clearly doesn't want to be a cop anymore,"
chuckled Yemi as he shuffled the folder in approval.

"Surprise you about Lyle?" asked Karen.

"Nah," Yemi said as he shrugged. "I always sensed he's creating an image in our heads to distract us from something. But he'll work." Yemi picked back up the chopsticks as he was ready to listen as he ate. "So who's paying us next?"

From taking tear gas straight to the chest alongside his fellow student protestors back home to grinding his way into the US State Department, Chiedu's life work was the foundation of the Vienna, Virginia villa he sat in. The master's degree from Georgetown's School of Foreign Service hung with the same amount of pride next to the framed bachelor of arts from the University of Ibadan. But even with the presence of his veteran bodyguard, Obi, his young assistant, Sade Gazama, and POPCO Public Relations director Francine Van Zandt, it was an empty dark castle created by the sudden death of his only son. Chiedu didn't consider himself an alcoholic, but he had turned to taking shots in the daylight once Sade reluctantly revealed to him the Bazaar listing of Adamu and his wife, Halima. He didn't care if it was a staff member of his former employer or a disgruntled Popco contractor who leaked the documents. It was irrelevant to Chiedu whether the price on his head was funded by the Biafra Freedom Movement, which felt betrayed by their former student activist ally, or some terrorist group tied to rival oil interests. What drove him to the bottle of Jack Daniels was that if it wasn't for his line of work, the pride and joy of his existence would still be alive.

"October first?" Chiedu asked as he poured himself some dark whiskey.

"Yes, that's what our research has revealed," Francine said, watching with quiet concern as the shot glass got filled. Although both she and Sade sat with more poise than Chiedu, Sade seemed more relaxed in her shoulders while Francine puffed out her chest with each sentence as if she was eager to get to the bottom of the purpose of their meeting.

"Imagine this, Miss Van Zandt. On the right day, anybody from a trained killer to an ambitious busboy can make a few dollars off a bullet to your head or..." Chiedu took his shot. His face grimaced from the hard liquor burning his throat as it went down. "A little cyanide in your glass."

"That's why we're here, Mr. Attah. Your protection is a high priority for Popco." A snort of a laugh that came from Chiedu hinted he didn't have high regard for the true intentions of his formerly covert business partners.

"Obi, come in here." The 6'4, 280-pound Obi had been waiting outside the office as he always respected the privacy of his boss's business meetings. "I want you to hear this... Miss Van Zandt, tell him that if you had stuck to the jobs agreement, we would not be here today."

"Chiedu—"

"Tell them!" The sharp outburst rendered cold silence for several seconds.

"I can't imagine—" Francine cleared her throat. She breathed and realized she couldn't take offense as she sympathized with Chiedu. "We have been informed that our executive security partner, Titus, has an initiative already in motion to address the threats posed by this type of new age threat."

"Titus..." Where had Chiedu heard this name before?

"They consulted on the Harcourt incident, sir," reminded Sade. During Attah's term as ambassador, Nigeria's oil pipelines had been attacked by gunmen in speedboats, upset at what they viewed as a parasitic economic relationship between American businesses like POPCO, the government, and the people of the Delta. While Chiedu attempted to use his connections to the Biafra Freedom Movement to see if he could get a channel to cool tensions with the militants, POPCO covertly hired an eight-man squad of Titus contractors to intercept them. The team vastly underestimated the well-organized Niger Delta Defenders and ended up as hostages along with a half dozen employees of a refinery at Port Harcourt. The operation was a miserable failure, and its secrecy destroyed any negotiations between Attah and the BFM.

"I'm not leaving my life in the hands of Western games anymore," demanded Chiedu.

"I have a company we should look at," Sade said before Francine could respond to Chiedu's concerns. "It's a small startup based in Prince George's but I read an article online about the founder, Karen Uzunma." That was a Nigerian name, Chiedu noticed. Sade definitely had his attention at this point. "I contacted her, and she is actually about to launch an executive protection program that caters specifically to the Bazaar. Her brother, Yemi, is the detail leader and used to work for State Security Services."

"He was one of ours..." Chiedu remembered the name. Yemi's contingent of DSS authorities nabbed Peter Ikwe, who wasn't just the financier of the Delta Defenders but was the architect of organizing several other guerrilla forces in the region under a single political movement. Yemi's efforts exposed a web of arms deals, hired guns, and open-sourced warfare that outflanked the dated combat waged by the Nigerian government or their multi-national corporate partners. It was the same technology-driven chaos coalition forces dealt with in Iraq, except without nearly as many casualties. Yemi had studied these concepts and knew exactly that the State going after a central entity like the rebellions of the 1970s was a waste of time. Yemi's foresight greatly impressed Chiedu.

"Yemi Uzunma. Yes, I know of him. He worked for Titus until recently. What's the name of this firm?" asked Francine with as much genuineness as she could, but Sade had the fine-tuned bullshit detector, and she could see Francine would shut down any talk of an alternative to the wishes of the establishment she represented.

"Raptor."

"I like that name," said Chiedu as if he had already made his decision. "Miss Van Zandt."

"Yes, Mr. Attah?" asked Francine, but she already knew where this was going. Her superiors weren't going to be happy but convincing Chiedu would be impossible at that point.

"This is the man I want in charge of protecting me on October first." Chiedu spotted a smirk on his loyal bodyguard. "My apologies, Obi. Of course, I know you have always been my trusted guardian."

"No need to apologize at all, sir. My ego will never get in the way of your safety."

"My man, have a drink with me."

"Only if you insist, sir." Chiedu pulled out four glasses.

"Oh, I'm fine, Mr—," Francine blurted out.

"Nonsense. You will need it when you tell your bosses they're going to be sending their check to Raptor Security." Francine couldn't help but smile as Chiedu's mood was on the up-swing.

"Your safety is our primary concern, Chiedu." She accepted the drink, it would help her deal with the fact her upcoming promotion was nonexistent.

CHAPTER 3

Aaron's father always talked about how fun the early 80s were. It didn't matter how much the news would yap about heroin or how high the crime rates were back then. According to him the neighborhoods had everything they needed to enjoy the company of their fellow people to party together through the hard times. He would drive his son from the suburbs to get his hair cut all the way on the old block in Temple Hills just to try and infuse some culture into his son stuck in a world of nonstop message board trolling in between Call of Duty sessions.

Aaron reminisced, sitting on the front porch and wheeling his father's body to the ambulance with his crying mother following behind. He walked through the courtyard of Marlow Heights, three blocks from where Errol Williams grew up. But it wasn't a trip to his father's barbershop that time. Aaron was walking back to the apartments under the housing authority he and his mother had called home since the foreclosure.

The joyous community unity Errol had described to his son seemed to be long gone. The face of Denise, a woman Aaron saw every other day, said it all. He only knows her name because she was almost always in her outfit that represented a different fast-food franchise each time. The previous year, it was Subway, but Danny and he pulled up to the Rally's drive-thru a few months prior to see her working as a manager. Every time she gave him the same courteous smile covering a longing desire to find better living conditions for her children. They rarely spoke, but neither needed to.

Aaron walked past her and spotted a group of five men around his age hanging out by the building entrance. They were all sharing a blunt of some top-grade cannabis, as Aaron could tell by the smell, a knowledge he had acquired from hanging around Danny so much.

Aaron saw them multiple days a week and their interactions had been minimal. This time, though, the face-tatted Qasim stared straight through to his soul like an owl scouting a field mouse. Aaron profiled Qasim to be a street lieutenant in a crew that sold substances far more addictive and harmful than the one he was smoking.

Whatever, Aaron thought. Deep down, Aaron was ready for anything at any time. If Qasim made a move for the $1,200 stuffed in his inner jacket pocket...the tatted-up gangster would end up like Adamu Attah, plain and simple. To Aaron, Qasim was no different than the countless teachers who gave up on his dyslexic tendencies so he knew the way up for him was either mining crypto coins or what he pulled off a few days ago. One hobby Aaron never let go of was discovering the corners of internet economics, whether it be the white, black, or gray markets.

Qasim said nothing, he just kept his eyes occupied with Aaron's presence. The crew watched Aaron step through the glass doors but he just ignored them and checked the mailbox. Most were bills, probably the cable television his mother refused to cancel because no level of poverty would stop her from HGTV. Aaron figured covering that would certainly make his mom happy. He made his way through the center of the decaying beige interior to the second floor.

Nobody promised life would go as planned, but Aaron knew Errol worked so hard to give his family the American dream in one of the richest African-American zip codes on the East Coast that figuring out how to approach Aaron's learning disability appeared to be their biggest hurdle, not paying for his education. For that reason, he was caught off guard discovering his father's body swinging in his parents' closet from a noose made with the zebra-colored tie he had worn to work for the previous decade. Aaron would have never guessed that a man so confident in his abilities as a system administrator would break under the financial and mental consequences of the pandemic shutting off his employment. Getting immersed into the limitless potential of the income to be made from cryptocurrency was therapeutic for Aaron, while the cheap vodka from behind the bulletproof glass at the local corner store seemed to somewhat ease Rita Williams's pain, albeit only temporarily.

The door swung open.

Aaron hated that his mother had become a drunk, grieving widow, but he knew he had to continue to shower her with love until the day he would surprise her with keys to a place far from nightly gunshots and crackheads knocking on the front door at 3 AM.

"Got something for you, Momma." Aaron handed the mail to Rita, and a plain white envelope rested on the top. She lifted the seal and took out the wads of 20s. She didn't even bother to count them.

"He would've beat your ass if he caught you getting in trouble again," stated the unamused Rita, remembering the days of driving to the court with her husband for all of Aaron's computer hacking escapades in high school. The last straw for the system was when he used a backdoor to deface the school's website.

"Not doing anything illegal, Mom. Remember what I said about my online business? Don't worry, though... We'll be out of here soon." When that same conversation took place months ago, Aaron had successfully highjacked the servers of a local unsuspecting IT firm to mine cryptocurrency. He switched careers from cryptojacker to a crypto-paid hitman, however, when they finally hired cyber forensics experts to delete his malware after they reviewed their electricity bill.

Rita still had no clue as to what her son did to pay their electric bills.

"Mmmhmm, everybody trying to get out. Except for that Chinese friend of yours. He seems to love the ghetto."

"He's Vietnamese, Mama."

"What?"

Aaron sighed. He couldn't figure out if her hearing or attention span was declining — or both.

"Nothing, Momma."

Aaron figured he'd grab something from the kitchen and head back to his lab so she could enjoy watching new homeowners getting documented picking between mini-mansions and urban townhomes. As long as that TV stayed uninterrupted, she wouldn't raise too much of a fuss as to the source of Aaron's income.

"He was here earlier looking for you, by the way. First time I've seen him without that goofy ass smile on his face."

Aaron microwaved some black beans and rice before he headed back to his room. His mother would never bother barging in, but that didn't stop Aaron from deadbolting his room's entrance. Outside of bills, necessities for the household, and Danny's gas money, Aaron had mostly invested in what was in his space.

The desktop PC and monitor were a competitive gamer's wet dream. Multiple CPUs, power sticks of RAM in the single digits of terabytes. Multiply that by twenty, and you would get the system's hard drive space further increased by the server rack tower next to the computer. The highlight of technology in that room, however, was the machine that produced the Adamu Attah murder weapon as well as the half dozen other 3D-printed pistols and AR-15 rifles laying around the UltraMaker XT, the last of his major purchases before he pulled the plug on his cryptojacking exploits.

Aaron plopped down in his chair and swiped his mouse to bring up where he left off in his digital tasks. In the background were different listings on http://Bazaar.tor as well as firearm design files, but the primary window was the encrypted Transmit messenger app.

L1BERTY0RD3ATH: chiedu attah at 130 btc...wat u think?

Chiedu? That might be too risky. Aaron knew nobody was going to be guarding Adamu. The Bazaar listings weren't taken seriously on any global scale before the previous 48 hours. Even the mainstream news may not have unraveled the real motives behind the murder, but Chiedu wasn't going to take any risks. He'd certainly have a full-blown security detail once he got wind of a date that had a price on his head. L1BERTY0RD3ATH was the handle of Doug Vanderville, a 23-year-old Jewish man who lived somewhere in Western Maryland. Through crypto-related message boards, they realized common interests in things ranging from their plastic arsenals to how the Bazaar would impact their side of the world. While Aaron's motivations were mostly financial, there was always a slight political edge to Doug's chess moves, but he still couldn't figure out how to follow up Aaron's shots heard around the dark net. They hadn't met in person, but they both knew each other's real identities when they found flaws in the other ones firewalls and realized they lived in the same state.

KrispyAttux: You know a date yet?

L1BERTY0RD3ATH: sum1 in a forum said oct 1st

KrispyAttux: Thats in a week lol

L1BERTY0RD3ATH: ... yeah lol

That was less than a month away and didn't leave much time to plan. At the same time, if Aaron could flip his thousand-dollar bid to a deposit that finally got them out of the projects, it might be worth finishing off the patriarch in the Attah family. Maybe if he threw a scope on one of his rifles and secured a solid getaway, he could pull this off. Maybe.

L1BERTY0RD3ATH: i can help lmk if u wanna do anything

Loud, panicky knocks came from the front door in the living room.
"Aaron!" his mom yelled to him.

KrispyAttux: Appreciate that bro. I'll let you know by this weekend.

Aaron rose out of his chair and locked up his room. He knew it was probably Danny and confirmed it through the peephole. Aaron opened the door halfway, keeping Danny's antics in the hallway away from the sanctity of his home.
"What's up?"
"You wilin moe. I don't know how to use that damn encrypted messenger joint or whatever bullshit—"
"Yo, chill." Aaron nodded his head toward the living room. Danny peeked his head in and saw Rita staring at them like they were disturbing the classroom of a catholic school teacher. She hated slang, especially when it was loud.
"Hi, Mrs. Williams!" Danny said with all the civility he could muster up. "Sorry just wanted to see if Aaron can fix my computer. My bad if I interrupted anything earlier—" Aaron

shoved him out and closed the door. "Man, what the—"

"I don't want her to be bothered right now. What's up, Danny?"

"Okay, okay. My fault, my fault. But I gotta show you something." At that moment, Danny was walking a little faster than usual, but Aaron followed him close by as they reached the stairs.

"Alright, but I'm not trying to be out all night." A whiff of the same top-shelf cannabis smell from earlier hit Aaron's nose.

"I'll drive you back." They started to walk down the stairwell.

"We going to your crib?" The second Aaron stepped off the last stair he became surrounded by Qasim and the entire crew like a moose at the center of a pack of wolves. A man drenched in black and white Helly Hansen attire quickly secured the front entrance to prevent any immediate escape. Even though Aaron was vastly outnumbered and most of them were probably armed, Aaron clenched his fist to get on guard. But he realized Danny didn't react at all. He'd either be ready to throw down with his best friend or at least make a run for it. Even if he broke down crying like a coward, it would at least be a reaction. But Danny couldn't even look in Aaron's direction or even Qasim's. He had a look of sudden shame like the previous few minutes of common friendship was a charade. Danny walked off to the side as Aaron realized he had been betrayed.

"Aaron, look—"

"Fellas. I don't want any problems. We can all just stick to our own business and go on about our way." Screw Danny, but Aaron realized he had to try to get out of this alive.

"When you move five bands on my territory, it's my business," said Qasim. "Don't matter if it's drugs or Girl Scout cookies." That was a threat. Screw the first plan. Aaron was prepared to sacrifice the remaining consciousness he had on this planet. Someone would hear a gunshot, and the police would get called. That would at least prevent Qasim's crew from storming his mother's place.

"Your territory? You own this building?" Some in the crew were shocked by this flippant response. Most people cowered before Qasim's threats by the time they were outnumbered. To the surprise of everyone, Qasim only reacted with amusement.

"Let's take a ride," Qasim said as he flashed the .45 caliber pistol on his waistband. "O-G wants to talk to you." That gun would definitely make enough noise, thought Aaron.

"Fuck you, shoot me right here."

"Wow," laughed Qasim. "It's about a job. Watch what you say, boy, but nobody gotta get hurt tonight. Come on, let's go." Aaron stood there. They were not going to let him leave, but something about the tone in Qasim's voice made it seem like an assault was no longer imminent. Qasim stepped to the side of the entrance and opened it, exaggerating as if he were a doorman at the Ritz-Carlton. Aaron walked forward and headed out with the crew, refusing to look at Danny. Danny stood alone in the lobby. A tear rolled down his cheek, and he broke down crying, not caring who in the building saw him.

"Shit!" Aaron heard his friend-turned-traitor from the stairwell. Just the other week, they were calling each other brothers, the dyslexic anime nerd and the only Asian against every wannabe street bully, whether in the crowded school hallways or at the basketball courts. Aaron knew Danny right then wished Qasim had just put a bullet through the side of his head.

––––––––

Aaron looked around from the back passenger seat as the early 2000s Camry passed through an automatically opened gated fence. The "O.G." lived in a three-floor playboy manor with a fully lit pool on a street that made Aaron's old neighborhood look like the one he was just kidnapped from. The blocks weren't lined with cookie-cutter McMansions like where his father had purchased a house for the Williams family. White oak trees flourished across the acres between the houses and each home design seemed like they had their own distinct architect. Qasim walked Aaron up the marble steps, and Aaron stared at the stone lions in the front yard.

A man in his late 40s opened the front door. He was 6'2, with a well-combed lion mane of a beard against a dark complexion, and he wore a red flight jacket issued by the DC Department of Health. He was probably the fastest linebacker in high school or competed for some type of golden gloves despite his gut. He was grinning at first, happy to see Aaron.

"Hello—" The man suddenly got a whiff of Qasim's marijuana habit and immediately reversed the direction on his face. The kid's eyes were bloodshot red off a blunt ride the whole trip from Temple Hills. "Inside. Now."

A spiral staircase greeted them in the living room. The interior solidified that it was the highest-priced house Aaron had ever stepped into. Paintings of resistance leaders ranging from Haitian revolutionary L'Touissant Overture to Queen Nanny of the Maroons hung on the walls.

"Q, how many times are we going to have this conversation?" The tone was frustrated and angry but disappointed more than anything.

"Yo look—"

"Don't bring up how it's legal again. That's irrelevant. I don't want to embarrass you in front of your crew." Qasim's gulp popped the inflated ego that had been floating on top of his neck the whole day. "If I haven't already."

"I'm—" Qasim had to take a breath as if to cool his head from reacting with an outburst. "I'm sorry."

"It's okay." The man placed his hand on the shoulder

of Qasim, as if to assure the young man he was still held in high regard."We are in a new direction now. With what I have planned..."

Aaron took his attention away from the lecture and noticed a 7-foot wall of books behind one of the goons. Everyone seemed to have figured Aaron wasn't a threat at that point, and they let him through. He scoped the library. Marx, Kropotkin, Chomsky, Guevara, Fanon, even from the other side of the revolutionary spectrum like Rothbard and Sowell plus the combat theory gods like Sun Tzu and Machiavelli. All authors that Doug would tell him to read. He then saw the more technical-based books around military concepts as well as historical titles covering wars they never mentioned in history class in places like southeast Asia, Eastern Europe, Africa, and South America in the 20th century. One book, *The OODA Loop and Other Theories of John Boyd*, caught Aaron's attention. He remembered Doug sending him the pdf file. He never imagined the hard copy print version.

"Observe, orient, decide, act," the man in the jacket said after he finished his conversation with Qasim. There was a strong hint of admiration in his voice. "The OODA loop, remember?"

"Yeah." Aaron wasn't in the mood to entertain long, drawn-out philosophical conversations. The brief answer got the man to take notice, but his body language showed that he would cater to Aaron's decision to keep the topic strictly business.

"Respect, respect. Aaron, right?"

"Yup. What's up?" Rold could not help but laugh at the tension built into Aaron. Qasim wasn't amused, though, and his owl eyes were back on Aaron. But Aaron realized the ball was probably in his court, and he was no longer defenseless prey. He'd keep things quick, but he certainly wouldn't mind trolling Qasim if he could.

"Relax, my brother. Name is Rold. Rold Jenkins." Rold stuck out his hand. Aaron gave a relaxed shake, enough to keep respect from Rold but also enough for Qasim to think the opposite. Rold took notice of the hostility. "He had to flash the chrome to get you to come, huh? Stubbornness is the sign of a true revolutionary."

"Revolutionary?" Aaron shook his head, chuckling to himself. "I don't play games of ideological crusades."

"I understand. But at the end of the day, I know it felt good to put that envelope in your momma's lap." Damn, Aaron thought, Danny told them everything. Aaron didn't take kindly to people knowing about his personal life.

"That's the last time you will bring up my mother." Qasim wasn't going to tolerate this kind of disrespect anymore.

"Alright," he said as he quickly drew the gun from his waistband. "I've heard enough out of this pussy ass ni—"

"Q. At ease, soldier," demanded Rold. Qasim had dealt with enough embarrassment in the last ten minutes, and Aaron knew a bullet in his forehead would put Qasim's mind at ease, but the muzzle stayed pointed to the ground. Qasim relented and put the gun away, but he refused to take his eyes off Aaron. "I saw you looking at my library. Clearly, this is about more than money for me."

"What is?" asked Aaron. Rold chuckled slightly at Aaron playing ignorant, but he decided to go along with it.

"The Bazaar. It's a paradigm shift in human interaction with control over the society we're forced to live in. Crowdsourcing every little dime from whoever wishes to shake up the status quo. The political elite already take dollars out of our wallets and spend it on their spoiled children to shove us off our own blocks for condos and coffee shops. But now, watch pissed-off constituents collect their pocket change together and put the scumbags on the free market with a six-figure price tag on their head. It's the beauty of democracy and the expression of the individual in one."

"And this gets you out of the drug dealing business, right?" Aaron casually asked.

"I gave these kids opportunities, but nobody in this room is going to die selling that shit to our community. Yes, we make a profit but not without real gains to our liberty. We're entrepreneurs in the spirit of our freed ancestors. "

"So," Aaron said as he put the book back. "You placed a bid?"

"I did, and others did too. Others who are paying for the operation. I've reached out to several interested parties, and after talks, I have gotten funding for our team and whatever we need to pull it off. Body armor, compact assault weapons, escape routes, you name it."

"I'll take a guess these donors are not the constituents from the sermon you just gave about exercising their democracy." A chuckle from Rold, although Qasim was still tired of Aaron's tone throughout the discussion.

"They are internationals who don't know your name or have any idea what you look like, yet they worship you like a rock star. Mentioning the fact that someone who shares my area code pulled off the first successful dark net assassination got me the deal in the first place and why everyone here is going to be well off after October first."

"I haven't agreed to anything."

"Aaron. I know you can't resist going after that ambassador. The Lord knows he has it coming, but there's already word that someone may have leaked the date to intelligence officials. We're lucky he's not backing down from the speech, but best believe he'll have a detail attached to his every move."

"I work alone."

"Look around you. These are soldiers ready to go to war. The State isn't ready for an attack this sophisticated. We can strike while the iron is hot without the risk that will be forthcoming once the system starts catching on." Aaron gave Rold a listen and did a slow 360 turn with his head. They did look battle-hardened from the wars in the streets, but exchanging gunfire with trained bodyguards who are possibly fresh out of Iraq or Afghanistan is a different level than stick-up crews going after their stash of dime bags.

"They're not soldiers. They're mercenaries now, just like the ones protecting Attah."

CHAPTER 4

The dream of becoming a young millionaire turned into an everyday checklist after Lyle saw the island paradise his father created in the Caribbean. Lyle's two sisters and mother would switch between spending weekends swimming in the clear blue waters off the coast of Ochos Rios or hiking through the Blue Mountain waterfalls, avoiding the Negril side of Jamaica infested with tourists. He remembered when Kimauly Patrick, one of the island's most notorious distributors of cocaine, would invite them to his lavish parties, and Lyle would sneak away from the loud dancehall speakers just to look over the porcelain balcony to gander at Kingston from the top of a luxurious fortress. The last time he looked at Kingston was right before the crackdown. Right when he was ready to transition from being another one of his father's hired guns to the youngest retailer of computer equipment in the country.

But there he was, three months shy of thirty, and dragging on a handmade cigar outside the Raptor office. His friend, who was supposed to open up a recording studio, ran off to the Dominican Republic with two of his paychecks, the cryptocurrency he invested in crashed through the charts, and the Washington Nationals sued his clothing line into bankruptcy. The only thing he felt he succeeded at over the past decade was catching fugitives in the Deep South and protecting property owned by the people with the wealth he desired.

A bright orange vehicle that was barely distinguishable from a fuel-efficient hybrid forklift pulled into the space next to Lyle's solid blue BMW 3 series. Lyle puffed some clouds and watched a college kid with a backpack step out who had the same pigment as Blake Griffin but a few dozen pounds less muscle than the bright-skinned NBA player. He seemed somewhat athletic still, so Lyle assumed he may have done the 1600 in track or another sport to suit his anatomy. But Lyle's biases solidified him as a man-child when he took notice of a giant robot gripping some type of futuristic cannon on the front of the kid's black hoodie.

"You on Battle Storm, bro?" asked the kid, clearly eager to find another first-person shooter connoisseur.

"I don't play no bomboclaat video games." Lyle's island patois could be subdued at times after being in the States for so long, but it came out in full force when he was mad or annoyed.

"Sorry, saw you looking at the shirt." He seemed a little surprised by Lyle's hostility. "Anyways, you here for Raptor?" Lyle slowly nodded a 'yes' as he focused more on his nicotine than making new friends, even if they were going to be his partner.

"I'm Nick Rice. I think we're going to be team members." They shook hands.

"Lyle." The young man was polite, so Lyle decided to cut him some slack.

"Oh, okay. I heard the accent, and I thought you were Yemi." Lyle shook his head. Maybe he should have gone with his initial assessment of Nick, who seemed like he had a high GPA in his academic career but his social was so limited that he couldn't tell a Caribbean voice from a West African.

"No, definitely not him." Lyle scrunched the tobacco and made his way to the stairs.

———

Lyle entered the meeting room first, with Nick keeping a safe distance behind, getting the hint they didn't quite hit it off well. Two men were seated across from Karen, who was organizing the pamphlets for the icebreaker. If Lyle's body frame was a first-generation hummer, the guy closest to Karen donning prescription sport glasses was a Porsche 911 Carrera, streamlined for quick-thinking movement, not beach mass. His clean cut, posture, and notepad in his palm hinted he took authorities seriously wherever he was stationed before this job offer. The other man, a heavy bearded middle-aged man of Hispanic origin, was almost the opposite to the point Lyle wondered if there was a Harley Davidson he missed in the parking lot. But Lyle didn't make the mistake of assuming the man was unqualified. His build was stocky with even more mass than Yemi, but he was still no sloth. The physique was most likely just a product of slamming down beers and barbecue in between lifting weights or combat duty.

"Quiet, quiet, they just walked in!" the easy rider said jokingly, making the Jamaican and undergrad feel like they crashed a party. "Just playing. Lyle and...Nick, right? Victor." They had never met before, but the man's nature seemed genuine, and Lyle gave him a dap of solidarity. He stared in Karen's direction, who seemed to have been laughing along with Victor about personal topics and decided to embrace the vibe.

"Oh, she been talking about me again? Trust me, you don't want to get too deep in that."

"Stop it!" Lyle fabricated any kind of relationship outside of work with Karen, but she still blushed. Victor and Lyle immediately cracked up. The man in the glasses stood up straight, smiling, but Lyle could tell the man was not too interested in spectating flirtatious conversation.

"Mr. Rice," he said with esteem. "Word is you're a young genius." He exchanged greetings with Nick as they shared a cordial laugh at the compliment. "Terry Blackwell."

"Yeah, he doesn't seem to get out much," interrupted Lyle. Terry and Lyle exchanged glances. Lyle could tell he didn't find it particularly funny. Nick seemed to ignore the comment and shrugged toward Victor, who still cracked a smile to keep the joyous mood going. The brief awkward moment broke quickly when Jasper and Yemi filed in through the door with packed black duffel bags like airport concierges. They were certainly carrying at their max capacity as they slammed them on the table.

"Hey, everyone. Our first assignment is in less than a week, so we're jumping straight into it." He and Jasper zipped all the bags down in a fluid motion. "Over here, you'll find your issued firearm with holster. Jasper's got your Kevlar, and Karen will set up your radios." Lyle was expecting more formality, but they all also knew immediately Yemi was right. Moving as a unit in a week's time needed no further introduction to the urgency. "When we get to the range, we'll have time to introduce ourselves." Lyle saw that Raptor decided to go with the Glock 22 as the squad's standard pistol, a significant upgrade from the Egyptian Beretta knockoff he was given for perimeter patrols. He released the magazine, slid it back, and cocked it as if he only wanted to hear the gun's trademark click-clack.

"You didn't send an address," said Lyle as he stared at his new lead companion.

"Terry's taking you to the location," Yemi stated as he slipped on his ballistic vest. "Victor, you ride with Jasper and I."

"Where—?" Terry seemed confused, but before he could get his full inquiry out, Jasper tossed him some car keys.

"Sorry didn't include this in our correspondence," Yemi spoke to the whole crew. "We might as well practice our driving formation and get you guys used to the vehicles. Nick... You got your laptop, right?"

"Always," Nick said. Lyle figured he was attempting a better first impression.

"Sit behind Lyle and Terry for today. During the assignment, you're going to be next to the client with his private bodyguard, Obi Ngozi, in the front passenger. I want you to be remotely monitoring surveillance, both C-C-T-V and drone until we arrive at the convention center. From there, Karen can handle it."

"Excellent. If you ever need to check anything in the field, I can always whip out my phone."

"Who's dispatch?" asked Terry as he placed the .40 caliber pistol into his holster.

"Me!" Lyle could tell Terry had to confirm what he couldn't seem to believe. Karen was smiling. Lyle knew Karen was taking courses at Prince George's Community College in public safety communication and surveillance operations. It turned out those were more useful to her than almost any of the core curricula for her degree that she was still paying off.

"That seemed like a question better fit for the interview, brother," chuckled Lyle. Terry's faux grin seemed harder to maintain with Lyle's jibe, but he half chuckled as he finished securing his radio.

"I hope that's not an issue," Karen commented. Lyle could tell she was a bit sensitive and sensed some doubt in her abilities from Terry's reluctance to speak after her answer.

"Not at all. I guess you'll have your hands full."

———

Driving big SUVs on Columbia Parkway was a breeze compared to speeding 90+ miles per hour on highways outside Riyadh, but Lyle turned the radio to max volume and it distracted Terry's concentration on preparing his mind for the field training.

"I swear if Drake does one more reggae song, I'm going to put his bitch ass on the Bazaar. Mother fuckers gotta stay in their lane, don't care how many yardies he claims to know in Toronto."

"I can't hear you with the music."

"What?"

"The music. It's too loud."

"Oh." Terry decided to twist the knob and lower the decibels.

"What did you say?"

"Just talking shit. Nothing important." Lyle turned the music back up. Terry didn't understand why this guy was listening to an artist he despised so much. Either way, he was not going to tolerate it anymore. Terry switched the frequency, and Lyle's body shot up, visibly offended by the gesture.

"Sorry, gotta see what traffic is looking like before we go on ninety-five."

"I can check my phone," insisted Lyle.

"It's fine." Terry landed on an anchor updating listeners on developments regarding the death of Adamu.

"Saturday's incident raises the total number of homicides in the district to two hundred thirteen. This marks the first time the homicide rate has surpassed two hundred since two thousand four—"

"Hey, can you change it if you don't mind?" asked Nick from the back seat.

"How the hell are you on your laptop?" asked Lyle. "Don't tell me you're on the internet."

"Satellite," responded Nick, eyes glued to his screen. "And Karen's password doesn't seem to be working. But I'll figure something out."

"They do the traffic report every ten minutes," said Terry. "After that." Nick nodded.

"Ten minutes?" laughed Lyle. "I could've found that shit the second after you brought it up, easy." Inside Terry's head was the notion to take the next exit, pull over in a secluded area, beat Lyle into a coma, and do a U-Turn on this whole career venture. Nobody on the force had that many micro-aggressions so early in their professional relationship. But he conceded. He would never let someone else compromise his own ethical volition. He would do the Chiedu mission and then make his way right back to behind the badge.

"My bad. I swear I'm not an asshole." Terry realized Lyle must have noticed his inner conflict through his facial expression.

"Really?" Terry laughed, and Lyle joined in. Even Nick smirked at the obvious in the back.

"Fuck you laughing at, college boy?" Lyle stated in a humorous yet overly alpha deep voice.

"What's wrong with college?" Terry decided to go along with the jest, but he wouldn't demean somebody he had respect for, at least on paper.

"Nothing. A little joke from earlier..." Lyle looked at Nick in the rearview mirror. Through their eyes it was now going to be a truce, but Terry could tell Lyle still didn't change his overall view on the recent undergrad. "Right?"

"He doesn't like video games," Nick snuck in.

"Me neither, to be honest," chuckled Terry who had surprisingly found something to agree with Lyle on. "Waste of time."

"Are we going to be doing like squad-based operations and stuff at this place in Hagerstown?" inquired Nick as he viewed the desolate warehouse they were heading to through installed cameras on his laptop.

"Operations?" mockingly laughed Lyle. "We're just bodyguards, kid. This ain't War Storm or whatever." The car cracked up. "But honestly, I have no idea. Welcome to Raptor, where they don't tell you shit, and you got to figure it out as it comes."

"So you've been with them for a while?" asked Terry.

"Six months strong. Since inception."

"How is it?" Terry realized that every reference to their company from Lyle had been a negative one. He liked the idea of leaving the world of bike patrol in between SWAT training sessions for the growth potential in the startup sector. Out of all his job offers, he decided on Raptor the moment Karen and

Jasper had brought up the dark net's connection to international security in their conversation.

"Can't lie. Jasper's a smart dude. He's probably the best thing they got in their corner."

"Yemi, Karen...how are they?" Nick asked from the back, distracted from his assignment by the topic of conversation.

"Karen's cool, I guess..." Lyle took out his cigar. "Mind if I?" Terry slowly took his hand over to the side window button on his panel. Lyle's was cracked halfway open for him to blow out smoke. With a flick of the lighter, Lyle began to finish off his original session in the parking lot. "Yemi... He's never going to tell you what he's thinking."

"But he's solid, though, right?" inquired Terry.

"Sometimes he knows what he's doing. Just make sure you have an exit plan."

———

The only farms Aaron knew about growing up were the elementary school trips that led to hayrides or the family reunion on his father's side in North Carolina. The Eastern Shore of Maryland reminded him more of the vast Southern fields his grandfather told him about than the local petting zoo with a red barn and apple tree rows.

"I know we can split that car exit time in half." Rold orated to the band of eight as they walked on a straw-laden path at the center of the livestock part of the property. The group had spent the past two hours practicing jump-out tactics with their vehicles on the other side of the one-hundred-acre estate. They never worried about police since a soul couldn't see any of the training beyond the woods from the roadside, and it took a quarter-mile dirt road to reach the main entrance. The property was also thirty miles from Ocean City or any major mecca of Mid-Atlantic society, so they could screech as many tires or fire off as many rounds as their preparation required. "But overall, we're on a good track. We'll be ready on Saturday. They won't be."

Aaron looked at the open chicken coop on his right side. A black fowl stared back at him, standing out amongst the others as they clucked around aimlessly. Aaron wondered if the birds were being raised for eggs or if they would encounter the same fate as his new team if they killed Chiedu but didn't escape. He paid attention to the encouraging words coming out of Rold's mouth but Aaron knew at the time of the mission the veteran wouldn't be by his side on the street.

"He's really proud of that one," Rold said when he noticed Aaron staring at the animal. "Breed is called Sumatra."

"Is kama sutra or whatever target practice?" snarked Qasim. A couple of the pack laughed but were immediately silenced when they saw the stone-cold reaction in the face of their superior. The same expression when Qasim's reek of ganja reached Rold's nostrils.

"The next person who disrespects me like that will be target practice." The threat was real to all of them, even Aaron. When Rold disciplined Qasim at the house, it felt more like a coach straightening out his players to focus on the second half of a game. This was a general in the barracks explaining that death was punishment for insubordination. "The range is right beyond those trees. I'll join you in twenty minutes," the commander said, pointing to a couple hundred yards from their position. "Aaron, come with me."

Aaron followed in the direction of the manor, ignoring the scorn of envious rage in Qasim, who watched Aaron get a hand-given higher level rank in his outfit of five years in 24 hours.

"The people I mentioned at my spot... Some of them are inside that house."

"You expect me to introduce myself to them?" Aaron stopped walking. Blowing his campaign to stay anonymous in his Bazaar assassin escapades was not part of the deal to join

Rold on this operation.

"Aaron... Relax. A few of these individuals are even banned from entering this country. I assure you they are taking the brunt of whatever risk is involved in being in their presence." None of this put Aaron's mind at ease. It was a risky operation from the beginning involving more than a single person. Any of those foreign figures crack under an investigation and Aaron would be on the Secret Service's Most Wanted. The idea of just taking Chiedu out as a single sniper seemed like the better idea now, but Aaron realized he might be too deep into Rold's grand plan for global notoriety to step aside.

"This whole idea was a mistake."

"Excuse me?"

"You're risking all of our lives for your silly game of trying to be remembered in history."

"Aaron..." Rold understood the skepticism but, at this point, had put up enough with the young man's smarter-than-thou attitude. "If you doubt me, state your reason, but this tone of yours isn't going to fly. Not anymore."

"You want me to waltz in there like I'm your prized racehorse." Aaron decided he was going to push the limits of Rold's tolerance. Aaron thought his age had fooled Rold into thinking he was looking for a mentor. Well, he was going to set any idea of that kind of relationship to a cold rest. "I've covered my ass every step of the way before I met your puppet over there, and you're telling me to risk losing it all for a charade show. I was learning how all this shit works while you guys were destroying our community with wars over crack rocks —"

A flying fist went straight into the jawline of Aaron. The raised voice of Aaron was enough to warrant a sucker punch from Qasim. The running start to the blow wasn't enough to render Aaron unconscious, however. A follow-up hook from Qasim got blocked, and a cross was ducked by Aaron, who quickly was able to regain focus.

"Quit it!" Before Rold's words could have any effect, Aaron was able to grab hold of Qasim's collar, who was still failing to land another effective hit. Aaron drove his forehead straight into Qasim's temple, putting the assailant's body in a sleeping limp. Aaron tossed Qasim onto the grass for Rold to tend to.

"He attacked me first," Aaron stated to get the record straight before things got further chaotic. Qasim attempted to rise, but his legs were gone, and he tumbled into the arms of Rold, who straightened him.

"Enough, Q."

The source of a rumble in Aaron's side pocket was a text Aaron had been waiting for since the car ride across the Chesapeake Bay. He tossed it over to a bewildered Rold, who got revealed a bombshell by Doug, aka L1b3rty0rD3ath: HALF OF THOSE NAMES ALREADY HAVE OPEN CASES WITH INTERPOL. HIT ME IMMEDIATELY WHEN YOU GET SOMEWHERE SAFE.

"I had no idea." Rold was in disbelief, but the severity of the situation calmed him right after having to halt a brawl that raised his blood pressure. He handed the phone back to Aaron. "You have to understand, I've known Altavius my whole life. He's never been this sloppy but it's impossible he would have known and still bring me on board."

"Remember the guy who led Qasim to me?"

"Yes, of course."

"He was the closest thing I've ever had to a friend in the physical world."

"That was my understanding. Stay here. I will handle this." Rold was going to be a man of his word and briskly walked straight into the main house. He snuck in through the glass door and caught the bath-robed Altavius right in the middle of a mid-afternoon sip of top-shelf white wine to escape from entertaining his several guests in the next room over. Rold stared back at his former partner. The two sold plastic-wrapped powdered bricks decades prior, but Altavius managed to exit the narcotics game clean and branched off into international finance in the Cayman Islands. He tiptoed back into the illegal markets when he saw the potential profits in his eager, loyal customers looking to play into an online dead pool to possibly shift the geopolitics in their home countries. Altativus didn't care for the motivations or consequences of his clientele. He had far more concern for the colonial style designed kitchen floor on which Rold had a .357 Colt Python pointed to his head.

"You either betrayed me, or you're incompetent. And both of us know you're way too educated to do the latter."

"Like I said." A gulp interrupted Altavius' sentence. The Marlow Heights days were decades ago, and even back in 2003, it was Rold who handled any disgruntled rival looking to kill the better competition. "Your man's source is lying. I promise you I screened all of them before I brought you in. Now put the gun down before one of them steps in here."

"If I confirm what I just heard..." Rold slowly stowed his pistol back into his jacket. "A few things will come back to mind." The subtle threat forced Altatvius to reminisce. Upon discovering that their supplier Raymond was inflating the cost of their cocaine purchases to more than two times its actual price, Rold was able to convince most of his fellow street lieutenants to ambush the kingpin. Even though Altatvius was going to benefit directly from the confrontation, he took a one-way plane ticket to Tampa for business school the day before the hit was supposed to go down. Others in the crew wanted Altavius' head next to Raymond's, but Rold was able to convince everyone that their former comrade was not a threat to their future. Rold knew the deed had been a weight on Altatvius' shoulders that seemed to lighten each year since the incident until Rold shifted it all back with his comment. But the fact that the two of them were the only ones left not living the rest of their lives in an orange jumpsuit or a coffin six feet under the surface had submerged into his psyche.

The door to the kitchen from the back suddenly slid open. It was Aaron, followed by a no-longer-hostile Qasim. They glid through the space toward the front of the house like they knew their destination.

"I told you to wait outside," Rold stated.

"Talked to my guy on the phone. Said we have a way out of this." Rold noticed Qasim was in cooperation with Aaron. He would celebrate the newfound unity among his young subordinates if he wasn't so confused about what shifted Aaron's decision. "I want to meet them."

Altavius seemed almost eager to accommodate Aaron even though there was a brief pause from both him and Rold on the situation.

"They're in the living room, follow me." Aaron followed Altavius through the house. There was a colonial style to the place. Even though the house he grew up in was half this size, Aaron remembered his father preferred this kind of look over the Monopoly board game starter homes that were the trend with their neighbors in Prince George's County.

The seven older gentlemen could be a smaller version of the United Nations Council evidenced by their diversity. Whether from the Middle East or Latin America, the hors d'evours in their hands hinted at a privileged background safeguarded by bodyguards back at their homelands. Aaron looked into the eyes representing the new wave of financing on the Bazaar's assassination market. They stared back in admiration of the one whose shot was heard around the cyber criminal underworld and, at that moment, held their extravagant bets on death in his palms.

"How old are you?" The question came from a heavy and

heavily bearded Jordanian man right across from Aaron.

"Eighteen," he confidently replied back. They were visibly impressed.

"So young. I speak for all of us when I say it is an honor to be in your presence. My name is Omar." He extended his hand to Aaron. The teenage hitman just smirked, a signal to his new comrade behind him.

"And my name is Aaron Williams," Aaron responded to the cordiality by raising a silenced Makarov automatic pistol from his inner jacket. Aaron and Qasim sprayed the entire living room, splattering the colonial-style decoration with blood of colonized descent.

"Stop—!" Bullets sliced Altavius' face and halted him from interrupting the massacre. Within seconds, the living room had become the opposite of its namesake as eight corpses lay strewn across the hardwood floors. Rold's eyes cut through the bodies to see if there were any investors of his grand plan that were still twitching, moaning, or showing any sign of life.

"What I said about the next person who disrespects me applies to you as well. And this is a pretty fucking big lack of respect." Rold directed his comment toward Aaron who didn't have a care for any more of Rold's preaching.

"There was no other option. And I knew you'd understand, or you would be lying amongst them." Rold smirked. Aaron knew the older man had no shame to be countered by an outsider in front of his young lieutenant by a superior strategist. He also realized that very few people even knew about this address and that burying the bodies wasn't an impossible task. He comes to the quick conclusion. Aaron figured this all out the second they stepped foot on the property.

"You trust him, don't you?" Rold asked Qasim, who was hesitant to answer right away. It wasn't an easy decision to partake in this, mostly being of Rold's potential scrutiny in

Qasim's eyes.

"He knows some things we don't, feel me?"

"Clearly," acknowledged Rold. "Well, Mr. Williams. I guess we are at your disposal for the next few days."

"Good to hear." Aaron stowed his gun away. "We need to grab a few more things. Can somebody drive me?"

"Where? Like a hardware store?" inquired Rold.

"After a farmer's market. Gotta grab some peppers."

"For what? You cooking or some shit?" Qasim was confused.

"Not exactly."

———

When Yemi's plane landed at Regan National, it was his first time stepping foot on the ground of the United States since his sophomore year of high school. He was perplexed by how much the urbanization in the D.C. metro expanded deep into suburbs of Virginia and Maryland, with developed downtown business. But he remembered those states were also home to the mountainous terrain in Appalachia perfect for the squad's impromptu training.

Yemi stuck to the basics before getting to the more complicated side of combat drills. Raptor's Executive Protection Team was not a government-sanctioned special ops team, but they were going to train like one, according to the former SSS commander. Lyle and Terry displayed the most athleticism of the six-man team, subtlely making it a competition on every warm-up ranging from the 2-mile run to the last burpee. Nick kept up with them on the run, but he struggled with anything involving his upper body. Although Victor was the anchor of every exercise, the whole squad was impressed by the older man's raw strength with his ability to pump out ten full pull-ups at his wide body frame.

Jasper shined on the make-shift target range. Nobody matched his aim. The years of sniper training he received from

US Marines made him a bullseye with anything from a pistol to a scoped .50 cal. Yemi knew he'd be the one in charge of one of the black long guns they'd keep stashed in each vehicle. In case their small motorcade got ambushed, Terry would be the other one with his hand on the trigger of the firearm that had the farthest firing range. Maryland had some of the strictest gun control in the country, so it was a pain in the ass to get an assault rifle registered for use, a move usually only reserved for the bigger fish like Titus or the Vienna-based RexCorp. However, Yemi convinced Karen the tedious filings were worth it to avoid being caught off guard by criminals he predicted were sometimes the first to technology and always the first to exploit it for profit. The ambassador was insistent on going through with this speech to convince one of the fastest-growing Nigerian immigrant communities in the world he wasn't betraying the interests of his home country. Yet, no kind of patriotism drove Yemi. It was the knowledge that he'd be at the edge of a new dimension in international crime and becoming one of the first to develop real-world counter-dark net operations. All the strategy and research he'd gather would be under his name, not lost in the bureaucratic mess of his former state or multi-national employers.

What brought Yemi back to reality was watching the overall weaker performances on the vehicle tactics. Yemi wanted the team in place within four seconds of stopping their motorcade. Nick's lack of coordination, combined with the fact that he was forced to start from a position with a computer in his lap was making Chiedu potentially vulnerable.

"One more time!" Karen called from her megaphone several yards from the dirt-gravel mixed "parking lot" they found deep in Alleghany. She counted to 10 and pressed the horn.

The doors flew open, and within a few seconds, each Raptor member was in firing position from behind their bulletproof doors... Except for Nick, who was late yet again, and he knew it. He cursed to himself amongst a loud sigh from Lyle on the opposite side of the car. Yemi walked over to Lyle's car like a pissed-off boot camp instructor.

"Step forward."

"Me?" innocently asked Nick to his superior.

"The guy who failed to protect Morgan State from shootings on campus and now can't be pried from his laptop fast enough even on the third freaking try. Yeah, you." As Yemi closed in, Lyle stepped over to Terry, so it was now just Nick and Yemi on the right side of the Toyota 4Runner.

"Sir, I'm sorry, but it's not like I can throw down the machine. I was thinking maybe I can guard him from the back seat—"

"You're delusional if you think I'm going to allow that." There was nothing in response but silence. Nick realized he had forgotten the chain of command for a moment and now must pay the price. Another typical rookie mistake he had been hoping to avoid.

"I'm sorry, Mr. Uzunma—"

"Apologies are not necessary right now. Results are. Your resume said active shooter training and an active shooter would have lit up your whole car by the time you close a browser window." Nothing could come out of Nick's mouth. He just nodded, and Yemi turned back toward his car. Jasper caught up to him to pull his comrade to the side.

"You do know Morgan is in Baltimore, right?" asked his long-time friend from the other side of their home continent. "I know what you're trying to do, but you can't lay that on the kid."

"Attah would be safer in Baltimore than with us if we don't get this down."

"I think that got through to Rice. He'll get it down within a few more attempts. Just relax." When Yemi couldn't look him in the face, Jasper knew that meant he was struggling with questions in his head about their progress. "Wanna take a walk?"

"I'm alright. Let me talk to Karen. Everybody," he called to the rest of the team. "Fifteen-minute break, then let's get it right." Yemi stepped over to the side of the parking lot to rendezvous with his younger sister.

"Everything cool?" she asked him. Her refusal to let go of staring at his face hinted she was concerned. "Holding a twenty two year old responsible for the state's leading city in homicide was a little harsh."

"Jasper already brought that up." Yemi sighed. "I gotta do a better job at making my doubts less obvious."

"You've been working hard, it's understandable."

"Lawyers of their family members won't take that as an excuse if we slip up."

"Yemi." Yemi knew those were the subjects Karen wanted him to stray away from. Insurance and legal claims were her realm of expertise, not to mention her actual academic background. "We're covered on that end, I've told you that multiple times." There was silence between the two siblings as Yemi attempted to gather his thoughts. He realized he needed to say something quick, though, because he saw this as an open entry for Karen to chastise his life choices, a habit she formed when her older brother quit his travel agency job fresh out of college to start a career in law enforcement that would lead to intelligence.

"Look what's done is done, and I support your decision." He was too late. She beat him to it. "But avoiding any legal traps was one of the areas Kirk could've helped in. Just saying."

"Also, if we cut a deal with him, you'd be all set to get back to day parties on the wharf and mimosas with your friends," he quipped back to his sister. Yemi saw her face and saw how that comment dented Karen's armor a little bit. Yemi never said anything in return to all the times she complained about her college friends' dream lifestyles of new Loudon County houses or townhomes blocks from Congress. He must have been saving his commentary for the moment she second-guessed his choice of full independence.

"Don't talk to me that way. You know how much work I've put in." He nodded back, realizing he didn't need to sprinkle salt on his last comment.

"Any news from Chiedu?" The question produced an unexpected snicker from Karen.

"He wanted to let us know he believes in our services, but he has no qualms with what the creator chooses for his fate so he fears nothing. And yes, he really did get that deep."

Yemi shook his head and looked toward his crew.

"Told myself a long time ago I had no interest in politics. Too bad even when you don't give a shit, politics finds an interest in you."

"We're in charge of his life for twenty-four hours, not organizing on his campaign committee."

"Our new venture won't even last twenty-four hours if I don't get these guys in shape." A smile rose over Karen's face. She had always admired that Yemi displayed a real focus away from the distractions of the modern world, a quality she never saw in any of even the most intellectually gifted men at Wake Forest. Her brother got his code of sticking to action over talk from his father, who also made sure his ego never put them in a situation where integrity was compromised.

"This is the dream, though, right?" she asked him.

That question hovered in Yemi's head. In his eyes, Karen was the dreamer of the two, always planning her life to play out a certain way five or ten years ahead. Granted, her ideals changed from becoming a decorated public attorney helping juvenile delinquents to a potential blossom in the D.C. startup scene. Yemi, on the other hand, took each day as its own brutal puzzle, knowing any hour could be his last breathing if a kidnapper or other armed criminal was on to his investigation. A feeling not so far off from the clientele he and his sister now served.

"You've always been the ambitious one. I'm just happy to be out of the cubicle." Yemi stepped away and got back to his team. They were going to get it right by any means necessary. If the mission failed, he wished the confined space he'd return to would be the office at Titus rather than a jail cell if they operated with enough negligence.

———

The drive back to the HQ started much quieter than the first journey earlier. It also was past ten P-M, three hours after either Baltimore or DC's economic rush hours, leaving open lanes for the interstate up to the beltway. Lyle looked in the rearview mirror at the defeated Nick in the back seat.

"Don't worry, young bull," Terry heard Lyle say. "This is all part of the growth period. If we don't learn hard now, we won't even live to regret it on the battlefield." There was no answer from Nick. The silence Terry heard seemed to mean it didn't inspire Nick too much.

"I actually have to agree with that," said Terry who was again surprised at another moment he saw eye to eye with the man who pushed him to almost quit on the spot on the first trip. Terry glanced at the rearview mirror and saw some life emerge in Nick.

"I've done everything right since ninth grade. I told myself I'd excel at everything I do, from programming operating systems to playing video games on them. I know I have a ways to go in tactical training, but in all my years of campus patrols, I've never had a superior come down on me like that before." Lyle shrugged his shoulders.

"Things can't always be mapped out, kid. You gotta learn to adapt to the situation. Flow with water."

"Observe, orient, decide, and act," stated Terry.

"I guess you're right," muttered Nick.

"We are right. No need to guess about that," said Lyle. "Some facts in your head only come from banging it up against a wall."

CHAPTER 5

The official protection period began at 12:00am and ended a full 24 hours before the team would exit the premises fifteen minutes after midnight the following day. However, Yemi and Karen established the perimeter of the Attah castle a full six hours prior to the top of the day.

Chiedu's street in Vienna was lined with mansions filled up by lawyers, CEOs, and others who had various ties to the taxpayer money pot across the Wilson Bridge. Chiedu's house stood out with the gargoyles staring back at the six-man squad as they walked up the front yard and mini statues at the center of the wrap-around driveway. From the entrance, Yemi and Jasper were greeted by the distrusting attitude of Obi. From then on, every request from Yemi on the pre-checklist had a smart alec response or something to delay the squad commander from the tasks at hand.

"He's fine with cereal for breakfast, correct?" asked Yemi, his patience at a low point.

"Don't you think the former ambassador to Nigeria deserves a more proper meal than frosted flakes?"

"If you want to take this to a new level, we can take it to a whole new fucking level. Otherwise, get the hell out of my way before you get hurt." Yemi rarely cursed, but he had enough with Obi. The extra four inches in height and thirty pounds in body mass did nothing to intimidate Yemi. Although Chiedu was still asleep, he knew Nick and Jasper being witnesses was enough for Obi to be pushed into escalating the bravado.

"We can do whatever you wanna do, commander," challenged Obi, refusing to back down. Jasper quickly jumped in to separate the two and grab his partner off. He was glad only Nick saw this and not Terry or instigating hype man Lyle.

"Relax, brother. Relax." Jasper didn't have to repeat himself much. Yemi knew he had to cool down. He stepped away and headed outside to help his team finish checking the perimeter. Jasper decided to be the mature one.

"What's going on with your boss?" asked Obi.

"He's trying to save yours. Let's cut this ego-tripping bullshit right here, right now." Obi stared off against Jasper for a few moments. It was a subtle hint for Obi to realize he was in the wrong without externally getting his ego bruised. Obi grunted and walked away. Yemi figured he was going to check on the former ambassador.

The property remained secured until the clock ticked 8:00 am. The team escorted Chiedu to their three-vehicle motorcade. Obi drove Chiedu's Black Mercedes AMG GT-4. Nick had his navigation and surveillance software booted up next to the man in the back seat whose life had reached its highest bid set to end on that day. The 4Runners were manned by the rest of the squad just like they practiced. The caravan pulled out of the driveway and Chiedu watched his castle left alone as it disappeared out the frame of the window. His wife had chosen to stay with her aunt in Maryland for the time being. It didn't offend Chiedu one bit, especially if October first was going to be his final day on Earth.

———

An open flame burned from a large ditch in the vast farmland behind Altavius' house. In the back of the Camry, Aaron vividly remembered the Rolex hanging off the arm of a corpse. Rold was against the idea of robbing victims. Aaron was, too, but not for the morally righteous political reasons Rold clung to. Pawn shops asked too many questions, and preliminary tomb raiding wasn't his style.

The crew split into two four-man groups. Rold left each car

with a $5,000 stipend for food and emergency costs. He, on the other hand, drove home alone to spectate the news. In the back of Aaron's mind, that was a tad suspicious, given it was Rold who left them with the war speech, and he figured Rold would be the one to lead them into battle, but he brushed it off, confident that his new team would still emerge victorious. After all, it wasn't like the ambassador had SEAL Team 6 escorting him.

The cars stopped at a Royal Farms to feast on a last meal five hours before their mission.

"Hey, chill on the speeding fam," said one of the group's drivers to the other car's chauffeur. He swallowed a bite of his hot dog purchased from the warmer near the front register. He was careful not to get any ketchup on his throwback #1 John Wall jersey from the mid-2010s Wizards seasons. "Feds pulling us over before we even get to the joint ain't the move."

"I think you need to chill with all that meat in your mouth, nigga," retorted the other driver. "Over there looking like the glizzy globetrotter and shit." The reference to both DC's staple street snack and the theatrical Harlem basketball team sent the group into a roaring laughter, with some even damn near falling off the bench. Even Aaron couldn't help but smirk.

"What you gonna do when you get your stack, Q?" asked one of the hired guns to Qasim after the hysteria subsided. Qasim thought about it as he dipped his potato wedges in the jalapeno cheddar sauce.

"Don't wanna do the typical shit like throwing it away at a club or something," he said, still pondering. "Lay low for a bit, then figure out a legit business to start. Been debating between a convenience store and a laundromat."

"Shit, I never thought about a laundromat."

"You ever been out to Wheaton or Langley Park? It's a whole different country. They have their own laundromats, restaurants, markets... It ain't like our hood where the Asians and

Arabs run everything. Time to change that."

"Damn, you starting to sound like Rold for real."

"Hey, he can get annoying, but O-G knows what he's talking about. Community economics is key." Qasim looked at Aaron, who had his head down nibbling at his chicken salad wrap, unengaged in the conversation.

"What about you, Aaron?" asked Qasim. Aaron chewed and swallowed, then wiped his mouth with a napkin.

"Same thing I've been doing. Just take care of my mom."

"Respect, respect. But you don't have any other ambitions? I mean, how are you gonna take care of her? Gonna get her a new crib?"

"Maybe. We'll see, I guess." Aaron went back to eating his wrap, a man of few words. That didn't go unnoticed by Qasim.

"Hey man, look. I'm sorry for how we pulled up on you, alright? I recognize now none of these blessings we're about to receive would have been possible without your input. Rold was right about you." Aaron paused from eating.

"Appreciate that." Qasim smirked. The silent truce formed before the farmhouse massacre was still intact. He went back to his potato wedges.

"Let's finish up and bounce outta here in five."

———

Route 29 turned into Colesville Road, and it was a straight shot into downtown Silver Spring for the motorcade. Chiedu watched the residential houses creep closer into the commercial center. He looked at the aerial footage on Nick's laptop.

"Aren't we in illegal airspace for drones?"

"Bypassed," quickly remarked Nick. "Yemi's got connects."

"He sure does, huh?" Chiedu could see a grimace on Obi's face from the rearview mirror on any positive mention of Yemi. Chiedu looked out the window in reflection. He was in slight disbelief he had reached such a point in life. Two decades prior, he was organizing the people of the Niger Delta to fight for their land in the voting booths against POPCO and the oil dynasties, who saw nothing but black gold in the region. Now, he rode in riding in luxury in the homeland of the oil barons, where he was marked a traitor by the Biafra Freedom Movement and was their #1 target.

"Where am I now on the list?" he asked the computer whiz next to him. Nick was a bit hesitant to answer.

"What list, sir?"

"You know the list. Why else would you be riding with me scanning for snipers on the rooftops?"

"Uhm..." Nick used his satellite internet to open up an internet browser Chiedu had never seen before with its minimal, early 2000s-esque layout. "I don't mean to sound rude, but does it really matter at this point, Mr. Attah?"

"Do as you're told," Obi said from the front.

"Relax, Obi," stated a calm Chiedu. He looked at Nick. "Whatever you do with your life, kid, don't let it be something where you have to pay people to stand up for you." Nick nodded as he browsed the page.

"Seven hundred seventy bitcoins, sir," Nick stated. "That's equivalent to roughly three million U-S dollars. Today, you've cracked the Bazaar's top five." Chiedu smirked to himself.

"How old are you, young man?"

"Twenty-four, sir."

"When I was your age, all I had to my name was my big mouth, but I didn't fear death. Now I'm in the back of a Mercedes surrounded by bodyguards in a foreign land being shoved along with my tail in between my legs."

"Don't be scared, sir. Let the tabloids gossip and the terrorists spread their lies. Most people don't understand the cost of true leadership." Chiedu turned back towards Nick with a sarcastic grin on his face.

"Remember what I just said."

————

Downtown Silver Spring, Maryland, had been known as "Little Ethiopia" since the 90s. However, by the 2020s, it had evolved into "Little Africa" with a presence of countries from the Western portion of the continent along with the diaspora in the Caribbean, creating a vibrant corridor for international commerce. For every three restaurants selling tibs and injera, there was a spot where one could get a generous serving of jollof rice with some egusi stew. For that reason, the Civic Building at Veterans Plaza was selected as the location for that year's Naija Fest in celebration of Nigerian Independence Day. Right across the plaza was the parking garage Chiedu's caravan would be pulling into.

Yemi scanned every angle as they drove up each level. The attack could come at any moment and at any location. The CCTV footage they tapped into provided a good start, but nothing beat the accuracy of an eye that's used to scouting ambushes from delta boat militants. Once they parked, the squad swarmed the Mercedes as if Chiedu was a baby elephant at the center of a herd. Yemi immediately began dividing up the duties.

"Victor, help Jasper do another sweep of the garage," Yemi said. Once you're done, join us inside while Jasper stays here. Nick, your phone ready?" Yemi knew Nick had Veterans Plaza and their section of downtown Silver Spring available to monitor remotely.

"Yes, sir."

"Alright, let's roll out." He had been resistant to orders all morning, but Obi abided, and the five squad members set up a pentagon formation around the former ambassador.

The Civic building opened in 2010, the same year an armed environmental activist made national news when he held multiple people hostage at Discovery Channel Headquarters down the street. Along with the rest of the Silver Spring revitalization, its goal was to be a cornerstone for community activities and organized events that brought the locals together. On the day of Naija Fest, members of the Nigerian diaspora in the area decorated the interiors with white and green colors in a show of pride for their origin. Chiedu, Yemi, Obi, Terry, Lyle, and Nick walked past the vendors setting up shop. They were looking for the person in charge. A woman who bared a strikingly similar profile to Karen stepped forward from a group of organizers.

"Mr. Attah!" she called out.

Before she could get close to the client, Obi closed the space. She backed up, clearly a bit surprised yet not all the way intimidated.

"My apologies, but I hope you know these kinds of precautions are necessary given recent events," Chiedu assured the young woman only a few years removed from grad school.

"We appreciate you joining our organization's special event today." Yemi watched her eyeball the security detail again. The sentence seemed like a cop-out as if she really saw his presence as a nuisance. But Yemi knew she was perceptive enough to know it'd be a waste of time to convince the ambassador of any alternative plans for the day.

"Thank you, miss—?"

"Efemena. I corresponded with Sade over e-mail."

"Oh. Sade spoke very highly of you... Yemi."

"Yes?" He snapped out of his owl mode of scanning the civic center for perceived threats.

"You two should link after this is over," Chiedu insisted. "Sade found out about Raptor through Efemena's database on local Nigerian-owned businesses." When Raptor was first launched, several blogs promoted the idea of a security startup being fronted by a young Black woman. Yemi rolled his eyes at these early accolades, but it seemed to have actually paid off. He gave Efemena a friendly nod to acknowledge her contribution.

———

Two cars arrived at a stop light on Georgia Ave at the Northwest D.C./Maryland border. Rold's team was inching near their Silver Spring destination and Qasim gave off the vibe to Aaron that he couldn't be more excited. In the backseat of the Camry, he shoved the magazine into his Glock modified for fully automatic fire and examined his weapon. Aaron saw Qasim out of the corner of his eye, eyeballing it with admiration, knowing his dreams of fortune were packed in each bullet.

"Y'all ready for this shit?" he asked the car's occupants. The driver and front passenger immediately responded with expletives followed by a "yeah," masquerading their nervous energy with excitement. Aaron didn't react. He stayed quiet like he had been this entire road trip.

"You ready for this, fam?" Qasim asked the silent assassin.

"Yup, just thinking."

"Shit, my mind racing too. All I got in my head is them M's, nam saying?" Aaron had difficulty with slang sometimes, but he knew the M stood for millions.

"I feel you, but it's not that." Qasim hesitated for a moment.

"What is it then?"

"Just crazy that I took this man's son... And now I'm about to end the whole bloodline." Aaron took another look at his main tool for the job. He chose the Mini Talon again over the offers for automatic pistols from Qasim and Rold. If he died on any mission, he wanted to go out with something created by his own labor.

———

"I am here with all of you in solidarity. In solidarity with the same spirit that gained our country's independence over sixty years ago..." Yemi and his squad stood in position, piercing through the crowd of the Nigerian diaspora to look for any potential threats.

A man reaching into his inner jacket put the squad on alert, but it ended up just being a tissue for Fall allergies. Feedback came into Yemi's earpiece.

"Yemi...a pair of heavily armed vehicles have just arrived at Colesville and Georgia."

Back at Raptor HQ, Karen monitored the aerial footage. Yemi figured she was able to identify the weapons by running through infrared scans. Raptor didn't have the highest budget, but they clearly knew the areas to spend for their protection.

"Models?" asked Yemi.

"A Crown Vic followed by a beat-up gray Camry."

"Okay. Nick, get eyes on 'em."

Nick and Victor guarded the exterior of the Civic Center, parallel to each other at the front glass doors. He whipped out his phone and pulled up the footage.

"I spot them, sir."

In the garage, Jasper peered over a railing at the side. He saw the two cars around the corner.

"I have them in sight," he said into the radio. "They'll be within our vicinity seconds after that light changes."

Yemi nodded to his fellow guards surrounding the podium. Everybody heard Jasper over the radio.

"He's only got a few words left," Obi stated into his earpiece. Yemi knew how important the speech was to Chiedu. After all, he could have just spent that day on his couch in the far more safe confines of his own home.

"And he needs to make them within the next fifteen seconds," Yemi responded. The two traded looks, but underneath their egos was the reality they both knew they had to get Chiedu into the bulletproof Mercedes as soon as they could.

"Yes, my days of protesting in the streets of Lagos are behind me," Chiedu projected behind the mic. "But I am still the same man who puts the love for his people above anything else.

God bless you all."

Behind the applause of the audience, Victor and Nick snuck onto the premises from outside. Back at a six-headcount, the squad surrounded Chiedu's space to guide him from the podium.

Chiedu could see in their facial expressions that they were acting with the urgency of an immediate threat. He made eye contact with Obi, which cemented the assumption to be true. Yemi started to dish out directions in the hallway.

"Victor, you and Nick escort Chiedu around back and get him to the garage."

"They go with ME," chided Obi. Yemi knew Obi never wanted to give up the authority he had over his boss' well-being. He traded eye contact with Yemi once again. He looked away and started to move with Chiedu toward the back. Nick and Victor leaned in toward Yemi before they followed Obi.

"Watch him," their squad leader warned.

Chiedu, Lyle, and Terry made their way out the front door. Despite it being a sunny afternoon, Veterans Plaza was rather clear of civilians at the moment. About fifty yards from the entrance was the intersection of Fenton Street and Ellsworth Drive at the corner of the garage, right where the two armed cars were heading toward. The three Raptor guards rushed to take positions, drawing out their pistols in the process.

The Camry and Crown Vic made their way down Fenton. Yemi looked through the windows of the Chic-Fil-A that was based at the corner. He could see many of the occupants sporting gas masks.

"Get ready!" he said to Terry and Lyle.

Something caught Terry's attention at the corner of his eye. He turned left and Efemena was walking in the middle of the street right toward their direction with a Chipotle-style paper bag in her hand. She sipped her drink with her shades on, oblivious to the chaos that was about to transpire. The inner police officer in Terry kicked in, and he dashed for the clueless organizer.

"Miss, get back!"

The driver of the Camry saw the pistol in Terry's hand as he sprinted toward Efemena. Sensing the ambush, the driver immediately whipped out his own handgun and lit up the Chic Fil A glass to the crosswalk, shooting through his dash window. He screeched the vehicle to a stop, and all the members of the car jumped out to take positions behind the car doors. The Crown Vic reversed and peeled down a connecting street to the garage.

Terry got Efemena to safety at the entrance to the mall. Once she got inside, he crouched down behind one of the pillars and helped Yemi plus Lyle return fire at the Camry.

Aaron grabbed one of his homemade teargas bottles and quarterbacked it over the door riddled with bullet holes. It broke by the crosswalk. The Ellsworth/Fenton intersection became completely covered in smoke clouds.

Blood splattered the windshield of the Camry. Even through the clouds, Yemi could tell the driver had been hit.

"I'm gonna intercept them from the garage," Yemi heard Jasper's voice through the radio.

"Aaron, we gotta move!" yelled one of the assailants from the opposite side of the car.

"Q! Above you!" yelled another one. Automatic pistol fire followed, and Yemi saw sparks on the railing several levels above his position to the right.

"Alright, let's go!" yelled one of the voices from the car they were engaged with in the shootout.

"Jasper?! You good?" Yemi called into the radio. He saw his comrade take cover but was unsure if any of the shells hit him. A few seconds of silence evolved into anxiety over the status of the Ethiopian sharpshooter.

"Yeah, yeah," Jasper finally answered back through the

earpiece. "Chin caught a ricochet, but I'm fine."

"Head back to the car. One of their vehicles took off to storm the garage. Two ran into the mall. We'll pursue and try to stop them from getting to the skywalk. Once it's clear, get Attah out of there. Don't wait for us."

"Copy."

———

Ellsworth Place was first opened as City Place Mall in 1992. Prior to Silver Spring's revitalization in the 2010s, City Place was mostly a hub of discount shopping and a slight destination for lower-level street crime like shoplifting, robbery, or the occasional stabbing. On Nigerian Independence Day of 2025, a much more severe crime was in progress once Aaron and Qasim burst through the glass doors. Patrons were hiding from the commotion outside but immediately ran for their lives to other sections of the building once the gas-masked gunmen came in from the Fenton entrance like a pair of school shooters.

Still recovering from the teargas, Yemi, Lyle, and Terry entered from the Ellsworth Drive side. Scared mall-goers ran from them while some ran past toward the exit, falsely assuming Yemi's team to be some sort of law enforcement. The three took cover at the end of the first hall. Yemi peeked around the corner and saw the two criminals heading for the stairs.

"Three O'Clock," They prepared to engage.

"Yemi!" the voice of Karen shouted into the radio. "Hostile coming from the South side of the mall!"

Yemi looked across the center court of the shopping center. On the opposite side, the hostile was a young man of Asian descent and a modified AK-47 with a drum round pointed toward their position.

"Get down!" Yemi yelled to his team members. Automatic gunfire shredded the second floor of the North Side, hitting store windows and scattering shards of glass. None managed to wound the three Raptor guards, but they were still unable to return fire.

———

Danny was intent on causing as much chaos as he could, screaming at the top of his lungs while he pulled the trigger.

"Danny!" Aaron called out to his neighborhood friend from the stairwell. Danny paused the shooting for a brief moment. "What are you doing?"

"I always got your back, bro!" There was a short pause between them. For that brief moment amidst the pandemonium, their fragmented friendship may have been salvaged.

"Go get that money, boy!" Danny yelled one last time. Before Aaron could even respond, Danny let it rip some more against the opposite side of the mall.

"Let's move!" Qasim's words broke Aaron out of his rekindling trance. They sprinted up the mall's stairs and headed for the skywalk.

———

"Jasper!" Yemi called into the radio as they retreated back toward the North entrance. "We had to fall back. They're heading to the skywalk."

"Copy." Jasper immediately headed to the trunk of the 4Runner. He got the hatch open and reached into a compartment hidden where the spare tire would be. He took out two civilian-standard Sig Sauer MCX-Spear assault rifles and handed one off to Victor, who was positioned right by him. Obi motioned for Chiedu into the Mercedes. He then went for the driver's seat, but Jasper stopped him.

"Can't go yet. They're moving in on us from all possible escape routes."

"So we just sit here and get ambushed?"

"Staying here is how we prevent an ambush," said Victor. He aimed toward the opposite end of the garage, ready to engage with the incoming enemy.

"Nick, guard the sidewalk," ordered Jasper. "Two of them are coming through the skywalk."

"They'll be too close to Chiedu by that point." Obi slid, cocked his pistol on point with his line like he was calling himself to action. "I'm going to intercept them." Chiedu's right-hand man headed out on his own to the nearby stairwell, eager to handle the threats to his boss on his own. Jasper and Nick made eye contact.

"Follow him. Be careful," he told the young recruit. At that moment, they could hear the screech of a car speeding up the garage ramp from the opposite side. "Go!"

Nick ran after Obi, getting his own pistol out in the process. Victor and Jasper took cover behind cars. The Camry appeared, and immediately, two occupants fired out the windows in their direction. Their small arms, however, weren't able to match the range of the assault rifles in Raptor's hands. Jasper and Victor could hear the obscenities from across the way as one of the shooters got hit by the 5.56mm ammo. The Camry skidded like a severely scratched LP record while reversing direction. Victor pushed forward, unloading his clip onto the car. Taking some hits, it still managed to scurry back down the ramp. Jasper fell back to directly protect Chiedu while Victor continued to pursue the Camry.

Qasim and Aaron finally arrived at the hallway that led to the skywalk over the center of downtown Silver Spring. However, once Qasim decided to continue jogging, Aaron halted him. Qasim was bewildered by the actions of his comrade.

"Bruh, we're running out of time," he said while looking down the walkway that led right to the garage. "We gotta get him before the Feds surround the place."

"Just wait one second," Aaron responded back to him. The future freedom depended on every moment and every decision, big or small. Two of their own weren't even alive anymore to make that choice. But the look on Aaron's face staring off down the hallway hinted he knew something Qasim didn't.

———

Finishing running the two flights from Chiedu's location, Nick barged through the push doors. A surprised Obi pointed his gun straight at him, unsure of who it was that just came from the stairwell. Within a few seconds, Obi eased up to let Nick take position parallel to him on their side of the skywalk. Each peeked around the corner to see if anyone had arrived at the opposite end yet. It was clear. Suddenly, both heard a ding from an elevator next to the stairwell. The two exchanged looks, deciding on who it would be between them that checked it. Obi decided to take the initiative, and he backpedaled to the elevator opening. The two walls opened, and Obi looked down at the floor. It was a paper bag designed for what was probably an American franchise fast casual restaurant. Something filled it, and the opening was tucked in.

KA-BOOM!

———

The ground shook beneath the feet of Jasper. Something just exploded above his immediate position. Yemi's voice tore through the earpiece.

"Jasper? Talk to me!"

"I'm good," the Ethiopian marksman responded. However, his main concern was for the young one he just sent upstairs. "Nick...Nick?"

"Just get Chiedu out of here," assured Yemi. "We'll check on Rice."

"Copy." Jasper ran to the Mercedes and swung open the back door. Chiedu was in the fetal position, a reasonable reaction to the automatic gunfire and explosion that was going on around him.

"Sir, we have to go into the S-U-V," Jasper barked at his client. "Now." The ambassador scrambled up and abided to Jasper's command. They rolled into one of the 4Runners as Jasper jumped behind the wheel.

At the opposite end of the garage level, Jasper watched Victor keep his rifle tactically pointed forward as he tiptoed down the ramp. Around the corner, Victor let off some shots toward what Jasper assumed was the Camry camped on the floor below. When there was no further return fire, Victor wove to Jasper signaling it was clear to pass.

————

His Raptor-issued blazer and slacks now covered in debris, Nick's damaged ear drums could barely hear himself crashing through the doors to get into the stairwells. Still, he had survived a much better fate than the large Nigerian man he dragged with him. Shrapnel protruded from Obi's face, and crimson red drenched his lower body with his limbs barely intact. Sparks flew on the door by gunshots from the opposite side of the skywalk.

Once they reached one flight down, Obi raised his hand to stop Nick. The wounded warrior used the last bit of his strength to reach into his inner jacket and reveal a second pistol, a hand-sized Beretta Pico.

"Fire department should be here any minute," he muttered. "Protect Attah by any means." Nick nodded and set him down. He patted Obi on the back, unsure of how else to send off the broadly built bodyguard to his likely demise. Nick didn't waste another second, and he sprinted down the rest of the flight of stairs. He heard a quick exchange of gunfire above him. Some more footsteps followed a corner above Nick's position. Nick fired in their direction. He missed but it managed to still send whoever it was in retreat back up the stairwell. Not wanting to wait around for a shootout in an enclosed space, Nick busted through the door and sprinted with all of his energy toward the

Raptor SUVs. Jasper was already in drive and was pulling out of the parking space.

"Jasper!" Nick yelled to the 4Runner, hoping the driver could hear him. Jasper stepped on the brake and waited for Nick to arrive at him. However, at the same moment, Nick could hear the hunting stalker from the stairwell enter the space through the second level door. Nick could almost feel the iron sights aiming for his body running through the lot.

POP, POP, POP. Nick noticed Yemi had arrived at the parking level just in time to catch the would-be assassin off guard. The gas-masked figure collapsed by the doorway like a deflated balloon as Lyle provided cover fire for Terry to get to the other SUV and for Nick to safely hop in the back of Jasper's. Another gas mask bandit saw the body of his comrade and unloaded his magazine in Lyle and Yemi's direction.

"Come on!" Nick could hear shouting from the figure to their brother-in-arms. Raptor secured their side of the garage while returning fire to the gas mask, using whatever energy they could to get up and be led back into the stairwell. The door slammed behind them. Nobody among the Executive Protection side was hit, so Lyle and Yemi jumped into Terry's vehicle. Victor slid into the front passenger seat of Jasper's. Ditching the Mercedes, the Raptor motorcade sped onto the ramp and exited the garage.

As they started their withdrawal from downtown Silver Spring, Nick closed his eyes. He didn't even have the power to wipe the debris off as he attempted to get some rest after the long day of turmoil.

"Rice," Victor said as Nick's eyes opened back up. "Your ears ringing?"

"Not anymore," the recent college grad responded. "I'm good." Victor gave him the thumbs up. Chiedu looked over at the bombing remnants on Nick's blazer, remembering who was upstairs with him when the explosion happened.

"Is Obi in the other car?" Nick could barely shake his head.

"No." Nick's reluctant body language solidified the fate of the ambassador's right-hand man. Chiedu nodded his head in recognition and stared back down. Nick knew the ambassador and his bodyguard were close friends in addition to being colleagues. A year prior, the poor politician probably thought the most action Obi would see would be settling disputes of who people cutting in line to get a picture with the country's most popular diplomat. But after the Afrileaks fiasco and his son's death, he knew that Obi was just standing in the bullseye of the bounty on Chiedu's head. The thought of Obi triggered Nick's memory of that elevator. Who could've snuck such a device into the garage, and who knew their exact location across from the skywalk?

"We'll have Karen run the footage back and see where the hell that came from." Jasper could tell what was on their minds.

"I'll help, too," added Nick.

CHAPTER 6

Aaron wasn't one for spirituality, but if there was a higher being at work in his life, his prayers were answered when he saw that 1996 Honda Accord on the fifth level of the parking garage. His knowledge of hotwiring older cars came from the internet, just like everything else he learned regarding his career as a hitman tied to the Bazaar. He threw Qasim in the backseat and sped out of the garage before any emergency services arrived on the premises.

"Stay with me, man," he remarked to Qasim, who was slowly bleeding out on the leather. The nurse who worked for Barry was in Beltsville, less than twenty minutes away from his location. Qasim could make it, and that was the only mission Aaron cared for anymore. As he drove off of Colesville onto I-495, he dialed Rold's number. It rang seven times.

"You've reached Rold Jenkins. Sorry, I couldn't come to the phone right now, but if you leave a message..." Aaron motioned like he was about to spike the phone down in angst. He composed himself to keep it in his hands. He didn't conclude that Rold betrayed them just yet, but it was not a good sign, given how things were panning out. Rold was adamant about contacting him after the mission, whether it was a success or not. This was pretty out of character for someone so concerned about honor amongst "warriors." Sirens blared on the beltway in the opposite direction as fire trucks, ambulances, and Maryland State troopers raced toward the location of the attack. Montgomery County's finest was definitely going to need backup in the 48-hour search for Aaron's crew.

When he reached the apartment complex in Beltsville,

Aaron turned around to see Qasim passed out. As he dialed the number, he shook his legs to wake him up. The eyelids rose up, and Aaron breathed a sigh of relief that there was still hope.

"I'm outside," he said to the nurse once she picked up. "Blue Honda Accord."

"Alright, give me a sec."

"Please hurry if you can. My friend is dying." He hung it up. He turned the radio to the news.

"Three dead, multiple injuries in a shootout and explosion in downtown Silver Spring," the radio anchor dished out over the air. "Police have one suspect in custody while two have been confirmed as part of the deceased. We will keep you updated with the latest developments as information comes in." There was no way to avoid the fact that what took place in Silver Spring was going to be the top news story in the region over the next week at minimum. Outside of 9/11, only the D.C. sniper incident from the early 2000s rivaled that kind of response. But Aaron refused to get put behind bars like John Allen Muhammad or Lee Boyd Malvo, even if the Feds managed to bring Danny in for interrogation. He was going to drop Qasim off for treatment and then make his way to Cumberland, where sanctuary was at the home of Doug Vanderville. He was on the clock.

A middle-aged woman still wearing her scrubs from her shift at the local hospital waltzed out of the building without the sense of urgency Aaron was pushing for and arrived by his window. Aaron quickly winded it down.

"I'm sorry, honey," she said in between gum chewing. "I want your friend to live, but I never received my deposit."

"Wait..." Aaron was in disbelief. "Barry was supposed to—"

"His phone is off." It became official. The bastard in charge of the whole operation betrayed his own outfit. Aaron smacked the steering wheel in frustration. No wonder Barry had no issues with the death of Altavius. But unless he wanted to go on an immediate pursuit of vengeance, he had to focus on the issues of the present moment. He looked in the backseat. Qasim was the present issue.

"Five hundred. Can five hundred dollars cover him for now?"

"Sweetie, look..." Aaron remembered that he had some crypto left over from selling some of his 3-D printed assault rifles.

"I can Cash App you two thousand within a few days." She thought for a second.

"By Monday?"

"Yes! Please just help him."

"Okay. Pull up around back. I'll meet you there in a few." She headed back inside the building as Aaron whipped the car around to the back lot.

"Just leave me," Qasim managed to mutter as Aaron looked for a parking spot.

"No! I'm not abandoning you like that punk bitch, Barry." He found a space and pulled in.

"They're gonna find the car. Save your money and get... Get..." Aaron had never watched someone die slow, but he knew what that meant as the words started getting choked up. He knew if Qasim passed out another time, he wouldn't wake up.

"Qasim!" he yelled to his partner as he pushed him again. This time, the eyelids stayed closed. With the fate of Qasim sealed, Aaron checked his phone. He received a CRYPTEXT from Doug:

L1B3RTY0RD3ATH: brooooo u good? it's all over the news

KRISPYATTUX: they prolly got my crib, need a place to lay low. Can u help?

There was a brief pause. Aaron looked out the window

and the nurse still hadn't shown up.

L1B3RTY0RD3ATH: get a burner and call 2406523365.

Aaron didn't waste any more time. He ditched the Honda and started to walk briskly toward another building. He would get an Uber to take him to a cheap phone store on the other side of the county where he would ditch his current one and get a prepaid cell to call Doug on. He looked behind him before crossing the street and finally saw the nurse approaching the Honda. As he continued to walk away, he knew she'd come to realize quickly that her services were no longer required.

———

The evening had set in. The Raptor motorcade was finally in Virginia and they were supposed to arrive at Chiedu's house with enough time to secure the perimeter before nightfall. Nick had switched to the back of Terry's car, where his laptop was located. However soon after they had pulled over for Nick to hop in the other vehicle, a set of three law enforcement vehicles began to file behind. Once the blue and red shined, they pulled over yet again. Nick watched Terry look at the rearview mirrors.

"Locals?" asked Lyle.

"Nah," said Terry. "I don't see Fairfax County colors." Solid black Chevy Suburbans meant federal, so Nick assumed it was either the FBI or Secret Service. A Caucasian man in his late 50s, who at around 5'5" had the physique of a welterweight boxer half his age, stepped out with an intercom in one hand and a pistol in another. Nick could spot the five-point star on the hat, hinting that it was the law enforcement agency that handled protecting the president. Soon, other agents flanked him with rifles and small arms pointed forward.

"All occupants, please exit the vehicles slowly with your hands raised," the figure demanded. Nick saw Terry look at

Yemi for approval, and the squad leader affirmatively nodded back. One by one, each Raptor member stepped out of the 4 Runners and onto the shoulder of the road. After the battle that was waged that day, none of it seemed to phase any member of the team, and they all knew Yemi would want them to cooperate. Nick was surprised. It was the first time they encountered police of any kind the whole day.

"Can Chiedu Attah please step forward," the man requested.

"Who are you?" the Raptor commander asked. The man paused as Nick saw him as a silhouette against the flashing lights.

"I'm Assistant Special Agent in Charge Chris Towers with the United States Secret Service Cyber Fraud Task Force." Nick had come across some white papers by the CFTF during his Bazaar research since joining the squad. It was formed in 2020 as an amalgamation of the Secret Service's Electronic Crimes and Financial Crimes Task Forces. If there was any division in American law enforcement keeping track of assassination markets outside of the FBI, it would be them. Still, though, he thought the private sector was ahead of the curve up until now.

"We're Attah's security detail," Yemi responded.

"We know. Again. Mr. Attah, please step forward!" Yemi turned toward the first car and nodded to his client. Chiedu started to begrudgingly walk toward the flashing lights. Nick was sure Chiedu was familiar with the Secret Service but was fascinated that all of a sudden, they showed interest in the former ambassador's safety when his son had been killed months ago. Once he got to the other side, two special agents escorted him inside one of the Suburbans.

"Cloud. Rodriguez. Search them and the cars." Two agents in tactical gear stepped forward and began patting down each member of the Raptor team. Nick looked at them, and they reminded him of Rainbow Six. Campus police at Morgan State didn't have a SWAT team. The agents removed the pistols and set them all on the roof of the cars. Once they finished with Yemi and Terry, Chris Towers holstered his weapon as he marched towards Terry.

"Talk to me here, Blackwell." Nick raised his eyebrow, realizing Terry and Towers were familiar with each other. "What the hell happened in Silver Spring?"

"We were ambushed, and our team leader made the right call." Nick knew Chris was trying to play the buddy cop game, but he also knew Terry wouldn't allow his boss to get disrespected, no matter how much of a soft spot he had for those behind the badge. But Chris didn't seem to get the signal after he looked over at Yemi, made eye contact with Nick, and then back at Terry.

"If it's going to get this violent, it'll fall all under the law, or they'll only let RexCorp or Titus get these kinds of contracts. I understand why you didn't take my offer, but be smart."

"Officer," interjected Yemi from the other side of the vehicle. He walked over.

"According to our intel, you had advanced knowledge of Bazaar bidders in connection to today's events. Is that correct?" asked Towers.

"Yes." Nick knew Yemi to be cordial but he never heard the Raptor commander ever issue any 'sirs.' "It's a part of our job duties to protect our customers from any possible danger."

"Okay, well, now it will be a part of your job duty to disclose to the Joint Terrorism Task Force any information in relation to an attack by a group listed as a terrorist organization by the United States Department." Nick knew he was referring to one of the vocal sponsors of the attack, the Biafra Freedom Movement.

"In addition to a violation of my Fourth Amendment right, safeguarding my intel is necessary to guarantee my contracts."

A twisted look formed on Towers' face. Nick smirked a bit at the federal agent, realizing he was talking to an immigrant who clearly passed his citizenship test.

"Get your clientele to adjust or violate the Patriot Act? Make the right choice, Mr. Uzunma." Yemi didn't utter a word. Nick knew Yemi was the type who didn't enter the startup sphere to take orders from a hierarchy. He just returned a 'I farted in your car' smile back to the special agent.

"Sir!" Chris and Yemi turned toward Special Agent Rodriguez, who held the two MCX rifles. "Found these."

"Permit?" Chris asked. Almost in a manner that Nick assumed he hoped for a negative response.

"Of course."

"Let's see it."

"Jasper!" Yemi's right-hand man was already paying attention to the conversation and reached into the front S-U-V. He dug out some documents and handed them over to Rodriguez as well as Cloud.

"They're clear, sir," Rodriguez confirmed. Chris waved for them to return to the side of the law. Chris started to backpedal once they passed him.

"Attah will be under our supervision the rest of the night." From the Secret Service side, an agent winded down Chiedu's window at his request. He exchanged looks with Yemi. Chiedu raised his hand up in a gesture of appreciation for his former protection chief. He signaled a job well done even with the loss of his primary bodyguard of over half a dozen years. Within a minute, the CFTF vehicles peeled off and left the vicinity. Nick hopped back in the backseat as Lyle lit up a cigar and placed himself in the front passenger seat of the second 4 Runner. Yemi, Terry, Jasper, and Victor congregated at the center in between the cars.

"The organizer. The one you grabbed out the way, Terry,"

said Yemi. Nick could hear them with his windows rolled down "She was walking from the scene when we rolled out the garage." A look of surprise came over Terry's face. Nick couldn't imagine how the ex-cop must feel saving the life of a possible terrorist when he was trying to be a hero.

"After he rests up," Jasper added. "I can cross-check all the personnel from the event with Nick and pinpoint her that way. I think Chiedu said his aide knew her."

"Efemena Kanu," shouted Nick from inside the car. He had already taken the initiative. "Pulling her up now."

"Victor," Yemi stated. "Can you provide me with a report on the explosives possibly used by the end of the week?"

"A-SAP, boss," the Venezuelan assured his superior.

"Good stuff. Let's roll out of here." Nick watched Terry catch up to Yemi before they headed into their vehicle.

"I'm your employee and that's where my loyalty is. Towers is just following through with this homeland security mess. I hope you didn't take our side talk personally."

"I'm familiar with Chris." Yemi's answer surprised Nick, and he could tell it also surprised Terr, who stood there in silence for a few moments. Yemi got to his car before Terry returned to Nick's vehicle.

"Everything good?" asked Lyle. Terry took a breath.

"Yeah."

Nick sat alone in the backseat, clicking away at his laptop. He minimized a 'Chiedu Attah' folder as he returned to scanning CCTV footage. In the background, he had a subfolder open. Its filename read 'POPCO Docs.'

CHAPTER 7

There was a time when Cumberland was the second most populous city in the state of Maryland as a transportation hub during the Industrial Revolution. Back when the C&O Canal meant more to the American economy than just a hiking trail. By the 2020s, Cumberland was eclipsed by Hagerstown as the economic hub of Western Maryland and was one of the poorest metropolitan regions in the United States, ravaged by manufacturing downsizing combined with a meth epidemic. Still, though, the three-hour drive felt worth it as Aaron looked over at the downtown from Route 68. Just like the Eastern Shore with Rold's crew, Aaron had never been up to this part of the state. The architecture and rustic Appalachia reminded him of Danny virtually roaming through the wild west of Red Dead Redemption 2.

Property in Cumberland was far more affordable than anything in the D.C. area. Aaron was nevertheless impressed by the single-family house Doug was able to purchase for himself with crypto flips. To the average district socialite, such space seemed only habitable for a backwoods percocet dealer or some other stereotype that fell into their view of anyone beyond the exurb of Frederick, Maryland. But Aaron saw what Doug saw. Inconspicuous. Hidden amongst a forgotten America. Perfect place to plan out a for-profit war against politicians.

Aaron knocked on the door. He looked around to see if anyone was looking. No nosy neighbors, it seemed. Doug chose wisely.

"He's here," a voice from inside said as steps grew closer to the door. Soon, it flung open, and standing there was a sleek backed, neck-length hair cross country build of a man in his early twenties with an Iron Maiden t-shirt. Doug Vanderville immediately went in for a hug with his long-time CRYPTMESSAGE buddy.

"Come inside." A pair of .50 cal bolt action rifles hung on gun racks. Cartridges and the last six issues of Guns & Ammo were laid out on the coffee table. The place reeked of high-quality cannabis like someone in the house was selling it by the pound. Doug led Aaron through the living room as Aaron looked at the heavy metal posters and war memorabilia from different eras hanging on the walls. He knew Doug was a history buff and not just a typical Civil War re-enactor. Doug studied every armed engagement of the United States and paid special attention to when the insurgents or guerrillas came out victorious. While the interior may not have been the most pleasing to the eyes, it wasn't particularly messy and just rather expressed Doug's personality.

The living room led to the kitchen. A round table was tucked in the corner close to the back door. A man with a shaved head around Doug's age was seated eating a bowl of cornflakes that reminded Aaron of an albino pitbull digging into its wet dog food. A Maryland flag tattoo stretched across the center of his neck that went along with ink up and down both of his arms. The man looked up and nodded nonchalantly toward Aaron.

"Aaron, this is my man Bobby Z. We go all the way back to middle school. Bobby, Aaron." Aaron remembered some stories about Bobby from his messages with Doug. It was a similar dynamic to Aaron and Danny where it was Doug who primarily handled all tasks tied to the digital realm. Bobby just liked to shoot, which would come in handy.

"Watched what you and your people pulled off on the news," said Bobby in between bites of cereal. "Or, well, almost pulled off."

"Chill, Bobby."

"What? I'm giving the man props." Bobby looked from Doug to Aaron. "I'm serious. That took some serious balls. Hope you join the team." Aaron nodded respectfully, but he wasn't convinced it was genuine. Didn't matter much to Aaron either way because he had nowhere else to go at that point.

"Whatever. Aaron, want something to eat?" Doug asked his new house guest. Aaron realized he hadn't eaten since that Royal Farms trip. He had burned quite a bit of energy since then.

"Wouldn't mind, to be honest."

"Cool. Gonna order a pizza, not in the mood to cook or anything."

"Always waiting until I make some bullshit before you order out. I swear," laughed Bobby Z as he looked down at his cold cereal.

"You know damn well that ain't gonna stop your fat ass from grabbing a few slices."

"Fuck you." Bobby Z wasn't actually that fat, just a little on the stocky side. Aaron was hip to the fact that Doug just targeted the greedy antics, like when Doug complained about Bobby using up more ammunition than they planned last time they were at the gun range. Even though it was Doug who made the most money, it was Bobby's brain who happened to always know where it should go. Bobby finished up his cereal and ditched it in the nearby sink. "I'm about to roll up." Bobby grabbed a nearby tray with crushed green on it and ripped out an EZ Wider paper. He looked up at Aaron. "You smoke?"

"Aaron doesn't chief." Doug gandered over at his new house guest, awkwardly standing, unable to speak for himself just yet. "Do you?"

"Shit, I'll hit it." A surprised look came over the face of Doug at the initiative, but Bobby was eager to support Aaron's decision. The tatted-up urban Appalachian tightened up the joint and sparked it with his Zippo. Two puffs, and he passed it over to Aaron. The newbie pecked at it and immediately blew clouds out with his mouth.

"You gotta inhale, bro," directed Bobby. "Suck it in." Clearly, it was his first time, and he never paid much attention to the hundreds of tokes Danny had done throughout their friendship. Aaron breathed it in, and he immediately hacked up a lung. Doug and Bobby couldn't help but laugh at the violent coughing.

"There you go," chuckled Bobby Z. Aaron continued to cough loudly and had to grab a chair to support his body going into convulsions. Doug grabbed a glass and poured him some water.

"Here," he said, handing his friend some nourishment. Bobby continued to chuckle as he took the jay back and puffed on it.

"I thought D.C. had that good gas?"

"It's his first time."

"Oh, right."

Aaron sat down, and his coughing finally ceased. His eyes were bloodshot red. Everything felt like it was going in slow motion. He was definitely high. Doug and Bobby stared at him.

"So, uhm." Aaron could barely form his sentences together. "What's the plan? Who on the uh...Bazaar do you guys want to hit next?"

"One day at a time, bro." Doug smiled at Aaron, trying to remain focused. "We're just chilling today. Sit back, make yourself at home. I'm gonna call in the food." Aaron nodded and decided to sit back in his chair while Doug dialed away. He was finally in a space of relaxation and comfort after a day of gun battles. Bobby flicked on a television across from them near the living room. The local news came on, and downtown Silver Spring was on the screen. Police tape and emergency crews were on camera. Within seconds, mugshots of the crew appeared as they were taken into custody. Aaron looked at the face of Danny, who decided to smile mischievously when his picture was taken. The same face Danny made when he would troll Aaron about his lack of knowledge of popular rappers.

"That your mans?" asked Bobby as he hit the jay. Aaron paused.

"Yeah." Bobby passed Aaron the joint. The news flashed Danny's rifle on a police evidence table.

"Damn, he was packing," Bobby said, eyes on the TV. Aaron smoked. He felt himself getting higher, both from the substance he ingested and from looking at his work on the television.

"He sure was."

———

"This a celebration or some shit?" Lyle seemed to mock the joyous mood of his fellow squad at the Ethiopian bar recommended by Jasper. Only Karen and Nick heard him. The rest were too focused on tales from previous jobs over beef tibs and beer.

"Oh, Lyle." She rolled her eyes.

"What? I'm just confused," he said as the bartender slid him a cold one. Nick glanced at Lyle, checking out the beautiful mahogany-skinned woman serving him the drink behind the bar. The smile on her face signaled she was into tall Jamaican men built like 80s action movie stars. Lyle took a sip before finishing his response to Karen. "The Feds took him before we could close out the night. That doesn't seem like a successful ending to me."

"I'm just celebrating being alive," Nick added. He swirled around the cherry in his Shirley Temple with a straw. Karen patted him on the back.

"You did a great job, Mr. Rice. You should be proud," she said. Lyle meditated for a moment with his drink.

"Eat something," Terry said to Nick. He must have noticed Nick's head down most of the conversation. "You've been through a lot."

"I'm good." Nick finally took a sip. He looked toward Jasper, who was conversing with Victor and Yemi about the materials used in improvised explosive devices. "I want to talk about Efemena."

That grabbed Jasper's attention, especially since it revolved around the same topic.

"Whatever," Lyle said. "I'm heading back to the bar." Lyle rose up from the table and walked back over to flirt with the bartender. Jasper took a bite of some injera and tibs before he focused on Nick.

"Talk to me, Nick."

"Efemena Kanu. Pulled up some of her essays from her grad school days and yeah, it looks like she sympathized with the Biafra Freedom Movement. Even defended the boat attacks on the oil rigs as the Delta people asserting their right over the resources on their land from Western imperialists."

"She was friendly to Chiedu at the event, though," Terry added. "He even wanted to connect her with Yemi."

"It was all a front." Nick took a sip of his soda. "She was gauging to see the security Chiedu had around him. Probably reported back to the opposition before they arrived."

"Someone contact the police about this information?" asked Terry.

"You would ask that," Yemi stated. He slightly chuckled as he took a sip of beer. Nick could tell Terry struggled to not look offended and he managed to carve out a smile as he cheered his glass with Yemi. "But you're not wrong. Once Victor and Nick finish their reports, I'll forward what I got over to Montgomery County's Fire Investigations."

"Good stuff, big brother. Now, who's ready for shots?" inquired Karen.

"Still partying like the college days, huh?" the big brother responded back.

"I didn't drink like this in college. You know I was broke."

"True, you didn't get a cent from Mom and Dad unless it was for a textbook."

"Yeah, my parents paid for my meal plan, and then that was it. Hence, why I looked to the campus police for work." Nick could relate to the college reminiscence. After all, he was the most recent graduate out of all of them.

"Shoot, I didn't get a dime from my family," said Victor before he gulped down some ale.

"Where'd you go to college, Victor?" asked Karen. She raised her finger for a waitress.

"Don't matter. Useless in the States."

"Same," Jasper said. "The only training I use from back home was the exercises instructed by the U.S. Army."

"Neocolonialism," said Karen as she passed around shot glasses full of Jack Daniels.

"Hey, we've never been colonized," clarified the proud Ethiopian sharpshooter. "Don't forget that."

"The only one." Yemi backed up Jasper's comment as he took his glass. "If only the rest of Africa learned."

"Throw South America in there, too," Victor chided in.

"Okay, that sounds like something to drink to." Karen raised her glass. "To all the friends and colleagues we get to meet through European conquest." They all laughed and swung back their shots.

"So what's next, boss?" asked Terry. Yemi traded looks with Karen, and they both shrugged.

"Hang tight. Something will come up soon. This area is a hotbed for Bazaar targets. Once word gets around, it was Raptor defending Chiedu, who knows what opportunities will come about?"

"You know who's rising up on the list?" commented Nick.

"Ryan Frost."

"Who's that again?" asked Victor as he dug back into the tibs.

"Attorney general of Maryland," answered Terry. "Why is he so high up all of a sudden?"

"He wants to expand the Undetectable Firearms Act. He's really pissing off the anarchists online who want their 3-D printed guns."

"Interesting. I thought they'd always be more concerned with the Federal Reserve or something."

"It's much easier to cut ties with centralized banking. But if Frost succeeds in convincing legislators, you'll see web hosts pressured to take down sites hosting the files."

"Well, I wonder if Mr. Frost will be hitting us up," Terry said. Nick had his hopes up, too, but Yemi was quick to squash the client dreaming.

"Nah. If he's not already under protection from the state, either Titus or RexCorp has him on lock." Terry nodded in response.

"He's supposed to be speaking in Hagerstown in a couple of weeks at a conference about the Western Maryland opioid crisis," said Nick. "Judging from what seems to be the most popular bid date on his profile, I think he should reschedule."

"Never underestimate the size of a politician's ego," responded Yemi. Nick saw Yemi's eyes shift their attention to the bar. He turned around to look over at Lyle starting to fail at his advances with the bartender. Nick's dreadlocked Raptor squadmate raised his arms up like she said something that touched his own ego. Lyle took out a twenty dollar bill, crumpled it up, and chucked it at her breasts, not the most civil way to close out his tab. Nick and Yemi watched a nearby male patron confront Lyle about the manner.

"Mind your business, fat boy," Lyle said to the heavy-set

man trying to defend the bartender's honor.

"This fat boy will fuck you up, believe that."

"Oh, really?" Yemi started to get up, and Nick put his drink down. They saw where this was going. "Touch me and see what—"

The man actually threw a reasonably fast, well-placed left hook straight to Lyle's chin. It knocked him off balance, but Lyle was able to return with a jab and a cross that grazed the big dude, but he didn't go down. Stools slid out, and some glasses broke as the two started a full out brawl in the middle of the bar. Yemi, Terry, Jasper, and Nick sprung into action and jumped in the middle of the commotion.

"Calm the fuck down!" yelled Terry into his squadmate's ear. Jasper broke them apart as Yemi grabbed the other man off of Lyle. Lyle's lip was swollen.

"Nice shot, mother fucker, but—"

"Go outside!" yelled Jasper. By then, the entire bar was looking at the situation. Terry let go of Lyle. He straightened out his shirt in an attempt to keep his confidence intact after just getting snuck by a seemingly much more out-of-shape man. "Go!" This is the angriest anyone had ever seen the usually mild-mannered Jasper. Lyle sighed and begrudgingly started to head to the exit.

"Batty boy!" Lyle barked his country's trademark homophobic insult at the good samaritan. A round two of the fight was about to start, but Jasper grabbed ahold of Lyle before he could make full contact. Jasper was strong in his own right, but Nick knew even his underbuilt frame could still be of help to getting the Jamaican grunt outside.

Outside, Nick and Jasper finally let him go. Lyle took out one of his cigars and tried his best to keep a cool persona after just causing a violent drama. However, Nick watched Jasper snatch the tobacco stick right out of his mouth, leaving his hands slightly twitching.

"What the fuck, Jasper — ?"

"What's wrong with you?"

"He got in my face."

"You got emotional with the bartender." Jasper handed Lyle back his cigar. He paused before he lit it.

"Emotional?" Lyle retorted. "That bitch — "

"You're pissing away this opportunity I set for you."

"It was a fight, bruh," Lyle said as he lit it. "Men fight. It's been like that for centuries."

"Fights over females crumbled empires," Jasper said. "What makes you think you're so special?" Lyle couldn't find an answer, so he just went ahead and finished lighting his cigar. He even glanced at Nick, but Nick knew better than to make eye contact at that moment.

"Get it together, man," Jasper added. "I'm going back inside." Jasper did as he said he would. Nick watched Lyle puff away. As he exhaled the smoke, Nick also realized his trademark ego was leaving his body as well. The team sharpshooter had exposed him. At least to Nick.

"What the fuck do you want?" asked Lyle. Nick shook his head rapidly, having been frozen in awe about what had just transpired in front of him.

"Oh, uhm. You okay?"

"Of course I'm okay. That Krispy Kreme-eating pussy bitch didn't do shit. Go check on his fat ass or something." Nick sighed.

"I'm just making sure my squad brother is good, Lyle. That's all."

"Listen, kid." Lyle raised his voice a bit, and then he faced directly toward Nick. "This ain't the fucking Marines or a boy scout troop, alright? For those twenty-four hours, we're on the clock, we're COLLEAGUES, got it? That's it. Meaning our bond is only as strong as your capability to get the job done. Save all that brotherhood bullshit for your butt buddy Blackwell or if you wanna keep trying to impress Yemi or whatever. But even he can see through your facade, and all it's gonna do is get you terminated or even one of us killed." Lyle turned back around to continue hitting his cigar. "Hopefully, the former."

There was something in Lyle's voice that Nick hadn't heard before. Maybe it was insecurity or just trying to build his persona back up after it got torn down by Jasper in front of the rookie.

"Lyle."

"What?"

"What did you do before Raptor?"

"How the fuck is that relevant?"

"I'm just asking. Relax." Lyle inhaled and exhaled for a couple of beats.

"A bunch of things," he said.

"Like what?" asked Nick.

"Doesn't matter," Lyle said. His body seemed to relax all of a sudden. Nick was unsure if it was the effect of the nicotine or if the question forced Lyle into a place of reflection. "None of them worked." Nick nodded and sighed again. He checked the time on his phone.

"Might head out soon. I'm going to head inside to say bye to everybody." Lyle didn't respond verbally. He just nodded his head affirmatively as he looked across the street at a street parked with Teslas, Mercedes, and BMWs.

"But I ain't done yet," Nick heard Lyle mutter to himself. "Sure as hell ain't gonna end here." Nick decided it was time to leave the man alone outside with his entrepreneurial dreams.

———

"Can't believe my daughter wanted to go to school up in these parts." Ryan Frost looked over the Stonehenge limestone architecture of downtown Hagerstown as his motorcade pulled into the city.

"Where? Mount Saint Mary's?" inquired Assistant Attorney General Darryl Busiek.

"No, Frostburg."

"That's about an hour away."

"Still in bumblefuck." Darryl couldn't help but laugh a little bit at his superior's lack of knowledge or enthusiasm for the Western part of his own state. Obviously, Darryl knew Frost was going to change his tune the second he got behind that podium. They were expecting families of heroin addicts in attendance, so Frost knew his mask of empathy was going to be required soon. He had made a number of public talks across the state of Maryland, but most could agree that only Baltimore had a more severe opioid crisis than the Cumberland Valley. Frost had spent the previous day trying to think of a way to relate to the crowd on a personal level. He had a hard time trying to pinpoint a relative with addiction but decided his best choice was a distant cousin who got hooked on painkillers after a skiing accident. The cousin was close enough to rally support yet removed enough from his immediate family to avoid being targeted by the media or opposition.

RexCorp was the firm in charge of his security detail for that day. While their executive protection services had always existed since the company's inception as an attachment to their overseas armed contractor services, the recent domestic events tied to the Bazaar sprung up their newly formed VIP Security Unit. (VSU) It was their response to Raptor's squad and the Digital Market Response Team (DMRT) over at Titus.

RexCorp had eight agents assigned to the conference hall on Potomac Street. Two were already outside the building, securing the perimeter as Frost's motorcade pulled into the parallel garage. Local police were alerted to Frost's presence and had some patrol cars nearby, as one uniformed officer would stand by the presentation along with the RexCorp guards.

Frost was escorted into the hotel and toward the conference room. The audience was already in attendance and he was given a round of applause for his appearance.

———

The whole event was captured on the hotel's CCTV cameras. Unbeknownst to the staff or any of Frost's security detail, someone else watched from several blocks away in a townhome garage.

Doug, Aaron, Bobby Z, and a fourth young man by the name of Ethan all awaited in a solid black Chevy Silverado pickup. Doug had hacked the hotel's closed caption system and watched the event on his phone.

"Okay, he's just starting now," he said to the group. The four were packing serious firepower. Doug straddled a 3D-printed AR-15 in between his legs, Ethan had a ghost SKS rifle ready next to him as he awaited in the driver seat, and Bobby had two pistols. One was a .357 magnum revolver, and the other was a Glock 19 with an extended mag for automatic fire, similar to how Aaron's former team had modified their handguns. Aaron was armed with another 3D-printed assault rifle like Doug. They all had vests reinforced with armored plates to lessen the impact any of the RexCorp agents' sidearms would have.

Aaron felt a different vibe amongst his new crew than Rold's from the jump. Whereas the nerves of Qasim and the others were obvious with the shouts and pep talk, the cold silence of Doug's group hinted at some experience or more thorough training for such a mission.

Bobby ripped open a protein bar and chomped on it. He offered another one to Aaron, who politely refused.

"So what this dude do again?" asked Bobby Z in between bites.

"He wants to ban 3-D printed guns," remarked Doug as

he studied the footage.

"So that means either you or Aaron gotta shoot him," laughed Bobby.

"You said eight guards?" asked Ethan.

"Yeah," responded Doug.

"And watch out for Feds, of course."

The four sat ready. Bobby pulled up YouTube on his phone and passed the time with some gun range videos. Aaron glanced over to get a glimpse and listen to the commentary from a mid-20s redneck describing the benefits of DIY hollow-point bullets.

"You subscribe to this guy?" asked Aaron.

"Subscribe? I went to high school with this mother fucker. He's from Boonsboro." The YouTuber started to load the bullets one by one into a magazine. "He's where I got this pistol from," Bobby said as he tapped his Glock at the side.

"Maybe you should get him to join us next time," remarked Aaron. Bobby laughed at the idea.

"He makes a decent amount from all these views. When you can talk about guns instead of using them, why put your ass on the line?" That made Aaron think for a minute. What exactly was his plan B for being a Bazaar-tied hitman? Even if he wasn't on the run from the incident in Silver Spring, he didn't even have a high school diploma. Maybe he could funnel some money into some storefront businesses like Qasim had planned on doing. Somebody else would have to run them, as Aaron knew deep down he wasn't much of a people person. He thought about this topic for the next forty-five minutes until Doug watched Frost step away from the podium.

"Okay, get ready." Guns cock as the team locked and loaded. Ethan pressed the garage door opener.

CHAPTER 8

The RexCorp personnel secured the perimeter around the hotel, hovering at their assigned posts and scanning the area for potential threats. Their client still hadn't made it outside yet.

"How'd I sound?" asked Frost as he walked through the lobby.

"I think the cousin story worked," responded Darryl. "But why didn't you want to stay for Q and A?"

"Caps versus Pittsburgh at seven. I never miss that series."

"Not even for your constituents?"

"I watch hockey and basketball. They watch their meth foil. They'll be fine." Darryl shook his head as Frost laughed at his own crude joke. They made their way out onto the front of the building. His chauffeured Mercedes was waiting for him and Darryl at the front of the building. Two field agents stood by it with one holding the back door open. A few others stood at points around the entrance to keep his perimeter covered. Frost was looking forward to the ride back to Montgomery County, where his wife Kelly, two daughters, and four-year-old husky waited for him. Hopefully, they wouldn't bother him with details of the event and just let him watch the Penguins lose. He and Darryl hopped into the back seat.

———

Two blocks over, twenty-seven-year-old Hagerstown Police officer Aithen Matthews tried to enjoy his unseasoned chicken sandwich as his Sergeant Bruce Simmons snacked on mozzarella sticks. Aithen was really hoping to check out the new fast casual Mediterranean franchise that sprang up downtown, but Simmons was stuck in his appetite for cheap items that were kept in a warmer. Many times Aithen would hint that his superior would be saving his wallet, and health for that matter, if he took his advice in learning how to meal prep. But Simmons didn't want to partake in the tasks he had left to his ex-wife. His waistline which seemed to have expanded four pants sizes since the divorce, was enough evidence to Aithen that his brother-in-blue heard him but refused to listen.

"What's supposed to be happening on Potomac again?" asked Aithen in between bites.

"Something with that douchebag attorney general," answered Simmons. "Can't believe he's in office."

"Should we go check on it?"

"Are we his security detail?"

"Not really."

"Then we're good. No need to rush through lunch. I'm starving." Aithen nodded and smirked in agreement. He looked forward and up the street. He watched a tinted black pickup truck cross the intersection. He reached to turn on the siren.

"What are you doing?" asked Simmons.

"That truck ran the light. You didn't see that?"

"Did you not just hear me say I was starving?" said Simmons as he continued chomping on his meal. Aithen shook his head and switched off the siren. He took a sip from his drink and the sweetness hitting his taste buds was enough to convince him he made the right choice in ignoring the minor infraction. For a gas station menu, the smoothies were pretty damn good.

––––––––

"We taking off or what?" asked Frost to the driver.

"One second, sir, security is just doing one final sweep." Frost sighed and looked out the window. He saw one of the RexCorp field agents glance inside a parked Hyundai about thirty yards behind the Mercedes. In the side rearview mirror, he noticed a pickup truck speeding down from the opposite end of the street.

Its speed attracted the attention of a RexCorp guard by the entrance. He stared it down through his sunglasses as he placed his hand on top of the hammer of his pistol.

KA-BOOM.

A massive explosion ripped from the Hyundai, engulfing the inspecting field agent in flames.

"What the hell?" Frost yelled at the top of his lungs.

The black Silverado screeched to a halt. Two men in ski masks were the first to jump out, and they sprayed the guards with automatic fire. Two RexCorp guards went down immediately as four others took cover behind walls and nearby parked cars unaffected by the explosion.

Frost immediately ducked into his seat as chaos erupted around his vehicle. Within seconds, the back window of his Mercedes shattered from the assault. The guard in the front passenger seat stuck half his body out the window to fire back in the Silverado's direction. His brain matter exploded onto the side of the Mercedes, and his body was riddled with bullets. The corpse hung out the window and slumped against the car door exterior.

"Fucking go!" yelled Frost to his driver, who was cowering in the front driver seat in an attempt to be safe from the chaos.

————

Aithen threw the sandwich down and put the patrol car in drive.

"Shots fired, shots fired," barked Simmons into the radio dispatch. "Need backup immediately. Sounds like automatic weapons, and we heard a possible explosion." Aithen whipped it around the corner as they headed to the intersection of Potomac.

"Turn the siren off," ordered Simmons. "They're probably waiting for our arrival. Park at the top of the street, and we'll push on foot."

————

The Mercedes they were firing at started to pull out, but bullets ripped into its tires. Its driving turned to sliding down Potomac Street.

"Pull up!" yelled Bobby Z to Ethan. Ethan put down his rifle and drove the pickup to be parallel to their target. Bobby immediately kicked open his door and unloaded a whole mag into the passenger side of the attorney general's vehicle, shredding whoever was ever in the left side of the car.

Aaron saw an occupant of the back of the Mercedes push himself out the right side door opposite the assault squad's side. The man crashed onto the pavement and started to crawl on the street toward the hotel. That might be Frost, thought Aaron.

————

Aithen and Simmons arrived at the top of the street. They spotted the Silverado a couple of blocks down.

"I'll get the shotgun," announced Simmons as they filed out of the squad car. Aithen ducked for cover behind the vehicle, gripping his 9mm handgun. Simmons soon jumped right in front of them, and both of them crouched down.

"Let's move." Simmons led Aithen down the sidewalk, staying covered by the parked cars. As they passed each vehicle, Aithen kept his attention glued to the truck. The back passenger door swung open, and a ski-masked assailant got out, wielding two pistols.

"Cover me!" yelled the ski mask as he started to march toward the Mercedes. By then, only a few RexCorp guards were left, but they were tucked into the hotel, looking for any opportunity to fire back without getting sniped like their dead colleagues. Ski mask stepped around the front of the Mercedes and looked down at the attorney general like a hunter descending onto its wounded game.

"Please." Aithen could hear the attorney general begging as he looked up at Ski Mask. "You don't have to do this." Aithen could even spot tears rolling down Frost's face. The two members of Hagerstown's finest crept around the side of a parked Nissan to get as close to the standoff as possible without risking obvious discovery. Simmons steadied his Remington toward Ski Mask with the pistols.

———

"Sorry, but I got two million and a half reasons to do this."

"I have a family." Frost tried one last appeal.

"Close your eyes," ordered Bobby Z. He raised his .357 and aimed right at Frost's head.

From the back of the Silverado, Aaron spotted a shotgun muzzle peaking from the front of the Nissan.

"Bobby! Your back!" Bobby immediately turned around, and the distance was perfect for the close-range gun. The blast from the cop's gun impacted Bobby's Kevlar vest and sent him to the ground, the magnum pistol flying out of his hand. Aaron took his assault rifle and burst fired toward the front of the Nissan. A bullet went through the window shield and caught the shotgun wielder in the neck, sending him to the cement.

Bobby's .357 landed a few feet from Frost. The attorney general scurried over to it. Once he was able to grab the gun, he lifted it toward Bobby. For a moment, one could almost say it was divine intervention to give him an upper hand. But the assassin had a quick draw and recovered fast enough to spray Frost in the face with his modified Glock, sealing their mission. Grimacing through the pain, Bobby picked himself back up and joined Aaron in firing upon the Nissan. The wounded police officer's partner dragged him to safety behind the car while simultaneously returning fire.

"Officer down, officer down!" Aaron heard him bark on the radio. "Need that backup!"

"We gotta roll, Bobby!" yelled Doug from out the window. Bobby stepped over to the dead Frost and picked up his revolver.

Out of spite, he delivered two more shots from the Dirty Harry to split open Frost's cranium, forcing a closed casket funeral for Maryland's ex-attorney general. Bobby Z jumped into the back of the truck. Ethan hit the gas and the crew took off down Potomac.

They sped through downtown Hagerstown. Sirens could be heard in the not-so-far distance. Soon, Ethan turned left into an alley. A parked Kia was waiting for them. They ripped off their ski masks and quickly hopped out of the Silverado into the Kia. From the new vehicle, Doug grabbed a beer bottle filled with gasoline and stuffed a handkerchief into it, creating a makeshift Molotov cocktail. He took out his Zippo, lit it, and threw it into the Silverado. He then grabbed a red spray paint can from the backseat and sprayed the letters 'N' and 'P' on the pickup's back window. He jumped back into the Kia and the team peeled off from the alley. Bobby could see the interior of the truck was engulfed in an inferno before they turned a corner.

"You good, Bobby?" asked Doug. Bobby Z felt around his rib cage area up to his chest.

"Definitely some bruises," Bobby responded. "But I don't think anything is broken, so yeah, I'm straight." Bobby sighed and looked over at Aaron next to him. "Good shit, bro." The two exchanged fist bumps. The car went quiet as a Hagerstown police cruiser zipped past them. Once the coast was clear, smiles formed back on their faces.

"So we millionaires now?" asked Bobby.

"Sort of," answered Doug. "But we ain't finished yet."

"What else we gotta do?" asked Ethan.

"You'll see. Just need to get to a computer."

———

Police tape went up all around the hotel. The crime scene was swarmed by state and federal law enforcement along with other emergency personnel, such as the fire department tending to the charred remains of the car bomb. Media from all regional levels were also on sight, given the magnitude of yet another assassination not so far from the nation's capital. Chris Towers stepped out of his SUV and surveyed the scene. He looked at the bullet-ridden Mercedes and the blood on the road. He tried to pinpoint how the shootout played out. He knew it was tied to the Bazaar, and his team had been tracking Frost but left it up to the attorney general's private security for protection. He wondered if their intervention could have made any difference as the shooters evidently packed some serious firepower.

"Sir." One of Towers' agents got his attention. Chris turned toward him. "We have one of the officers who engaged with the suspects." The agent directed Towers over to the medical station. An officer of the Hagerstown Police Department sat at the edge of the ambulance as he was looked at by a paramedic. Towers guessed he was in his mid to late 20s. His head was down, and his whole body language seemed deflated. Not surprising at all, given the circumstances. Chris approached him, and the officer looked up.

"Good evening, officer. Chris Towers, Secret Service." The officer slowly nodded his head and shook Towers' hand, but the body language displayed by the local cop showcased he would rather be anywhere else at that moment. "Do you mind if I ask you some questions?" The officer shook his head 'no.'

"First off, you have my condolences as I learned about your partner, Sergeant Simmons." The police officer nodded with acknowledgment, still choosing to express his reactions in silence. "When you exchanged fire with the suspects, did you get a good look at them?" The paramedic handed the cop a bottle of water and he took a sip before he responded.

"They had ski masks on. The one who shot Frost point blank was a White male. Probably early to mid-twenties. Wasn't able to get a good glimpse of any inside the truck." Towers' colleague returned.

"Sir, we've got an update. A group has claimed responsibility."

"Okay," Chris said as he turned back to the local cop. "Give me a second, Officer—?"

"Matthews. Aithen Matthews." Chris stepped off to the side for a debriefing.

"What we got?" The agent pulled out a phone and showed Chris a message board thread.

"They call themselves The New Patriots."

"Right-wing nationalists?" asked Towers.

"Pretty much. Says Frost was targeted for the firearms legislation he was pursuing."

"How do we know it's them other than some online post?"

"We found the truck burning about eight blocks away in an alley. It had the letters 'N' and 'P' spray painted on the back."

"Fair enough. Okay, let me finish up with Officer Matthews, and in the meantime, get an analyst to dig up what we know about the group or if they're fresh off the block."

"Got it," said his subordinate before he left. Towers turned his attention again to Aithen.

"Were you and your partner aware of the circumstances surrounding why Frost may have been targeted?" Aithen raised his eyebrow.

"We just knew he was speaking here. Why? Do you have info on these assholes?" asked Aithen with a hint of animosity.

"I'm with the Cyber Fraud Task Force. Ryan Frost was listed on a site on the dark web called the Bazaar, where individuals can predict the dates of deaths for various high-profile individuals. He made himself pretty high up on the list within the past few months. The assassins who killed him and your partner most likely had placed a bet on this particular date." Aithen meditated for a moment on this new information.

"Are you going to check the registration of the truck?"

asked Aithen.

"We are in the process of that now. But, judging at how well-planned this attack was, I doubt we'll turn up much." Aithen thought some more.

"Why wasn't this information shared with my department?"

"We just knew Frost was a target. We didn't have intel on a particular date. We're still a little new to this entire process."

"I'm sorry, I can't accept that as an excuse." A look of confusion came over Towers at Aithen's attitude. "When you Feds don't share intel about domestic terrorists, it's us who end up getting slaughtered in the streets." Towers sighed.

"Look. That's the FBI," said Towers. "I can't speak for their past fuckups with the Sovereign Citizen Movement, but I promise you that we're taking these threats very seriously."

"I hope so," said Aithen. "Cause more are gonna die if you don't. Especially since you said money is involved."

"Roger that, Officer. I'm sorry how your day has gone, but I hope you take comfort in returning to your family." Towers saluted Aithen and headed back to the center of the crime scene. He knew there was some truth to Aithen's concerns. Back when the FBI was funneling countless resources into investigating radical Islam, domestic right-wing terrorism was a lower priority. The consequence was West Memphis police officers getting shredded by an AK-47 belonging at a traffic stop turned deadly. But the difference between the Sovereign Citizens and this new group, New Patriots, pulled off a lucrative move in addition to a victory for their supposed ideological stance. And also, unlike the rifleman who shot the Arkansas officers, they got away with it.

CHAPTER 9

Nick didn't visit D.C. often while growing up in Prince George's County. All he remembered were the Smithsonian tours when he was in elementary school or when his father would surprise him with Wizards tickets. As a grown adult, he found himself on K Street standing in front of the offices of the Middle Eastern-focused online news site, Al Noor. He looked through the pristine glass doors and into the newsroom. Keeping up with the alternate news blogs throughout college, it was the type of environment Nick had dreamed of being in upon graduation. However, places as high as Vox Media and The Intercept weren't impressed by his crime reports for The Spokesman at Morgan State or his time as a campus cop. But he saw his position at Raptor as an opportunity to get access to VIP information that some of these blogs seemed to be hungry for.

A man around Nick's age of Sudanese descent approached the entrance to let Nick in. It was his point of correspondence, journalist Abdallah Kalfat.

"How was it getting here?" asked Abdallah as they stepped into the lobby.

"Can't tell you the last time I took the metro, but I found it okay."

"Aren't you from around here?"

"Grew up in Clinton."

"Oh, haven't been out there."

"Don't bother. Nothing but an air force base nearby, some black folks with money, and a Walmart." Abdallah chuckled as they entered the main offices that Nick was gandering at from outside. He looked at the decorations throughout the space, including a water-colored painting of murdered journalist Jamal Khashoggi. 'Free Julian Assange' hung from some of the journalists' cubicle walls. The two stepped into an office, and Abdallah shut the door behind them. Abdallah pulled out a roller chair for his guest, and the two faced off at the side of the conference table. It almost felt like an interview, according to Nick.

"Can I get you anything? Some water?" asked Abdallah.

"Nah, I'm good." Nick revealed a metal water bottle tucked in his backpack.

"So." Abdallah cleared his throat. "I thought it'd be good for us to finally meet in person."

"I agree." Nick took a thumb drive out from his backpack and handed it to Abdallah. "All the POPCO files or anything else related to Chiedu is on here." Abdallah became enamored over the small piece of hardware, looking it up and down like Gollum from Lord of the Rings.

"Your hard work is very well appreciated, Mr. Rice." Abdallah tucked the hard drive into his pocket. "I was worried about you last Fall after what I saw on the news."

"Yeah, well, that's what the job entails sometimes," responded Nick. Abdallah nodded back, respecting Nick's sacrifice.

"What was he like?"

"Who? Chiedu?"

"Yeah."

"He's cool, I guess. He seemed to treat me pretty well. I wouldn't call him humble, but not really a total dick like you'd expect some wealthy African politicians to be."

"Did the Popco stuff seem to bother him?"

"It did, actually." Nick reflected on the conversation in the back seat of Chiedu's vehicle. Abdallah nodded his head again. "So, what are your plans with this information?"

"Well, we're going to do a follow-up piece to what was revealed from AfriLeaks. We'll go through what you provided and see what's worth reporting. Better sooner than later since the whole shooting was relatively recent."

"What about the Frost incident?"

"What? You have some documents on him, too?" Abdallah was intrigued.

"Nah. He wasn't our client. That was RexCorp."

"Oh." There was a few seconds of silence between them. Nick didn't know what to say next, and it didn't seem like Abdallah knew either.

"So I was wondering," started Nick. "Are there any openings?" Abdallah paused, a bit hesitant.

"For what? Like on the staff?"

"Anything. Journalists, contributors, interns. I'll do whatever." The working journalist scratched his head like it was a topic of conversation he didn't expect to have.

"You're looking to leave Raptor?"

"Raptor is my paycheck. Journalism is my passion. I wrote for the school paper, but nobody wanted to take me on when I graduated, so I took what I could get with my resume." Abdallah nodded, but he stayed quiet. "These leaks are just the beginning of what I can dig up on this new trend with the Bazaar. Al Noor can be a leader on this subject matter. I just need my shot."

"So, look." Abdallah cleared his throat. "Budget is tight all across media right now, and we're no exception. However, why don't we just continue this relationship we got going?"

"So I'm like a Snowden, and you're what? Glenn Greenwald?" Abdallah laughed a bit, but he noticed when Nick's face didn't budge.

"Yeah, pretty much. That's actually the perfect comparison." Nick sighed in slight disappointment. "But hear me out. In the long run, this will jump-start your career in journalism better than a Newhouse degree. Keep being our anonymous insider at Raptor and you'll be front line on this Bazaar revolution like you talked about." Nick thought for a moment. He wondered if Abdallah was sincere or if he was just watching out for Al Noor's bottom line.

"Fair enough. That's a deal." Abdallah enthusiastically shook Nick's hand.

"Excellent. Any hint at who your next client will be?"

"There's a team meeting next Wednesday so if I don't get an e-mail or phone call by then, I think that's when it'll get revealed."

"Good stuff, man. Let's stay in touch after that." Nick nodded his head and started to rise out of the chair. Abdallah led him through the offices back toward the entrance. Nick looked at the decorations across the cubicles and the staff hard at work at their positions. Nick couldn't help but feel some sense of envy to be in their seats. He hoped one day he got to be a part of DC's alternative political press scene. He just hoped he could survive whatever would come his way at Raptor.

———

Yemi stepped into the Raptor office with Peruvian chicken carry-out in his hands. He opened the door to the meeting room and saw that there was a guest along with Jasper and Karen. A smiling, well-groomed Iranian man no older than thirty was seated with his hands crossed. He looked like he had been entertaining the two of them for some time before Yemi's arrival.

"Yemi. This is Vash Ahmadabadi. He runs the company I e-mailed you about." Yemi placed the bags down at the table, and the two casually shook hands.

"Alla something?" replied Yemi as he sat down.

"Alamut," Karen said, correcting her brother. "I think you should hear what he has to offer." Yemi took a seat across from Vash.

"Talk to me."

"First off, thank you for having me here, Mr. and Ms. Uzunma. It's an honor and I am a huge fan of what Raptor has accomplished being at the forefront of the Bazaar phenomenon. Now, I have a question for you, Yemi. What was the biggest issue you ran into while protecting Chiedu Attah?"

"Well." Yemi hesitated for a moment. He wasn't too big a fan of this guess around game that Vash seemed to want to play. "It was our first assignment, so there were some holes we didn't foresee."

"Of course." Vash seemed to want to lend a sympathetic ear, but Yemi just knew it was only polite business manners.

"But I guess the ambassador choosing to give a speech on a day he's predicted to be assassinated may have made our mission a bit more difficult than it needed to be."

"Right. You go from his house to the roads to a parking garage and then a whole convention center. That's at least three to four different properties you have to secure, correct?" Yemi nodded his head affirmatively, albeit reserved.

"That's true."

"And the location is just one variable. There are all types of ways in which someone can penetrate your defenses and get to your client."

"What's your point?" Karen and Yemi exchanged looks like she didn't approve of her brother's impatience. Vash smiled as if to reassure her that it didn't bother him.

"I would like to offer my services to Raptor. My family has ownership over a few buildings in the Rockville and Bethesda areas. They can be secured for an entire twenty-four-hour period, where we have a full overview of everything the client has access to. Their workspace, food, you name it. We provide the shelter, and Raptor provides the security." Yemi took a second to think it over before his next choice of words.

"Can you excuse us for a moment, Mr. Ahmada —?"

"Ahmadabadi."

"Yes, sorry. I'd just like to have a word in private with my team." Vash kept his smile intact as he nodded affirmatively and stood up to leave the room. Karen looked at Yemi with slight scorn at what she expected to be a negative reception to the proposition.

"So why do we need this guy?" asked Yemi.

"Yemi. Tell me one thing he said that was wrong," his sister responded.

"How do you feel, Jasper? Does he seem legit?"

"His points seemed valid to me," Jasper remarked. "But I also understand your skepticism. We're still early in our development, so we do have to take each offer for collaboration with a grain of salt." Yemi meditated for a moment. When he started Raptor with Karen, he envisioned an opportunity to be free of external pressure to become a hierarchy. Being a small startup, they were able to be nimble and adapt to rapid change, the type of change the Bazaar marketplace exhibited. With Vash, Yemi was unsure if that was adapting or going in the direction of becoming another Titus.

"Let him back in."

"Vash!" called Karen. Vash waltzed back in and enthusiastically took his seat.

"Can you e-mail Karen a list of your properties?"

"Already done."

"Good. We'll take a look, and we'll make a decision before the end of the month."

"Sounds like a plan. Thank you for having me here, everyone." Vash shook each person's hands and stepped back outside. There were a few moments of slightly awkward silence. Jasper and Karen were unsure of Yemi's take on their possible new business partner.

"So... Do we have a new client?"

———

"I can see this isn't your first time," said Bobby as he sipped his Blue Ribbon can and watched Aaron cast out into the Savage River.

"Pops use to take me to the Patuxent all the time," replied Aaron as he straightened out his line.

"Nice," Bobby said. "Gotta return the favor before he goes. Y'all ever go to the bay?"

"Nah, we never got the chance to," Aaron said in a tone with a lower octave. Bobby already could tell what that voice change revealed. Before Bobby could reply, he made eye contact with his lifelong best friend. Doug shook his head, signaling to Bobby to end the conversation. Ethan had another rod out while Doug tended to a grill. Bobby leaned over as Doug flipped the burger patties like they were sharing a word that needed to be kept hush-hush.

"Scottie hit me up yesterday," whispered Bobby. Doug paused for a moment like that name rang a bell.

"Scottie from Elkton?"

"Yeah." Doug hesitated some more as the juices seeped through the holes of his utensil.

"The fuck you talking to him for?" 'Scottie' was Scott Wilkins, an activist for the Maryland chapter of the Western Renaissance Movement. Far-right and secessionist, the group denied being lumped in under the white supremacist label. However, many of Cecil County's ex-Klansmen found a comfortable home in their ranks after Scottie's public meetings, where he spoke about the danger of the influence of Baltimore's darkness reaching their communities.

"Possibly get some more bodies for the next job, you know?" said Bobby.

"Hold up, Bobby." Now Doug took his focus off cooking ti

face off with his partner in arms. But he kept his voice low. "We talked about this. The whole New Patriot thing is supposed to be a front. A ruse to distract the media and authorities while we get paid. Now you talking about recruiting idiots who actually believe that kind of bullshit?"

"Look, man. I understand your concern. Especially after your little affirmative action move." Doug exchanged an annoyed look with his comrade as both glanced over at Aaron before they returned to their conversation. "But we just got away with taking out the goddamn attorney general. Whenever you want to ride back out for round two, the opposition is probably going to have a little bit more than just some pistols and walkie-talkies, if you know what I mean."

"The fewer people involved, the less chances of having a rat." Bobby sighed but shrugged knowing Doug was right on that point. "But look, let's enjoy our time off, alright? I don't like Scottie, but if you really think someone like him can be of assistance, then we can talk about it when we get our next hit. But for now, how do you want your burger? Please don't say well done." Bobby finished his brew and picked up another cold one from the cooler.

"You know I hate any hint of pink," Bobby said as it cracked the can open.

"No wonder you don't get any pussy."

"Suck a dick." Doug laughed as he flipped the patties.

"Hey guys, I think I got a bite!" yelled Aaron with excitement. The arched rod confirmed something was indeed pulling hard on the other end of the line.

"Reel that sucker in, then! Let's go, Aaron!" Doug cheered back to his comrade. Whatever it was, it put up fierce resistance as Aaron pushed down on his reel. Within a minute, the line was close to the shore, and a large fish splashed at the surface.

"Bobby, get the net!" exclaimed Doug. Bobby placed his

beer down and ran to the fishing pole net. He headed over to Aaron's spot and helped bring in the catch. The crew looked at the 22-inch channel catfish that Aaron reeled in.

"Damn!" exclaimed Doug as Bobby dumped the fish onto the land. Aaron picked it up by the line and studied it. It was the perfect position for a photo op. Doug whipped out his cell and snapped a picture of the catch.

"Ain't seen a catfish that big since Doug's last Tinder date," joked Bobby.

"Yeah, I was blown when that happened," Doug chuckled back. "I was expecting your mom."

"Mother fucker!"

"I mean, that was the goal—!" Bobby tackled Doug as the rest of the crew laughed at the impromptu grappling match between two former honorable-mention all-county wrestlers.

CHAPTER 10

Carlos was almost a third of Merlin's age and was only hired the previous year, but he had already progressed to the rank of store manager given his bilingual upbringing as opposed to Merlin, who still struggled with English outside of basic greetings he had learned trying to flirt with women of the various other ethnicities in the diverse region.

Three hours had passed since Americas Mercados had opened, and Merlin knew he was due for a lunch break soon. However, the open door chime went off and he looked toward the front while he was sweeping the floor. It was a young Salvadoran girl with curves that would break any straight male's neck if she walked past them. She had a liberal use of makeup on, but it perfectly complimented her natural beauty, like she was ready to be the star of a hit VidaPrimo music video. As she stepped over to the section for fruits and vegetables, Merlin noticed the skinny and shy Carlos. The young man also seemed infatuated with the voluptuous spectacle of God's creation that had just walked in. Once she disappeared into an aisle, Merlin snuck up behind Carlos.

"Keep an eye on that blue moon, my boy," Merlin whispered in Spanish, referring to the color of her leggings that amplified her gluteal muscles. "She's got the walk of a killer. Some Adobo will disappear off the shelf, and we'll be too distracted to see it tucked in her shirt." Carlos was caught off guard by Merlin and shook his head in an attempt to go back to counting the register. But the blushing red was hard to hide from the older man playing Cupid.

"Or did she already steal something?" laughed Merlin as

he palmed Carlos' chest.

"An angel like that never needs to be a thief," Carlos responded quietly. "Probably has her boyfriend's credit card." Merlin looked outside through the front windows. Some cars were in the lot, but they were all empty.

"No car waiting, no man outside," Merlin said as he leaned in again. "Make a move."

"No way," muttered Carlos as he continued to try to focus on balancing the dollars and change.

"Why not?" The girl started to head to the checkout with her basket half full of items. Before she could reach the register, Merlin watched Carlos retreat to his laptop several feet behind the counter, facing another direction at a 90-degree angle.

"Merlin." He beckoned for his co-worker to handle her order. Merlin shook his head as he approached the register, laughing to himself at the lengths Carlos was willing to take to avoid interacting with his newfound crush. She placed her basket down and started with a roll of toilet paper, followed by some canned black beans and bags of rice.

"Did you find everything you were looking for?" Merlin asked in Spanish. The girl looked over at Carlos and smiled. His eyes wandered a bit toward her, but he resisted turning around. Merlin could see his nerves were getting the best of him.

"Maybe," she said with some carnal undertones. Once the last item got scanned, she presented a credit card to Merlin.

"Gabriel Jimenez?" he read before swiping.

"My brother," remarked the girl. It seemed like she made sure Carlos heard that.

"Ah," Merlin stated as he swiped the card. A brief moment before a message popped up on the screen. "I'm sorry, beautiful, but it declined."

"Ugh," she exclaimed. "He probably bought all his stupid friends bottles at the club last night." She shook her head in slight shame and utter disappointment, but soon enough, Carlos spun around with his employee card in hand.

"She's fine, Merlin," the young manager said quietly as he scanned his card to override the order.

"Please, you don't have to do that."

"No, no," said Carlos as he typed away at the register. "I insist." He finally worked up the courage to make eye contact with her. She returned a bright smile that pierced through his face and gained control of his whole nervous system.

"That's so sweet of you. What's your name?" Carlos cleared his throat, now looking down after her radiance seemed to overpower him. Merlin smirked at the whole exchange, not a care in the world for the store's loss in revenue.

"Uhm, Carlos."

"Well, Carlos. I hope I can get the chance to pay you back for this gesture." She continued to smile in his direction. Merlin could tell this was hard for Carlos to digest. Despite graduating high school, he confided to Merlin he had never had a girlfriend let alone even danced with one at the countless notorious mixers at Montgomery Blair High School. And even Merlin knew there were not many members of the opposite gender in the Computer Science department at George Mason University.

"Why don't you write down your number on this notepad, and you pay him back by letting him take you out Friday?" Merlin interjected to the embarrassment of Carlos. He swiped at the yellow notepad to the apparent humorous delight of Merlin, and even the girl had a few chuckles.

"Notepad, Merlin?" Carlos tucked the notepad into the shelves below the register. "I'm sorry, he's old."

"He's not old, just old-fashioned. Give me your phone," she said as she stuck her hand out. Carlos paused out of surprise at her insistence, but he snapped back to reality after Merlin hit his shoulder again. He handed his Android phone over to the young woman. She continued to smile as she scrolled through the apps.

"You got I-G?" Merlin only had a Facebook account that he hadn't checked in years. But even he was aware Carlos avoided social media like someone openly coughing on a Metro train a week after COVID lockdown.

"Oh, uhm. I can install it if you'd like?" Carlos said, almost panicky. She laughed.

"Underscore diamond angel two four two, all one word," she said, handing back the phone to Carlos.

"Okay, one sec." A whole minute later, Carlos was still fumbling with his phone, his face grimacing in frustration. She smiled and shook her head.

"I'll just stick with old-fashioned," she said snatching the phone back from Carlos' hand. She input some digits into the keypad and handed it back over to Carlos. He read the saved contact.

"Reina?"

"Yes, like the singer." Merlin was done with listening to any new music the previous ten years, but he had heard one of his nieces talk about a new Dominican artist named Reina. But he only heard a form of hardcore rock when Carlos had his headphones turned up. And it wasn't the Slayer or Iron Maiden he remembered that was popular with his cousins. Instead, it had emotional melodic singing intertwined with growls over heavy guitars.

"Oh, cool," Merlin could tell Carlos was only pretending to know of this Reina sensation.

"Respond to my texts, okay?" Carlos tried to nod nonchalantly. Merlin knew it would be Carlos who would be sending a 'hey how r u?' before the sunset that day. "See ya Friday."

Reina waved her fingers as she winked in his direction

and exited the market. Right as the door closed after the chime, Merlin gave Carlos a hard congratulatory smack on his upper back for accomplishing a task that seemed impossible for Carlos, even with the availability of countless dating apps.

"She likes you, my boy." Merlin grabbed a nearby broom and started to sweep around the register. The line between lovestruck and stalker became thin as Merlin glanced over at Carlos' attention to the rows of pictures on Reina's Instagram.

"If I mess this up, I'm going to put my name on the Bazaar my own damn self."

"The what?" asked Merlin. Carlos sighed, making Merlin realize it was another casualty of a generation gap.

"Here, I'll show you." Carlos turned around and grabbed his laptop. He placed it from behind them to the front counter for Merlin to look over his shoulder.

"I don't want to watch any of your porn."

"Shut up, Merlin." The two laughed as Carlos connected to the wi-fi. He clicked on the Tor browser icon on the desktop and went to the homepage of an icon that had Bazaar.tor as text under it. Merlin looked at the list of names with Bitcoin signs next to their portraits.

"Isn't that the president?" asked Merlin, looking at one of the list's top ten.

"Yup, that's forty-seven, alright. And he's not even number one on the list." Merlin kept looking at the list, and he saw more familiar faces. "Look," said Carlos. "Even the vice admiral is on there." The Navy of El Salvador's vice admiral Jorge Cuevas was also the country's minister of defense. Merlin was quite familiar with him but was still confused about what exactly this digitally compiled list of individuals was.

"Why are these people on here?" asked Merlin. A smirk with a secretive dark underbelly emerged on Carlos' face. He looked around to make sure the coast was clear before he revealed the figurative punchline to answer Merlin's curiosity.

"People place bets on a date for each person you see here. The more money put under your name, the higher you are on the list."

"A date? What's supposed to happen on this date?" Another pause on Carlos' end like he still hadn't ripped the surprise out of the bag.

"Nothing is supposed to happen, but if they were to say, 'go to sleep and never wake up,' on the date somebody predicts, they win the pool." Merlin went silent for a moment, putting together in his head that this was a prediction market for homicides.

"And who are the people making these bets?"

"You know," Carlos said, still with a sinister smirk on his face. "People like you and me." Immediately after that last line, an enraged Merlin grabbed Carlos by the collar of his shirt and swung him with such force up against the wall behind them that it nearly knocked over boxes of cigarettes. Whatever confidence in Carlos' face had been wiped clean, and he was now quivering in fear, visibly shocked at the turn of events.

"Merlin, what the —"

"People like you and me?" recited Merlin. "You and me are nothing alike, my boy. Death is not a game. It wasn't a game when I had to shoot back at esquandrones de la muerte massacring our women and children."

"Okay, Merlin. I'm sorry! Please, you're hurting me." Merlin looked directly into the soul of Carlos. He realized the young man had no understanding of the years of random nephews, nieces, friends, and even grandmothers going missing into the night as the civil war raged into the early 90s before Merlin finally left. He let go of Carlos, who shook uncontrollably from being confronted with the PTSD of the 14-year conflict that tore apart their home country. Merlin started to case up. He patted Carlos on the shoulder to reassure him it was out of love.

"You have every opportunity at your grasp in this land," he said as he fixed the young man's collar. "We made all these sacrifices to raise your generation better, but all you guys want to do is bring that Mara shit over here and kill each other like animals."

"I hate MS-13," said Carlos as his shakes started to calm a bit. "I want nothing to do with those assholes. Or Latin Kings or any of them."

Merlin shut the laptop screen down.

"Then you want nothing to do with that nonsense you just showed me. Understand?" Carlos nodded in agreement.

"I know, Merlin. I'm sorry I just came across it while doing some work for school. That's all."

"My man. One day, you're going to own this whole block. You get that degree, become the Latino Bill Gates, and make our people proud," Merlin laughed as the two exchanged a masculine hug.

"Bill Garcia," Carlos chuckled back.

"I think I like Carlos Mateo better," Merlin said as he handed the laptop to Carlos to put in his bag. "Now let's talk about where you and the future Mrs. Mateo are gonna do Friday night."

"What she doesn't know is that I'm broke too." The joyous mood was back in Carlos' voice.

"If girls at your age are seeking partners for money, you ditch them where you found them," exclaimed Merlin as he took out a card. He handed it to Carlos. He read the words 'El Tigre Grill' in extravagant letters, sitting between a soccer ball, margaritas, and utensils. "Take her there and tell the manager, Miguel, to put your whole date on my tab."

"Really? Merlin—"

"I insist, my friend. It's a good spot over in Gaithersburg. Never saw one of them MS-13 idiots there. They got some pool tables, too."

"Damn," Carlos reflected as he looked at the card and put it in his pocket. "You're like the uncle always looking out, I swear."

"I'll be gone from this world while you're still changing it," said Merlin. "But until then, I'm going to protect you and your dreams. It gives my life purpose." Carlos damn near got teary-eyed at the heartfelt admission. The door chime went off as a couple walked in as customers. Merlin left the register, and the two got back to work.

CHAPTER 11

U.S. Representative of Maryland 4th Congressional District Desmond Ellis remembered his final conversation with Attorney General Frost. Congress had passed the Undetectable Firearms Act and it was the first bill from national Congress to target 3-D printed guns, having been a snowball from all the efforts from state senates. He remembered Frost bringing up his name being on the Bazaar and out of his own curiosity, Ellis went back home that night to look up the list himself without his wife or anyone in his family seeing him hunched over the laptop on the dark web. To his horror, he saw his own name crack the top 500, officially making his death a decent profit for any interested party. That was why he was now on a tour of an office building in North Bethesda, Maryland. It was very similar to the setting he was in for over a decade as an HR specialist until his involvement in local politics finally became a career. Congressmembers made well into the six figures, but to employ Raptor, many of his donors chipped in to sponsor his security on the anniversary of the legislation being passed, the day that is generally thought to be the most popular date for his targeted assassination.

––––––

Six weeks from that date, Vash, Yemi, and Karen showed Desmond, along with his aides, around the sixth floor. It seemed like a stroll down memory lane as they turned the corner from the elevators toward rows of cubicles. Even the color scheme matched exactly the same as the consulting firm Ellis worked for fifteen years prior.

"Your secured office will be at the end of this aisle," said Vash. "It does have a window to look out onto the floor, but it'll be blast and bulletproof, as well as the door, which also has a deadbolt."

"In addition to the uniformed guards on the first floor," Yemi said. "We'll have a few by the elevator, along with two members of our elite executive protection team who will remain positioned in the cubicle area."

"Where will you be?" asked Desmond toward Yemi, knowing he was the commander of the Executive Protection Team.

"In the parking garage with the four other members of my team," he responded. "We'll be in a vehicle, ready for a rapid response to any potential threat that enters the premises." Desmond turned to his aides.

"It's your responsibility that my location on July seventh does not get leaked to the public. I'm not threatening your job, but you may have to consider a different career path if any breach gets traced back to anyone right here right now."

"Let's head back to the ground floor," insisted Vash, attempting to ease the apparent anxiety taking shape in Desmond. "I know the circumstances seem stark, but I want to show how your stay here can almost be a vacation in your backyard."

The group entered the cafeteria area. Although it was the weekend so nothing was in service, Desmond took notice of the salad bar, hot bar, sandwich station, and soda fountain that was an updated Coke Freestyle machine. It was another blast from the past as he remembered his three egg omelet and fried potatoes he'd get every morning before setting up shop in his cubicle. If he hadn't taken up cycling at the behest of his wife a few years back, he would still be carrying the thirty-five pounds he gained from that period.

"I don't know how familiar you are with the cuisine in Rockville, Mr. Ellis," started Vash. "But in my opinion, we have the best Asian food on the East Coast outside of New York City, no question."

"Northern Virginia might give it a run for its money, especially around Eden Center," remarked Desmond as he looked at items listed on a standing board. It read SPECIAL: SMOKED SALMON AND MASHED POTATOES. "But I've heard good things about these parts."

"None of that bland slop will be on the menu while you're here, sir," Vash stated as he caught Desmond looking at the board. "You're going to get the opportunity to see for yourself which one is better because we're having chefs from half a dozen of the best local spots cater for you. Chinese, Vietnamese, Korean, Peruvian, you'll have the best cuisine from the pike right at your disposal for the entire period."

"And every meal, drink, item, anything that can possibly be ingested into your body will be inspected by my team," Yemi stated. Desmond noticed the Raptor commander was making sure the conversation stayed on the topic of the mission and not an Anthony Bourdain documentary. The politician nodded in approval, impressed.

"Well, since I'm clearly going to be getting my grub on, where do I get to burn it all off?"

"Follow me, sir."

Desmond was expecting an exercise bike, a treadmill, and maybe some free weights to be the sum of all the components inside the building's fitness center. But, the place appeared to be a few steps above his prediction. There were four weight machines, three treadmills, two ellipticals, two exercise bikes, a vast array of free weights, kettle bells, an ergometer, multiple mats and benches for calisthenics, along with a bathroom that included a full walk-in shower.

"We're not LA Fitness, but you should definitely be able to keep up your regimen during your time here," stated Vash as he fixed up the weight rack.

"I'm flattered that you think I have a regimen."

"You look good, Congressman." Desmond turned to the source of the compliment as it came from the only female voice in the room. Many in the press and several women colleagues of Desmond regularly remarked that his face seemed carved for Mount Rushmore before he ever took office. His granite chin beneath his symmetrical face, combined with his post-military workout regimen, made him an anomaly among balding, overweight, pale lawmakers.

"Why thank you, uhm — ?"

"Karen."

"Sorry, I'm bad with names."

"You're fine. If you don't mind me asking, what do you normally do to stay in shape?"

"Cycling. Mixed in with some light calisthenics when I can."

"Oh, you bike? I was thinking about getting into that. What made you start?"

"Needed some cardio to get back in shape, and running is a little hard on my knees, so I figured it was the best thing next to swimming." Desmond reflected to himself for a brief moment, questioning why he didn't mention his wife as the reason. He realized his attraction to the young CFO of the company he had entrusted with his life was already affecting his decision-making process.

"It's funny you say that because I swim."

"Oh? Looking at you, I would've guessed you're more of the track type." Desmond saw Yemi's eyebrow raise. The two made eye contact, and Desmond who got the hint that he wasn't as slick as he thought he was despite being a groomed politician. Desmond cleared his throat. "I mean, where do you swim?"

"Just at the Y by where I live."

"Cool, cool." As bad as Desmond wanted to invite himself

to dip in the water with Karen at some point, he knew he couldn't push the envelope any further than he already had. In an attempt to ease any possible tension, he directed a question to Yemi that he already knew the answer to. "Will I have protection when I'm in this facility?"

"Two guards, at an absolute minimum, will be at your sides at all times during your stay." Yemi had already moved on from the brief awkward moment between them. "Even when you use the restroom, one will be stationed outside, and one will have to be outside the stall."

"Were those details really necessary, Yemi?" Karen was still in a casual, joking mood. Desmond noticed Yemi wasn't.

"Very much necessary. King Edmund the Second was killed while using the toilet, Robert Kennedy was shot in a kitchen, and God knows how many pundits have been assassinated by deliberate food poisoning." The room was quiet for a brief moment. Between Vash's treatment of the tour like a stay at a Cancun resort and the congressman's own underhand flirting with Karen, it seemed like Yemi was the only one whose tone matched the severity of the situation.

"Well, it sounds like I'll be in good hands," remarked Desmond, breaking the silence.

"Very good hands," said Karen as the two made eye contact one last time. Yemi slightly sighed through his nose.

"I think this concludes the tour, Congressman, unless there is anything else you'd wish to see?" explained Vash.

"No, I think my staff and I realize this is the best option for me. We can go ahead and get the contracts signed."

"Excellent! Right this way." Vash led Desmond and the aides out of the mini gym.

———

Yemi and Karen traded glares as they slowly created distance behind their client.

"You know he's married with kids, right?"

"Keep your voice down!" she demanded of her brother. She looked forward as they walked and realized nobody had heard him. "What's wrong with you?"

"I was about to ask you that same question."

"Can we please just focus on the task at hand?"

"That's all I've been doing this whole time. Didn't realize I was a third wheel to a potential career-ending affair."

"Okay, Yemi. I know your detective senses are what make you good at your job, but now they're malfunctioning 'cause there's nothing there. You know I'm not that type of girl."

"Mmmhmmm." The two kept a wide gap between themselves and the rest of the group. "I know you'll be backstroking across the Atlantic ocean once the same blogs that called you the area's top Black female entrepreneur find out about you and Mr. Tour de France."

"I hate you sometimes."

"Just sometimes?" chuckled Yemi.

"There's gotta be something else in between since we share our profits."

"Ah, so it's just money keeping the family together. Dad would be proud."

"Just shut your smart ass up so we can make sure Ellis signs the dotted line."

"I hope he and the misses also signed a prenup—" Karen gave Yemi a hard yet playful punch in the shoulder as they followed the group into a room where Vash intended to get the paperwork done.

CHAPTER 12

When the Maryland House of Corrections Jessup closed down in 2007, the North Branch Correctional Institute and the adjacent Western Correctional Institute in Cumberland were left as Maryland's only maximum security prisons. NBCI was close to where Aaron lived now, but he knew he was still taking a risk to make a conjugal visit. He had filled out the visitation form with the alias Christopher Atlas, a tongue-in-cheek remix of his Cryptext username. He also had a fake ID and documents to match it. For all Aaron knew, there was a possibility of correctional officers handcuffing him at the entrance gates to turn over the real Aaron Williams to the Maryland State Police. However, by the time he was seated and waiting in visitation, he realized he was in the clear.

Within time, a line of the convicts allowed for visitation stepped into the parloir. Aaron scanned each one, and he was finally able to spot Danny in an orange jumpsuit. Danny had clearly stopped skipping meals as he added about ten to fifteen pounds of muscle to his formerly slim frame over the last several months and had gang-affiliated tats inked across his forearms. Danny's institutionalized deadpan face lit up in joy upon seeing Aaron. They immediately embrace, locking in for several seconds before they sat down across from one another.

"Man, look at you!" Aaron exclaimed as he flexed his arms. "Went from a starving pup to a pitbull."

"You already know. Gotta let 'em know ain't shit sweet from where we from." Aaron respectfully chuckled to himself, knowing Danny's infatuation with the streets hadn't changed a bit. He looked at the letters 'ETG' and skull designs tatted across his forearms. Aaron knew from a History Channel documentary those were affiliated with the Crips.

"So you good in here?" Danny realized what Aaron was looking at.

"Oh." He pulled his arms back, seemingly a little apprehensive on the particular topic. "Just how it is, ya know? B-G-F think my people are parasites in the hoods, and you know damn well I can't roll with them racist ass Aryans and come back to P-G. So yeah..." Danny casually flashed a 'C' with his hands. The two awkwardly laughed as Aaron shook his head.

"True."

"What about you? You good?" Danny leaned in. "Don't worry, nobody can hear shit."

"I know, I know. I wouldn't be here if I thought it was sketch," said Aaron. "But yeah, I'm up in Allegany County with a new crew."

"Allegany County?" a bewildered Danny asked. "I'm behind bars fighting white boys, and your Black ass joining up with them in the free world. Somebody explain this." They shared another laugh.

"Nah, nah. They're chill. Mad professional, actually. On a whole different level than anything Rold could imagine."

"Oh, hold up." Danny leaned in again. "That hit on the attorney general. Was that y'all?" Aaron paused for a moment in response to his friend's incriminating question. His eyes rose very slowly to Danny with a shade of a grin. Danny got his answer right there. "Bro, y'all WILD —"

"Shhh, shhh," beckoned Aaron as he couldn't help but chuckle at Danny, possibly bringing them attention from his energy. Once it settled, Aaron continued. "So yeah, fam, things are operating a different level now out here."

"Dawg, Aaron —"

"Yo!" Aaron again asked through his body language to

keep it down. "Christopher, remember." Danny snickered.

"Ight, Chris," laughed Danny. "Just remember to get out of this shit, bro." Aaron's face shifted a bit, not expecting this from the guy who appeared in public with no mask and fired off multiple rounds of a fully automatic assault rifle.

"What do you mean?" There was an awkward pause between them.

"Fam, you really want to end up in a place like here? It ain't worth—"

"I just said things are operating at a different level."

"And I get that, bro, but you're smart—"

"Exactly. I operate at a different level. I always have, ever since we've known each other." Another awkward pause.

"What are you getting at when you say that?" asked Danny. There was an unfamiliar tension between them.

"Danny." Aaron breathed in and out. "I'm here out of respect for your sacrifice, but you did that out of your own volition. Come on, dude, you react with emotion. You're swayed easily—"

"Whoa, whoa. Do you hear what you're saying, bruh? Watch your mouth." Now, the temperature had risen. They made eye contact. Aaron's stare pierced right through Danny's newfound persona.

"I'll say whatever I want, got me? Especially to somebody who set me up and put me in this situation in the first place." Danny kept his composure, not flinching despite Aaron being able to tell his head was running in opposite directions, trying to keep his ego intact while also admitting to the truth in Aaron's insult. Eventually, Danny just kicked out his chair and stood up. He kept his stare on Aaron.

"Don't bother coming back here again." Aaron realized this escalated too quickly as a pissed-off Danny headed back to the guards waiting for him.

"Yo Danny—"

"Fuck off." Within seconds, Danny was being led back to his cell. Aaron sat there, wondering where that burst of arrogance came from in his exchange with Danny. He thought he had written off the betrayal by now, but he realized he never had the chance to confront Danny about it, and it came out when his own ego felt threatened by what was probably just a concerned friend. He looked around at the infrastructure that surrounded him. Right behind those walls were essentially human cages. He swore right there to himself to never set foot in one of these environments again, even preferring death. Aaron got up and headed back out of the prison.

———

It was 2:30 PM. Merlin realized he had made the right choice to arrive at work twenty minutes early that morning because nobody else was there to unlock the doors and open up the store. Carlos was supposed to start his shift six and a half hours ago, and Merlin hadn't seen his skeletal frame come in through the entrance all day. He called the young manager's phone number again, and it rang multiple times before going straight to voicemail, the case it had been the whole morning. As customers piled, including the occasional passerby who didn't know Spanish, Merlin realized he was going to have to reach out to the owner to give them the lowdown on the situation. He was only hesitant to make the call because the last thing he wanted was for Carlos to lose his job, which he needed to help pay whatever his scholarship didn't cover.

Finally, after Merlin checked the last person in line out, he dialed the number for the Las Americas Mercado founder.

"Crystal Santos speaking."

"Crystal, it's Merlin from the Wheaton location."

"Merlin!" exclaimed Crystal. "What's up?"

"Pretty backed up over here. I've been on my own since

the morning."

"What? How so? Where's Carlos?"

"I don't know." Merlin paused, trying to quickly think of a way to boost Carlos' credibility. He wasn't going to mention Carlos' date the previous night. "I was hoping you may have heard something?"

"No, he never called in or anything."

"Okay. This is very unlike him."

"It is. I like Carlos, but he can't leave you hanging like this."

"It's all good. I think I'll be able to get through today. I think he's got mid terms coming up, and my guess is he slept past his alarm with all the studying." A low chuckle came from Crystal's end.

"Maybe. Let me know if you hear from him. None of the other managers are free, so if he's still not in tomorrow, I'll just come down there myself."

"Thank you, Crystal."

"Any time, Merlin. Talk to you soon."

———

Four more hours passed by, and there was still no sign of Carlos, so Merlin's concern grew. The last call he made to Carlos went straight to voicemail, so that meant his battery had either died or Carlos' phone had been purposely turned off. Gaithersburg was on the other side of the county, but Merlin wanted to do some light investigation into where his young manager could have gone. He had been to the El Tigre Grill numerous times, even without a car, so that evening's dinner plans would no longer be his usual bowl of Top Ramen. Merlin finished closing and headed to the Wheaton metro station, where he hopped on the 48 toward the west side of Montgomery County.

———

Flags of El Salvador, Mexico, Guatemala, Honduras, and

Nicaragua draped the walls. All the mounted TV screens blasted international soccer games narrated by high-strung Spanish commentators. El Tigre Grill was about half full, mostly with groups of men with dried paint on their cargo pants coming in to watch professional athletes kick around a tether ball as they washed down plates of pupusas with Corona Extras. Merlin walked in and scanned the hole in the wall he was accustomed to. He didn't drink anymore, so it had been about a full year since he had been back. As he sat down, he didn't see much had changed, but he did notice a new breed of customers across the floor on the opposite side. Unlike the day-laboring regulars who seemed to prefer to sit at the bar, Merlin took notice of three or four boys who couldn't be older than the legal drinking age limit sitting in a booth in the farthest corner. They were loud, cursing, laughing hysterically, and they were all covered in tattoos from the arms to even the face. Despite his age, Merlin had 20/20 vision and could even tell one of them sported multiple inked tear drops below their eyes, the sign of someone who had bodies under their belt.

"Would you like a menu?" Merlin was so focused on the gang of youth that he didn't even notice the pear-shaped beauty of a waitress approach his table.

"No, it's okay. What's your name, gorgeous?" She slightly blushed, but she had the confidence of a grown woman, not just an undergrad picking up a part-time shift.

"Diana."

"Sopa de mariscos and a glass of water, Diana. Please."

"No pupusas?" Merlin watched the gang get loud as they cheered one of their members into chugging a can of Modelo. The drinker was unable to make it to the bottom and flipped the can from his mouth, splashing beer all over the booth causing a huge mess as they continued to laugh loudly. The waitress rolled her eyes as she focused back on Merlin.

"Who are they?" inquired Merlin.

"Just assholes," she casually remarked. "Sopa de mariscos. Anything else?"

"Two pupusas, actually. Both beans and cheese." She jotted the full order on her mini notebook. "And is Edgar here today?"

"Yes, he's in the back."

"Tell him Merlin's here. Ask him if he's free to have a word."

"You got it." Diana smiled and stepped away as Merlin continued to watch the wild pack on the other side continue to turn up in the vicinity. All four pairs of their eyes became glued to Diana's backside as she turned the corner to go behind the bar. A couple of them whistled in her direction, and two yelled out some cat calls in Spanish.

"Ay, mami!" one of them screamed. "Bring your sexy ass over to our table." Merlin continued to study their behavior. Eventually, one of them flashed a devil hand sign towards one of the regulars, who looked over at them for a brief moment. Merlin thought El Tigre was free of any gang activity, but clearly, over the past six months, a Mara Salvatrucha chapter had set up shop in Edgar's club. The owner himself soon came from behind the bar and made his way to his table. Merlin stood up, and the two enthusiastically greeted each other before they both sat down across from one another.

"Where you been, old man?" Edgar said, despite being only a few years younger.

"I can't drink anymore," shrugged Merlin. "Trying to live as long as I can."

"Well, it's looking like you might outlive me. Doctor said I have to get part of my liver removed. All those damn beers over the years have caught up." Merlin watched Diana serve another round of Modelos to the table of young gangsters. Merlin could tell she was in a rush to leave them after dropping off the drinks, but one grabbed her hand to pull her in. She resisted and strutted back to the bar as they continued to whistle at her.

"Speaking of beers," said Merlin as he nodded in their direction. "I don't remember those types being around when I was here." Edgar glanced in their direction. Immediately, he shook with head with frustration as he turned back toward Merlin.

"I can afford a police officer Thursday and Saturday nights, but every other day I don't know how to cast away those damn demons." He sighed. "They're like a virus messing with my bottom line."

"Just like COVID, huh?" said Merlin as Diana brought him his water as well as a glass for Edgar. He leaned in so she could hear him discreetly.

"If those kids continue to bother you, just let me know," assured Merlin. She smiled.

"They're just drunk and horny. Don't worry about it, papa." Edgar pat Merlin on the back, almost like he was showcasing his old friend to the girl.

"This guy right here. He'll send them all to the E-R with a flick of the wrist, I tell ya."

"Stop it, Edgar." Merlin wasn't one to blush, but sometimes, it was involuntary while trying to keep his humility intact.

"Merlin was on his way to being the best Salvadoran boxer since Carlos Hernandez."

"We have boxers?" inquired a surprised Diana. "I thought it was all Mexicans."

"These youngsters don't know their own countrymen," said Edgar as he shook his head side to side in disappointment at the lack of athletic knowledge of the younger generation. Diana smiled at them before she headed back to the bar. "That reminds me. A kid last night brought you up. I think his name was Carlos, too. Said to put his order on your tab."

"That's actually what I came here for," said Merlin as he took out two twenties to hand over to Edgar, but his old drinking buddy held his hand up to refuse the cash.

"He ended up not getting anything besides a Coke with lime. Think he was waiting for someone, and they never showed up."

"There wasn't a girl with him?"

"None that I saw," Edgar stated as he sipped his water. "Then again, these days, I don't even know what a woman is supposed to look like with this generation."

"So he left alone?" asked Merlin, staying on topic and not wasting anymore precious time with random quips.

"Now that I'm not sure. At some point, I came out from the kitchen, and he was gone." Edgar paused, trying to jog his memory. "As a matter of fact, he disappeared at the same time as those jackals last night." Edgar used his thumb to point in the direction of the group that occupied the booth across the restaurant. Merlin stared in their direction. He traded looks with one of them, face tats and all. The kid, who could have been a third of Merlin's age, stuck his tongue out and made a hand gesture with his face like something of demonic origin. Edgar sighed, seeing the exchange.

"Let it go, Merlin. I don't know how many more bar fights I can afford with the lights staying on."

"Been coming here for eight years and think I have seen two fights max. And all of them got broken up before the cops showed up." Merlin watched Diana approaching the two of them with his food ready.

"Well, since the corner over there has become the official meeting spot of the Gaithersburg chapter of MS, multiply that number by ten in this year alone."

"Jesus," responded Merlin. Diana sat the hot soup down with the two stuffed corn tortillas. A hungry Merlin quietly said grace to himself and dug in. "Well, your mom's soup recipe hasn't changed."

"She passed in January. Rest her soul."

"Oh, Lord. I'm sorry, Edgar."

"It's alright. She was happy to go while seeing her son still having a business under his watch. Now, if she were to hold off until next year, that would be a real tragedy."

"Don't say that," Merlin said in between scoops full of boiled crab and shrimp in a tomato base. "This place isn't going anywhere." He took one last look over at the kids in the corner. "But they are."

———

Merlin was up early again the next morning. Without drinking, it was easier for him to get a full night's rest prior to work. On that day, he was joined by the 44-year-old Crystal, who stepped in to replace Carlos while they figured out where their rising star went off to the past two days. She seemed reluctant to be there, and rightfully so, figured Merlin. It was getting to the point where she would have to hire a new manager. Usually, the TV in the store was turned to sports like El Tigre Bar, but Crystal preferred having C-SPAN on. Merlin watched as Congressman Desmond Ellis introduced legislation in honor of Maryland Attorney General Ryan Frost to officially ban the creation of plastic guns on a federal scale.

Within fifteen minutes of the store being open, in walked a pair of men in blazers, dress shirts, ties, and slacks. The badges around their belt buckles identified them as law enforcement. One of them approached Merlin while he was sweeping the floor as Crystal was in the back taking inventory.

"Hello, sir. I'm Detective David Dykes with the Montgomery County Police Special Investigations Division."

"No habla ingles," responded Merlin, only knowing the words 'Montgomery County Police' from what Detective Dykes just said.

"Ah," said Dykes as he motioned for his younger, fitter, browner-skinned partner to step forward. "Palacios." The other man approached Merlin.

"Detective Alejandro Palacios with M-C-P-D, sir. How are you today?" the man asked in Spanish. Crystal decided to put inventory on hold as she entered the front of the store before Merlin could give an answer.

"Can I help you, officers?" asked Crystal, visibly a bit sketched out by their presence. Detective Dykes stepped to her, realizing she could speak English.

"Did a young man named Carlos Mateo work here?"

"Did?" asked Crystal. She traded looks with Merlin. He didn't know what the officer said, but Merlin could see the concern on Crstyal's face. "He still does work here whenever he decides to show up, that is." Now it was the detectives who traded looks like they were about to drop a bomb on the whole conversation. "Oh my God. Is Carlos alright?" The two members of Montgomery County's finest paused again, not sure which of them was going to unveil what they came there for.

"Carlos was found this morning in Malcolm King Park in Gaithersburg." It was Dykes who broke the news. Crystal stood in shock, her body frozen in trying to digest the information.

"Found?" was all she could manage to eke out in her state.

"He was stabbed over eighty times," Palacios added in Spanish, making sure Merlin understood what was being said. "He was pronounced dead at the scene. I'm sorry." Merlin had the same reaction as Crystal, the ability to move or even react was muted.

"I know this is hard to take in," said Dykes toward Crystal. "But we want justice for Carlos, and it's imperative that we start tracking his series of events on Friday as soon as possible."

"If any of you can tell us anything about what his plans

were that day or who he was with," Palacios announced in his native tongue. "It would be of great help and can lead to the apprehension of whoever may be responsible faster." Merlin twisted tight on the broom handle in his grasp, all the recent conversations he shared with his former manager running through his head like a daydream turned nightmare.

"Carlos was never involved in violence," stated Merlin in an attempt to make sense of this situation. "He stayed clear of la Mara or any that foolishness."

"Carlos is only a victim in this situation," Palacios responded. "We don't have any reason to believe he was a willing participant in what we think may be a ritual."

"A ritual?" asked a horrified Crystal.

"We're not positive that this is connected to MS-13 just yet," said Dykes. "But the signs are there. They have been known to launch violent attacks on random civilians as part of an initiation for new members. A chapter down in Manassas stabbed a pregnant woman to death a few years back." The example provided by Dykes only pushed Crystal down into a well of despair, still in disbelief at the whole situation.

"He might have been lured to that location under the guise of some kind of transaction," Palacios continued in Spanish. "Like maybe a weed deal or—"

"Carlos didn't touch drugs," a stern Merlin made clear to the detectives. "He was clean and was on the Dean's List at George Mason."

"It could've been something else. Maybe a friend he trusted? Maybe a girl?" Merlin paused again, squeezing the broom even tighter as he connected the dots to who may have set Carlos up.

"Listen, I know this is probably a lot for the two of you," said Dykes as he reached into his pocket and handed a business card to Crystal. "But please give us all a call if you have any information."

"You can reach out to us at any time to get an update on the case," followed up Palacios in Spanish. Merlin nodded a faint 'goodbye' to them as they proceeded out of the store. As soon as the door chime went off, Crystal broke down into tears. Merlin leaned the broom up against the wall and embraced her to provide at least some sense of comfort, not only for her sake but his own, in order to counteract the violent urges that were rising within him. Urges he had kept dormant for decades since battling the paramilitary forces in his home country.

"Lucas is only a few years younger than Carlos." Lucas was Crystal's son who worked as a cashier at the Langley Park location of Las Americas Mercado. "How am I going to talk to him about this?"

Merlin didn't have an answer. He just stood there in silence, cradling a woman in mourning over a fellow mother's child. The only thing on the former guerrilla's mind was underscore diamond angel two four two.

CHAPTER 13

Abdallah was restless, sitting in the cushioned chair right outside his editor's office. Reading the text about the impromptu meeting was so anxiety-inducing that his Benzos prescription could barely bring him down, and it was only an emergency call to his therapist that eased him enough to get him out the door of the basement apartment he was two weeks late on rent for.

He couldn't remember doing or saying anything that would suddenly get his job slashed. However, as he already explained to Nick, the media realm was no stranger to waves of layoffs in this post-pandemic labyrinth of trying to monetize people's attention spans. He thought all those years of grinding on articles late into the night after shifts serving tables in Dupont Circle were steps toward better job security, but the doomsday LinkedIn updates from many of his colleagues at other outlets were signs he would have to enter a whole new field if he wanted a stable future.

"Okay, Abdallah, you can come in," announced a mature female voice from behind the office door. Abdallah shot up out of the chair but slowed down when he twisted the knob, realizing it was his nerves acting out again. He opened it and sat down across from Al Noor's DC Bureau managing editor-in-chief, Dena Shabruni. He had only been in this office once before for the second stage of the interview process. Some more press awards had been added to desks and walls since then. He actually felt a bit more intimidated than he did when he wasn't even on the payroll.

"How are you, Abdallah?" the Palestinian national in her late 40s asked her young Sudanese journo.

"Well, if I'm being honest." He cleared his throat. "I'm a little nervous."

"You have nothing to be nervous about."

"Oh." Abdallah breathed a sigh of relief. "Sorry, I just know there had been budget cuts, and a lot of my friends at CNN, MSNBC—"

"Don't even worry about any of that," she assured him as she shuffled some papers. "The creators of our content are what keep Al Noor going. We get rid of you, we might as well shut down the bureau." There was an awkward chuckle between them. "Maybe I shouldn't joke about that... But anyways, no, you're fine. I'm actually here to let you know I'm moving your beat."

"Really?" The energy had shifted in Abdallah from dark anxiousness to a promising light of excitement.

"Yes, almost like a promotion, if you will."

"Like a pay raise?"

"Not yet, that's why I said almost. But we feel it's best to sunset your AfriLeaks column and think it's time for you to step in as Al Noor's first full-time White House correspondent." Abdallah was visibly elated, shocked at how wrong his prediction for the turn of events would be.

"Wow," he mouthed after waiting a moment for the news to settle in. "I don't know what to say other than thank you so much."

"It's very well earned. Keep up the great work, Abdallah."

"But, uhm. What, uh." It was hard for Abdallah to counter good news from his employer with concerns, but he had to know the future of some of his work. "What about my reports on the Bazaar? Wasn't my Attah piece one of the most viewed articles on the website?"

"Yes, and still is. That's part of why you were our first choice when this opportunity came up," she said as she fixed her spectacles. "But I've gotten the memo from higher up that there are some major security concerns."

"What? Like that al Noor might be targeted or something?"

"Well, not quite in the way you phrased it. No one here is in physical danger. But some in the intelligence community have warned us that your reports have been cited as possible fuel for future Bazaar-related attacks."

"Wait, wait." Abdallah paused, realizing that this conversation might go from good news to bad. But he didn't become a journalist to just climb the media employment ladder. "I'm a bit confused about how that's even relevant. My story is the truth, and my sources are legitimate. Since when did we cave into what the government thinks? This is an independent publication." The face on Dena shifted as if he somehow crossed a line of respect between them. "Sorry, I'm just trying to get clarity on this."

"You're fine. But look, Abdallah, I hope you understand we have to be careful now. We pride ourselves on our autonomy, of course. And we will continue to do that. But we also know the environment we're in. RT America had its headquarters down the street only a few short years ago, remember."

"But we're not backed by a foreign entity." There was a pause on her behalf as if she knew something he didn't. "Or I didn't think we were."

"You start down at Pennsylvania Ave next month," she said, taking the topic back to the positive news. "Want to give you some time to prepare. I hope you're as excited as we are."

"I am, and again, thank you, Ms. Shabruni." She nodded. "Of course."

"But just to confirm," Abdallah added. Dena breathed hard out of her nostrils, possibly tired of the subject Abdallah couldn't seem to shake. "I've been in contact with an inside source to one of the original executive protection firms that have clients who are on the Bazaar. Is this just getting canned?"

"I've been in news for over twenty years, Abdallah. Most ideas, even some of the best ones I've heard, don't make it to publication."

"I understand."

"Keep on blazing trails out there. I'll email you the process on how to get your credentials."

"I appreciate you." Abdallah and his boss exchanged farewells before he exited the office. He pulled up Nick on his phone and started writing a text message explaining the ending of the partnership. After a whole paragraph, he arrived at his own desk and thought for a moment. He then closed down the chat and whipped out his laptop. He examined the article he had been working on for several weeks with the title INSIDE RAPTOR: THE HEAVILY ARMED SQUAD PROTECTING DC'S ELITE. He hovered his index finger over the 'delete' key.

After a few moments, he withdrew his finger and saved it to an external drive, remembering the journalism undergrad who wanted to change the world would not want it to change him.

———

Yemi focused mostly on strength workouts during the week, but he dedicated at least three days to endurance training to balance out his regimen. For long trail runs, his favorite location was Seneca Creek State Forest, where he remembered the horror film The Blair Witch Project had been filmed a few decades prior while he was still in middle school. He was on his second lap around Clopper Lake, and a quarter mile away was the finishing point for his workout at the land bridge where a few fishermen preferred to have their lines out. On that time around, he brought his sister along since she had wanted to try something different from the YMCA she had rambled on about to Congressman Desmond Ellis.

As he got closer, he saw she was bent over on the walls, still catching her breath. His run was completed once he arrived next to her.

"Damn, how long was that?" she asked while looking up at him. Yemi caught his breath, but he was not quite on the brink of collapse like she was.

"Around the lake twice is a little over seven."

"Good Lord," she said in between deep breaths and calculating her brother's fitness level. His slight pouch of a belly around his midsection sometimes misled shallow perceptions of how seriously he took fitness. "I barely did half that."

"Three and a half miles is pretty damn good," said Yemi. "I guess the swimming really is working for you." She waited a few more seconds to catch her breath before speaking.

"I was waiting for you to reference the Congressman."

"You're my sister, but not a punching bag for my ego. You know this."

"I do." She patted him on the back. "Big bro."

"So Vash, you trust him?"

"I mean, we're a little late in the process to be second-guessing aren't we?"

"You're making me a little nervous now," Yemi said, but he stayed cool-headed.

"Of course, he's reliable. Nobody I'm recommending for our only shot at this is gonna get us a situation like in Hagerstown."

"I'm glad you brought that up," replied Yemi as he began his routine stretches, starting with the quads. "What was your take on that?"

"You want MY opinion?" a surprised Karen said as she started her own stretching. "This whole time, I didn't bother bringing it up, given that's all you and Jasper strategize about."

"It is what we work on. But I want your two cents. If nothing else, from a financial point of view. Your specialty."

Karen stayed quiet as she focused on her hamstrings while trying to address an issue she didn't know her opinion was valued on.

"Well, it's profitable," she started off with. "Very profitable. From the assassin's perspective. And on the opposite side, it's a total net loss given that they failed to protect the client, and I can't imagine the life insurance costs for all those agents, assuming the Frost family doesn't sue, by the way. And this is all in addition to the entire thing being a P-R nightmare on several fronts. I'd say RexCorp is looking at halting all VPS assignments until further notice."

"Which benefits us, right?"

"What I wonder is if it's a blessing..." She exhaled and looked out toward the picturesque lake, seeing what the Nacotchtank people saw of her home state centuries ago. "...Or a warning."

"We're not RexCorp. The same thing would have happened to them in Silver Spring."

"I agree, but let's not act like protecting Chiedu was all smooth sailing."

"I'm not," he said, now focusing on stretching his arms. "I just see the same dated patterns that I saw back in Nigeria. My subordinates and all their Western advisors were trying to interrogate innocent poor oil workers while Peter Ikwe and his boat bandits were spearheading fifth-generation warfare." Karen's mind was visibly lost now.

"I don't even know what any generation of war looks like," she stated while going into a lunge position. "I'll just stick to analyzing the impact on our profit margins." Yemi rocked his head back and forth as he couldn't help but smile at his sister's reluctance to express her opinion.

"Which you're great at," he insisted. "Nobody's touching Congressman Ellis." He made eye contact with Karen, where he still had a smirk on his face, and she knew something else was coming out of his mouth. "Without consent."

"Oh, shut the hell up, Yemi." She delivered a kick to his shin. He pretended it hurt, and the siblings laughed.

———

Only twenty minutes driving distance from where he went to elementary school, Nick watched the heavy police presence across the street from where he was parked. He was on a stakeout of a residence that Prince George's County law enforcement was raiding. He also noticed a federal branch overseeing the whole situation when he recognized Chris Towers and his Secret Service CFTF team on the outskirts, letting the local SWAT unit handle the apprehension of the suspect. Despite the bright colors of his fuel-efficient vehicle, he was well hidden from sight by any of them, including a small group of local reporters.

When the front door swung open, he quickly raised his phone to zoom in, acting as his binoculars. Sporting a Howard University sweatshirt and sweatpants, Efemena Kanu was led out of her townhome in handcuffs by PGPD officers in full tactical gear. Her head was held high, almost proud of being discovered as a conspirator against Chiedu despite the lengthy terrorism sentence that would be coming her way. Nick watched a microphone get shoved in her face in front of an ENG camera, and her facial expressions hinted she delivered some passionate words before Towers stepped in to take her into custody from PGPD. She got placed in the back of one of the solid black Chevy Suburbans. He spotted the large Channel 9 logo on a van outside the house.

Nick opened up the X app, formerly known as Twitter, on his phone and immediately went to the feed of Channel 9's account. He refreshed it every thirty seconds until he saw a new post:

BREAKING: AUTHORITIES RAID HOME OF SUSPECT IN ASSASSINATION ATTEMPT OF EX-DIPLOMAT.

The headline was posted with a short video clip. Nick hit play, and he got to hear what Efemena had said five minutes earlier.

"Ms. Kanu, do you have anything you wish to say about the accusation that you were involved with the attempt on former Ambassador Chiedu Attah's life?" asked a female Channel 9 field reporter.

"Free the Delta! Long live Biafra!" The reporter was a bit taken aback by the energy, but she still quickly jumped to the next question.

"Is this tied to the documents leaked about Popco and the Niger Delta region?"

"Chiedu Attah is a traitor, but he's just another low-level puppet for Western colonial interests. Anybody who contributes to the oppression of my people will have the wrath of God delivered to them." Efemena looked directly at the camera. "The money you capitalist bloodsuckers worship is now your downfall. More deaths will come!" That's when the arresting officers handed Efemena over to Towers' team and blocked out the news camera.

Nick copied the hyperlink of the X post and opened up his text messages. He pasted it into a message and sent it to Abdallah.

Abdallah Kalfat: Whoa.
Abdallah Kalfat: This just happen?
Nick Rice: Yeah. I'm right across the street.

Nick uploaded his own recording to the chat.

Abdallah Kalfat: Okay now, Mr. Journalist!

The Raptor mole smiled to himself, loving the affirmations of his long-term career goal.

Nick Rice: Told ya I'm built for this!

Abdallah Kalfat: Never said you weren't.

Abdallah Kalfat: Btw we need to talk soon. Some shit going down at Al Noor.

Nick Rice: Oh damn. What happened?

Abdallah Kalfat: Not all bad.

Abdallah Kalfat: I'm going to be covering the White House starting tomorrow.

Nick Rice: Oh snap. Congrats fam!

Abdallah Kalfat: Thanks, brother. But yeah, we might need a new outlet for our story.

Nick Rice: Damn.

Nick Rice: Fr?

Abdallah Kalfat: Yeah... But don't trip. I got an idea.

A short spurt of knocks on Nick's window startled him, and he shoved his phone into his pocket as he looked up. It was Jasper, dressed completely differently than Nick had seen him on any of their missions or training sessions. Usually, his squadmate was either in a full-on tactical outfit, looking like one of the SWAT members Nick just witnessed, or he was dressed in a business casual polo khaki outfit, ready to talk intel. This time, he had on a black sweatshirt with the word ADDIS in Ethiopian colors. He wore photochromic sunglasses that sat below a gray Dickies beanie.

Jasper motioned for Nick to wind down the window, and the young man followed orders immediately.

"How'd you know where to find me?"

"I figured you to be the type who likes to admire their work," said Jasper without any hostility in his voice, to the relief of Nick. "I was right."

"Look, okay—"

"Let's go for a walk. There's a trail around the corner." Nick paused. He looked back over at the scene across the street as the police and media closed down.

"I could use some fresh air."

"Come on."

The sun was out, and the weather was rather warm for early Fall. There was a minimal amount of people in the park as Nick trotted along the pavement next to Jasper. Nick watched a sharp-shinned hawk soar above their heads and land on a tree branch above them.

"Look," Nick said to Jasper as he pointed up at the hawk. "Our patriotic company logo." Jasper looked at the bird of prey and smirked.

"It does look kinda like it," said Jasper. "Especially with the sun behind it causing a silhouette."

"I mean, it's not a bald eagle," said Nick. "But close enough, I guess."

"Yemi, Karen, and I actually based it off the African Fish Eagle, no relation to the American one."

"Oh, where are those found?"

"In Africa," chuckled Jasper.

"Africa is a big continent, I meant, what country?"

"I know. I'm messing with you," assured Jasper as he patted his young co-worker on the back. "They're found all over Africa. Growing up in Ethiopia, I'd watch them hunt at a nearby lake."

"What was it like growing up there?" asked Nick. He looked at Jasper's shirt. "You're from Addis Ababa?"

"No. I grew up in a town called Shashamane. It's about one hundred fifty miles south of Addis."

"Oh, cool. I've never heard of it, but I like the name."

"It's where Bob Marley stayed when he came to Ethiopia. A lot of Rastas from the U-S and Jamaica still live there."

"Jamaicans? Does Lyle know about Sha-sha-uhm?"

"Shashamane. And I doubt it. Lyle's spirituality begins and ends with a dollar sign."

"You could say the same for a lot of pastors."

"I guess you could," laughed Jasper. "That's one thing that stays consistent from Africa to America."

"So how did you end up from Shashamane to DC? Were you forced to join the military or something?"

"Not every kid from across the Atlantic is a child soldier, Mr. Rice."

"Oh, I didn't mean anything by that." A few steps of awkward silence, but Rice could tell Jasper wasn't offended. "But I guess maybe I watched the Kony 2012 trailer too many times in elementary school." Jasper shook his head, but he couldn't help but laugh at the ignorance Nick was becoming aware of.

"I joined voluntarily. Lots of my friends were poor, but my parents had a decent income. I was just bored. Wasn't really a big fan of soccer, running, or many sports Ethiopians were into. I did like gebeta, though."

"Gebeta?"

"You might know it in the States as mancala."

"Oh, nice. Yeah, we played that," said Nick as he watched some kids sprint ahead of their parents, racing each other on the path. "Around the same time I was watching Kony 2012." Jasper palmed his face before he continued.

"I signed up for the Ground Forces once I was eighteen. Right away, they put me in action. Was getting in firefights with shifta, not even a year after boot camp."

"Who are the shifta?"

"They're either bandits or revolutionaries, depending on who you ask. They occupy many of the less governed wilderness of Ethiopia, Eritrca, or any part around the horn of Africa. The army doesn't always like to engage with them, but sometimes their raids will kill a few farmers, so if it's our side of the border, we'd get involved."

"Didn't you get training from the U.S. Marines?"

"That's where I learned how to be a sniper, yes. And then I made the move from the Army to the Republican Guard."

"And I'm assuming that's where you met Yemi?"

"Yeah. About a year into my service protecting the prime minister, I met Yemi for the first time when we collaborated with S-S-S on a Nigeria-Ethiopia joint commission meeting in Addis."

"And that's where he convinced you to battle terrorists in the Western hemisphere instead of the East." Jasper paused.

"I never called the shifta terrorists."

"Oh, right. They sound like they fought for things more honorable than just money."

"I didn't call our opposition terrorists either." A pause between the two as they continued to walk.

"What? Do you agree with what Efemena is saying or something?"

"Of course not," remarked Jasper. "But a disagreement doesn't mean I'm in the position to classify a movement I myself might not fully understand."

"What exactly did you want to discuss with me today?"

"I didn't have an agenda."

"But you tracked me down on a day when I was off. There must have been a reason."

"You're more than a decade younger than me, and yet your knowledge about the potential of the Bazaar is greater than anybody on the squad. By far." Nick was a bit speechless at the compliment. He was in potentially hostile territory with where the conversation was going until that statement.

"I appreciate that, Jasper."

"But one thing I'll say from my years of tracking shifta. Stick to keeping the peace. Don't end up adding unnecessary violence. We're bodyguards, not soldiers." Nick started to realize maybe what Jasper had been trying to show him.

"I don't view Efemena or anybody as some kind of prey. If that's what you think."

"I just want you to be aware. Hopefully, there will not be too many more gunfights in the future. But if there are, remember you don't know who's behind that other trigger. And you don't need to know. Because their reasons for being there might make you question yours." Nick nodded his head up and down, intently listening to the veteran of executive protection next to him. He looked up again and saw the same sharp-shinned hawk in a different tree. He studied it closely and realized there was a whipping long tail attached to a patch of fur gripped between its talons belonging to an unlucky native forest rat.

CHAPTER 14

Merlin didn't have a bachelor's degree or any type of document that could help him with seeking higher employment. He dropped out of high school during the unrest and never had the opportunity to enroll in any of El Salvador's twenty-four universities. However, a few years prior, Crystal offered him to attend Montgomery College for ESL classes in hopes he'd pursue an associate in Business. Merlin Erazo was a hard worker, but he never flourished in a classroom, so she gave up on sponsoring his education after he failed his first semester. From that experience, Merlin was familiar with both the Rockville and Takoma Park/Silver Spring campuses of MC. For the first time, he found himself at the Germantown location. He reflected on his brief attempt at higher education during the entire ten hours he had been hidden in the nearby forest reserve, studying carefully who entered and left the Bioscience Education Center.

It was 5:07 PM, about 8 minutes before the time Reina had shared she had just finished class on her Instagram Story exactly a week prior to Merlin being there. The area around the Bioscience building looked the most similar to the background in her video as Reina and her fellow classmate did an impromptu twerk to a popular rap song. The Instagram post stayed etched in Merlin's mind. As the clock ticked closer to 5:15 PM, he took out Detective Palacios' card for the twentieth time that day and read it. Merlin never joined a gang, but refusing to talk to police was still a mantra he stuck by, whether it was tied to criminal activity or ICE looking to deport him or a friend. But the temptation to inform Palacios was great. If Reina didn't walk out of the building within twenty minutes and he headed back home with no leads, he may just give the young detective a ring.

Soon, people started to file out of the Bioscience Center. It was a community college, so it was a very diverse mixture of age groups, genders, and colors. Like a crouched lion looking for a baby amongst a herd of elephants, the eyes of Merlin scanned the crowd for the girl he was after. A few more minutes passed until he finally spotted her, and she was walking quietly by herself, unlike the joyous IG story where she was getting down with a friend. Merlin could tell she was heading toward the nearby Ride On bus stop. He straightened his snapback hat and threw his hood up to conceal his identity as best as he could before he stepped out of the woods to stalk her from a safe distance.

She chose to sit at the bench, which suited Merlin's goals perfectly as he was able to freely stand around the bus stop out of her view. Her phone ringtone went off, and Merlin listened in on her side of the conversation.

"What's up?" she asked the caller in Spanish. "I'll be around the way in about thirty. Just got out of class." The sigh and tone hinted to Merlin that she was not eager to be talking with this person, let alone meet with them. "I mean to keep it real, I got a lot of school work to do, so I don't know how late I can chill." Merlin slightly turned his head from facing away so he could see some of Reina's reaction. She grew flustered.

"No, I haven't talked to anybody about it," she said. "Please don't bring that shit up with me again. Especially over the phone." The 55 Bus started to appear down the street. It approached its stop as Reina started to get off the bench.

"Okay, my bus is here, I gotta get off. Bye!" She clicked the red button at the bottom of her phone and scanned her Smart Trip app at the front of the bus. Merlin let the three other riders waiting at the bus stop go ahead in front of him to avoid suspicion as he hopped on the public transit.

He kept his head tucked as he walked toward the back of

the bus, but Reina was already looking straight out the window, so she didn't take any notice of Merlin. He headed to the back corner of the bus, but he selected a seat that faced the opposite windows so it was less likely for Reina to just turn around and see him or possibly spot the vigilante detective in the bus' convex mirror. In fifteen minutes, she finally pressed the stop button for Clopper Road and Cinnamon Drive.

Montgomery County was one of the wealthiest counties in the country. Although Germantown wasn't quite the posh pastures of Potomac or Bethesda, it still had a median household income near six figures, well above the average middle-class American salary. However, there were still pockets of poverty spread throughout the county, made possible by a variety of factors ranging from section eight housing to decades of economic disenfranchisement. Despite its name, Cinnamon Woods was not the sweet part of MoCo, according to local residents. While in the land of prosperity that is the DC suburbs, it may be considered a ghetto, such a classification was laughable to Merlin, who came from a third-world country where millions had to leave their homes just to fetch clean water. He hadn't been to this part of the county much, so while following Reina from a far distance, he took time to appreciate all the parkland. Maybe there was still time to own a house someplace out here, he thought to himself. He all of a sudden wondered if he was risking the rest of his life in an attempt to avenge another life that was already gone.

Before he could dwell on his decision for too long, a Honda Civic with spoilers and flame decals roared up right next to Reina like a dragon with dark scales descending onto a vulnerable princess. He heard some tense exchanges between her and the occupants of the car in Spanish. He could tell they were of the male gender, and she was refusing to go along with their demands. Within a moment, a shirtless, tatted-up occupant of the backseat jumped out and grabbed Reina by the arm. She resisted pretty well. The skinny gangster clearly only relied on weapons without any kind of weight lifting or adding protein to his system. Two more got out of the other passenger seats and helped their fellow man finally overpower her and get her swallowed into the pit of their mechanical beast. Merlin watched the Civic start to bust a U-Turn. He quickly spun 180 degrees to walk in the opposite direction, always careful to keep his presence minimal. The black dragon sped down the road parallel to Merlin's sidewalk, and his eagle eyes were able to snap a picture in his head of the license plate.

Before he introduced Merlin to the Bazaar, Carlos showed him a site to look up addresses by license plates so he didn't have to chase shoplifters. Merlin plugged in the seven digits into the search bar. Within seconds, he pasted the listed address into Google Maps on his phone.

The map showed it was a forty-five-minute walk. They were close enough that he could get there, realized Merlin, but he knew he was greatly outnumbered despite his superior strength and combat skill. He was expecting things to get messy on this path, just not quite on the first day of his investigation. Nonetheless, he gripped the utility knife in his pocket, the only tool he owned that could practically be used as a weapon.

Merlin slowed down as he got closer to his destination, making sure he didn't just stumble upon a potential ambush. The listed house was the plainest structure on the block, with grass that probably hadn't been cut for years and all the blinds down to block any nosy onlookers. Parked right in front was the four-wheeled black dragon. Merlin realized he had to make one of two choices now. Either figure out a way into the house or cancel the whole endeavor, go home, and call Palacios to tell him everything he had witnessed.

He studied the windows from a safe distance, and he realized nobody was watching the outside. He marched through the overgrown field of a front yard and snuck his way into the back. There was no guard dog, cameras, or much external security at all for whatever property this was for the gang, so Merlin figured this probably wasn't a trap house unless MS-13 was really feeling the recession like ordinary civilians were.

Merlin arrived at a patio that connected to the basement of the house. He stood at the back door. He gently twisted the knob and noticed it was locked, something Merlin was more than prepared for. He slightly shook the door to also realize there was no deadbolt. Like clockwork, he whipped out the utility knife and stuck the blade between the crack of the door and the doorframe. He dug in with his knife to find the latch. Once he felt metal touching metal, he started to leverage his tool and push the latch back into the door.

Suddenly, the door swung open. Knowing this could have startled somebody, Merlin leapt to the side of the entrance, hidden with the blade in his hands. He didn't hear any movement on the other side, but he still slowly peered over the door frame to scan the immediate area beyond it.

His knife steadied in his grip like he was back in his guerrilla days, making his way through the rainforest with a machete. Merlin entered the basement interior. A stench penetrated his nostrils, and he had to stop himself from choking on its odor. It was a smell of old, stale urine and excrement. He tactically moved through the hallway. It was decorated in crude demonic drawings depicting the skeletal deity Santa Muerte, and a few feet from the sketch was a light switch. He checked around the corner, but there was nobody on the side of the perpendicular hallway. Still, it was getting hard to see, with only some evening light shining through a small cinder block window in the top corner at the end of the hall. Merlin flicked the switch, yet nothing came on. More graffiti lined the halls. 'M' was drawn extravagantly with devil horns coming out the sides and the number 504, the area

code for Honduras, written next to LOCOS along the walls as
Merlin saw some stairs at the end of the hallway. He got close to
one door. However, once he cracked it open, he realized it was a
dilapidated bathroom where most of the smell was coming from.
He still checked it and silenced his gag reflex once he saw the pile
of fecal matter in the rusty bathtub. Realizing the floor was clear,
he got to the bottom of the wooden stairwell and carefully went
up step by step.

Merlin was familiar with what the house was. It was
a 'destroyer' house. An abandoned residence flipped into an
MS-13 sanctuary where they could stash guns, throw parties,
pimp prostitutes out to johns, or whatever the gang preferred
until it got discovered by authorities. More common in LA, a
few existed in Maryland, especially around Langley Park, and
one was stumbled upon by a Metro transit employee in Silver
Spring in 2017, where he was held at gunpoint until he managed
to escape unharmed. The place proved the gang had expanded
well into the West side of Montgomery County, returning to their
dominance in the area from back in the mid-2000s. Unlike most
destroyer houses, though, this one was evidently legally leased
under the name of the person who owned the black Honda.

Merlin reached the first floor of the house. The odor of
human waste had decreased, but now he started to see far more
litter scattered across the floor. Beer bottles, porn magazines, used
lighters, discarded fast food bags, and other trash items lined the
short hallway around Merlin as he exited the stairway entrance.
The artwork on the walls was even more detailed now, with
color added onto the hoods of the depicted skeletons to make
them look like the Grim Reaper and pointed Satan tails wrapped
around the figures.

Out of the corner of Merlin's eye, he saw movement and
ducked behind a wall corner he just stepped from. He peeked
around and watched the skinny teenager from the backseat of

the Civic step into the hall from a room as he lit a joint in his mouth. Merlin closed up his utility knife and crouched low to sneak behind the 'MS' and skull tattoos across the young man's amber-colored body. The kid took a puff, brought the rollup down to his waist, and immediately, Merlin snatched him into a suffocating headlock. As evidenced by his inability to subdue Reina earlier, the Salvatrucha was no match for the veteran who went toe-to-toe in armed and even unarmed combat with US-trained paramilitary forces. Within a single minute, the gangster in Merlin's grasp went from struggling and squirming to a limp sack of flesh. He laid him down on the floor of the hallway, below a sketch of demonic-looking hands flashing the same horn gesture one of them had done toward Merlin at his friend Edgar's bar. Staring at his comatose face, Merlin realized that it was indeed one of the teenagers who were in the gang-designated corner of El Tigre Grill.

Merlin got his knife back in his grasp and continued his descent into the dungeon. Around the next corner, he saw an open area that would likely act as a living room if the place was properly furnished. Instead, a miniature skeleton outfitted in a light blue skirt and purple hat hung from a ceiling fan. Below it was a pair of dirty mattresses surrounded by more trash like it was an altar for a Satanic sacrifice. Laid out on one of the beds with bruises along her legs, arms, and a swollen face was Reina. Merlin quickly strafed over to her and saw that her hands and feet were bound with rope. Her eyes were open but twitched like an injured butterfly. Her lips were so puffy from repeated blows to her face that she could only breathe in through her nostrils. She was not too close to death but left like that for another few hours, and she could submit to her injuries. He kneeled down and started to cut the rope. He could tell from some of the blood on her upper inner leg below her jean skirt that she was the victim of a vicious gang rape. Being gentle with her body but fast, he quickly got her limbs free. He softly grabbed her back and leaned over to talk to her.

"Are there any more in the house right now?" he asked in a low, empathetic voice. She shook her head from side to side in a 'no' response.

"They m-m-m." She was having issues with speaking from all the damage she had taken. "They might be back soon."

"Are you able to stand up?"

"Maybe," she managed to say with all the energy she had left. He used his right arm to scoop both her legs up, and he lifted her from the layer of foam she had been a sex slave from for the past hour. One leg at a time, he steadily got her feet to touch the floor. While still leaning on him, she was able to stand. Through her right eye, which was almost sealed shut from the repeated blows, she saw one of her rapists incapacitated in the hallway. She whispered into Merlin's ear.

"They killed Carlos," she said as she broke down into tears. Merlin consoled her as he attempted to help her stand on her own.

"I know."

"I'm so sorry."

"It's okay. You're safe now." He knew they had to get moving fast, but he also realized this may be his only chance to get a word with her. "Do you know why they killed him?" Fighting the pain throughout her body, Reina lifted her arm up to point to a corner of the underworld shrine that made the center of the destroyer house. Merlin looked in that direction and spotted Carlos' laptop propped up in the corner. Its screen was up, but it was turned off, and it sat on the floor.

"Okay. Let's get you out of here." Merlin peeked through the blinds and saw that there was nobody outside. He straddled Reina, ripped open the front door, and escorted her to the Honda Civic.

"Hang tight." With his welted leather work boots, he kicked the outside edge of the driver-side window. The tethered glass shattered all at once from the powerful force delivered to the right spot. He reached in to unlock the door, and with his left arm, he wiped off all the broken shards from the seat. He sat her down upright before immediately going to work with his utility knife on hot wiring the vehicle. Within seconds, the engine revved up.

"Do you know where the closest hospital is?" She took a second but eventually nodded affirmatively. "Are you able to drive?" She gave the same response. They hugged each other before he shut the door.

"God bless you," she projected in between tears rolling down her face. He folded his hands and did a prayer gesture to let her know her gratitude had been received. The car took off down the street. Merlin headed back inside the destroyer home.

He re-entered and immediately went straight to the laptop. He hit the power button, and thankfully, it still had half its battery left. It went right past the startup screen and straight to what was last loaded up. It was the Bazaar.tor website, but instead of the full list, it had one single profile pulled up. Merlin recognized it as Desmond Ellis, the man who was on TV when Crystal took over as manager at Las Americas Mercado. He suddenly heard something hit the floor and turned to see the victim of his sleeper hold coming back to life. He pounced on him like a jaguar on a stubborn deer in the jungle and threw him up against the wall.

"How many people are coming back?" demanded Merlin.

"Fuck you, pendejo." Wham! Merlin shoved his blade into the MS-13 recruit's shoulder. He screamed in agony as Merlin twisted until he cooperated.

"How many?!"

"Two, man! Two!"

"You swear on your mother?"

"Yes!" He continued to grimace through the pain of the knife being lodged into his upper body.

"Tell me why you bastards killed Carlos."

"Who's Carlos?"

"Carlos Mateo, asshole." There was a pause. Soon, an evil hyena-esque laugh came out of the gangster. "What the hell is so funny?"

"He died like a bitch." Merlin responded to the insult by digging the knife deeper, eliciting more sounds of agony from the kid he was interrogating. Merlin saw a door cracked open next to their position, the same room his captive had originally come out of.

"What's in that room?" asked Merlin.

"It's where we dump all the whores after we destroy their clits, and they suck us dry," chuckled the gangster recruit. "And then the beast gets to ravage their souls."

"You're all sick.".

"Go on in and check," the boy said with the same smirk on his face, not paying any more attention to the pain of the knife. "I'm sure your mother's in there." Merlin delivered his signature powerful left hook to the man's jawline, harkening back to his amateur boxing days that Edgar hinted at in the restaurant. The impact knocked him back unconscious, and Merlin tossed the boy to the ground. He then entered the dimly lit room. More dark underworld graffiti across the walls, but he focused on some black duffel bags sitting beneath the window sill.

They were pretty heavy, and from the click and clank sounds, as Merlin grabbed one of them, he could tell there were some metal objects inside them. He pulled down a zipper, and when he opened it up, it was revealed to be an arsenal of over a dozen handguns. Most were automatics, but there were a couple of revolvers. He unzipped the other bag and found more pistols but also one pump action shotgun. There was a third, last bag that, when he unzipped it, he uncovered a few more handguns, but it was full of far more 9MM ammunition, along with some machetes and knives. He went back to the first bag and picked up a Glock 17. He released the magazine and counted the number of bullets it held.

Merlin hadn't held a gun in his hand in over thirty years. During the conflict, the pistol he was handed was the Soviet Tokarev. Certainly, a different generation of weaponry, but the mechanics of loading a magazine and preparing to fire still rang true. The difference was that the Tokarev was used in a mission to liberate his people from tyrants who had no issues with shooting down humanitarian priests during mass and following up with sniping over forty mourners at the funeral. But at least those murderers were convinced their side would bring order to El Salvador. Now, he found himself in the country whose government not only sponsored those same tyrants several years ago but also served as the birthplace of the gang he was now waging a vengeful asymmetrical warfare against. A gang that, unlike those death squads entrenched in their fascist ideology, didn't care about the future of their homeland but actually worshipped deities of death and chaos.

He heard fidgeting with the front door. He reached around the corner and grabbed the young man he had repeatedly subdued. He retreated back into the room as the other two gangsters from earlier burst into the central room of the house.

"Where the fuck is my car?!" yelled one of them, presumably the driver. Merlin had a tight grip on his hostage with one arm and the Glock in his other hand. His back was against the wall.

"And where the hell did the bitch go?" the driver demanded.

"Maybe he bounced with her," suggested the other one, whose voice was not as wound up as the driver.

"I'm the only one with the key!" Merlin listened to him

march around and kick some of the trash across the room. "Fuck!"

"I mean, he could've hot-wired it." Merlin heard the speaker flick a lighter to spark a joint. He also realized his captive was fully awake at the moment. "I been warned you about trusting new blood, homie."

"Wait." Something else had caught the attention of the driver. "Why the hell is the computer on?"

"He's in the storage room!" screamed the man in Merlin's grasp. In a single motion, Merlin took the utility knife shoved into the shoulder and swiped it across the neck. The jugular got sliced, and the cut-open carotid artery was exposed, spraying blood onto Merlin as he pushed the now-deceased body off of him. He ducked down and grabbed heavy duffel bags to protect his body as the driver fired off rounds from his own gun into the walls of the room Merlin was in. Merlin kept his low position as bullets flew through the wall, and a few hit the bag, clinking on the metal of the weapons inside. He counted every shot. Once it got to sixteen, Merlin spun around the corner of the room's entrance. The driver fired off his last bullet right into Merlin's makeshift shield. The former revolutionary fighter returned fire, and the driver took two to the chest and one to the head, sending him to the ground. The other one had a knife in his hand, with smoke rising from the joint he dropped next to him. The kid looked at the dropped automatic pistol.

"Stay where you are!" demanded Merlin. The youngster made a move for the firearm, and Merlin rewarded his decision with two shots to the lower limbs. He fell over in agony, dropping the knife, and even winced again when his inked-up shirtless back touched the lit spliff.

"Please, please!" the man, who couldn't be over 22 years old, begged as he threw his hands up from the ground. "That's where all the guns are, I promise." Merlin dropped his shield and approached the wounded MS foot soldier.

"Get up."

"I-I-I can't."

"Try." The kid used his hands to try to stand himself up. He crawled over to the nearest wall and was able to elevate himself. Merlin speared him with his palm and put him at gunpoint.

"Why is my friend's laptop in this house?" The man with teardrops tatted on his upper cheeks now had real tears forming in his pupils. His eyes shifted in the direction of the laptop turned on with the Desmond Ellis profile brought up.

"Look, okay," he started off. To Merlin, he seemed already to be far more flexible on giving info than the first one he killed. "Diablita sent orders from Honduras that he wanted to place a bid on Ellis, and he wanted us to carry it out." Diablita meant 'little devil' in Spanish, and Merlin figured that he was one of the higher-ranking leaders of MS who had oversight on the East Coast operations.

"Why didn't he just place it himself?"

"He didn't know how. He had just heard about the Bazaar. None of us knew how to access it. So this bitch Yulan was messing around with said she knew somebody who knew all about that internet computer shit."

"Who's Yulan?" The dude at gunpoint shifted his head toward the floor next to their position. Merlin realized he was referring to the driver with three bullets in his corpse now. "Oh."

"So she got him to go on a date, and we met them at the bar. Told him we'd pay him and smoke him up if he showed us how to place a bid. He didn't want to smoke, but he still told us everything. Smart guy he was, not going to front."

"And then what happened?" demanded Merlin. The kid paused before he answered, like he was a bit reluctant to get to the next part of the story.

"Next thing I know, Yulan gave us the green light." Merlin and him made eye contact. Merlin knew what green light meant. "Look, I didn't want to do it, alright? But it would've been my body next to his in those woods if I didn't, you understand, O-G?" Now, Merlin was the one who paused for a moment, his gun still pointed forward.

"What did Reina do while you all killed him?"

"Who? The bitch?" Merlin shook his head, realizing this dude didn't even know her name.

"Yes, the girl."

"She waited in the car during the whole thing."

"Did she know you all were going to kill him?"

"I have no idea. Yulan was the one who talked to her."

"The three of you raped her."

"No! I didn't. That was only those two, I swear. I don't do that shit, bro. I just be hitting the gas and chilling. I been trying to get out this lifestyle for real." Several things ran through Merlin's mind. Nobody deserved sexual abuse and torture, according to any sane person, but he wondered if he had made a mistake in freeing Reina. He looked at the tatted teardrops and questioned if this man was telling the truth or just trying to not experience the same fate as his two comrades.

"What's your name?" asked Merlin.

"Luis."

"Luis, I want you to show me what Carlos taught you." Merlin spun Luis around and forced him toward the laptop. Luis slowly got on his knees. He clearly was uncomfortable with this position, but he was staying cooperative. Luis started to click around at the Bazaar tabs.

"Do you know what Bitcoin is?" Luis asked.

"Yes."

"He said that's what you need to make a bid. This is how you do it." Merlin studied Luis as he clicked a tab beneath the profile shot of Representative Ellis. It took them to an input-based menu that allowed the user to upload their cryptocurrency and select a date on a calendar. Merlin watched every movement.

"Who's money are you using?" Luis froze. His seemingly open-book personality was now hitting its epilogue. "Tell me," Merlin demanded as he shoved the pistol into the back of Luis' head. "Or you join your friends in hell."

Luis breathed in through his nostrils and exhaled.

"MS sponsors."

"How many other chapters in this area know about this hit?" Another pause on Luis' end.

"Look, bro—" Blood splattered after a gunshot across the smiling portrait of Desmond Ellis beneath the altar of Saint Death suspended from the ceiling. Merlin stepped over to the front windows and bent some blinds to peep at what was in the front yard.

A sedan far less extravagant than the black Honda Civic earlier was parked parallel to the mailbox. Merlin realized that Yulan wasn't the only driver in the house. He walked back over to near the laptop and ran through Luis' pockets. Wallet, rolling papers, some ganja, various credit cards from several different names, and then the last item he pulled out was Toyota car keys. He headed back into the arsenal room and started the process of loading all these weapons, ammunition, and Carlos' laptop into his newly confiscated vehicle.

CHAPTER 15

"Hello? Who is this? Why do you keep calling my phone?" The confused voice of a senior woman didn't get a response for several seconds.

"It's me, Mom," Aaron finally managed to work up the courage to say. He sat on a bench outside of Rock Tavern, a dive bar on the outskirts of Cumberland.

"Aaron?" Her tone changed. Aaron hadn't heard empathy in his mother's voice in years since the passing of his father. It appeared now.

"Yes, Mom." His tone had changed since their last conversation as well. The confidence in purchasing a new house didn't seem to be present in his demeanor, resisting long, optimistic conversations. "Did you get the money I sent?"

"Son. I don't care where you are or what you did. Just come home." Silence took over the conversation for a few moments.

"I love you, okay? I'll be back before the end of the year. I promise, just hold on." It took him a minute, but some of the forward-thinking of his character returned back to his voice.

"Are you safe?"

"Yes, I promise."

"Your friend was on the news again."

"Who? Danny?"

"The Chinese one."

"He's Vietnamese, Mom."

"They said he said he stabbed a man death in the prison."

"Wait, what?"

"Newsman said it was a prison gang type thing. I warned you about that boy..." As Rita rambled on, Aaron just remembered that last look on Danny's face at the visitation. He realized that his friend may have had a cooler head if they ended on a better note. Aaron attempted to rationalize and started to think maybe it was inevitable, given that those types of killings are usually organized from the top of the different prison factions. Or at least that was the conclusion that was going to let him sleep at night. "...And he always wanted to be about the streets or whatever. Guess he's finally is, but it won't matter 'cause he's never going to out onto any street as a free man again."

"Mom." There was some defiant anger in Aaron's voice. "Don't say that." She paused.

"I don't want that for your future, my son." Even with his attitude, her new empathetic attitude continued.

"That's not going to happen, Mom."

"I know it won't, my beautiful boy." Aaron sighed.

"I gotta go."

"Okay. Love ya."

"Love you too."

―――――

Click. In the living room of her apartment, Rita looked up from her phone to Agent Towers. He was flanked by five other officers of law enforcement. Two from his unit, two FBI agents, and one Prince George's County PD officer by the doorway.

"Why does he have the number blocked?"

"My son is terrified," insisted Rita. She was also referencing her own feelings being in the presence of that much legal authority. A few members of the FBI's Evidence Response Team exited Aaron's room. The first two had plastic assault rifles in their grasps. One followed behind, holding the entire 3D printer in his hands.

"Ma'am, help me out here," Towers said as he sighed at her denial at the deep involvement of her only child. "I have a source telling me your son was there in Veterans Plaza last October. We get here, and we find illegal plastic firearms, ammunition, body armor, unmarked cash—"

"Aaron was a great kid. Never got into any trouble up until those criminals calling themselves counselors at his school wanted to put him on all those drugs—"

"Ma'am." She exchanged glares from her dining table seat with Towers, who was positioned like his last name in front of her while standing. "Let's stay on topic."

"I don't know what to tell you. Go catch him if you're so sure he's guilty." Towers shook his head and sighed.

"Were we able to track that call?" He asked a man in an FBI jacket near him.

"I doubt it. Our best bet is whatever E-R-T found in his room. There may be some chat logs on there."

"Okay." Towers turned his attention to Rodriguez from his team. "Any word on discussions with Danny Phat or his father?" Rodriguez air-cut his neck with right-hand fingers pointed straight, signaling a negative answer.

"They threw life at him, and he didn't budge. He refuses to talk about Williams," Rodriguez responded. "His pops ended any further contact with him after that recent stabbing he carried out behind bars. Sorry, captain." Towers sighed.

"Think it's time to go to the public with his information?" asked Rodriguez.

"Let's trace the envelopes of money he's been sending, and then we'll go from there," the superior agent said while looking toward Rita, who didn't return any eye contact and remained tight-lipped. "If E-R-T is good to go, let's roll out."

"Roger, sir." The silent Rita stared across the living room at the photos of her former husband and her son that she didn't want to join him. Her face didn't budge as the federal agents filed out.

———

Aaron put his phone away and headed into the bar. It was the local watering hole, but on a regular weekday evening, not many Cumberland residents populated the stools or dingy interior that hadn't been touched with any new remodeling since the tavern's opening in 1973. Rock Tavern survived the final major factory closure in the area with the shutdown of the Kelly Springfield Tire Company's plant in 1987, but the bar ended up being a miniature model of the city itself. Hanging with whatever it had left onto a declining population trying to numb the pain of harsh economic realities with substances, whether through drinking or opioids.

Doug sat in the back corner of the bar beneath the framed black and white photos of Cumberland in its heyday of the first half of the 20th century before World War II. Smiling proud factory workers, railroad construction, and other archaeological evidence of a grander time period for urban Appalachia sat above Doug, Bobby, and a third man around their age at a tall table. Doug raised his arm up toward Aaron, beckoning him to join them for drinks. Aaron walked past the few locals at the bar and a young obese couple at a booth. He was an unfamiliar face to the middle-aged lady bartending, but Aaron exchanged a friendly nod to her, which eased the tap pourer of over twenty years, no longer assuming Aaron was an out-of-town dealer or anyone looking to cash in on the addiction epidemic.

"Can I get a glass of half Sprite, half water, please?" requested Aaron to the bartender, never one to drink alcohol.

"We got Sprite Zero. You don't just want that?" Aaron shook his head, refusing the alternative proposed by his server. She shrugged her shoulders and poured up his carbonated beverage. He took it, left a $5 bill on the counter, and continued to his destination at the other side of the bar.

Doug and Bobby were wearing their typical Walmart-bought outfits. Doug was head-to-toe in solid-colored Dickies work pants and hoodie. Bobby had similar attire but in a hunting camo color scheme. The third man at the table stared right back at Aaron like he was profiling him. He had a slim frame, blue eyes with a green tint and dirty blonde hair sticking out from beneath a white hat that had a hand gripping an axe on a black and white shield as its center logo. Aaron recognized it as the official symbol for the defunct far-right college student group, the Youth for Western Civilization. It dissolved in 2012, so despite the man's appearance, as he could be around Doug and Bobby's age, he was probably in his mid to late 30s.

"Scottie, this is Aaron," introduced Doug. "The original Bazaar trigger man. We wouldn't be here having this conversation if it wasn't for the likes of him." Scottie slightly nodded. There was approval in his body language, but there was still a cloud of skepticism between the two. Scottie stuck out his hand to shake Aaron's.

"Scott Wilkins. Maryland Chapter president of Freedom Legion." Scott had a strong grip.

"Aaron Williams. Uh, that's it."

"He's being humble as usual," laughed Doug. "He's our MVP."

"That means most valuable player," said Bobby to Scottie. "Given that I know you don't watch any professional sports 'cause that means too many minorities on the screen."

"Shut up, Bobby," Scottie said, hinting to Aaron that he and Bobby had a history.

"Ignore that," Doug said to Aaron as the group laughed it off. "Bobby's just being stupid. Scottie ain't racist."

"Realist, not a racist. There's a difference." Scottie looked toward Aaron again with suspicion, but that time, Aaron didn't return the energy. He looked away to stay in his own world and just sip his drink.

"Got nothing to do with me," said Aaron, refusing to make any more eye contact with the man he was most unfamiliar with at the table. An awkward moment for a few beats until Doug spoke up.

"Scottie brought up Desmond Ellis," said Doug. Bobby eagerly nodded up and down. "What you think?"

"The date that's the most popular right now apparently is coming up a little soon," Aaron said after he took another gulp of his drink. "We haven't really been training the past few weeks, and I'm assuming we're going to have some new folks with us."

"My people are always ready," Scott responded with the utmost confidence. "We're like the original minutemen if the British tried to invade again."

"Here he goes," a buzzed Bobby chuckled.

"I don't doubt that the Legion hits the gun range regularly—"

"Gun range?" Scott was now a bit offended by Aaron's presumed assumptions now. "Try close-quarter battle scenarios, squad movement tactics, improvised explosives, long-range capabilities, you name it, we have it on our checklist. Not even the local National Guard regiment would stand a chance against my chapter."

"I wasn't trying to offend you if you thought that was my intention," Aaron said.

"None taken."

"But you have to realize that all that training you just named was done without us," continued Aaron. "Our teams combined is a whole new unit, and therefore, we need to start from scratch to analyze all possible situations that can occur on the date of the mission. Personally, I'm thinking we should be looking at a late winter date for our next outing."

"That's kind of a long time," commented Bobby.

"With your spending habits, sure," said Doug to the annoyance of his long-time bald friend. "But what Aaron is saying makes sense. We can't rush something with so many implications if things go wrong."

"I agree," said Scott, still keeping his focus on Aaron. "But most of the ones on my side who'll be taking up arms echo Bobby's sentiments. They want to make a move soon. We wait too long, and who knows? The market might not even be as popular, and it won't be the goldmine it is now." Aaron glanced in Doug's direction during Scott's talking and noticed a slight facial change, like he was annoyed with being pushed into another operation sooner than he anticipated. Aaron then looked in the direction of Scott but still avoided having their vision pointed directly at each other.

"This isn't something that should be rushed into," Aaron said.

"Right," Doug added to boost Aaron's point. Scott sighed and finally took his attention off Aaron. He sipped his IPA.

"What type of firepower do you all have?" asked Scott after his gulp. Doug and Aaron took a second, not sure if they wanted to reveal that type of information at the moment.

"I always carry two pistols with me," Bobby said after another big gulp of his own beer, the alcohol seemingly fueling his bravado. "Got a Glock and a magnum."

"Oh, nice."

"Yeah, bro, that kickback—" Doug gave Bobby a light shove on the shoulder. It almost knocked his beer over.

"Yo Doug, what the hell, bro—"

"We're in the middle of switching things up," Doug said with his attention on Scott. "You know, we never go out twice with the same gear."

"Well, in that case," said Scott. His tone switched to almost like a salesman. "I need to get you in contact with our supplier. Full auto, no serials, made in this country. I'm not just talking about some plastic AR 15 bullshit." That last line raised an eyebrow on Aaron. Did this patriot just lie, and he actually did know what they used in the Frost hit? If so, did he just throw shade in Aaron's direction? He had a lot of questions in his head, but he'd just download information to answer himself. Aaron made sure to never let his assumptions turn into emotional reactions. "I'm talking AKs, Galils, SCARs, any rifle you've seen in Call of Duty, you can get. And for explosives —"

"Let's discuss these aspects another time," said Doug.

"And at a different location." Scott turned his attention back to Aaron, the source of the last sentence. He was feeling a little challenged now, even though that wasn't Aaron's intention.

"Where you from, Aaron? Baltimore?" asked Scott. That comment noticeably pissed off Doug, but Aaron kept a cool head.

"No. P-G."

"Oh, okay," responded Scott. Aaron was sure the majority-Black Prince George's County was a place Scottie avoided while growing up. "I only went out there for like a Redskins game when I was little. That's about it."

"You from the D-M-V?" asked Aaron, pretending the hostility was nonexistent.

"I grew up in Poolesville." Of any top 10 most ethnically diverse cities listed in the USA, the blogs almost always included multiple towns in Montgomery County, Maryland. None of those would be Poolesville. Scott checked his phone for a brief moment. He then chugged the rest of his beer and started to rise up. "I gotta start heading back." Doug had informed Aaron that Scott had property in Rising Sun out in Cecil County. It was about a three-hour drive from Rock Tavern.

"We'll be in touch," said Doug. Aaron was unsure if that was actually going to be the case. Each of them shook hands with Scott on good terms until he headed for the door. Once he made it past the bar, Bobby turned straight to Doug.

"Bro, what type shit you on?"

"Bobby, you can't be serious about trusting that dude."

"What you mean?"

"Talking about guns, his so-called 'supplier,' he's trigger happy, asking us all these questions. What does that sound like?"

"An informant," said Aaron.

"Boom," Doug said. Bobby looked at the two of them for a moment.

"Whoa, whoa. Okay." He decided to ignore Aaron and just focus on Doug for a moment. "Dude, we know Scottie."

"Do we?"

"We've known Scottie for five years. When has he ever got popped for anything? To be a snitch, you gotta get turned into one. Come on now."

"Not necessarily," remarked Aaron. Bobby sighed and just stared at his glass of beer. "What type of work does Scottie do?"

"I think he's an accountant," said Bobby as he finished his drink.

"So why is a C-P-A getting involved with extremist politics when his career is constantly on the line."

"Do you know where he works?" rhetorically asked Doug to Aaron. Cecil County made Poolesville look like D.C. when it came to demographics, and it was one of the red counties in a blue state. In other words, Aaron knew Doug doubted any of Scottie's clientele would report him to the Southern Poverty Law Center.

"Doesn't matter. It's still a risk. Working a white collar job and dabbling in an armed second American revolution is something to be skeptical about."

"You're right on the money," Doug said as he finally took a sip of his own drink. "You've been right all night."

"But that being said, I think we should still consider his partnership if he checks out."

"Welp, until you said that."

"Come on, Doug," said Bobby as he raised his empty glass

up to the bartender to signal for another one. "That's two against one. Now you're against democracy."

"Look at Bobby here all of a sudden getting ideological and shit," said Doug.

"Stop acting like I don't read."

"You read the comment section of YouTube gun porn and heating instructions for Hot Pockets," Doug responded. "That's about it." Aaron cracked up. Doug smiled, and Bobby hissed his teeth.

"But I don't know," said Doug. "I was all for Scottie until today. I just know to trust my gut. That's all I can say."

"Despite what Bobby said," remarked Aaron. "We can't move forward with him until you're fully on board. So listen to your gut, but also look at our manpower. Ethan might not even be willing to go again." Ethan had been M-I-A for a couple of months due to a new girlfriend, followed by a pregnancy. He was considering a move to central Pennsylvania to chart a new path in life that didn't involve risking incarceration. Aaron figured life behind bars with his son and mother on their own on the outside didn't appeal to him, no matter how many millions another assassination would bring. "Also, keep in mind this might be our last assignment for a while. Because if, no, when we are successful, there's going to be a total crackdown even more severe than the one now."

"Oh yeah," said Bobby as a server handed him a new beer. "They caught that African girl round your parts, right? That ain't gonna come back to us, right?" Bobby directed the question to Aaron.

"Bobby," warned Doug.

"What? A second ago, you were saying Scottie could be a rat, we gotta be careful, this and that. Your man over here might be tied to some bitch who actually got pinched—"

"You're drunk, bro," said Aaron. "Relax."

"Excuse me?" The temperature had risen.

"People talk a lot when they're not sober," Aaron calmly but sternly stated. "Let's change topics."

"No, I like this one," an increasingly drunk Bobby spit out. "Back to this Wakandan chick. You know her, Aaron?"

"Alright, I think it's time to—"

"Hey!" Bobby yelled when he interrupted Doug's peace attempts, and immediately, all the patrons in the bar turned toward the direction of the outburst's source. "I asked a question, and I want a God damn answer!"

"Bobby. Chill the fuck out." Doug had to put his alpha foot forward, and he was not going to back down. "You're making it hot right now." Bobby simmered for a second and breathed out. He went for a sip of his beer, but Doug snatched it away. "Nah, I think you've had enough. Let's bounce."

"Bro, that's my drink—"

"I think you need a blunt, not a beer." Bobby shook his head and got up with the rest of them.

"Fine, let's go," Bobby said. Aaron threw a twenty dollar bill on the table, and the three headed to the front doors of Rock Tavern. The whole bar watched them as they left.

Outside, Aaron took the lead as they headed toward Doug's pickup.

"Yo, Aaron," said Bobby. "I didn't mean to start anything by all that." Aaron sighed, and he started to turn around.

"It's cool—" Bobby surprised him with a right cross straight to the face that threw Aaron's equilibrium totally off, and he stumbled across the parking lot.

"Bobby!" screamed Doug as he rushed toward his raging alcohol-induced psychotic friend. Bobby was too fast for Doug as he got a running start to spear Aaron in an attempt to throw him to the ground.

His lip was already fat from the initial contact, but Aaron

maintained his balance. He did a sprawl right in time to offset Bobby trying to get him in a lock. Aaron quickly hooked his left arm around Bobby's neck and started to punch the pale face of his fellow hitman. Aaron's skinny frame didn't stop him from delivering powerful blows that Bobby had difficulty in defending against. In desperation, Bobby went to eye gouge Aaron as he tried to push him toward the pickup truck. In a swinging motion, Aaron quickly delivered a whipping elbow straight into Bobby's jawline that sent him to the gravel.

"Fuck!" yelled Doug as he looked at the damage to Bobby's face. Bobby Z started to have trouble breathing as he ventilated, now laying on the parking light like road kill. "His jaw is broken."

"Let's get him to the E-R," said Aaron as he fixed his own face.

"Urgent Care," corrected Doug. They weren't on any wanted posters, but the small private practices were always less conspicuous than the general hospital's police stayed coming in and out of at all times of the day.

"Fair enough." Aaron and Doug crouched down to help Bobby into the truck.

CHAPTER 16

U.S. Representative Ellis lived inside a luxury townhome in Laurel, Maryland, an area which he represented in his position. At 10:30 PM, ninety minutes prior to the day of his predicted assassination attempt, Raptor's Executive Protection Team was at his front door to escort him to the ALAMUT office building, where he would stay under their close supervision.

The door opened. Flanked by his whole family, he was dressed in a suit and tie, gripping a rolling suitcase like he was about to travel to a different country instead of a county. While holding their baby daughter, she leaned in for another hug, almost teary-eyed from what could happen to her husband. Their five-year-old son, Jarvis, sensed the mood at the moment and wrapped his arms around one of the tall legs of his 6'3" father.

"They met in law school," Terry whispered to Lyle. There wasn't an answer for a few seconds. "They were one of the few Black people in their civil procedure class at Catholic."

"Okay," Lyle said while barely cracking a shrug. He could sense Terry rolling his eyes at him.

Desmond and Lisa kissed again before Congressman Ellis started his descent down the brick stairs.

"Don't forget to FaceTime me at lunch," she said to her husband.

"It's on my calendar, sweetie," Desmond announced back. Lyle rolled his eyes. What was in front of him was a life he never pictured for himself. Neither the monogamy nor the children, although the six-figure salary Ellis made would be nice. None of Lyle's Tinder matches or nightclub pickups were able to convince him to settle down. Eventually, the appeal of the muscles and

Jamaican swag would fade, although the good sex would cause them to relapse every so often with the 3 AM 'wyd' text.

On the other hand, he noticed Terry looking on with total admiration, even cracking a fanboy-esque smile when the Congressman nodded in his direction. Lyle knew Terry had a fiance, but it seemed her maternity clock was having an effect on Terry. Lyle also wondered if age wasn't even a factor, and instead, the shootout on Nigerian Independence Day scared one of them from commitment to supporting bringing in another life into this world.

There was no third car on this mission as Desmond filed into the back of the 4Runner. After making sure the perimeter was clear, the team packed into the vehicles. Just like last time, Nick sat next to the VIP. However, on this trip, he wouldn't have to do any aerial surveillance.

Desmond Ellis was quiet most of the ride to North Bethesda. But then his voice jolted Lyle up from passing out when they were five minutes away.

"Shoot. I forgot to ask if there was a place for me to sleep in there," Desmond announced as he palmed the front of his face. Lyle noticed Nick looking up toward the back of he and Terry's heads, waiting for someone to say something.

"Uh," the intel expert said. "Terry, you know if there will be anything available?"

"I'm sure we can pull out a cot or something," Terry said while behind the wheel. I'll radio Karen to contact that guy Vash or whatever."

"A cot?" asked a disappointed Ellis. "Y'all don't have a like an air mattress in a closet or something?"

"Sir, this is a facility outfitted for your protection," Lyle said. "Not a vacation." Terry turned his attention from driving for a brief moment to slightly scorn Lyle from the side, but he didn't care.

"That's not the vibe I was getting on the tour," said Desmond. "Your boss and his people made it seem like I was about to be staying at the Four Seasons."

"If by his people, you mean Vash Ahmadabadi, well," Lyle said. "That's part of his job, from what I understand about him. Ours is to make sure you're safe. And a cot, air mattress, or a sofa in the snack room makes little difference to Yemi as long as you're healthy." Lyle watched Desmond nod his head through the rearview mirror.

"Appreciate your concern, uhm—?"

"Lyle. Agent Lyle Evans."

"Good to meet you, Lyle, and..." Desmond shifted his body toward Terry.

"Terry Blackwell," he said as Desmond saluted him through the rearview mirror.

"And I'm Nick Rice," Nick told him before he even shifted ninety degrees.

"How's Karen doing?" Several seconds of silence passed in the car.

"Karen's on dispatch," Lyle finally said. "so she'll be up with us the whole time."

"Oh, okay," said Representative Ellis. Another few seconds of silence as Lyle saw Desmond look out the window toward the moonlit corporate campuses of Montgomery County's District 1. Lyle did the same. "Tell her I asked how swimming went this week."

"I'm sure you can ask her yourself after you get some rest, sir," Terry said. Why the Congressman was so inquisitive about another woman fifteen minutes after just kissing his wife farewell was a question Lyle was going to avoid for the next twenty-four hours. A Raptor property patrol guard was already stationed at the check-in gate. He knew who occupied the black SUVs, so he raised the barrier arm, and the Executive Protection

Team drove another two kilometers into the campus. They parked in a garage next to the ALAMUT building. There was still an hour until midnight, so while they surrounded Ellis as a precaution, Yemi had let them know an ambush was unlikely to happen during that period. The squad made their way through the front entrance. Two uniformed Raptor guards occupied the front desk. One was veteran property guard Mark Sowell, and the other was Gen Z Trinidadian-American Rana Singh. It was only his second week in a Raptor uniform. Lyle knew the Ellis assignment was a change of pace for the extra guards from patrolling shopping centers throughout Prince George's and Howard County. For a pay bonus, Karen enlisted Lyle to be the one whom Rana shadowed on the drives. Unlike Nick, Lyle took an immediate liking to the kid of the new generation. Like Lyle, Rana had experience as an armed response security guard in the Caribbean. Unlike Lyle, though, Rana told him his family wasn't tied to the business. His father abandoned him before he and his four siblings reached elementary school, leaving his mother to push Rana to pursue higher education. Wanting to move out on his own, he dropped out of the University of the West Indies in St. Augustine and answered a job posting for a security guard at KFC. Singh worked for Trident Security Services for a year before he had saved enough to move to DC, where he immediately found employment at Raptor.

Rana saluted Yemi, a gesture that Lyle was sure Yemi thought was way over the top, but he nodded back nonetheless. The other guard at the desk checked in Desmond, who handed over the valuables in his pockets before he went through the metal detector.

"Not sure what the reasoning behind checking me is, but I guess it's just procedure."

"Correct, sir," the gentleman said as he siphoned through the Congressman's wallet. Lyle noticed the exclusive

Congressional Federal Credit Union credit card. "We knew you wouldn't possess anything to harm yourself, but we want to cover all bases." Once Ellis got his stuff handed back, Lyle dapped up Rana as the squad headed toward the elevators.

"You good?" asked Lyle to his young protege.

"You already know. Another day, another dollar," Rana stated as Lyle started to slowly backpedal to carry on the conversation while following his team. "Wanna see if the Congressman could shout me out on I-G."

"Give me your phone," demanded Jasper, who overheard the comment and barged past Lyle to get close to Rana.

"Oh, I was just joking around—"

"Now!" The raised voice got the attention of everyone in the area, including Ellis himself, who looked back as they got closer to the elevators. Rana looked down in shame as he reached into his pocket to hand over his brand-new Samsung Galaxy to his Raptor superior. Jasper snatched it out of his hand and looked at the home screen. "Did you go Live at any point tonight?"

"No, sir."

"Nobody on any of your social media accounts knows about Ellis' location, correct?"

"Correct, sir."

"Okay. You'll get this back in a few hours. But I'm going to have Rice disable all Wi-Fi or 4G connectivity until Ellis leaves. Understand?"

"Understood." Rana, whom Lyle knew had prided himself most of his life on carrying himself like someone far beyond his years right then, looked no different than the kids who ended up getting disciplined by the sisters in front of Lyle's class in Catholic primary school.

"Let's keep moving," Jasper told the squad as they resumed their march to the elevators.

The sixth floor looked the same from the tour as Desmond

exited the elevator with the executive protection staff at his sides. One Raptor guard stood at the corner of the lobby, and Lyle acknowledged two more stationed around the cubicles as they headed toward his office.

"Where's Vash?" Lyle heard Desmond ask Yemi. Right on cue, the door to Desmond's designated workspace swung open, and standing there was ALAMUT's hyperactive CEO.

"Welcome to your safe haven, Mr. Ellis!" As Desmond got closer, he spotted a blown-up air mattress in the space next to his desk. The politician smiled. Lyle figured he was happy that his demands were actually being met. "I heard you requested a place to rest."

"I am a bit exhausted. It's been quite a day."

"In that case, we'll leave you to get some well-earned sleep. I know you plan to get a lot done tomorrow, and we couldn't be happier to host a public servant of this great nation," announced Vash, advertising his patriotism.

"Thank you, Vash." He turned to the leader of the squad that surrounded the entrance of the office section. "And thank you, Yemi."

"You're welcome, Congressman," Yemi said. "Nick here, along with Lyle will be the two of our executive protection unit that'll be on this floor."

"And you said you'll be in the parking garage?" asked Desmond.

"Yes, sir."

"The whole time?"

"Yup. The perimeter is where the highest chance of a threat will come from, so that's what we'll be watching. Your office is outfitted with a radio that goes directly to our transmitters, so you can contact me whenever you please."

"Sounds good." Desmond yawned. "Okay, well, I'll see some of you in the A-M for breakfast, I guess."

"Have a good night, Mr. Ellis. Enjoy your rest." Desmond stepped into his office and closed the door. Yemi, Jasper, Victor, and Terry headed to the elevators. Lyle and Nick took their positions amidst the cubicles as Nick whipped out his laptop.

"Playing your little video game or something?" rhetorically asked Lyle.

"No." There was bass in Nick's voice. Somewhere between the gunfight experience in their last mission and his hidden frustrations with Abdallah, Lyle saw him transforming into a man who didn't tolerate being trivialized from a boy looking to please everybody he shared an employer with. Lyle took notice of both the tone and the brief response.

"It was a joke, Rice. Relax."

"Doesn't seem like there's much to laugh at over the next twenty-four hours," said Nick as he booted up his control panel of all the CCTV footage within the building. "Except for your career, I guess."

"What the fuck did you just say to me?" Lyle stepped over to Nick's seated position so the Jamaican hovered above him. The Raptor guard nearby glimpsed at the looming confrontation but stayed in his position. Nick sighed.

"Just let me do my job without always having to throw in your little side comments." Nick was still holding his ground, but his voice was slightly more diplomatic now. "It's getting old. Just like you." Now Nick looked up, and the two made eye contact. The animosity was hot for a moment, but soon Lyle smirked.

"Alright, I admit that was funny. But thirty ain't old, bitch."

"Happy belated birthday, Lyle." The mood had completely U-Turned. The guard in the back shook his head, thinking he was about to witness two of his co-workers throwing down thirty feet from their client.

"How'd you know?"

"Jasper told me."

"Uh-huh. You turning into Jasper's lil' pupil, aren't you?" Nick shrugged.

"He knows a lot about things I don't know much about. Usually, when that happens, I just listen."

"That's good." Lyle nodded up and down, reflecting on all the advice Jasper had given to him over his time at Raptor. In addition to recommending Lyle for the Executive Protection Team, it was Jasper who kept Lyle's family history with the drug trade hidden from Yemi until he realized it would be of their benefit. "Jasper's a solid dude." Lyle wondered why Jasper looked out for him with nothing much to gain other than maybe a more composed brother-in-arms on assignments.

"Very solid," echoed Nick as he checked the cameras monitoring the driveways outside the building. Lyle started to wonder. Was Nick his replacement for Jasper's student? Did he give up on Lyle after the fight at the Ethiopian bar? Lyle snickered to himself, trying to subdue any feeling of jealousy he had for a mentoring relationship between two other grown men. Class was over, and he didn't need any teachers, he rationalized. He peered over Nick's shoulders at his screen.

"It's not too dark to see the entrance?"

"I got eyes everywhere." Lyle nodded again and headed to a nearby cubicle. He took out his phone and opened up a sports betting app to see if he could make some extra money before the weekend.

––––––––

The doors were open, but the walls were closing in on Crystal. She was in a corner behind the Wheaton location, balled up against the floor and counter, the top of her polo shirt wet from sobbing for the past fifteen minutes since opening. The stress of the situation had got to her. Carlos being gone was enough to put her over the edge, but Merlin had also disappeared. And it was the same pattern as Carlos' disappearance. The phone rang the first several times, and by the morning, it had gone straight to voicemail. She'd ask her son to take over, but she refused to let him see her like this during work hours.

The only thing that was able to bring her back to sanity was the echoing bell of the door chime. She slowly stood up, wiped her face, and looked forward at the same Montgomery County detectives from before.

"Are you alright, ma'am?" asked Palacios. Dykes handed her a Kleenex from his inner blazer pocket. She accepted it and dabbed her eyes.

"I'm not," she said in between sniffs. "But you can't unscramble eggs, right?"

"My grandmother used to always say that," said Palacios. Crystal didn't fully buy into the truth of his reference, but she nodded in approval nonetheless.

"The past always haunts us, but it's the future that we can change," remarked Dykes. "We have a young woman in custody who checked herself into a hospital out in Germantown. She said she was with Carlos right before he was killed."

"She had been repeatedly raped and beaten almost beyond recognition," added Palacios.

"Carlos would never do something like that," Crystal said defensively.

"We know. What we believe is that she may have been the one that led him to his fate." Crystal stalled in her thoughts, putting together the fact that someone deliberately misled the sweet, polite boy she entrusted with her business.

"Somebody set up Carlos?"

"Yes, she admitted to being on a date with him the night he went missing," informed Palacios.

"Was she part of a gang or something?" asked Crystal, still wiping away at her pupils.

"Not a direct member," answered Palacios. "But she was targeted by them along with Carlos. For different reasons, obviously. They were hoping to use her for sex trafficking in addition to being an unwilling girlfriend to the leader."

"Which brings up another reason why we're here," stated Dykes. "Merlin Erazo is the other gentleman that works here, correct?" Crystal was a bit confused at what they would want to know about the older stock clerk, who she couldn't imagine even hopping a Metro turnstile.

"Yes, he does."

"Is he off today?" further questioned Dykes. "Or is he coming in later?"

"I haven't been able to get in contact with him," she said, still bewildered. "Why? Did he have something to do with this?" Palacios and Dykes paused. They looked at each other, similar in vein to how they looked before revealing Carlos' passing.

"The young lady said the man who rescued her from the gang worked at this store with Carlos," said Palacios.

"I don't know if you've kept with the news, but three bodies of MS-13 members were found in Germantown earlier this week."

"The ones who killed Carlos?"

"We suspect so. But we're still investigating." Crystal was done crying. She looked Palacios dead in the eye.

"Then they can burn in hell with my ex-husband."

"So, when do you think—"

"I have nothing else to say to you, gentlemen. Enjoy the rest of your day."

"Ma'am—"

"Please. I'm using my right to remain silent."

"Miss, we're just trying to get justice for Carlos."

"Don't try to emotionally blackmail me."

"Miss Santos—"

"Get out!" Dykes sighed. He motioned for Palacios to begin their exit. Palacios got one last word in before they headed out the door.

"Just so you know, next time we come, it'll be with a warrant. It might not look good to your customers to have a bunch of Montgomery County police officers rummaging through your grocery store." The 'good cop' routine was gone from Palacios' tone, and the threat seemed legitimate. Crystal just stared them down as they filed out of the market. She had changed her tune like Palacios, but for her, it was from melancholy to a serious suspicion for the authority she had been trusting. She figured she should have just treated them like immigration officers from the jump. And if Merlin was on the run for killing those sociopaths, she would hide him in the same exact way.

———

It didn't matter how much the threat of an assassination loomed over his head. Desmond refused to ever do his routine morning workout on a treadmill or an exercise bike. He didn't quite have the "Lions never stretch" mindset of some of his more hardcore friends who found themselves getting injured trying to mimic endurance athletes on social media with far better genetics, but he at least subscribed to the belief that humans were meant to do cardio outside. After all, exerting energy over long distances was one of the areas in the animal kingdom where homo sapiens remained supreme. Sure, on any given date, a motivated Bazaar bidder could just blindside him during a daily ride on the roads. Cycling was pretty much a sport that involved pedaling a vehicle at 20+ MPH on streets shared with cars going double the speed with what amounted to a diaper on your head for all your protection in case of a crash. But Ellis didn't care, and on the day he was most likely to meet an early demise, he was still sticking to his motto. That day was free weights and calisthenics, which suited the Congressman just fine since he didn't want his newfound hobby to put him into the stereotype of elite cyclists who needed their wives to carry the groceries.

He finished within forty-five minutes and headed for the bathroom to take a shower. Every step of the way, he was shadowed by Lyle and Nick. Even though Nick had the footage pulled up on his laptop on the sixth floor, Desmond learned it was Karen's primary duty to monitor all the footage along with Rana's partner at the front desk. Nick was just a third set of eyes to back them up.

As expected, the morning was quiet. Ellis had booked the entire building to himself, and the rest of the campus was empty with ALAMUT requesting all other occupiers to work remotely in exchange for a reduced rent of that month.

The shower and his office were the only locations in the whole structure where Desmond felt like he wasn't directly being watched. While rinsing off the sweat, that was when he realized he still hadn't contacted Karen since the start of his session. Why was he even thinking about this? He wondered to himself as the hot water hit his body. The Bazaar nonsense was already stressing out his poor, beautiful wife as it was, and there he was about to masturbate in the shower to another woman. He remembered how proud Lisa was when he won a seat on the New Carrolton City Council only a year after they graduated from Columbus School of Law. They shared a studio apartment and had a mountain of student debt after he had turned down a lucrative offer to be a junior partner in one of DC's top law firms. But she never doubted the vision. She was probably more proud of the fact that she was about to marry the second youngest elected official in Prince George's County history than if they were a couple ready to appear on HGTV's House Hunters.

"You okay in there?" asked Lyle from the locker room area of the bathroom.

"Yes, yes. Finishing up." Desmond didn't realize how

long he had been stuck on these thoughts about the options and consequences of infidelity. That fact alone made him realize how much his political ascent was corrupting his soul. He turned the faucet all the way to the right, palmed his face, and stepped out to change into his clothes for the day.

Walking into the dining hall for breakfast reminded Desmond of another reason to stay faithful to his law school love. When he committed himself to get back in shape, Lisa always had his avocado toast and salmon ready for him before he headed out the door to Capitol Hill, even with a full-time job of her own in addition to being a mother. The temptation was there, and every active person had a cheat day, but he wasn't going to slide back into the three-egg omelet and fried potatoes habit. Vash greeted him as he walked up to one of the chef stations.

"This is from El Sol Cafe in Wheaton," showcased Vash with pride. Desmond knew he personally selected the restaurant to cater to the elected official. "You ever had a baleada?"

"A what now?"

"Bally-AY-Da," pronounced Vash. "You need to try one. It's delicious. And healthy."

"What is it?"

"It's similar to a quesadilla but a better fit for breakfast, in my opinion. Flour tortilla, refried beans, crumbled cheese, crema, scrambled eggs, and avocado. Shoot, I'm about to order two for my own greedy self." The word 'avocado' got his attention. With the carbs of the tortilla, that was close enough to his standard early-morning diet.

"Yeah, I'll take one of those. Any plantains back there?"

"Oh? You eat plantain, sir?"

"Are you serious, Vash? What, you think us Black folks just order soul food all day?" An embarrassed, flush-faced Vash was unsure of how to respond to what he hoped was a joke. Lyle loudly snorted in a laughing manner while Nick smirked at the unexpected turn of conversation.

"No, no, sir—"

"I'm just messing with you, man." Vash and Desmond shared a common laugh, much to the relief of Vash. Desmond shook his head and nodded to the kitchen staff to go ahead with the order. For a brief moment, he caught one of the cooks staring right at him, almost like he had been studying Ellis during his back-and-forth with Vash. The older Latino man in a face mask slowly saluted Desmond and got to work on the grill. Desmond was caught a little by surprise by the sudden eye contact, but he shrugged it off and waited for his food.

————

As he sat at the kitchen table with a joint in hand, Bobby Z watched a pop culture talk show on the screen. "What's Really Good?" started off as a podcast filmed on YouTube but had recently been picked up by one of MTV's rival networks still keeping the television game alive. As he watched rappers long past their prime in the spotlight debate nerdy Gen Z influencers about daily topics, Bobby craved a large pizza with double pepperoni and an order of wings to smother in the Hidden Valley ranch that was tucked on the side door of the fridge. But he would never dial the number that was on the paper menu right in front of him because unless he wanted to put all of that into a blender without the chicken bones, he wouldn't be consuming any solid foods for the next 6-8 weeks due to his jaw being wired shut.

Aaron walked in with an undershirt on and sweats, having just woken up. He nodded respectively toward Bobby but still stayed on a fast track to the refrigerator for a glass of orange juice. He grabbed a granola bar, too, which was a bit strange to Bobby. Aaron usually ate cereal for breakfast, but maybe he avoided that this morning because that would probably require him to sit at the table with the man he put in a maxillomandibular fixation. Aaron turned his head from the fridge to the counter next to them, where a large container of Whey protein sat.

"You need a shake or anything?" he asked Bobby. Bobby Z's eyelids dipped, and he turned to Aaron to give him a 'Did you just seriously ask me that' look. "My bad." Bobby sighed through his nostrils. He was over the hostility himself.

"You good..." Bobby Z held up the jay. "Wanna hit this?" Aaron took the orange juice out and grabbed a nearby glass.

"Fa sho." With his glass of OJ, Aaron joined Bobby at the table. The rolled-up cannabis got passed, and Aaron puffed a few times.

"You smoke this much back in DC?" asked Bobby Z. Aaron took a moment to respond, reflecting to himself for a moment.

"Not really. My boy Danny would spark every hour, though."

"Danny?" asked Bobby. "The Asian dude that was on the news?"

"Yeah," Aaron said after a pause. The two heard the word 'Bazaar' uttered on the television. They both turned their attention to it.

"In other news, there are still no arrests yet in the shooting of Maryland Attorney General Ryan Frost. This has further thrust an online prediction market known as the Bazaar into the spotlight," said 26-year-old host Cerius. "Where Frost was apparently in the top ten of the most valuable persons listed on the website."

"See? That's what I don't get," chimed in 42-year-old early 2010s top charting rapper Young Loose. "Why is it just political muh fuckas on this joint?"

"As opposed to...?" A third host was present, a woman in her early 30s, and her lower third on-screen read 'Kyra Kash.'

"As opposed to dudes who actually need to get capped out here." Loose's voice grew in passion. "Like, how bout we put some of these police getting away with murder on the list? Them people that killed George Floyd, Breonna Taylor, man, I could go on. All of them cops still walking around freely."

"Shit, I'd put my own money up," stated Kash.

"Right?"

"I mean, look y'all. I'm all about the movement or whatever," chimed in Cerius. "But do you know how much chaos this thing can cause if it keeps getting more clout?"

"Clout?" asked Kash, visibly a bit offended at the terminology. "This is a free market to kill people, Cerius, not a hashtag."

"And while we're at it, I might add your barber to the Bazaar, letting you leave the shop with your head like that, ya Jackson five perm having-ass boy!" laughed Young Loose.

"Can you believe these fools are joking about this?" remarked Bobby Z, grimacing through his wires. Aaron shrugged as he hit the joint.

"I don't really be watching this type of shit for real." Bobby nodded.

"Yeah. I kinda feel what they were saying, though," Bobby said. "I just wish people remembered that the pigs be killing us, grimy white boys, too, know what I'm saying?" Aaron shrugged again, not changing his face at all.

"I just need to get paid. That's all I care about." Bobby Z never thought he'd meet someone more apolitical than him, and that person was right across the table from him.

"True." That was the only thing Bobby Z could find himself to say, and it was also something he entirely agreed with. The front door to the house swung open, and in trudged a sweaty Doug, who just finished his morning long-distance run.

"How far you run?" inquired Bobby as Aaron passed him the joint.

"Was going for twelve or more but had to stop at eight."

"Oh damn, why?"

"You'll find out in a second." Doug dipped right into the bathroom close to the kitchen and shut the door. Within a few seconds, Aaron and Bobby Z heard an extremely loud burst of flatulence. They cracked up at the table, combined with some exaggerated looks of disgust. After the toilet finally flushed and they heard hands washing, Doug stepped back out into the living room area with a towel wrapped around his shoulder. He continued to wipe away the sweat as he approached the kitchen.

"That sweat from the jog or the shit?" asked Doug.

"Jog? I run, fool. Ain't no weekend warrior bullshit round these parts." Bobby Z took some puffs and exchanged a look of sarcasm with Aaron.

"He always gets butthurt when I use that term."

"You don't break a 19-minute 5k from some Sunday stroll in the park, is all I'm saying," Doug stated as he grabbed bottled water from the fridge. He chugged it as he hovered around the table.

"No wonder you never had a problem making weight," muttered Bobby, remembering their high school wrestling days. Doug was a multi-sport athlete who competed in cross country in the Fall before wrestling season, while Bobby Z only stuck to the mat. He didn't even bother with football despite the insistence of his father, who was part of the state champion team in 1975 at Fort Hill.

"Any decision on Scottie?" asked Aaron, refocusing the topic of conversation to the current times. Doug breathed through his nose and out of his mouth before he took another gulp of H2O.

"I went through every informant database for the state of Maryland and didn't see his face anywhere."

"A well-protected C-I will never get his profile found on the internet regardless," Aaron responded.

"I thought I was the one who was skeptical?" Doug said

as he crushed his current bottle, tossed it into the recycle, and went to the fridge to grab another one. Bobby assumed Aaron was on board with Scottie joining the next mission, so he raised his eyebrow toward their comrade as well.

"If Desmond Ellis survives today, he's probably only going to rise on the charts even higher," Aaron said as a confused Bobby passed him back the joint. "If the number next to the Congressman's name crosses the five million dollar mark... And after we get info on his potential location and our training regimen is solid, I'll give Scottie and his crew the green light." Doug nodded affirmatively, already three-quarters done with his second bottle.

"That message board still active?" Bobby referred to the Reddit-style website on the dark net that served as a gathering for many users of the Bazaar. The popular prediction dates, rumored locations of targets, and other tidbits of information regarding those unlucky enough to be on the market were discussed. He also knew it was where Doug and Aaron initially found each other online.

"It is," said Aaron. "But we may have a new source of intel." Aaron pulled up an app on his phone. He pressed a bit on the screen and then handed it over to Bobby Z for him to see. Bobby was staring at the news-generator app, but it only focused on stories related to the Bazaar. He realized that he was reading under a section called 'Targets in the News.' Other tabs at the top included 'Date Guesses,' 'Security,' and 'Culture.'

"What is this?" asked Bobby.

"Nobody knows who launched it," said Doug as he finished off his second bottle.

"And it was released only a week ago. Blew up quick."

"I guess this makes things easier research-wise," said Bobby Z as he continued to scroll past headlines. He pressed the 'Security' tab. "What's it even called?"

"Hitter," answered Aaron.

"Already got 5-K downloads."

"Interesting," said Bobby as he looked at an article profiling the rise of Raptor and how they partnered with ALAMUT to protect Desmond Ellis. "Ain't Raptor the team that y'all went up against, Aaron?"

Aaron paused after he puffed on the jay.

"Yeah."

"That's who's assigned to Ellis, apparently." Bobby Z looked at photos of Karen and Yemi. Karen was a business portrait fit for a LinkedIn profile. It was ripped from the blogs highlighting female entrepreneurship. Yemi's picture was one when he was in his early 20s in a Nigerian police uniform. Underneath the pic, a line read: 'Before Raptor founder Yemi Uzunma came to the USA as a consultant and before he was a member of Nigeria's elite State Security Services, he was a young recruit in the controversial SARS unit of the Nigerian Police.' Bobby Z continued to read, fascinated by the Yemi character.

"This Yemi Uzunma dude is a savage," Bobby said. "But I know you probably looking to take this dude out, right Aaron?"

"Huh?" the man across from him asked.

"His team killed some of your folks, right?" Bobby asked as he continued to look at the photos. It took a few seconds for Aaron to answer like some kind of PTSD had hit him.

"Yeah," Aaron finally responded.

"His sister is pretty hot," Bobby remarked as he looked at Karen's pose with her arms crossed with an enlarged Raptor logo behind her. "I wish I could see what that ass looking like, though. I know African girls always got something in the trunk."

"I thought you didn't date foreign girls," Doug said as he rolled his eyes at Bobby's blatant thirst.

"Hey," Bobby Z responded as Aaron handed him the joint. "I was never with that building a wall bullshit Ethan was

talking about. It would keep too many hot Mexican bitches out."
Aaron sighed and shook his head. Doug did the same and started
to leave the kitchen.

"I'm taking a shower. I'm guessing Scottie is a go? But
under probationary terms?"

"Yeah," said Aaron as he looked back up at the television
screen. Young Loose and Cerius seem to be getting into an intense
argument. "Just gotta keep our eyes and ears open as always."

"Right on." Doug entered the bathroom again, and the
shower turned on.

"You never take me seriously!" yelled Cerius at his older
co-host. "You know I'm speaking facts right now, and you just
wanna cook me."

"Cause you make yourself a target! You missing the whole
reason why this Bazaar shit even exists in the first place."

"What do you mean? I just said I understood—"

"But you don't understand though. People bidding on the
Bazaar because they're fed up with those in power getting away
with that shit that would send any of us to prison for the rest of
our lives. Or just abusing their power, period, to infringe on our
rights, and we deal with all the consequences, not them and their
bodyguards that all their money buys."

"See you trying to make me into an apologist for the status
quo, and I never defended them—"

"Cause you don't know about the struggle, boy. You
talked about the streets from a mic in your college dorm while I
was fighting attempted murder cases."

"You don't know me, Loose!"

"I know that you a BITCH!"

"We're going to go to a commercial break and let these
two simmer down," interjected Kash, sensing the confrontation
was about to go from verbal to physical. "Coming up, do
antidepressants actually work? Popular actor George Jonas has

recently taken to social media to speak out against what he calls the mental health industrial complex. More on 'What's Really Good?' when we come back."

"Shit, she can get the D too," said Bobby staring at the rap video model-turned-talk-show-host. "At this rate, I think my future kid might look like you," Bobby joked in reference to Aaron's light caramel skin tone. Aaron snorted a minor laugh. Bobby offered him to hit the jay again, but Aaron raised his hands up, signaling he was tapped out.

"I don't want to get too high," Aaron said. Bobby laughed.

"I don't know what too high is," Bobby Z said. "Maybe that explains some of my bad decisions." They shared a slight chuckle.

"Qasim smoked a lot," Aaron said.

"Who's Qasim?" asked Bobby. There was another drop to silence like that name brought Aaron back to the darkness of the PTSD a few moments ago. "You good?"

"A dude who Yemi killed," Aaron said back to him. Bobby Z nodded in respect, now knowing what had triggered Aaron.

"Y'all were homies?" asked Bobby Z. Aaron nodded affirmatively. "I know wherever he is, he knows you're holding it down."

"Yeah," Aaron said. "I'm sure he does."

CHAPTER 17

The day couldn't have gone smoother for Representative Ellis. He called his wife three times that day. Once at 10 AM to check in, another right after lunch to discuss what he ate that day, and at 9 PM, he called to help read a bedtime story to little Jarvis and baby Regina before Lisa tucked them in for the night. He was also proud of himself for never resorting to calling Karen despite the temptation that crept into him the night of his arrival. His aides gave him plenty of work to do, such as reviewing a brand new study put out by the gun violence prevention organization, Everytown, on the danger of 3D-printed guns such as the Mini Talon. When he had drafted the original legislation, he cited an older white paper put out by the State Department, but the Everytown study went far more into detail. 'The Danger of Downloadable Guns' cross-examined previous White House administration's efforts to ban home-manufactured firearms and how none of the efforts seemed to amount to anything, in turn creating an environment for the Mini Talon to flourish. Desmond smiled when he read the line about how the most major development was his own legislation he pushed to Congress, along with public support from the late Maryland Attorney General.

When he didn't feel like working, Ellis read one of the earlier books put out by one of his idols, former Maryland governor Wes Moore. But as it got closer to midnight, Ellis was winding down from anything that required brain activity. At 10 PM, he turned on a stream of a boxing match headlined by a fighter from the trenches of Suitland, Maryland. If the 28-year-old pulled off the win over the Dominican pugilist, Ellis would consider doing a photo op and maybe even join the new governor in declaring a state-wide holiday for him. It'd be a nice change of pace from all the discussion on gun violence and racial issues that took up most of the mental and physical space in his offices.

———

"Yeah, that's enough," said one of Congressman Ellis' guards to Teresita's co-worker as he dabbed some guacamole next to a quesadilla in a to-go container. The man closed it up and stacked it on top of three other boxes by the counter. "Do I take this to the cashier, or do I pay you or...?" The tall, slender armed guard didn't see anyone manning the register station at the front of the dining hall. Teresita stepped forward to talk to Terry since she could speak English.

"All the meals for today have been paid for, my dear," she said in a sweet voice like she was feeding her own son, who hadn't been home in ages.

"Oh, didn't realize that," responded the mercenary. "I didn't come in for breakfast or lunch, so I had no idea." He took out two ten-dollar bills from his wallet and set them on the counter. "For the great service," he commended.

"God bless your soul, young man!"

"I turn 40 next year," chuckled the guard. "But I'll take it."

"You're a baby," Teresita said back to him. "Your best years are ahead of you."

"That's not saying much, given I spent the past two decades between getting shot at in foreign land and chasing schizophrenics around Union Station." Her eyes widened from the sharing of his life story. "But anyways, the two of you have a great rest of your night." The man stepped away, and Teresita took the cash from the counter. She offered one of the bills to the man next to her, but he gently held his hand up, refusing it.

"This is yours," she insisted in Spanish.

"No, no, senora." The man pointed to a locket necklace dangling above her apron. "I heard you mention your grandson earlier. Get something for him."

"Aw," she said as she gripped her locket and brought it into her chest as she tried to stop her emotions from taking over. She exchanged a hug with the man. "What's your name?" she asked as she let go.

"Carlos."

———

Terry walked through the first floor of the parking garage with his full plastic bags. Yemi watched him approach the vehicle.

"Finally," said Victor. "I'm starving."

"Why didn't you head in when it was dinner time?"

"Most assassinations take place during the daytime," answered Victor from the backseat as he eagerly waited for Terry to arrive.

"But most violent crime happens when it's dark," corrected Jasper. Victor was one of Venezuela's combat elite. However, Yemi knew that the oldest member of the squad was just being lazy. Such a trait didn't really bother Yemi much, and if anything, it gave the team a needed relaxed touch to their chemistry without leaving room for a fatal error. The back passenger door opposite Victor swung open, and Terry stepped in. He removed the boxes from the bag and began to check them for each of his comrade's orders. The smell of lime and corn flour seemed to excite Victor the most as he set eyes on his three empanadas.

"Did you get the name of this place?" asked Victor to Terry.

"Nah, nice lady, though. Is it good?"

"Phenomenal. I can tell it's a saltena and not just an empanada."

"What's the difference?" inquired a curious Jasper before he started to bite his quesadilla.

"Saltenas are shaped more like a football and filled with stew. Nice and juicy. Sometimes regular empanadas can be a little too dry."

"That was the perfect setup for a Lyle joke," laughed Terry as he started his own meal. Yemi knew what Terry meant, assuming Lyle would have related Victor's sentence to the reproductive organs belonging to the plethora of women he'd slept with. "It was a blessing he got stationed on the sixth floor. Poor Nick." Victor and Jasper followed up with a low, polite chuckle but clearly were not trying to share the same level of animosity Terry had been incubating against their squad's criminology expert.

"They call this thing a silpancho," said Terry, changing the subject back to food as he stared at his pile of potato, fried egg, rice, beef, and tomatoes. "Never had it before—"

"Hostiles at the front gate!" yelled Karen through their earpiece. The boxes were tossed to the side with no care in the world for whatever mess it caused. Victor and Terry sprang out of their respective doors with assault rifles while Yemi and Jasper filed out with their automatic pistols. Within a moment, all four were tactically moving forward across the first floor of the parking garage, with Yemi leading the pack.

"Talk to me, Karen!" barked Yemi. "Nick, do you copy?"

———

Nick played eeny meenie miny moe between the pack of Haribo Goldbears and the gummy LifeSavers. He heard the dispatch from Karen once he landed on the multi-colored fruit-flavored carnivores.

"Shit!" he cursed to himself as he spun around to the stairwell and sprinted up from the fifth floor. Once he got to the middle of the steps, he heard Yemi. "I copy! Getting back to my station now."

"Come on, Rice!"

"I'm sorry, one second." He pushed through the stairwell entrance to the sixth floor. Pointing a Glock straight at him was

Lyle, who was in a position to secure the area of the Congressman. The other Raptor guard was on the opposite side of the elevator lobby, also ready to shoot whoever invaded their space.

"Nick!" yelled Lyle as he shifted his gun back down. "Communicate! I almost shot you."

"My bad, my bad!" Nick ran toward his desk, doing his best to avoid pissing off any more of his squadmates. He wiggled the touchpad on his computer to get past the screensaver and straight onto the cameras. He immediately scoped the surveillance camera focused on the front gate of the campus. A sedan packed with baklava-clad individuals skirted from the booth toward the main building. Nick noticed the glass windows of the gate entrance security guard booth were riddled with bullet holes.

"They're speeding towards the main building now," said Karen, beating Nick to breaking the news.

"I counted at least four of them in the vehicle," added Nick.

"Okay, we'll intercept them before they get to the lobby," informed Yemi.

––––––––

Yemi eyed the late early 2000s Toyota Crown Majesta zoom past the garage, but none of the occupants spotted the executive protection squad blended in with the darkness on the first level. Yemi had requested for the lights to be shut off for that very reason. The team arrived at the pillars near one of the garage's side entrances.

"Terry and Jasper! Push forward from the other side. We'll cover you and then do the same from here."

"Roger!" As the Toyota screeched to a halt at the driveway in front of the main ALAMIUT building, Jasper and Terry sprinted across the narrow street to take firing positions from behind a concrete wall.

Yemi could spot Rana and his fellow Raptor guard, Mark,

in the lobby with their pistols pointed toward the Toyota from behind the front desk. Yemi knew Rana's heart was probably racing, realizing this was about to be the first gun battle in the young security officer's career. He had informed Raptor on his resume that he never had to fire his weapon in Trinidad, although he definitely drew out his gun a few times to shoo away serial loitering vagrants.

"Stay covered, Rana," Yemi told him over the radio. "Just hold them off from entry. We're engaging them from the back."

"Copy, sir."

The doors of the Toyota flew out. The car was filled to capacity as five bandana-masked men jumped out. Three were armed with fully automatic AK-47s, and the other two wielded pump-action Remington shotguns. The one from the driver's side yelled out orders in Spanish right before they sprayed the entire front of the lobby. Rana and his partner were overwhelmed by the rapid gunfire, so Yemi saw them duck behind the security desk, unable to return fire.

Almost immediately after the first shot was fired from the hitmen, Yemi took a shot toward one of them, who was armed with a shotgun. He hit a bullseye at the center of his target's back on the first trigger pull, and the man collapsed onto the pavement.

"Behind us!" yelled one of the MS-13 members in Spanish. Two of the gunmen turned their attention toward the Executive Protection Team, and the two sides exchanged hails of gunfire.

Bullets penetrated the bumper, car windows and deflated the tires as the gangsters used the car doors to shield them from the onslaught. Now that the Raptor detail had the opposition surrounded from both angles, Rana and Mark were able to deliver better-aimed shots at the Mara-occupied vehicle. Another gang member went down after his shotgun failed to effectively reach Yemi's squad due to the range.

"Go!" yelled Yemi to Victor. The Venezuelan sprinted to

take cover behind a structure closer to the Toyota. Yemi effectively provided cover fire as Victor made it to his destination safely. "Reload!" Yemi ducked behind the wall, released the magazine, and slid another one back in.

Resorting to even more desperate measures, the driver of the assault car hopped back in the driver's seat. He yelled at the other two in Spanish to jump in the car as well. They traded fire with both sides of the Raptor defense and made their way to their respective car seats. Yemi heard the Crown Majesta rev up. He pushed forward next to Victor's position as he let off some rounds toward the car.

"Rana! Careful, I think they're about to ram the lobby!" warned Yemi into the radio.

After the wheels briefly burned out on the asphalt, the driver floored the Toyota toward the building. The other two gunmen continued to fire out the window until it crashed through the locked doors and windows.

The damaged car was only a dozen feet from the security desk. At close range, Rana dumped his mag into the driver's side, managing to hit the assailant once in his shoulder.

"Reload," yelled Rana.

"Sowell?" inquired Yemi into his radio, checking for the well-being of the other guard stationed with Rana.

"Mark's down!" Rana yelled into the radio.

"Hang tight! We're pushing in." Looking forward at the lobby, Yemi saw Rana stick his pistol above the counter and blindly shot toward the car. Automatic fire continued to penetrate the desk.

Terry carefully strafed outside the driveway, making his way to get a clearer shot of the crashed vehicle along with Jasper. Yemi saw him take out one of their enemies.

The man fell to the floor of the lobby, his head smacking the car on the way down. There were only two of the hit crew left.

Victor and Yemi started to close in.

"Surrender now!" Victor yelled in his native language to the remaining gunmen. "Or you will die."

"Mother fuckers!" yelled one from behind the front passenger seat. The face-tatted dude raised his AK to the roof of the car toward Victor and Yemi. Before he could let anything off, he was sniped by Jasper at the side of his face, and a second bullet sliced his jugular. That rendered his body limp, and his life met its end on the tile floors of the ALAMUT lobby.

———

The dining hall workers were all hiding in the prep area behind the serving stations where most of the non-perishables were kept. As the gunshots grew louder, especially after the sound of the car crash, a few even slipped into the walk-in cooler, not taking the chance of security guards on their floor losing the battle. Teresita knew the cold temperature would be too much for her developing arthritis, so she stood by the shelves of seasonings and assorted canned beans. A few of her fellow cafeteria staff stood in the vicinity, some of them from Vash's favorite Vietnamese restaurant in Rockville. They were also skeptical about taking refuge in freezing temperatures, but Teresita could hear the panic in their language with each succession of gunfire.

Carlos stood by an opposite shelf and finally lifted his head up. Teresita had been watching him pray for the last ten minutes, his head bowed the whole time. She assumed he was asking the Lord to protect them from any crossfire down the hall, but there was no hint of fear in any of his demeanor like the rest of her co-workers. Not a single tremble of any limbs, no frantic phone call to a loved one, just a calm stationary pose and a long private conversation with his God. Suddenly, Carlos made his way to a bunch of white 1-gallon buckets of corn masa at the end of the shelves. He scanned the top of them and picked up two. He carried them over to a nearby sink and started the process of unsealing them.

"Carlos," she said to him. "What are you doing?" He paused before he took off the first top. For the first time during their entire time of interacting with each other, he removed his face mask and then made eye contact with her.

"My name is Merlin." In his pupils, she saw the thousand-yard stare. The same stare her brother Oscar had forty years ago when he came home for a brief period after battling the Salvadoran Army in the jungle of the Chalatenango province. He had left her and the rest of the family to take arms after news of the village massacres of El Mozote and Los Torilles spread.

Merlin got back to his task and finished unsealing the bins. He dug into the cornmeal and revealed ziplocked plastic bags that he quickly rinsed in the sink. As he worked rapidly and unzipped them, she realized they were handguns along with ammunition magazines.

Once the Vietnamese workers nearby saw the contraband Merlin had snuck past inspection, they finally walked briskly away and entered the large refrigerator they didn't want to risk hiding out in earlier. Teresita didn't want to leave, though. Even though she didn't know Merlin, as he loaded bullets into his pistols, she wondered if Oscar's motivation to forego the future of his livelihood to pick up arms was any similar to the man in front of her who lied about his identity.

———

The remaining MS-13 member continued to recklessly fire his AK. However, he traded between hitting the desk in the lobby and Yemi's squad continuing to press into the car's violent entry point.

Finally, the wannabe hitman pulled the trigger and heard a click. The banana clip was empty.

"Push in!" yelled Yemi. "He's out!" The gunman tossed his rifle aside and took out a butterfly knife that was submerged in his pocket. At that point, Yemi doubted he would be able to reach his target, but Yemi knew the stakes were too high for the man to be expected to raise a white flag.

Rana spun around the corner of the desk to continue exchanging fire. The MS gunman was charging full speed at him with the raised balisong ready to slash or stab. Rana immediately fired a succession of three bullets into the deranged man's torso and arms, but it didn't even slow him down. Yemi figured he was high on PCP, and the feeling of invincibility translated into action as he powered through the pain and reached Rana to stab him right in the shoulder.

Rana yelled out in agony but grabbed the angel dust-induced man, trying to kill him by the arm to try and stop more repeated stabs. Yemi was the first of the crew to reach the lobby and spotted them tumbling into the desk, hitting the surveillance monitors. He tried to get a clear shot of the gangster, but he didn't want to risk adding any further injury to Rana despite the urgency. Jasper, Terry, and Victor arrived.

"Take the shot!" he yelled to his comrades, who were all better marksmen than him, not to mention that Victor and Terry were equipped with actual assault rifles. Rana saw his Executive Protection Team encroaching on the struggle. With all of his strength, he managed to shove off the assailant for a brief second. The whole squad lit him up, but it was a HEADSHOT from the opposite angle that put the failed assassin into a permanent sleep. Yemi and Rana looked down the hall and noticed it was another Raptor rookie, Joseph. When Jasper had taken the new crop of Raptor property guards to the range for some training, Yemi remembered it was Joseph who impressed the EPT's primary sharpshooter the most. Joseph had claimed his father was in the military and taught him, but there was a rumor floating around that he was a young enforcer for an Oxon-Hill-based drug trafficking ring that was busted before he went legit with Raptor.

"Yo Singh!" called out Joseph as he made his way down the hall. He had been primarily holding a position near the dining hall and elevators as a last line of defense in case one of the car occupants broke through. "You good?" The EPT started to gather around the desk. Terry immediately went to Rana. He saw the knife wound and immediately applied pressure, but Rana was conscious, his back against the desk.

"Yeah!" Rana called back out to Joseph. "Mother fucker stabbed me in the shoulder, but I'll be alright." Terry looked for something under the desk and couldn't find it.

"Where's the med kit?" asked Terry to his boss.

"There's one upstairs and one back in the car."

"I'll be fine," insisted Rana as he tried to stand, but Terry pushed him back into his resting position.

"Stay down, kid," said Terry. "We have to rendezvous up there anyways, right?"

"Yeah, let's just do a double-check of the bodies here, remove the weapons, and then make our way." Yemi spotted Joseph a dozen feet away with his gun still pointed forward. "Joseph," he said. "Go secure the elevators until we get down there."

"Yes, sir." As Terry watched over Rana, the rest of the team went to survey the damage caused by the Toyota and the heavy gun battle. The scene was reminiscent of a bank robbery gone wrong from either a mid-90s heist movie or a real-life scenario such as the North Hollywood shootout that was directly inspired by Heat two years after the release of the Michael Mann film. It was one of Kirk Fitzgerald's favorite movies and recommended it to Yemi once he arrived in the States. Reality often imitates fiction and vice versa, realized Yemi as he looked at a deceased face tatted man with tear drops laying next to the ever-reliable Russian-manufactured assault weapon, but it was an undeniable fact that humans could indeed name a price for their freedom or even life. Maybe the gang members from El Salvador weren't attempting to hold up a teller, but it was the same end goal with the same tools to kill U.S. Representative Desmond Ellis as the mission to rob a Los Angeles Bank of America thirty years prior.

"Yemi," said Jasper as he removed a shred of paper from the floor of the backseat of the car. "Check this out." He handed it over to Yemi, and the EPT detail leader looked down at a printed-out Capitol Hill portrait of the Congressman himself.

"Too many things could go wrong with them having to fiddle with a photo of Ellis on their phones," said Yemi. "Guess this was the one smart choice they made today."

"Guess so—"

"Joseph—!"

POP. POP POP. Their conversation was interrupted by Karen trying to warn the guard about something, but the noise of an exchange of gunfire from the hallway completely took over the halls. Immediately, the four EPT members in the lobby raised their arms and took tactical positions at their end of the hall, making sure they didn't turn the corner into a direct threat.

"Joseph!" Yemi called out to his young subordinate. "Talk to me!" There was no immediate answer. Despite being injured from a 7-inch blade, Rana spun around to the monitors and checked the CCTV footage.

"He's been shot!" Rana yelled out to his superior.

"Shit," Yemi said to himself. "Any eyes on the shooter?"

"Negative," responded Rana.

"Karen?" Yemi asked into his radio.

"I've been watching the whole time. Nothing yet. He must know all the locations of all our cameras."

"Lyle, Nick," Yemi demanded into his radio. "We probably had a mole amongst the staff. Between the two of you and the patrol guard, stay aimed at the elevators and stairwell. One of you plant yourselves right outside Ellis' door. No matter what happens, do not let anybody enter that office."

"Roger that," stated Lyle over the radio.

———

It was starting to feel like Silver Spring with Obi, thought Nick, as he stayed at the corner of the elevator lobby and kept his pistol pointed toward the elevators. Lyle was on the opposite side and had to maintain his sight on not only the same area as Nick's but also the stairwell entrance that sat right across from him. The two uniformed patrol guards assigned to the sixth floor were also on the same side of Lyle. Lyle realized he was going to have to be the commanding field agent until Yemi could get his way up there.

"Jason," said Lyle to one of the guards. "Head over to Nick's side to back him up. Be careful."

"Yup, yup." He briskly walked across the elevator lobby and joined Rice's side to crouch in firing position. Next, Lyle spoke to the other guard, another rookie like Rana and Nick named Michael.

"You. I can handle this myself. Go get in position around Ellis. Now." Michael nodded and jogged down the row of cubicles until he found one right in front of Desmond's suite.

All points of entry to the sixth floor from the bottom of the building were then covered. Unless the assassin was planning to rappel in through the windows, he was going to be forced to engage with somebody from Raptor upon his arrival upstairs. Lyle kept the door in his iron sights, waiting for the knob to twist or a bell from the lobby. Whichever happened first.

———

"I have movement!" announced Karen through the radio. "He just entered the stairwell."

"Let's roll!" Yemi motioned for his squad to get in a diamond formation and tactically proceeded down the hall. Yemi, Jasper, and Terry kept their weapons pointed forward while Victor periodically checked all their surroundings from the back. The stairwell door cracked open, and their adversary immediately fired in the direction of the squad. Terry took a shot to the chest that his Kevlar blocked from penetrating his body. He was able to keep his composure to join the rest of his team in lighting up the end of the hallway. The gunshots ricocheted off the metal door, but the gunman shut it almost immediately after the beginning of the exchange.

"Lyle, he's in the stairwell," barked Yemi into his radio. He pressed the button to call the elevator, and within five seconds, a bell rang, followed by the second one from the stairwell opening up its walls. Yemi signaled to Rana, who gave him a thumbs up and raised his fully loaded pistol to let Yemi know he would be alright as they proceeded with the mission to protect Ellis. "We're coming up on the middle elevator."

"Copy," answered back Lyle. "Radio me once you hit five."

"You got it," radioed back Yemi. Jasper and Terry were the first to step onto the platform and spun their position 180 degrees once they arrived at the corners of the elevator. Yemi and Victor made the same motion but occupied the front angles closest to the buttons and doors. The dim shadow of the moving walls encompassed the determined faces of each Raptor EPT member.

They were prepared mentally for any possibility on each floor the elevator may have arrived on. It showed in the dead silence among them. Yemi was too focused to let any mistakes take priority in his head. But submerged deep below his survival combat instincts was the concern that there was an insider who got past all background checks, screenings, and everything his sister plus Vash had put in place. Joseph's gun was found still lying next to his body once they passed him, so Yemi figured that the gunman had smuggled the firearms in. Victor helped with all structural and ventilation defense risk assessment, Jasper was in contact with Vash on all intel, but Yemi realized he and Karen made the mistake of entrusting the safety of all food intake to ALAMUT and a third-party food inspection firm called Nourish Safety Consultants. NSC was run by a James Madison University College of Business classmate of Vash named William Kim, who had met neither Yemi nor Karen.

Their anxiety levels were managed, but the second-floor bing raised the nerves up a notch on Yemi, Terry, Victor, and Jasper. The elevator rode past it. Another bing, it was the third floor. Not a sound as Yemi slightly tensed up his muscles from the anticipation. Elevators were rarely something he considered from all his experience, as a stairwell was always the preferred option for clearing floor-by-floor. But the situation wasn't a rescue or threat elimination goal at the moment. It was about swarming to positions around their VIP to guarantee protection, at least for the next two hours.

Bing, fourth floor... Bing. Fifth floor. Yemi grabbed ahold of his radio.

"We're on the fifth, Lyle."

"Copy. You hear that, Nick?" A slight delay.

"Yes, sir!" said the technical prodigy. When the final elevator bell went off, the doors slid open after a few seconds.

They knew they were safe, but the four still proceeded out into the elevator lobby with peripherals covering every corner around them. Yemi used his hands to signal for Victor and Jasper to go left to join Nick while he and Terry headed to Lyle's side.

"Sir," Nick said to Yemi in a low voice. He got his detail leader's attention and pointed to the red LED number above one of the elevators. Yemi watched the level rise to '4.'

"Get ready, everybody," Yemi said to the Executive Protection Team plus Jason. Lyle kept his Glock pointed to the stairwell entrance, but everyone else still had their muzzles in the direction of the left elevator. The unspoken intensity rose with the red number when it hit '5.'

Finally, the bell went off. As the elevator doors slowly opened, Yemi, Victor, Terry, and Jasper encroached on its perimeter. Once the doors finished opening, a loud series of POPS came from the platform. The team responded with a hail of gunfire into the walls and inside the elevator.

"Cease fire!" barked Yemi after a series of shots. Yemi and Victor continued to step forward. A bloodied Skechers sneaker was the first thing they saw upon getting closer to the elevator. As their view became clearer, the shoes became connected to crimson-stained cargo pants, and as they got a full view of the body, Yemi recognized the body as one of the Vietnamese staff workers who must have been killed before being placed there as a decoy. Another POP came from the area around the corpse. The sound caused Terry, Jasper, and even Nick to run up closer to the elevator, but Yemi waved them off, knowing it was not a weapon making the noise. The two of them looked at a small white paper bag that was lit on fire from the bottom. Some smoke rose, but Victor stomped on the bag to put out the fire. Underneath his boot, a rapid succession of pops went off.

"Bang snaps," Victor said to Yemi. "They were popular with protesters back home."

Suddenly, two gunshots came from Lyle's side.

"Fuck!" Yemi heard him yell in pain. The team shifted to Lyle's direction as Lyle fell back while delivering some shots of his own toward the stairwell entrance. They heard the gunman bust through the door while firing off a semiautomatic pistol. He quickly dived into a nearby cubicle to act as his cover while he engaged in a firefight with Raptor. Lyle regained his posture and backpedaled into another cubicle by his position. Yemi and the rest all took positions around the edge of the elevator lobby near Lyle's side, careful to not jump into the line of fire.

A Glock peeked around the corner toward Yemi when the

detail leader attempted to find a spot to aim back. Yemi fell back into the lobby as the gun unloaded toward him. Yemi heard the pistol get tossed. But soon, he heard a shotgun getting pumped, and one shot fired toward Lyle's cubicle. He saw the top corner of the divider splinter onto the Jamaican. He had to stay tucked underneath the desk both to avoid the 12 gauge onslaught and to check the damage he had taken. Lyle brought his hand up from his kevlar, and Yemi could see blood on his fingers. Another shotgun blast to the cubicle destroyed a panel.

Pinned in the positions from the assailant's powerful firepower, Terry moved up to near Yemi and tapped him on the shoulder. Without saying a word, he removed a small black canister. Yemi remembered they had upgraded their arsenal to include pepper spray bombs after their previous incident. Yemi immediately approved of its use. Terry ripped off the top and pressed down on a button. It started to shoot out a spray straight up into the air. He heard their adversary start to reload the shotgun, and at that exact moment, he leaned over the edge of the lobby to toss the pepper spray bomb parallel right with the gunman's cubicle.

The spray bomb hit its target and ceased the shooting for a few moments. But before Yemi decided to have his squad move in, the gunman blindly shot around the corner of the cubicle with a revolver to repel any of the Raptor agents from attempting to push further into his space before he took off down the hall. Keeping his body tight to the corner of the lobby and the cubicle area, Yemi exchanged gunfire with the assailant as he ran away. The gunman reached the end of the hall and bucked the corner. Yemi waved for Jasper and Victor to join him in pursuit.

"Terry, focus on Lyle! Nick, hold your position with Jason. Hold them from coming around the opposite side." Yemi, Jasper, and Victor pushed into the hall. They took cover in the cubicles every few steps, knowing that their enemy could return fire at any moment from around the corner.

———

Terry ran in the opposite direction toward Desmond's office. However, he stopped a few cubicles short of the door. Wielding his Raptor-issued Helwan pistol, Michael popped out from his hidden position in the cubicle closest to Ellis. Terry instinctively pointed his gun toward him, but the uniform stopped him from pulling the trigger. Both of them let out an involuntary sigh of relief.

"Step aside for a moment, please," ordered Terry. Michael nodded affirmatively and stepped outside the cubicle for Terry to dig in. He opened up a drawer of one of the desks and took out a bright orange zip pack with a red cross on it. It was the med pack. "Okay, get back in position." Michael traded places with Terry before Terry took back off down the hallway to Lyle's cubicle.

There was more blood now around Lyle's side, but Terry could tell already that an artery wasn't hit.

"The plate stopped one," said Lyle as he undid his vest for Terry to operate. "I didn't feel a bullet, so I think this one here went clean through."

"Either way, I'm going to patch you up. We'll get medical attention for you and Singh once we take down this asshole." Terry ripped Lyle's bloody undershirt.

"Rana got hurt?" asked Lyle. Terry nodded his head affirmatively. He got gauze out of the bag and unwrapped some.

"He got stabbed in the shoulder. But he'll be alright. You're more banged up than he is." Lyle watched Terry compress the wound and start to bandage it up.

"No rubbing alcohol or peroxide?"

"Nope. It can damage the tissue."

"You learned that in the Army?"

"Air Force," corrected Terry. "But yeah, treating bullet

wounds isn't the same as falling off your bike." Lyle nodded his head. He looked straight forward, keeping his ears peeled for any gunshots to come from the other side of the floor. Terry finished applying the gauze. He zipped up the medical kit, dropped it in their current cubicle, and swung his assault rifle back around front.

"Yemi," said Terry into the radio. "Lyle's secured. We'll flank him from the opposite side. Nick, we're coming to you now." Lyle loaded a fresh magazine into his Glock 22. Once Terry saw him upright and ready to move, he led them from the cubicle and through the elevator lobby. The veteran then formed a unit with him, Lyle, Nick, and Jason to clear the cubicles that lay on the northwest end of the floor.

"Go!" ordered Yemi. All three gun muzzles spun the corner of the northeast side of the sixth floor. Nothing was in sight other than rows of beige dividers formed into workspaces with an office plant near the center of the cubicles. Yemi, Jasper, and Victor then formed a three-man chain to proceed down the narrow path at the edge of the quadrant.

Their eyes scanned each row they approached as they tactically kept moving to reach the other side. They were not going to get caught like in the lobby, and each member knew they were dealing with a tier above the kamikaze gangsters they engaged with on the first floor. As outgunned as they were with the Rold's crew, fighting a man who effectively used the element of disguise and distraction in an environment they had spent several weeks running drills in demonstrated that their opposition had extensive guerrilla warfare knowledge. All the studying and experience in fourth-generation war had prepared Yemi for the situation, but the creativity of his adversary gave him flashbacks to dealing with the militants back in the Delta. If Peter Ikwe was a free man, he would be one of the primary architects in Bazaar-related hits, figured Yemi. His team's delayed reaction to the ambush earlier reminded Yemi of the stories from the security forces who had to respond to the bombings of the oil facilities and the hostage situations where they found themselves outmaneuvered by men from the local tribes on old fishing boats.

They continued to move through the north side of the floor. As they got halfway through the cubicle section, Yemi remembered there was a second bathroom near the center of the workspaces. Within a few minutes, Terry's half of the squad turned the corner, and the two sides spotted each other. They cleared the last remaining rows and realized the last spot to check was, indeed, the two restrooms across from each other on their current side of the floor. Yemi hand signaled for them to stay split, and each group stacked up outside of each lavatory. Yemi's half would take the Men's, while Terry's would clear the Women's. Lyle and Victor prepared their individual pepper spray bombs. On the count of three, Yemi and Terry kicked open their respective doors as the pepper bomb was thrown in.

Yemi, Jasper, and Victor burst into the Men's room with their guns pointed forward, scouring every corner of the tiles. They maneuvered around the spraying canister, avoiding the burning mist. Yemi observed that no feet were visible beneath the stalls, but they still posted up at each edge before checking because Yemi knew the assailant could be standing on top of the toilet waiting to catch them off guard yet again. Within a minute, it became evident that no one was in the restroom. And since no shots or commotion had been heard from the other bathroom, it seemed like that was the case with Terry's crew as well.

"Sir!" called Terry from the other restroom. "Come see this!" Yemi and the other two filed out to see what Terry was referring to.

Once they arrived in the Women's restroom, the other three field agents, plus Jason, were gathered around an opened air duct.

"He can fit in there?" asked Nick.

"Doesn't matter," said Yemi. "We need to get to Ellis. Now!" The seven-man squad exited the bathroom and began their trek back to the south end. The movies usually depict villains or spies crawling through ventilation shafts to sneak past enemies, but Yemi figured that, in reality, the ducts were too small, made too much noise, and had far too many sharp edges to make it a viable option for a path to pull off an assassination. The individual they were going up against had a clear determination to ensure they profit off of their prediction, not only based on their willingness to withstand the conditions of a building's dirty ventilation system but also the fact that they actually knew the ins and outs of ALAMUT's infrastructure.

When they got near the elevator lobby, the team marched past a vent cover lying on the floor that clearly wasn't there before the original descent into the north side. At that point, they knew that they not only needed to reach the Congressman as soon as possible, but the would-be assassin could pop out from any cubicle at any given moment. The moment they got past the elevators and were about fifty feet from turning the corner to head to Desmond's office, they heard three shots.

"Terry, Nick, Lyle. Cut through the elevators and flank them from the other side. Jason, hold here," ordered Yemi. "Go, go, go!" The squad split up. Once he arrived at the edge of the corner, Yemi whipped out his own pepper spray bomb, tore the top off, and tossed it down the south side hall. Victor was the first around the corner with his assault rifle aimed forward.

Yemi and Jasper spun around the corner. The top half of Michael's body was sticking out from a cubicle strewn across the floor. Right at the end was Desmond's office, and the reinforced door was still closed. Carefully checking each row, the three continued their pursuit, being extra careful as they approached the body of the deceased Raptor guard.

Suddenly, a loud shotgun BLASTED through a divider toward the three. Yemi saw that their opposition just missed Victor. Immediately, all three of the EPT members returned fire in the direction of the destroyed cubicle, still unable to see their adversary's exact location. The gunman dipped down in the opposite direction of the row while Yemi and his side held their position. Yemi heard him pump his Remington near the outside wall of Ellis' square office while they tried to hit him.

BOOM! A chunk of the wall scattered across the office. Yemi heard the shotgun cock again, and another loud bang made the hole in the office even bigger. Only a few more shots and the gunman would have created an opening that could disintegrate Desmond Ellis' skull.

"He's penetrating the office!" yelled out Yemi. "Push in!" Yemi saw the damaged wall of Desmond's office but didn't yet have a visual of the assassin. He fired four shots to the left of it, careful not to fire into the office and hoping one of them hit the gunman who was only a few feet from ending the entire future of Raptor, not to mention the political stability of the state of Maryland. The gunman turned around a cubicle corner and faced off with Yemi, who was at the end. Yemi didn't recognize him as any staff member in the building, but he did take notice of his significant age difference from their dead Mara Salvatrucha members in the lobby. Yemi quickly ducked into a cubicle, and the two exchanged gunfire. Jasper and Victor took positions behind Yemi's cubicle and added to the barrage of firepower shooting toward the graying gunman.

"Think I caught a piece of him!" yelled Victor. Victor's optimism was answered with gunfire from their adversary. He had switched from the shotgun to a .38 revolver.

"Don't let him get inside the office!" commanded Yemi to his entire team. Terry and Lyle pressed against the front of

Desmond's office. They knew the assailant was around the corner at the end of the pathway between the cubicles and Ellis, so they knew that not only was there danger around the edge, but they wouldn't be able to evacuate the Congressman until they could push the gunman several rows away or they ended his existence altogether.

"Anybody got any pepper bombs left?" asked Terry to his team.

"I do," answered Nick. BOOM! A third shotgun blasted into the wall. The man had switched back to the boomstick, and the squad had to act immediately.

"Throw it! Quick!" Nick made his way in front of Terry and got his pepper spray bomb canister ready.

"Nade out!" warned Terry to Yemi and the rest on the other side of the cubicle rows. Nick tossed the fog grenade down the narrow floor path. It nailed their opposition. He was disoriented enough to retreat back behind the last cubicle divider. Terry spun around the corner, pointing his rifle forward.

"Ellis is out of striking distance now, sir!" yelled Terry to his detail leader a couple rows over.

"Blackwell, stay in your position," responded Yemi. "Rice and Evans, get the congressman out of here. We'll keep this mother fucker pinned down." Yemi's strict Christian parents raised him to limit his cursing, but certain nuisances would bring the Navy sailor out of him, even though he never served in the Naval forces in America or even Nigeria, for that matter.

Lyle used a FOB on his keychain to unlock the office door. He and Nick quickly moved in. Lyle kept his gun raised toward the blasted holes in the wall.

"Follow me, congressman," Yemi heard Nick say when he found Desmond behind the desk. "Quickly." Representative Ellis didn't waste any time and lept up to get behind Nick. They started to backpedal toward the door —

BOOM! The gunman managed to hit the wall even from his withdrawn position behind the cubicle divider. Both Lyle and Terry unloaded in his direction. The blast froze both Nick and Desmond, who crouched down upon the impact.

"Get him the fuck outta here!" Lyle snapped Nick out of his statue, and he continued to lead Ellis out of the office. They headed in the opposite direction of Yemi's side and rushed toward the elevator lobby.

When Ellis was safe, Yemi knew they finally had time on their hands.

"Karen," said Yemi into his radio. "How long ago were the cops notified?"

"They should be there any minute," she responded.

Yemi was sure their adversary had been shot a number of times by that point. Yemi saw the man toss the shotgun in between the cubicles, but he knew the man most likely still had a number of weapons at his disposal.

From outside the building, the team could hear sirens approaching their location. Montgomery County Police were finally arriving after a thirty minute gun battle.

"You hear that?" rhetorically asked Yemi to the man they've been chasing all this time. "It's over. You still have a chance to live a life. But if you don't put don't down your weapons, it all ends here. I don't care either way, but the choice is yours." No answer. The gunman stayed in his position. Yemi wondered if the man had limited English like the first people they engaged with. He nodded for Victor to talk.

"The police are pulling up now, tough guy," declared Victor in Spanish. "This is your last opportunity to surrender peacefully." Yemi wondered if this guy was going to go the suicide-by-rent-a-cop route.

The man announced several statements in Spanish in response as the team stayed ready with their armaments. Victor followed up with a question to him in Spanish, and the man seemed to respond positively.

"He said if it means anything, he's not a gangster. Before the men he killed today, he never killed anyone who did no harm onto others. In the past, he only fought for justice." With all the chaos that had elapsed, the conversation had gotten strangely cordial. Victor repeated the gunman's comments in English to Yemi and Jasper. Terry and Lyle could hear him as well.

"Just now, I realized this makes me no better than the bastards under Monterrosa or those tatted-up devils downstairs," the man said to Victor in Spanish.

"I know that feeling, brother," said Victor. "Most men will never know what it means to risk their life for a cause instead of a bounty. What already happened is now in God's hands, but I sense a man with a good heart in you. Someone like that can always be reformed, no matter where they end up."

"What most men know is not of concern to me," the gunman responded in his home country's language. "I know that at this point, I'm dying, having lived a contradiction. But if hell is my destiny, then I will only take as many dark souls with me as I can." Suddenly, the gunman spun around, firing off dual-wielded pistols toward the Executive Protection Team. He was immediately riddled with bullets by Yemi, Victor, and Jasper. The impact sent his body backward, and he crashed through the window, the bullets also further sharding the glass. He fell over the sill.

"Hold fire!" demanded Yemi. The five squad members proceeded to the end of the cubicle row. Yemi and Victor looked out the window and toward the ground as Rockville and Montgomery County Police swarmed the driveway. Staring back at them six stories below was a deceased man who died with a smirk of internal satisfaction on his face as he lay at peace on the concrete.

CHAPTER 18

Two major assassination attempts in the same year, in the same state. One of them was successful. The news fed the notoriety of the Bazaar's influence, and its increasing popularity skyrocketed the value of the names on the market. Before answering any media-related questions regarding the incident at the ALAMUT building, Chris Towers apparently wanted to meet with the Uzunma siblings. Yemi never settled to handing off any intel to the CFTF, but the Joint Terrorism Task Force wanted answers on how a gang that the FBI had been investigating for years had a bid out for the death of Representative Ellis, and it took a private startup from PG County to stop it from happening.

Despite MS-13's involvement, all Bazaar-related crimes were still primarily handled by Towers' team within the Secret Service. Yemi and Karen were seated on a bench inside the headquarters on H Street. They had gone up the escalator and had been waiting outside the Cyber Fraud Task Force suites for ten minutes.

"What are we going to say to him?" asked Karen. Yemi sighed.

"At this point, I'm not sure what they expect out of us. That Hitter app or whatever is available to anyone with a Tor browser, so all the intel is open knowledge."

"Maybe it's good news?" suggested his sister.

"We don't have a missing relative, so I'm not sure how a federal law enforcement agency asking to talk is anything positive." Karen sighed.

"I'm just trying to find a bright side here, Yemi. Sheesh."

"You know me. I don't even like my cornflakes

sugarcoated."

"I can't with you," she chuckled. Agent Towers arrived by their bench, joined by Rodriguez and another agent in a suit. Towers shook their hands and opened the door to an empty conference room. The body language seemed to hint at good vibes, but Yemi knew veteran investigators had great poker faces.

"Let's head in."

The room was nothing like the vast executive chair board rooms that made up the Titus HQ down in Tysons Corner. The room was a round table with about five folding chairs, a plain white wall, and nothing else for decorations. It seemed better fit for an interrogation than any kind place to court a partnership. Yemi and Karen sat down across from the federal agents. Towers laid down a manila folder and took out some printouts related to Desmond Ellis, including his Bazaar profile.

"So, let's start off with... You," said Chris as he shuffled the papers and spread them out in an order that put the Ellis bid page first. "I want to hear your side of the incident. What happened, what went wrong, what was the plan, etc."

"What went wrong?" repeated Yemi. "Our mission was a success. Ellis is back working on the hill today, completely safe."

"Three guards killed, multiple injuries, hundreds of thousands of dollars in structural damage... Looks like a pyrrhic victory if I ever saw one."

"We were up against members of the most notorious street gang in the country armed with assault rifles. A gang that I thought your people were keeping track of," chimed in Karen. Although she was not quite as hostile to collaborating with the Feds as her brother, she was always going to back up her sibling. Especially when she felt he was right.

"MS-13 is FBI's territory, not ours," stated Chris for the record. "But the man who you all shot out the window, Merlin Erazo. There's no evidence suggesting he had any gang ties."

Yemi shrugged his shoulder.

"We're an executive protection firm, Mr. Towers. Not a criminal investigation unit."

"But this is why we need Raptor to share with us your information. If the Joint Terrorism Task Force knows Ellis' location ahead of time, we can share our resources to not only ensure that your client remains safe but that we can continue to track any pattern with these attacks connected to the Bazaar. The pressure is on now. Your own white paper put out by Titus, Yemi, was right. A lot of the capital being funneled into Bazaar bids is still tied to The Anat Network. The U.S. government is not going to sit back and let the nation's capital turn into a terrorist-created battleground between hired guns on either side of the law."

"Then do what you need to do and contact your local lawmaker or whatever," responded an annoyed Yemi. "I already told you on I-95 in October that we can only guarantee our client's safety if we keep our intel to ourselves. Now, are we here to discuss anything else?" Towers let out a long breath and exchanged a glance with Yemi. Yemi wanted to make it clear that Raptor wasn't like Titus or RexCorp. The cash-strapped startup from PG County wasn't looking to join in as a symbiosis of a public-private partnership, the type of relationship that had made the Red Line of the Metrorail the artery of the Beltway's economic infrastructure.

"Fair enough," said Chris. "Well, I also want to inform you that Chiedu Attah is asking that the Secret Service back down from being in charge of his security. Instead, apparently, he specifically requested Raptor to be back under contract."

"I'm confused." Karen sat up straight. "Why are we hearing this from you? I haven't heard anything from Attah's office."

"Because he made the decision this morning. Says you all saved his life. Therefore, he's only entrusting your brother to lead his security detail on a day that needs it." Karen and Yemi looked at each other. Turned out Karen was right. There was good news from the meeting. Just not what they expected. Towers continued. "Seems like the most popular prediction for him is now around December, right? December 11th?"

Yemi responded with an "I dunno" shrug. Of course, he knew. And he was sure Towers knew that he knew. Yemi also knew that Towers probably only brought it up to just test Yemi for a last-minute chance of some type of cooperation. The EPT squad commander wasn't falling for it.

"Alright," said Towers. "I guess that's all I need from you two. We'll be in contact." Yemi and Karen nodded to the person who invited them to come in that day despite the fact it didn't seem like they were welcome anymore. Besides Towers' crew, though, the staff was extra polite and friendly, contrary to the reputation of Social Security, the other government agency with 'SS' abbreviations in its title. They left Secret Service HQ and headed out onto the streets of downtown D.C. around the Chinatown area.

"Want to get some lunch?" asked Karen. "I could go for some dim sum."

"Where? Here?!" responded Yemi. "You and I both know DC's Chinatown is in name only. Gotta take the red line to Rockville if you want some decent Chinese."

"I know you hate Vash right now, but that's something he would say." Yemi needed a moment to shake his head.

"Hate's a strong word. I just need some answers."

"He promises to never work with William Kim again," said Karen. "That is if you ever want to do another contract with ALAMUT again."

"I'm surprised you're even asking me that question." They continued to walk, but Yemi was a bit concerned with what seemed to be Karen's lack of concern. "Karen, this Merlin dude snuck five weapons and ammunition in cornmeal. Imagine if he chose poison as his method? Ellis would be buried with everyone else we lost that night. I probably wouldn't even be having this conversation with you right now."

"But Yemi, right there, you're not giving Vash any credit. We were there for all the toxicology tests of everything that was prepared that day. I'm not expecting you to agree with me, especially right now, but I don't think we should throw away our partnership with Vash."

"Don't tell me this is another one of your crushes being involved in the decision-making process." Karen stopped in their walk. With the silence and halt of their movement, Yemi knew he may have overstepped with the teasing of his little sister. "Karen—"

"You know what? You go ahead to Gallery Place. I'll walk to Metro Center."

"C'mon Karen—"

"Or any of the other stops in walking distance where I don't have to wait next to an ungrateful asshole." Karen stormed off in the opposite direction down the street. Yemi sighed and rubbed his forehead. He prided himself on usually being the one in control of offhand comments and things outside of getting the task done. But he was heading to the office alone, having just pissed off the woman who was primarily charged with handling all their income. Although insurance rates were about to go up after the deaths of the three patrol guards, at least he could meditate on the fact that their next client was already secured.

———

The New Patriots crew never bothered finding another fishing spot. It had been kept a secret among Doug, Bobby Z, and a few fellow Fort Hill alumni. Aaron was the first person outside of the Cumberland metro area introduced to the location hidden from Appalachian voyagers and other tourists from out of town.

Scott Wilkins became the latest addition to be introduced to the exclusive site along the Savage River. Most of the fishing had been done for the day, and three of them sat in fold-out chairs while Doug handled the grill. He also had a portable fry cooker too.

"Alright, who wants trout, who wants bluegill, and who wants perch? Somebody might have to take the catfish, though."

"Shoot, I'll take the cat as long as it's fried," said Bobby. "Unless any of y'all want at it."

"Hell no," responded Scottie as he took a sip of his Busch Light. Aaron saw Bobby's eyebrows raise like he was caught a little off guard by the reaction.

"Oh, you're one of those people," stated Bobby before he took a sip of his own beer.

"What do you mean?" asked Scottie.

"Don't start any shit, Bobby," said Doug while he breaded the catfish. Aaron knew Doug couldn't deal with another situation like the bar that one night.

"I didn't even say anything yet!" a defiant Bobby joked. "I just want to know why white people up here don't like catfish. C'mon Doug, every summer we'd hit up Choptank, we'd come back with two or three twenty-inch cats just from folks giving 'em away. Aaron, you know what I'm talking about, right?" Aaron was a bit amused at the topic of conversation, but he just shrugged his shoulders.

"I didn't really start fishing for real until I started hanging with y'all, so I have no idea."

"Race got nothing to do with it," followed up a visibly annoyed Scottie. "It's a bottom feeder. I don't eat it for health reasons, if anything."

"It actually has some of the lowest mercury levels of any fish." Bobby, Scottie, and even Doug, for that matter, didn't expect Aaron to cite that kind of data. "Excellent source of protein and many vitamins. Matter of fact, Bobby, you want to split that?"

"That's what I'm talking about!" laughed Bobby as he chugged his beer.

"Whatever," stated Scottie as Aaron could feel him staring at his head with slight disdain. He then heard Scottie let out a sigh before he continued. "So, are you all ready to talk business or what?"

"Chiedu Attah has moved pretty high up," said Doug as he placed the battered filets in the fryer. "And he's still somewhat local, so that's my nomination."

"Ready for round two, Mr. Trigger man?" asked Bobby Z toward Aaron. It was almost as if their fistfight was a segue into a blossoming friendship at that point.

"In a way, it's kind of round three," Aaron responded as he took a sip from his Gatorade. He may have picked up a weed habit, but he wasn't going to pick up their consistent intake of alcohol.

"Oh, that's right," Bobby said. "You're really about to cut down the whole family tree, huh?" That was exactly the sentiment Aaron had shared with Qasim in the car en route to the attack on Veterans Plaza. Aaron reminisced for a few moments.

"Yeah, guess that's what it's looking like, isn't it?" There were days that Aaron's conscience ate a bit at him for the pain he had caused the Attah family, but the feelings were only temporary surges. Aaron didn't consider himself a sociopath, but he had learned to realize those were leftover sentiments he picked up from his father's moral compass before the patriarch of the family couldn't apply his ethics to his own decisions regarding his life. Following the rules seemed to only put him on ADHD medication while he grew into an able-bodied adult male who couldn't put food on the table for his mentally ill mother, dealing with losing her husband in his battle against depression. Chiedu made his choice to betray his constituents a long time ago. Aaron figured all he was doing was carrying out the democratic process, albeit a violent version, at the end of the day.

"Aaron, didn't you say you needed my people to undergo some training or something?" Aaron could sense in Scottie's voice that he took the catfish debate a little personally. "Because I'm just a little confused about how a group of experienced hunters and military veterans need pointers from some kids with no formal firearm training to speak of." Doug looked up from his cooking duties. He exchanged looks with Bobby Z and Aaron, all knowing that this educated redneck was pushing the line of disrespect.

"Explain to me how Hagerstown was pulled off with no formal training, Scottie," said Doug before Bobby could launch a verbal assault to throw the whole partnership out the window. Scottie straightened himself up. Aaron sensed Scottie realized he might need to re-evaluate his tone and let go of the minor grievance over his taste in seafood.

"I've always been impressed with the Frost hit. You know that. That's the whole reason we're having this meeting in the first place. I'm just saying you gotta look at it from my perspective. I have to convince a bunch of dudes who have been ready to bring the war for freedom home for years. And they've been preparing for it a long time as well." Scottie took a sip out of his brew. "So they might raise an eyebrow when they show up having to take orders from some eighteen-year-old—" Before Scottie finished his sentence, Aaron could tell Scottie was being careful about the word he chose so he could stick to his own rule of avoiding race in the conversation. "—Kid."

"I turned nineteen last month," corrected Aaron politely.

"Oh. Well, happy birthday." A couple of beats as Scottie took another sip. "But yeah, when we go public with the New Patriots movement—"

"Whoa, whoa. Hold up," beckoned Doug. Now, his focus

was totally off cooking the fish. "The whole New Patriots thing is a front, Scott. The whole point of that moniker is to take attention away from us, not claim responsibility."

"Yeah, what the fuck you talking about, Scottie?" aggressively asked Bobby. Aaron wondered if even Bobby was starting to second guess bringing this guy on board.

"Guys." Scottie cleared his throat. "I know you all like using our rhetoric to put up a nice show for the media while y'all cash out, but there are people in this country who actually believe in something. People who have actually suffered from tyranny. Hard-working Americans losing their businesses to bullshit audits, dairy farms getting raided for raw milk, and don't even get me started on the neo-Marxist bullshit they're forcing on our kids' public school education."

"Scottie." Doug sighed. "I get that you're passionate about your movement. But I thought we made it pretty clear from the get-go that we were just looking for bodies to back us up. Right now, it's just Bobby, Aaron, and I, so you know as well as I do that we could still use your help. But I'm sorry, we didn't create the New Patriots moniker as a flag to fight under."

"Just a little fucking trojan horse, huh? Nice little alternative to pushing meth to our families."

"Alright," Bobby Z said. "Now you're tripping, Scottie." The head-shaven, catfish-loving member of their crew put his beer down and started to rise from his chair.

"Bobby." Doug was back to trying to stop Bobby Z from getting physical. It was starting to be a repeat of the bar, but Scott calmly got up and raised his hand to halt Bobby as if to make peace.

"It's alright. No need for this to go any further. You have my number if you all want to re-address this. If I don't hear anything by next week, we'll go our separate ways." Scottie finished his beer and tossed it into a trash bag near the grill.

"Enjoy your meal, everyone." Scottie walked off from the group. There was a brief moment of awkward silence between the three. They were caught between the necessity for more hands to pull off a hit against heavily armed opposition and their own strategy for anonymity.

"I say 'fuck 'em,'" said Bobby, reversing his position from the bar. "Maybe you were right the whole time, Doug."

"I'm trying to figure out how he has any ideological reason to kill Attah," said Doug as he returned to focus on the fish fry. He started to make plates for his two comrades. "Chiedu Attah barely has anything to do with American politics. Especially not the stuff Scottie was talking about. Isn't it just Nigerian rebels that want him dead?"

"It's strategic for Scott, not ideology," said Aaron. "If he avoids arrest while claiming to be a spokesman for the New Patriots, he'll attract the attention of many global investors who'll like a face to a group that's reliable to carry out whatever fits the investor's agenda."

"Attention usually means money," agreed Bobby. "Across the board, whether we're talking the Bazaar, social media, entertainment, you name it."

"That's true," said Doug as he slapped some potato rolls on the plates and doused each dish with some potato salad. He handed meals over to Bobby Z and Aaron. "But is attention what we want? Need I remind y'all that if we fuck up once, that's it. This whole thing is over, not to mention whatever future we got planned for ourselves."

"Man, what?" asked a defiant Bobby as he dug into his fried bottom feeder. "What the hell is my life without this shit? They closed all the factories here, and what the fuck am I gonna do with a college degree anyways? Be another sucka putting in sixty hours a week to give all the money I make to corporate parasites?" Bobby Z bit and swallowed. It seemed to Aaron to be a subject he had contemplated deeply. "Keeping it real, that's why I say it's always worth the risk. We're the first mother fuckers on this planet to successfully pull off a hit from the Bazaar. That alone puts us in the history books. All the cornballs from our high school going off to be lawyers, doctors, doorknob technicians, whatever. None of them leaving the legacy we are on this world." Aaron saw Doug couldn't help but smile as he took a seat where Scottie was and started to work on his own meal.

"Damn, Bobby, listen to you being all inspirational," he said in between bites. "Never thought of it that way."

"I mean, am I wrong? Even look at Ethan's bitch ass. I bet twenty-five years from now, when he's fat sitting around the house, and his grandkids want to hear a story from the old days, what's he gonna tell them? Was he an all-star athlete? No. Some Boy Scout stories? Stop it. The peak of his life was with us, and that's facts."

"I feel you," Doug said as he tried out the potato salad. "Potato salad is kind of mid, not going to lie."

"This is the third time in a row you got the store brand," Bobby Z said, agreeing with Doug as he took a bite of the yellow-white slop. "We not poor anymore, but you forget where we live. Save-A-Lot ain't Wegmans." Doug laughed as he shook his head.

"But I can't get mad at Ethan for looking out for his family. I mean, I'd probably do the same thing if I got a girl pregnant."

"Wait, you want kids?" Bobby asked as Aaron watched him put the catfish into the roll to make a mini-fried fish sandwich.

"I don't know yet," responded Doug. "Haven't even checked any dating sites in six months."

"That's what I'm talking about," said Bobby Z. "No porn?"

"Nope. Going straight monk, bro."

"No hand banging either, right?" inquired Bobby. To that question, Doug paused.

"Well..." They all laughed at Doug's admission. Bobby Z

got back on the soap box.

"It's all about legacy, my man. Sometimes men get too caught up in the pussy that it distracts us from our true purpose in life. There's a reason Isaac Newton never got married, feel me?"

"Look at you educating me on history for once," laughed Doug. "You hear this, Aaron? I think you might have knocked some sense into him. You did a better job in a few minutes than thirteen years of Allegany public schools."

"Man, fuck you." Bobby Z hissed his teeth, but Aaron could tell he knew it was all jokes. "What about you, Aaron? You gonna settle down eventually?"

"Never crossed my mind," said Aaron as he was equally focused on his meal.

"No kids? No girl? Nothing?" pressed Bobby.

"I think about my next assignment. Anything beyond that is pure speculation." Aaron methodically ate his trout, never looking up as he talked. "At the first Attah hit, we stopped at a gas station for lunch before we arrived in Silver Spring. Everybody shared their dreams about what they were going to do after we got paid. Starting businesses, partying, giving back to their families, and whatnot. All of them are now either dead or in prison. And none of us got paid." The crew ate in dead silence for several moments. Aaron gave their lighthearted conversation about the future a brutal reality check. Doug spoke up eventually.

"We'll just kick back and chill today. And then, we'll make a decision about Scottie by Friday. Sound good?" The rest of them nodded their heads.

CHAPTER 19

Abdallah imagined the White House Press Briefing Room to be much larger than it was. The wide-angle lens capturing the reporters on the Live Feed always made it seem like it was as big as a committee hearing room on Capitol Hill. Instead, it felt more like a tightly packed Sunday service at a small church. Kalfat recognized the people he shared his bench with from their social media accounts. The balding Caucasian man built like the fat Gargoyle from the 90s Disney cartoon at the end of the row closest to the hearing room's entrance was the Washington, D.C. correspondent for the right-leaning New York Tribune, Kip Diggs. As the years went by, Abdallah noticed the Tribune seemed to care less about whatever political slant its readers were and had morphed into something barely a tier above a tabloid that went after anything from flash mob attacks on Asian or White citizens to having Diggs focus solely on exposing the potential pedophile rings tied to the power elite. At the other end of the bench was an elegant, well-groomed, slightly stout African-American woman, Jessica Reynolds, who had been covering the White House for over two decades. She had been recently awarded for being the longest-serving Black correspondent in White House history and made waves for leaving one of the big three cable news channels for an online startup owned by her friend, the Black billionaire Eric McKenzie. She caught a glimpse of Abdallah, and the two traded cordial smiles, Abdallah was a bit star-struck while he was sure Reynolds was just happy to see another dark-skinned journo before the podium.

Finally, White House Press Secretary Dawnn Sampson approached the microphone before the blue backdrop and

American flag. Sampson was a Guyanese American who ascended in DC's politics while coming from nearby Bladensburg, Maryland. Many believed being a lesbian and an immigrant would make her a target of Diggs, but there were so many things the Tribune's fanbase found problematic with the current administration that Abdallah figured he had plenty of other topics to bring up.

"Good afternoon, everybody." Nobody seemed to answer back. "Come on, guys," Sampson playfully joked with the press corps. The mood swung in the cheerful direction as most of the staff reporters, especially Jessica, returned the greeting. "That's better. Give a girl some love is all I'm saying," she laughed, and half the room chuckled along with her. "Some news. The president had a meeting this morning with Representative Ellis and his family. The president is eternally grateful that the Congressman is alive and healthy. He is proud to have supported Congressman Ellis' important legislative work in regulating the disturbing trend of home-manufactured plastic firearms that can escape metal detectors and contribute to the disturbing uptick in gun violence across our communities. The president wants to make it clear that the safety of the American public, along with its elected servants, is of the utmost priority, and he will be meeting with the heads of all major federal law enforcement agencies this week until there is a set plan of action. With that said, Jessica, how are you? It's been a while."

"Indeed it has been, madam secretary. I was on P-T-O for several days for my daughter's wedding," Ms. Reynolds responded back.

"Congratulations to her."

"Thank you, Dawnn. My question is on the topic of your introduction. Representative Ellis went on record to state that he will begin drafting legislation targeting websites on the internet similar to the one that was tied to his assassination attempt last week that was only twenty miles from here. Some civil liberties activists have expressed this bill could potentially violate freedom of expression and assembly rights. Does the president plan on signing this bill if it meets his criteria, or does he share some of the same concerns as its critics?"

"Like I said," started Dawn. "Right now, in regards to this matter, the president's primary concern is protecting the public from the pattern of violence we've seen connected to certain prediction markets. He is just talking with federal law enforcement, and he has no comment yet on Ellis' next potential bill." Sampson looked around the room.

"How were any of these MS-13 gang members allowed across our border?!" yelled a disruptive Diggs. Sampson ignored him as she picked on a correspondent in the front row.

"Thank you, Madam—"

"WHY IS THE WHITE HOUSE BEING QUIET ABOUT THEIR IMMIGRATION STATUS?! What does the president have to hide?"

"Sir!" quipped Dawnn. "We are going to carry out this briefing in a civilized manner as we usually do. Please wait until you are called upon. Thank you." Abdallah watched Diggs back down as the correspondent in the front continued with her question about a separate topic. Abdallah looked to his left and again made eye contact with Jessica. She rolled her eyes, giving Abdallah a hint that Diggs was a regular at interrupting the press briefings.

"...Let's see here," said Dawnn, looking for a new journalist to call upon. Abdallah kept his hand raised. It was hard for him to not act like a first-grader needing permission to go pee. She pointed in his direction. "Go ahead, you in the fourth row."

"Thank you, madam secretary. Abdallah Kalfat with Al Noor America. I'd like to circle back to the attack on Representative Ellis. With the shootout in Rockville, the Ryan Frost assassination, the attempt on former Ambassador Chiedu Attah last October, and the shooting of his son, Adamu, this makes four total incidents tied to the Bazaar, the prediction market you referred to. All in the span of a year. I understand the president is meeting with federal law enforcement officials to address what can be done to prevent another attack, but I wanted to highlight how the assaults were carried out by groups with totally different backgrounds. The group claiming to have killed Ryan Frost called themselves The New Patriots, while the recent incident was carried out by a local chapter of an international street gang with no political affiliation. Some experts have called such a phenomenon 'open source warfare' given how diverse the assailants have been. Is the White House able to provide any information yet from these meetings with federal law enforcement that address this terminology?" Dawnn cleared her throat. Abdallah knew she was always prepared for tough questions, but the young journo seemed to have brought the heat today.

"I will have to forward any questions on that matter to the Department of Justice, but the president will have a statement by the end of the week after his talks have concluded. Thank you, next question please..." Abdallah jotted down in his notepad to follow up with the Department of Justice. He caught Jessica glancing over in his direction. She nodded up and down like she was impressed with his preparation. Within forty-five minutes, Dawnn answered the final questions and exited from the podium.

Abdallah left the West Wing and headed down the path toward Lafayette Square. Before he got to the gate, he heard the voice of one of his icons calling after him.

"Abdallah!" Jessica said, walking a bit briskly as if she was eager to talk to him. "Did I get your name right?"

"Yup. And, Uhm, of course, I know who you are, the honorable Jessica Reynolds."

"Stop it, child," she chuckled at the formality even though

her slight blush showed she appreciated the young ones in her field who showered her with respect. Abdallah figured most were just looking to take her spot. "Great question in there. Too bad she wasn't prepared."

"Ah, I probably should have known better and just waited for someone from the D-O-J or Homeland Security to appear later this week."

"Don't ignore your instinct. It's what got you in that room in the first place, and if I ignored mine, I wouldn't be here talking to you today."

"Appreciate that, Miss Reynolds."

"Please, just Jessica." They shook hands. "You're at Al Noor?"

"Yes, ma'am."

"How long have you been there."

"About a year and a half. Today was my first time at the White House. Guess I made an impression, huh?"

"The fact that you even got called on on your first day is a sign, young brother." Of the esteem and reputation she had prior to their meeting, Abdallah felt like he was talking to one of the mothers of his college frat brothers. "But listen, I don't know what your contract is looking like over there, but over at The Boukan, we're on the lookout for gifted young reporters like yourself." She handed him her card.

"Wow, Jessica. I know I'm with Al Noor right now, but it'd be hard to turn down an opportunity to work alongside a legend like yourself."

"I swear if you continue like that, I might just have to pay your severance with Al Noor with my own salary." The two shared a laugh. "But no, don't rush. Take your time and check out our site. I'm texting Eric McKenzie right now to keep an eye out for you."

"Thank you so much, Jessica. It's really an honor."

"The honor is all mine. Get home safe now." The two parted ways once they got past the North side gate. Abdallah looked down at the business card. He was familiar with The Boukan. It focused primarily on issues relating to the African-American community, and Abdallah preferred more of an international direction for his career, but two years prior, he was on the verge of eviction while scraping pennies from whatever he could get from freelancing and whatever temp job he had at the time. And as long as the ad revenue kept rolling in from the Hitter site, he had a safety net for whatever path he chose.

───────

IN LOVING MEMORY OF JOSEPH HILLSBORO, 2000 - 2025. Yemi took a sip of white grape juice in the plastic wine glass as he stared at the funeral poster board. It was the third and final memorial service the Uzunmas attended for their employees who were killed in the assassination attempt on Desmond Ellis. Jasper had joined them in the previous two, but Rana was the only other person on the Raptor payroll to show up at the church in Forestville, MD. The insurance policy was covering all the costs associated with the memorial services, but Yemi dipped into the operating budget for a few gifts they could afford while still being in the green profit-wise. Joseph left behind a fiance, Toni, and his five-year-old son, Derrick. After letting space heal their previous heated argument in downtown D.C., Yemi and Karen presented Derrick with a year-long membership to an after-school program at the Sugar Ray Leonard Boxing Center in Palmer Park. Rana had informed the Uzunma siblings that Michael was a huge fan of the sport, having been a former champion on the Golden Gloves circuit, and was looking to get Derrick to lace up the gloves within a couple of years. The gift also provided Toni with a place she could have Derrick stay while she finished her shift as a paralegal.

While the previous two families kept their distance from

interacting with their loved ones' former employer at the other services, Toni seemed grateful to meet Karen and Yemi. Nothing could prevent the inevitable atmosphere of the sudden death of a life partner being in the air, and the concealer makeup on her face could only do so much to hide the recent sleepless nights. Yet she had warmly greeted the Uzunmas even before they presented her son with his new extracurricular option. Rana, in particular, gave her the longest hug. Yemi knew Rana had been over to Joseph's apartment several times over the course of their Raptor career.

"If there's anything else we can do for you, please just let us know," comforted Karen to Toni and her son.

"Thank you," she responded. "It's going to be hard, but I know the Lord is going to watch over us."

"Amen," said Rana. Yemi just nodded respectfully. The years of being forced by his father to cite Bible verses every dinner conversation, combined with observations of the behavior of many prosperous West African ministers, turned Yemi off from religion. But he understood almost everyone prayed when faced with uncertain times.

"He was so proud to work for you," Toni said to Karen and Yemi. "A month ago, he told me that it was his dream to get on the Executive Protection Team."

"Really?" Yemi would have never guessed. Joseph was no slouch at the job, but he seemed so laid back even compared to Victor's attitude. Yemi would have never considered Joseph until his display of bravery on the day he was killed.

"He would always brag to his friends that he worked at the firm that saved the ambassador on the news. After high school, he considered the military, but then Derrick happened, and he didn't want to leave his son like his father did his family." Rana waved to the young Derrick. Yemi could tell the young boy was still having difficulty with accepting that the man who would prepare his Cinnamon Toast Crunch in the morning and watch

Spongebob with him before he fell asleep was gone.

Looking at Toni and Derrick reminded Yemi about why he didn't want a family. He considered himself married to the Bazaar as the underground market's existence gave Yemi a sense of unique purpose to stand out among the combat analysts and strategic consultants he brushed shoulders with while at Titus. They all used their time in the military as a segway into a comfortable 8-hour workday that would allow them in their free time to spend their paycheck on their wife and whatever spawn came out of her. Nursery care, recreational soccer leagues, tuition for private education if the school district wasn't Fairfax County or Falls Church, Mercedes or BMWs once they hit 16, Ivy league or Little Ivy if their grades were good, SAT prep courses to get them into George Washington or Elon if their GPAs were low, and then shedding out enough cash for a studio apartment in whatever trendy urban neighborhood the next of kin chose to reside in. None of that appealed to Yemi, but he suspected such a lifestyle was a goal for Karen if she managed to find the right suitor from all her dating app matches.

"I have to talk to Joseph's mom," said Toni, a welcome interruption to Yemi's train of thought. "Please help yourself to a plate or any more drinks." Toni took Derrick by the hand and led her son over to the other end of the room, where a group of Michael's relatives had gathered. That left Yemi, Karen, and Rana standing around the poster board a bit awkwardly. Yemi checked his phone and wondered if it was the right time for them to exit.

"What does it take to get selected to join the Executive Protection Team?" asked Rana, approaching Yemi. Yemi finished up his white grape juice and basketball-shot the cup toward the trash bin closest to their position. It hit the rim and bounced off the floor, gaining the attention of some nearby attendees visibly judging Yemi for such a casual action during a serious affair. The fake wine glass landed near Karen, so she rolled her eyes and did her brother a favor by rebounding the plastic container and laying it up in the trash can.

"Why? Are you considering applying?" asked Yemi to one of his newest employees.

"Just wondering. Want to see what you look for in an agent."

"Well," started Yemi. "It helps to have an individual unique skill. Something that nobody else on the squad would have expertise in or just minimal knowledge about."

"Oh." Rana looked like he was reflecting for a moment. Yemi wondered what possible assets Rana could possess that could make him stand out. "Would getting a degree help my chances?" Yemi paused, reflecting on the fact that he himself did not have a degree.

"I guess it would depend on what you study and what we're looking for at the time. Hey Karen!" His sister walked over with a hint of an attitude from having to clean up after his missed shot earlier. "Tell Rana what we're looking for when it comes to E-P-T candidates."

"Well, we're not looking at anybody right now due to what our budget allows."

"Money aside. What stood out for you with the list that you sent me prior to my selection?"

"Honestly..." Karen took a swing at her own non-alcoholic beverage. "I just thought about what you would seek. Given that you're the team leader, you probably know the answer better than I do."

"She has a good point there," said Rana. Yemi laughed and sighed at the same time.

"What's your last name again, Rana?"

"Singh."

"Mr. Singh, how about we come back to this question in

a year or two? I'm not going to lie to you. Business is good, but we're still making sure this whole thing can stay above water." Yemi looked around at the funeral. He found Michael's family talking among each other. An older woman who must be his mother broke down along with Toni, and the two embraced.

"And with the least amount of casualties as possible."

———

"Damn, how much longer until we get there?" asked Bobby Z from the backseat of Doug's pickup truck. "Are we still in the same state? Like damn."

"Yes, Bobby, we are. Maryland is small, but it ain't Delaware," answered back Doug with eyes on I-495. "Like fifteen more minutes or so. Just chill, but don't light another jay, though."

"It's legal now, bro."

"I don't care. We're not coming into a meeting smelling like weed." Aaron couldn't help but be reminded of Rold's same hostility toward the plant around business matters as Bobby hissed his teeth and looked out the window toward the Southern Maryland landscape. Aaron had been doing the same most of the trip from the front passenger seat. Through his new profession, he had now been able to travel to every section of his home state. He remembered his mother looking at affordable housing options in Waldorf, Maryland, after his father's suicide. Aaron never came with her to the showings, and she told him there was no point in living in a mini-ghetto so far away from the opportunities D.C. had to offer. Aaron looked at the real estate opportunities outside of his window and had to question his mother's choice of location. It wasn't like she was working anyways. She rarely left the house for anything other than cheap liquor through all the years they'd lived together as just the two of them. The part of the state he was riding through seemed quieter and more spacious. Aaron had doubts that section 8 out here was as bad as back in Temple Hills.

They finally arrived at a modest single-story home that sat by a dock along the Western shore. Despite Doug's insistence that it was a formal business meeting, Scottie was in the front yard by the driveway with dirty torn jeans, sandals, his rail-thin arms sticking out of a white beater, and the same YWC hat on as before. Doug rolled down the window before they went further onto the gravel.

"Yeah, just park your Lincoln up ahead," Scottie said. "Few inside, but more are on the way."

"Cool," Doug said back. Doug steered his truck down the dirt path to the parking area next to the house.

"You weren't lying about this dude's dedication to his cause," said Bobby as he looked at the DON'T TREAD ON ME etched along the yellow Gadsden flag being pridefully flown from above the porch of the house. Aaron didn't care for the political message, but he wondered about Scottie. Didn't he live in Cecil County? Was this a second home of his or a house that belonged to one of his group's members? Doug hadn't revealed too much information other than that it was where final decisions were going to be made about any collaboration going forward.

They parked the car, and the three filed out of the truck, Bobby taking the longest as he was still doing his best to stay awake. They walked under the banner with the coiled snake before they arrived at the front door. Aaron tried to get a peek inside the house, but all the blinds were down. Being a bright sunny day, he assumed the occupants didn't want to risk anyone eavesdropping on any plans to alter the country's political landscape. Strolling like a cowboy in a Clint Eastwood western, Scottie joined them on the porch and proceeded to open the door.

While Doug's pad was covered in war memorabilia, this house's interior was straight out of an American Revolution museum. Portraits of George Washington, Patrick Henry, Thomas Jefferson, and numerous other founding fathers were posted around the room. The place was also far more tidy than Doug and Bobby's. No sign of any recreational drug use or beer cans anywhere on the property.

"Follow me, fellas," said Scottie as he led them through the living room and the kitchen. He opened up a skinny door and revealed a staircase down to a basement.

The four reached the bottom, and around the corner from the stairwell was a den fit for an all-male Super Bowl party. Trophy heads of Sika Deer, a black bear, and a full-sized stuffed opossum aligned the walls. There was no large flat-screen television set, though, and it seemed that the game of focus for this hangout spot was cards instead of football as three men decked in camo hunting outfits were gathered around a small square table playing a round of Texas Hold Em. All of them had beards that went past the bottom of the neck, and Aaron observed they seemed about twice his age, probably a decade older than Scottie or more. He guessed that at least two of them were ex-military by their solid physical stature but assumed the large man of at least 350 pounds was probably the gunshop owner Scottie had been talking about.

"Gentlemen," announced Scottie to the men at the card table. They had paused their game as soon as the four had reached the bottom step. All of the boys from Cumberland got stares, not just Aaron, making it clear that they had suspicions of any outsider, regardless of skin color. "These are the infamous New Patriots."

Bobby, Doug, and Aaron traded cordial nods with the men at the table. The three playing cards continued to study the crew from up north as Scottie grabbed another square table that was stacked against the wall to unfold and combine it with his housemates. He grabbed an additional few foldout chairs and invited the original New Patriots to take a seat across their potential new collaborators.

"Doug Vanderville, Bobby Zahl..." Scottie introduced each

member. "...And Aaron, uhm, forgive me—"

"Williams."

"Yes, Aaron Williams. This is who we're going to carry out part two of the American Revolution with."

"I like your group's name." The big red-bearded man was the first among the card players to speak. "Which one of you came up with that?" Aaron and Bobby shifted their eyes to Doug. He took a breath before answering.

"I did."

"What made you want to take up arms against the State?" Red-gray beard asked.

"Tom is a long-time supporter of the Delmarva secessionist movement," said Scottie in reference to the man asking Doug the question. "He's even got the flag tatted on his shoulder." The flag represented a campaign to have the Eastern shore of Maryland, most of Delaware, and a chunk of Virginia become the 51st state of the United States. Aaron knew from discussion boards that it was popular among liberty-minded activists for its calls for no sales tax like Delaware and other ways to cut it off from what they perceived as the parasitic bureaucratic swamp that bordered northern Virginia. Aaron wasn't as familiar with it as Doug was but nodded in fake admiration as Tom rolled up his sleeve to show the Blue Bonnie lone star tattoo on his shoulder.

"Once the state made it part of their agenda to go after our ability to create our own tools for liberation," stated Doug. Aaron kept it to himself that Doug was lying his ass off about having any kind of political motivation. "I figured it was time to act."

"They want to bar us from keeping what this whole country founded upon," said Tom as he folded his cards up. "And then get mad when we look for alternative ways to express our freedom. Can't even say nothing like this in public anymore without getting put on a Fed watchlist or something."

"Somebody once told me that the second amendment is

there for us to exercise when the government doesn't respect the first," commented Aaron, recalling one of the tidbits of knowledge Rold had dropped on him before the drug dealer dropped his whole unit altogether. The table was quiet for a few beats. Their faces hinted they were a bit surprised by where the very relevant statement came from.

"Right on, brother," said Tom as he put his fist out to bump Aaron's. Aaron exchanged the gesture of solidarity.

"So you guys put up the money yourselves?" asked one of the other beards at the table. Aaron read U.S. ARMY VETERAN with various stripes on the man's hat.

"We put a little bit," answered Doug. "But the majority of the money on the top ten of the Bazaar comes from international sources."

"Like terrorists?" inquired the same man. Doug paused for a brief moment. Aaron could sense that the individual was a skeptic, but he figured Doug would just tell the truth and see where the conversation ended up.

"Many different groups," Doug responded. "I'm sure some may be on some federal watch list."

"Isn't the Anat network one of them?" asked the veteran.

"I believe so," Doug said. "They've claimed responsibility for bids on their social media accounts." "We fought against those fuckers in the sandbox," the same man said with a triggered tone. "You telling me that hit on Frost put money in their pockets?" Now, there was an awkward silence. The hostility was certainly unexpected, and none of the New Patriots were sure how to respond. Scottie jumped in to try to save them, though.

"I'm sure nobody here is mad at that commie bastard Frost being six feet under," he said.

"Anybody with money can profit from the Bazaar," said Doug. "At the end of the day, that's how a free market is supposed to work anyways, right? Liberty is protecting an individual's ideology, whether we agree with it or not." The man didn't say anything, but he nodded quietly as if to give Doug a bit of respect.

"Mason here did a few tours overseas with the Rangers," Scottie said. "I don't think any of us here except Craig have witnessed the things he saw on the battlefield," Aaron concluded Craig was the other in-shape bearded man at the table.

"So sorry if my passion overflows sometimes," Mason said to them. "Don't take it personally."

"I didn't," Doug said. "And thank you for your service."

"Now that we are all familiar with one another, more or less," said Scottie. "I'd like to bring up two items. First thing first, the target and his location. This will be a major factor in how we train for this mission."

"Attah is employing the same firm from the first assault," Aaron told them. "Raptor, the company that also was protecting Congressman Desmond Ellis in the recent assassination attempt. For that attack, Raptor partnered with a commercial real estate property management company called ALAMUT. From my understanding, they're still under contract together, so it's a safe bet that for the December date, Attah will be stationed at an ALAMUT property."

"Any idea yet on the possible location?" asked Mason.

"I've been keeping track of recent acquisitions by ALAMUT in Maryland and any surrounding states. It looks like they purchased a remote cabin in Hampshire County, West Virginia. Don't see why a company interested mostly in office buildings in the suburbs would acquire such a property unless they wanted to keep somebody or something away from any potential danger. So if I had to make an educated guess, it would definitely be that."

"We've got people out near there," stated Scottie.

"We sure do," followed up Tom. "One of my suppliers is based in Winchester. We can stock up there and do some training runs in the George Washington Forest."

"Solid. That sound good to y'all?" asked Doug to Bobby Z and Aaron.

"Yes, sir."

"Hell yeah," a hyped Bobby got a word in the conversation.

"Good stuff," commented Scottie. "Now, the other thing. To follow up Aaron's research, a Beltway insider has actually reached out to me and is willing to update us on whatever moves Attah makes leading up to December."

"An insider?" probed Mason. "Like a Fed?" That word raised the hair on the back of all the New Patriots, given their original concerns about Scottie.

"So what am I supposed to do when our words inspire somebody behind enemy lines? Turn them away?" Some silence and sighs at the table from Scottie's people. Doug, Aaron, and Bobby just exchanged glances of concern with one another. "I'm keeping him in the dark about everything going on right here. But everybody here is a student of warfare, and what conflict in history didn't have spies on the other side? Tell me."

"So he's working for us and not the other way around?" It was Mason who gave the harsh inquiry.

"You calling me a snitch?"

"I didn't say that. You know what I mean." The tension was back, but the New Patriots remained quiet to see if it got settled quickly like the last time.

"If I was a rat, why would I be making this announcement?"

"Who's he with?" asked Tom, steering the conversation to the facts instead of a game of omerta. "F-B-I, State Department, Homeland Security, what?" Scottie paused for a moment, debating how he wanted to answer the question. Given Mason's comments, he'd keep it truthful.

"D-H-S."

"I voted Bush, but that department is a waste," Tom

replied. "They're definitely deep inside, though." He checked his phone for a text message he just received.

"I have my reservations," Mason said. "I hope he stays in the shadows, but I guess I don't really have an issue for now. If he was a plant, he'd be one of us at this meeting."

"Agreed," said Doug. Aaron could tell he was actually uneasy, but that was a feeling they would converse about later.

"My man out in Winchester just hit me back," remarked Tom. "Seems pretty excited. Said we're welcome whenever, even today, plus the whole weekend if you all are free." Bobby Z nodded, impressed. Doug raised his eyebrows.

"Where are we going to stay?"

"He's like the damn mayor of that town," replied Tom. "He can get you boys in any motel within the city for free. All meals are provided too. You know my fat ass ain't going to stay up there hungry." Some chuckles from around the table lightened the mood from any previous sketchy vibes from the discussion about Scottie's connection.

"You guys cool with that?" asked Doug toward his crew. Both Aaron and Bobby Z looked at each then nodded with approval. "Alright, let's get going. How long of a drive is that?"

"About two hours if you're driving like a normal person," answered Tom. "About ninety minutes or less if I'm behind the wheel," Doug smirked as he got up with Bobby Z and Aaron. The two crews shook each other's hands.

"Text me the address," Doug requested from Scottie as they made their way to the stairwell. Scottie nodded affirmatively and signaled for Tom to send him the information.

Doug, Bobby, and Aaron stepped out the front door to head toward the truck. Once they got in the cab and the doors were shut, Bobby Z spoke up.

"This man actually admits to WORKING with a fed?"

"Yeah, that threw me off too. If y'all want to cut loose of

this whole thing, now's the time. We can head back up north now and plan out this whole thing ourselves."

"They now already know where Attah is going to be hiding," informed Aaron. "If we split now and then see them in December at the spot, it might just spark a three-way firefight that I'm not so confident we can win."

"Fuck you mean?" an offended Bobby asked Aaron. "I merk all four of those bums. Especially Scottie and that Tastykake-eating mother fucker."

"One of them is an ex-ranger," Aaron calmly retorted. "The one next to him was probably also in special forces. I don't know Scottie's background too much, but that Tom guy seems pretty well-connected. So even in the unlikely event we came out victorious in a shootout with them, somebody would be after us for the rest of our lives."

"Aaron's right," Doug said. "We either drop the Chiedu operation altogether, or we start driving to Winchester. What do you guys want to do?" The car was quiet for a few moments as everyone figured out what choice to make.

"Shit, I'm not even going to lie," Bobby said while settling down. "I'm running on E with the bread from the Frost hit. I need this."

"Aaron?"

"I'm in. But let's keep our eyes and ears open. If anything seems off during training or leading up to December, we bounce and cut off all contact with Scott and his people." Doug nodded his head in agreement and started the truck.

"Always open."

CHAPTER 20

During his time at Morgan State, Nick flew out to California once to compete in a hack-a-thon representing his school against other HBCUs. He led the team to victory by designing a program to teach users about credit and won a scholarship that covered the rest of his tuition. However, he arrived in the Golden State on a plane, and the farthest west he had ever driven was Gettysburg, Pennsylvania, for a cross-country meet. That was surpassed once the Raptor EPT SUV he rode in crossed over the West Virginia border on U.S. Route 340. He knew they were on their way to visit the safe house for Chiedu. But there wasn't going to be any heavy tactical training, just a walkthrough for the squad to get familiar with the setting. So Nick had his laptop put away and kept his mind clear to enjoy the ride.

"How are you doing?" asked Terry toward Lyle in the front passenger seat. Lyle took a second to answer.

"Physical therapy's been good. I started lifting again this week. Still just walking, but I'll be able to run soon."

"Don't rush the recovery process," advised Terry. Whatever issues Nick noticed between Terry and Lyle had were seemingly out the window. "And honestly, it's not too late to see if we can put a temp in your spot in December," Terry added. "I think it's even part of the insurance policy that you still get paid if that happens."

"I'll be fine." The car was silent for a few beats. "But thank you."

"Cool. Just letting you know." Nick watched the Appalachian wilderness pass by them during the drive. It reminded him of some of the races he was in during his time as an NCAA Division I AA athlete. Some of the members of Raptor's EPT, especially Jasper and Terry, reminded him of his coach consistently trying to steer his gift of intelligence toward a productive direction. He got his heart ripped to shreds his sophomore year when the petite Brazilian weave-wearing Tanika, whom he fawned over since freshman orientation, ended up in a threesome with two wide receivers of the 0-11 football team who seemed to have a better game off the field than on it. It was his coach who told him to channel the emotional pain into the hack-a-thon if the physical exertion during the practices didn't do the trick. Nick still hadn't fostered that same kind of relationship with Yemi, however, and had doubts that he ever would. Yemi didn't even request for Nick to handle the video surveillance for Chiedu's new safe house.

"Do you know if Yemi is thinking about letting me go?" Nick asked the car, assuming Terry would be in the know about any of Yemi's major Raptor decisions. There was a definitive pause from the front of the car. Both Lyle and Terry were caught off guard by the question.

"What would make you think that?" asked Terry.

"I mean, I haven't exactly been on his good side since I've been here. I wasn't even monitoring the cameras when he called me during the hit on Ellis."

"Rice." Terry took a deep breath before he continued. "You have a gift, but it seems to come with a curse. All due respect."

"What do you mean?" asked the rookie bodyguard.

"You overthink things," Terry continued. "Granted, that's why you're a walking Wikipedia search bar, but you cloud your mind with things that have no relevance to your current situation."

"If Yemi doesn't like me, then that means I may not have a job. That affects my current situation."

"Where are you right now? And what are you doing?"

Nick paused before he could give an answer.

"I'm in a car that gets under twenty miles per gallon, and we just entered West bumblefuck."

"Okay, see, that's your problem. You're young, so I can see where the mentality comes from. Sizing up everything, nothing is good enough until you hit it big before you land on the three O. I get it. I'm sure even Lyle can relate."

"Leave me out of this mess," interjected Evans. "I mean, maybe Yemi doesn't actually like the lil mutha fucka."

"Why the hell would you say that?" a pissed-off Terry said back to his co-navigator. "I just explained how he overthinks, and now you just enabled his racing thoughts even more."

"It's a cold world," an unapologetic Lyle responded. "Shit, I thought your all-American ass would understand more than anybody on the squad."

"Look. Rice, don't listen to this guy, alright? He's mad at the world for some reason."

"There's a lot of reason to be mad at the world, Steve Rogers." Lyle just wouldn't stop with the cracks on Terry's service to his country. "I don't know if you've taken the time to look around lately."

"Jesus Christ," Terry said. "Am I in a car full of rabid pessimists? What made you people even sign up for this in the first place?" A couple silent beats as if Nick and Lyle were deciding who should go first.

"I mean. It was by far the most exciting job description on Indeed. At least at the time," said Nick.

"So what changed between then and now? You've been in two major incidents that have made national news, and you're not even twenty-five yet." Nick paused again.

"I never looked at it like that."

"See? It's all about perspective. Now it's your turn, Lyle."

"Fuck is this carpool confessions or some shit?"

"You seem to be pretty observational, given your outlook on the world," pressured Terry. "Now you don't want to share the reason why your ass is even that seat next to me?" Lyle hissed his teeth and looked out the window toward Shenandoah Valley.

"I mean... Shit, I can't front. I was tired of chasing crackheads off parking lots or whatever Yemi and Karen had me do on a nightly basis. Once Karen told me about Yemi forming a squad with all the tactical shit, it sounded pretty straight to me."

"Why is it so hard for you to admit that you actually like this job?"

"It's a job, dawg. Are you Raptor internal affairs up in here? I don't gotta like it, I just have to be good at making sure the property is secure and the person who paid us stays alive." Terry shook his head as he continued to drive.

"You're not as old as me, Lyle, but that mentality is only going to be a weight that gets heavier each birthday. Trust me on that."

"Whatever, just get us to the damn location before I put in my two weeks." Terry sighed. It could easily escalate, but Nick knew Terry was the type to let it go. Despite what he said earlier about possibly relieving Lyle of his duties to recover, Nick knew there would be too many variables in disarray if they replaced him. Especially if it was just someone from the patrol ranks who had even more limited combat experience than himself.

––––––

The long dirt driveway up to the safe house made some on the squad feel like they were driving to an early 1900s lynching. But the modern-day era became apparent once Yemi spotted Vash's 2024 Audi A4 parked in front of the porch. The ALAMUT CEO, himself, was standing on the highest step with his trademark 100-kilowatt smile, always excited to see his collaborators at Raptor.

Jasper parked first, and Terry steered to set it parallel to the first 4Runner. The whole EPT squad got out and gandered at the house. Contrary to the environment leading up to the structure, the 2-story cabin seemed very welcoming for a vacation rather than just a place to stow away a politician in danger.

"Welcome to West Virginia, everyone!" Vash exclaimed to the crew as they walked up to the porch like he was an over-excited tour guide to a bunch of primary school students on a field trip.

"Top of the hill. That's good," said Terry as he realized that the house sat on the peak of the small mountain they were on, giving them high ground. Yemi knew they would have a great advantage in terms of spotting any potential hostiles approaching the property as well as providing them with the upper hand in a shootout. That was if they engaged in one. The whole purpose of ALAMUT acquiring the cabin was to prevent something like the previous two situations.

"Let's head inside," welcomed Vash. "Coffee, hot chocolate, and baked snacks for anybody who wants some. I know it's been at least a two-and-a-half-hour ride." Only Nick and Victor seemed to care about any of the refreshments. Jasper and Terry scanned the windows for all possible sniping vantage points while Yemi went to check out the walled-in office Chiedu would be occupying. Once it met his approval, he joined most of his team back downstairs in the kitchen.

"They say around the time we start here, West Virginia will get more snowfall than average," Nick said in between mouth bites with Danish icing sticking to his upper lip.

"How the hell do you know that this far ahead?" asked a doubtful Yemi.

"El Nino." Yemi rolled his eyes at Nick's insight into air pressure and global weather patterns. Nick slowly sipped from his drink.

"How's the hot chocolate?" asked Vash. "The cocoa is

from Jamaica. I'm sure you can taste the difference from that Swiss Miss bullshit."

"It's solid," Nick said in a low voice. Yemi could sense that the warm drink may have been the only thing soothing his waning confidence. Maybe he should take it easy on the kid, he started to wonder.

"But this is a great spot, isn't it?" Vash asked the crew when they met back near the central room after they had gone off on their own paths.

"Bullets could rip this place to shreds," Yemi said, looking at the rustic aesthetic that was nice on the eyes but a cause for concern if they ran into any trouble. "Are the walls around Attah's office bulletproof, blastproof, or both?"

"Uh." Vash paused. Yemi knew he knew the answer, but it was a salesman's hesitation to reveal any shortcomings of the product. "We just purchased it. I can certainly talk with my engineers to see if it can be modified."

"Yes, please do that," insisted Yemi. Yemi took out his phone, flipped it horizontally, and started to record everything around him. He text messaged all the videos to his sister. Within a few minutes, Karen FaceTimed him. Over the video feed, Yemi saw his sibling tucked away in the corner of a restaurant's outdoor seating. A packed day party was in the background as a fully made-up Karen was wearing a long amber-colored dress for the warmer-than-average Fall temperature.

"It looks nice," said Karen in reference to the cabin's interior.

"We don't need it to look nice. We need it to be safe, and I'm having some doubts, if I'm being honest."

"Did Vash say he was going to reinforce the walls around Chiedu?" Yemi raised an eyebrow, a bit caught off guard by her accuracy.

"How did you know that?"

"I've been trying to tell you, Yemi. You don't give Vash enough credit. He wants nothing more than to impress you. He respects you more than you believe."

"Respect doesn't keep the client from getting shot," retorted Yemi.

"That is true."

"How's your little party?"

"Don't say it like that."

"What? You said it was a day party."

"It is," Karen said as she raised her mimosa glass near the screen for her brother to see. "But it's not just that. There are some major beltway connections at some of these tables. I swear this one guy is a V-P at Haliburton."

"Keep up the good work, sis. I'm proud of you."

"I'm proud of you too, big bro." Yemi had gotten tired of cracking jokes on her even though it was the perfect opportunity. Day parties in the district were what Karen would always fantasize about during summers from Wake Forest, but she was too broke to even afford an outfit that would attract complimentary drinks. Fast forward years later, she didn't need a man to buy those for her. And for that, Yemi was glad she had achieved at least a part of her dream lifestyle.

"Alright, we're going to finish up here. We'll link back at H-Q tomorrow. Jasper and I will give you a debriefing. And hopefully, you got some client leads."

"Not hopefully, I will," said Karen as she took a sip of brunch liquid and shut down the app to return to focus on networking. Yemi put his phone away and turned back to his squad gathered in the living room area. He focused his attention on Nick, who seemed visibly depressed and hadn't touched any more of the snacks provided by Vash.

"Rice," Yemi said. "A word with you."

"Yes, sir," the rookie gulped and stepped over to his detail leader. Terry exchanged looks with Nick en route. He motioned for Nick to hold his head up high and resist slouching. He did his best to correct his posture as Yemi led them through the door and outside. A few beats of silence as Yemi continued to stroll into the woods, and Nick followed behind. Yemi pointed up in the sky.

"Can you fly two drones at once?" Nick's whole demeanor reversed. It didn't seem like he envisioned himself being entrusted with any other kind of responsibility.

"Of course, sir. I can fly and monitor as many drones as you need."

"Just two. Even one might be plenty. But we need to make sure they have thermal imaging. I want eyes on all sides of the mountain." Nick was keeping a straight face, but Yemi could sense it was the moment he had been waiting for since first arriving in the Greenbelt parking lot.

"I still have the drone from the first Chiedu assignment. So is there room in the budget for a second one if need be?" Yemi looked through the trees. He nodded up and down, meditating on Nick's question.

"I'll talk to Karen tomorrow."

"Okay, I can come back out here next weekend on my own to run some tests if that'll help."

"That's what I'm talking about, Rice. Good stuff." Yemi turned around to head back inside. He could see through a reflection in the window Nick clenching his fist in moral victory before he followed his boss inside.

CHAPTER 21

After the 3 PM press briefing, Abdallah stood on the crowded platform at Farragut North while he waited for the red line Train to take him to his destination. He didn't have to transfer to Metro Center to take the Orange line to New Carrolton like he had been doing the previous few years, where he could find the only studio apartment with a rental price below a thousand a month without having a car. With his new raise, he had been able to move to a one-bedroom luxury suite in the gentrified NOMA neighborhood of Northeast. His fellow tenants had changed from families of blue-collar and secretarial workers to singles under the age of 50 walking furry toys with proud displays of their rainbow pride flags. And it was the third week in a row he had actually paid for his Metro fare. Hopping the turnstiles for a whole year saved him at least forty dollars a week, but he would have to be mindful of Transit police, who would be in the rare mood to issue the $50 fine. $100 and a citation if it happened in Maryland or Virginia.

The Glenmont train arrived, and he stepped into the car, managing to grab himself an open seat. It was only a short fifteen-minute ride at max, and he usually did offer a seat to any women standing, but Abdallah was eager to get to the next chapter of William Gibson's literary classic, "Neuromancer." He had been putting it off for some time now, despite how many times he had watched "The Matrix" and "Strange Days." Once the train pulled off, he eagerly wanted to devour how hacker Case escaped sociopath Riviera, but his anticipation got interrupted by loud trap music from a nearby cell phone speaker coming from what Abdallah profiled as a high schooler from one of DC's public institutions. It was obvious from the facial expressions of other passengers that he was not the only one annoyed by the disruptive tunes, but the teenager in his bright red Helly Hansen outfit paid none of them any mind as he recited the chorus with bravado. He was only a few rows from Kalfat, and Abdallah wondered if it was even worth the risk to try to convince the young man to turn the noise down. Just the thought of that made the young journalist think of himself as the grumpy single old man in the basement apartment shouting at the house party upstairs. Plus, it wasn't like he was even the confrontational type, having never participated in any contact sports in his life, let alone any organized athletics, period.

"Can you please turn that down?" asked a middle-aged woman in formal business attire. She looked like she could work at a law firm or was a policy consultant, not necessarily one of the humanitarian non-profits in Dupont Circle. "You're sharing a space with other people."

"Mind your mutha fuckin business, bitch," the young man yelled over the music. Suddenly, a clean-shaven, stocky man with military fatigue stepped forward and got in the kid's face.

"Watch your language, and she's right. The music is too loud," he lectured the youth. "You're on public transportation for Christ's sake."

"You think I'm scared of you?" the teenager looked up at the soldier.

"Make a move, and it won't matter if you fear me."

"I fear no man but GOD, nigga." The kid paused the music and stood up. He and the grunt were face-to-face. "I ain't scared of YOU, I ain't scared of ya ARMY, shit just look at the news. All it takes is a few lil bitcoins to put a hit on ya general these days, right?" The last sentence of the argument got Abdallah's attention. The Bazaar had evidently become a part of the social fabric of everyday interactions, even in the vein of threats being exchanged between strangers.

"Next stop, Judiciary Square. Doors opening on the right" beamed over the intercom before either challenger could raise a hand to the other. The face-off continued until the train came to a halt. Once the bell chimed over the speakers and the doors finally opened, the teenager dashed for it, but not before he stuck his hands up, mimicking pulling a trigger toward the soldier and the lady.

"Blah, BLAH," he shot bullets with his hands in the form of an air gun at them as he exited the train. The other car occupants seemed a bit disturbed by the brief incident, but Abdallah felt he may have gotten more inspiration from this encounter than his original plan to read the genesis of cyberpunk. He whipped out his phone and got to typing up notes for the rest of the ride all the way to NOMA Gallaudet.

Abdallah made his way through the lobby of the posh Market Square apartments. He waved to Darius at the front desk, but he had too much writing juice flowing through his body to make conversation that day. He jumped in the elevator and smacked the button for the seventh floor. A young Caucasian couple coming in from walking their Yorkshire Terrier was about six feet away. He was tempted to hit the button to close the doors, given how eager he was to write his new article idea, but he relented and held the elevator doors for them to enter.

Luckily, they were on the 10th floor, so it didn't delay him any further to get to his studio. He rushed out of the elevator, took out his key, and quickly opened the door to his new home. He rushed to his desk across from the door to sit at the only electronic device that existed in his apartment besides his phone, his Al Noor-issued Macbook. He hit the power key, but instead of starting from the loading screen, it cut straight to the login. Strange, Abdallah thought. He swore he shut it all the way down before he left that morning. Regardless, he opened up Libre Office and let his spirit of the independent-minded press guide his fingers to rapidly type away. 'All it takes is a few lil bitcoins...' was the perfect introduction to this article. It was perfect for Hitter, but he didn't really want to be anonymous for that particular piece, so he would consider submitting it to his editors at Al Noor. Suddenly, the sound of a pistol slide interrupted his typing from behind him.

"If you turn around, you will be killed. This is your only warning." Abdallah could tell that the authoritative voice behind him was using some type of disguiser. He also wondered where this person was hiding when he came into the room and realized they must be a professional since he didn't even hear a door creak. No other thoughts crossed his head except for trying to not defecate himself.

"Your name is Abdallah Kalfat, the creator of the Hitter app, correct?" Abdallah wondered how the hell the person traced him to Hitter, given he did all the domain registration, web hosting, and article posting through virtual private networks. From that fact alone, Abdallah figured this individual must have had some connection to the federal government. But only the CIA seemed like the kind of branch to have agents who would threaten to kill you in your own home with a gun pointed at your back, and it happening on domestic ground made that culprit unlikely. "Not answering will grant you the same fate as turning around in your chair." Say less, thought Abdallah.

"Yes, that is me."

"I am going to ask a series of questions. If I find out you are lying to me, I will know eventually, and you will be killed. Do you understand?" Abdallah gulped down a breath.

"Yes, sir."

"Have you been in communication with a member of the Executive Protection Team at Raptor Security?" Abdallah paused for a moment but realized, at this point, he wasn't ready to sacrifice his life for a code of silence.

"I was. Not any more, sir."

"What is his name?"

"Sir—"

"You have five seconds."

"Uh, uh, Nick. Nick Rice, sir," Abdallah uttered out. He paused again. "He handles their field communications."

"What information has he provided to you about Chiedu Attah in December?"

"Like I said, sir. We no longer communicate with each other." There was a long pause after Abdallah's sentence. The uncertainty of what would happen next drove up his anxiety, producing an almost involuntary slight shake in his body. He heard a zipper move like a backpack or some type of handbag was being opened. He then heard footsteps start to approach his back.

"Again, do not turn around." A black vinyl glove placed a red thumb drive on Abdallah's desk, right below the laptop. "Copy all the contents of your computer onto that drive. Everything."

"Uh, how big is that drive?" asked a hesitant Abdallah.

"It'll fit. Just do it." Abdallah sighed and proceeded to drag all the contents of his root drive onto what the unknown man just handed to him. He looked at the estimated time.

"Says it's going to be about an hour."

"That's fine, I have time," the figure stated as Abdallah listened to him return to the seat across the room. "Are you hungry? I can order us something." Abdallah was a little taken aback by the sudden gesture of hospitality from the man who was threatening to take his life a second prior.

"Uhm," started a confused Abdallah. "S-s-sure."

"You have utensils? Every time I order from these places, they forget." The situation was already frightening for Abdallah, and right then, it was getting even more awkward.

"In the kitchen."

"Never mind. I'll just put it in the instructions."

———

99% of the time Doug drove, it was his Dodge Ram, the prize of his hard work both before and during his career with Bazaar targets. He had inherited his mother's 2008 Nissan Versa but only took it for a spin when the Ram had to be in the shop for a coolant leak. For that reason, he had no issue with lending Aaron his mom's former trusted vehicle. After retreating to Allegany County for almost a year at that point, Aaron figured it was time to scope his home turf. Seeing his mother would be nice, but that wouldn't be possible, given she was probably compromised after the Efemena bust. He was taking a pretty big risk even being in the DMV, even more so than his visit to Danny in the prison. The main goal wasn't to see his last remaining parent, get any belongings from his previous home, or any kind of cheerful recollection of where he grew up. The only relic from the recent past on Aaron's mind was Rold Jenkins. He remembered Rold's house from that one ride with Qasim. It was about a twenty-minute ride, given Rold had moved to the more upper-middle-class Fort Washington once he was able to afford to get out of Temple Hills.

Aaron was behind the wheel, and it was in the early morning, only an hour after dawn. He turned onto the block and steered slowly down the street he remembered, almost like he was about to pull off a drive-by if it was the West Coast. He spotted the large mini-mansion where he was first introduced to the man who betrayed him, remembering the cement big cats in the front. An "Under Contract" real estate sign was posted on the front lawn. While that confirmed Rold no longer lived at the spot, Aaron's eyes locked in on a formally dressed African-American man with a neatly groomed lion's mane under his chin stepping out the front door. The man walked up to the post with some materials to change the sign from its previous wording to "For

Sale." Aaron immediately pulled over a few houses down and parked Doug's car.

Dressed in the basic hoodie and jeans he always wore, Aaron walked up the sidewalk to approach the real estate agent. The man noticed Aaron and politely nodded to him as the teenager approached.

"How can I help you today, young brother?" asked the man.

"Yes, I see the 'for sale' sign," responded Aaron. The man looked at the sign he just replaced. "Are you doing any showings today?" The man looked back at Aaron. He nodded respectively, attempting to hide the fact that he was shocked that a kid at Aaron's age was in the market for purchasing a $700k+ property. Also, Aaron was aware his attire didn't scream generational wealth, either. After reflecting for a brief moment, he grinned big.

"I can certainly show you around if you'd be interested," said the man. Aaron walked forward, and the man shook his hand. "Damien Hughes of Diamond Realty Solutions. Your name?"

"Christopher." Aaron stayed consistent with the same alias.

"Great to meet you, Christopher. Follow me inside."

The interior of Rold's old house looked the same, with the exception of how every ornament or piece of furniture had been cleared out. "It has a beautiful spiral staircase right by the front door. And then wait until you see the kitchen." Damien wanted to take Aaron to the left, but it was the library that used to have Aaron's attention.

"Mind if we check out that area first?" asked Aaron.

"Not at all. That room is quite unique." Damien stepped ahead to lead Aaron into the area. "The previous owner used this space as his library. Nothing but books were all along these shelves and walls. Made me wonder if he actually read all of them." Damien chuckled at his own joke while Aaron just continued to gander around at the empty space.

"Who was the previous owner?" asked Aaron.

"Uh, I think he worked for the DC Department of Health. That was his nine-to-five, but I'm pretty sure I remember him saying he ran some other businesses for residual income."

"Ah," said Aaron as his eyes still looked at each corner of the white room. "Interesting."

"And, uhm, if you don't mind me asking." Damien gulped down like he was not about to say something that could be interpreted as out of pocket. "What do you do for a living?" Aaron nodded, subtlely understanding the suspicion but not offended in the slightest.

"Crypto." Simple one-word answer that had a spot of truth to it.

"Oh wow." Damien was visibly impressed, and his perception of Christopher/Aaron seemed to change. "Makes sense now. Was wondering, given our age."

"Do you know why he sold the house?"

"Uhm." Damien paused, evidently not ready for the questions that early into the showing. "Not sure, honestly. He put it up for sale a year ago. It's just been tricky getting a buyer to follow all the way through since then." Aaron realized that meant Rold took off right away once the assault on Attah went sideways. "Would you like to see the kitchen now?"

"Did he say where he was moving to?" Damien couldn't help but laugh a bit at Aaron's investigative antics.

"You seem more interested in the previous owner than the house," the real estate agent observed.

"Because I am." Aaron removed one of his 3D-printed pistols that was hidden in his waistband. Damien's face morphed from a happy salesman to a deadpan hostage. Aaron put the Windsor knot of Damien's tie at the center of his Mini Talon's ironsight. "The man's name was Rold Jenkins. Do you have any knowledge of where he could be located?" Damien gulped down, closed his eyes, and then re-opened them.

"You're going to kill me if I don't say anything?" asked Damien. Aaron paused. That wasn't his intention, but he didn't want his captive to get bold.

"It's in your best interest to cooperate, I'll just say that." Damien took a second to assess the situation before he gave out any information.

"I don't understand this world," Damien said. "Before I got my real estate license, I had just finished a two-year bid for aggravated assault. Got right with Allah, ditched the streets, cut off all the toxicity in my circle, got engaged, and did everything to make sure I was going to build wealth for my family the right way. Even turned down half a mil 'cause I knew it was tied to what put me behind bars in the first place." Aaron kept his aim steady, and although he wanted intel, he wasn't intent on interrupting Damien's monologue. "Now here I am, in the middle of my business that's one hundred percent halal, and I still have a gun pointed at me." Aaron nodded and then respectfully shrugged his shoulders.

"Your mistake was thinking the profit motive ever gave a fuck about your spirituality," Aaron said. They traded stares. Damien had nothing to say in response. His face sent a message of disapproval but not so much disagreement with the facts. "Where's Jenkins?"

"He was brief with any kind of details. Almost seemed like he was suddenly on the run." Damien locked in on Aaron. "Guess you may have something to do with what he was running from." Aaron cocked the pistol to send Damien a message about getting to the point.

"I'm low on time, Damien."

"Yeah, sorry. He asked if my company had any properties

on the Eastern shore. Told him we managed to snag a fixer-upper in Cambridge from a police auction. From there, another agent worked with him, so I don't know if he ended up buying or not, but that's all I know." Aaron slowly pulled the gun down.

"I hope you didn't take me holding you at gunpoint in your own house personal."

"It's all good," Damien said. "Unfortunately, I actually do know how it is." Aaron nodded his head. He took out his phone and handed it to Damien.

"Can you put in the address of where that house is? Or if you don't know, just the general area."

"I got you." Damien typed away on the keypad. "You don't seem like a man who wants to reveal much, but you got me a little curious as to what this man actually did."

"Ran off on a deal," Aaron stated casually. "Like you said, you know how it is." Damien finished typing and handed Aaron the phone back.

"So it is personal between you and this Jenkins guy?"

"No, it's business."

"Business?" Damien asked rhetorically, as that was a subject matter Aaron knew he was familiar with. "Going on a vengeful road trip, risking detection... I hope it's well worth whatever you're getting paid out of it."

"It's complicated." Aaron thought he may have told the guy too much. "Don't worry about it."

"Take it from a fifteen year veteran of the trap, kid. That life wasn't for me, but if it's for you, you gotta set aside the ego so the brain can calculate the right moves. Don't make my mistake. Now all I can do is entrepreneurship 'cause my record will block me out of any H-R inquiry."

"Was real estate your destiny?"

"Yes, Allah guided me here."

"Then how were your actions a mistake? Seems like that's

just how fate works." Damien nodded his head up and down in recognition of Aaron's wisdom. "See you around, Damien." Aaron turned toward the door. After a few steps, the sound of a gun cocking turned him into a mannequin. Aaron slowly turned around to face Damien, holding a Colt .45 straight at him. His facial expression had changed to the cold-hearted street lieutenant he must have been before the lockup.

"Is Chris even your real name?" Aaron was not sure how to answer. A chuckle with dark undertones came from Damien, a transformation from the friendly real estate agent looking for a client a few minutes earlier. "Nevermind. I know it's not. Just get the hell off my property and make sure nothing you're about to do comes back on me."

"You got it." Damien kept his gun raised as Aaron continued his exit.

"If you're ever going to take a hostage, you gotta pat 'em down first." Aaron stopped again in his tracks and looked back at Damien. The last piece of advice was unexpected. "Remember..." Damien used his other hand to tap on his head. "Brains, young G." Aaron nodded again, somewhat nervously that time. It was the most threatened he'd ever felt, even versus being surrounded by Qasim's crew in the stairwell or rumbling with Bobby Z. Yet, the one person who could have ended his life was now letting him go and with some tips at that. He opened the front door and headed back to the Versa. He could see Damien through the window sighing, tucking his pistol back into his hidden holster. Aaron figured the man must be relieved that he didn't return to the antics of his past.

———

The file transfer finished at the same time Abdallah was done with his egg roll. He took the plastic red object out of his computer.

"It's done," he said as he held the thumb drive up for the man of mystery. A few steps came from behind him, and the black vinyl glove took back the drive.

"Thank you, Mr. Kalfat. Hopefully, you won't hear from me again."

"Yup."

"Once you hear the door shut, you're free to move back around your apartment without harm." Abdallah heard a bag zip, and within a few moments, the front door opened and shut. Abdallah quickly turned around to make sure the coast was clear and then immediately clicked frantically at his laptop. The first thing he checked was his webcam, which he set to constantly record whenever it turned on for situations like the one he just faced. He looked at the footage and saw that his own body took up most of the lens. However, a few times, Abdallah purposely shifted his head for the camera to capture the man behind him the whole time. When he came across a shot of it, he froze the frame. He could tell that the man was Caucasian, but he was wearing sunglasses, a face mask, and a solid black hat with a black and white American flag on the front of it. Abdallah opened up his internet browser and typed in a special URL. On his screen, it was apparent that Abdallah had hacked into all the CCTV for his apartment building, a technical ability he shared with his friend Nick Rice. Abdallah highlighted the cameras for the lobby, the elevators, and the seventh floor. From the seventh-floor camera, he saw the man jimmy open his apartment door at around 12:35 PM, a few hours before Abdallah showed up. However, by that time, he already had on his disguise. Abdallah checked the lobby camera around the same time. He spotted the hat and the backpack but still couldn't get a clear look at the face. His last chance was the elevator CCTV. He selected elevator two's camera system and watched the footage starting at 12:30 PM. He fast-forwarded until it landed on the home invader. He was able to get a full frontal shot before the man put on the mask and sunglasses. Abdallah screenshotted the athletically built middle-aged man and copied the image file. He opened up another browser tab and went straight to FacePatterns.ID, an AI-powered facial recognition database. Abdallah cropped the image to focus strictly above the neck of the figure. He exported it as a .jpg and uploaded it to FacePatterns. He waited patiently as it searched through its records to try to find a match.

Within a few moments, Abdallah got a result he hadn't seen before:

CANNOT DISPLAY INFORMATION. ERROR CODE 4120.

Error code 4120? Immediately, Abdallah pasted the message and put it in a search engine for a FacePatterns discussion board. He read his answer in one of the first replies to a thread topic:

FACEPATTERNS HAS BEEN BLOCKED BY U.S. LAW FROM ASSISTING IN THE IDENTIFICATION OF ANY FEDERAL LAW ENFORCEMENT.

————

Crossing the Bay Bridge and passing the Royal Farms from the original trip with Qasim really gave Aaron a flashback to the previous year. All eight of them thought they were on the cusp of entering into the 1% from a single hit. Aaron was one of the few left alive and the only one free. Aaron had rolled his eyes at all of Rold's ideological monologues about class warfare, the people rising up and overthrowing the power structure. But the whole time, he was a step ahead of Aaron on the cutthroat scale. Qasim's final breaths replayed in Aaron's mind as he entered the city limits of Cambridge, Maryland. Following the GPS, he passed by a dispensary and could even smell the aroma through the windows of an herb that had quality rivaling Doug and Bobby's back in Cumberland. But getting high was nowhere close to a priority at that moment. He hadn't even been smoking the past few weeks while his roommates got blasted off of bong hits on a daily basis. Wiping the arrogant smile off of Rold Jenkins' face was the mission, even taking up more space in Aaron's head than preparations for the next attempt on Attah.

"Turn left onto Race Street," said Google Maps. Aaron turned the wheel and drove onto one of the rougher-looking blocks he had seen on this trip. "In five hundred feet, your destination will be on the right." Aaron slowed down and began to scan his entire surrounding environment. One portly middle-aged African American was preparing his car for some late afternoon fishing, one hand full of rods and the other holding a tackle box. His son and daughter followed behind with a cooler along with some foldout chairs. "You have arrived at your destination." It was a couple homes down from the family. The slightly dilapidated one-floor single-family house clearly hadn't undergone much renovation. But there was a car parked out front. It was an early 2010s silver Ford Mustang, not a car Rold had owned at the time Aaron knew him, but a vehicle that fit the OG drug dealer's tastes. On the first pass through, Aaron didn't see anyone around the house, so he went down to the end of the block and parked at the side, similar to how he arrived in Fort Washington.

Aaron checked his Mini Talon and cocked it, making sure it was ready to fire. He didn't want any kids to witness a potential murder, so he looked down the street to make sure the fisherman left with his family before he began his march down the block. Within five minutes, the family of three pulled out of their driveway and exited Race Street. Aaron threw his hood up, stowed away his handgun, and got out of the Nissan. Walking down the street in a dark hoodie brought back a similar feeling in Aaron when he approached Adamu and Isaiah on Marion Street, even though in Cambridge, it was during the day. There was a financial kickback awaiting Aaron's completion of killing Chiedu's son, and unless he actually did take Rold's wallet, the only reward this time was a moral victory in memory of his original crew. Aaron was lying to himself, trying to block out Damien's warning about the path he was currently on. He was about two houses down when he watched the front screen door open from his target location. Aaron stopped in his tracks and carefully ducked behind a nearby Chevy Tahoe.

It was Rold. Despite the look of the house, he still had his expensive taste with his navy blue Balenciaga sweatsuit on and walking to his Mustang in his Yeezy sneakers. When Rold got about halfway through his front yard, Aaron looked around to make sure nobody was watching him, and he removed his pistol to get ready to attack. He took a few slow steps and got ready to aim once Rold grabbed the driver-side handle. The anticipation of finally ending the traitor's life built up in Aaron's body. But just then, the screen door opened again. Aaron quickly backpedaled to behind the Tahoe.

"Daddy!" The voice of a girl no older than nine came from the entrance of the house.

"What, sweetheart?"

"You forgot your lemonade!"

"Baby, I'll drink it when I get back."

"But it won't be cold, Daddy!"

"Just put it in the fridge, darling."

"But Daddy!" She started to throw a crying tantrum. "I made it for you." Aaron could hear Rold's loud sigh as he shut the Mustang door and headed back to the house.

"Here I come, honey." Damien's advice went from being submerged in the back of his head to being a throbbing migraine. The whole mission in Cambridge had selfish inclinations in the first place, but he was about to blast the brains out of a little girl's father right in front of her. Aaron stowed away the pistol. Just then, he felt his phone vibrate. He checked it, and it was Doug. Making sure Rold wouldn't be able to spot him, Aaron took the call.

"Yo."

"Everything straight down there?" asked Doug over the phone. Aaron could hear Bobby coughing in the background. They were clearly taking turns ripping the bong. Aaron took a look at the house again before he answered.

"Yeah. Mom's good, but she's worried, of course. I'm about to head back soon," he said as he checked his surroundings again, making sure the Tahoe owner didn't storm out. "Need me to pick up anything?"

"Let me check with Bobby."

"Pick up two large pepperonis. Hungry as a mother fucker up here," Bobby shouted from the other side of the kitchen table.

"He's not going to be here for another two to three hours, Bobby," laughed Doug.

"Shit, I'll still be hungry then too."

"Man, yo fat ass always hungry."

"Lick my nuts and hit this bong, fool." Aaron laughed over the phone at their conversation.

"Alright, bro. You don't gotta pick up the pizza unless you want to, but otherwise, I think we're good here. Get home safe."

"Thanks, Doug. See y'all later." Aaron hung up. He stared at the house again, giving himself one last time to reminisce about a past injustice he had decided not to correct. He turned around and headed back to his vehicle.

He wasn't quite ready to head back to Cumberland just yet, though. Aaron had spent the past 9+ months in the company of his newfound roommates and was enjoying some time to himself in a different part of the state. He remembered the dispensary and stopped by to pick up a few pre-rolls, a Clipper lighter, as well as an eighth of an Indica dominant hybrid he could take back to home base as a gift for his partners in crime. He drove to the nearby Choptank River and pulled into a parking lot. He spotted a fishing pier that would be the perfect location for him to light up one of his pre-rolls. Although the pier wasn't crowded, there were spots of people all the way down to the end. Aaron picked a bench shaded by a roof and not close to any children as his spot to spark up. He realized it would be the first time he had ever smoked by himself, always having done it with either Danny or his newfound Allegany County crew.

He sat down with his back against the picnic table and torched the end of his joint. He started to puff away, and immediately, the THC loosened up his body as well as his mind. He watched the seagulls fly above as some landed on the pier to pick up scraps. He was even more enamored with the occasional osprey that soared above the water, looking for the opportunity to grab a fish close to the surface. The more he smoked, the more he realized he made the right decision on Rold. He wondered if he would've made the same decision if he never met Damien.

About twenty yards from him, he watched a mid-50s sunburnt man in a John Deere shirt start to reel his rod in. The bend of the pole meant that he had something with some serious weight biting on his hook. Curious to see what the man was going to bring in, Aaron watched the battle between hunter and game as the fisherman continued to reel with all of his might.

"Got a big one, huh?" asked Aaron in between inhales and exhales. Aaron was never one for small talk with strangers, but it was a special moment for him for a number of reasons.

"Yup. Those bloodworms never fail." Within a few minutes, the battle finally subsided. The pole was still jumping, but the fisherman had his adversary out of the water and started to reel him up to get him over the ledge of the pier. Aaron watched the man land a fat 26-inch catfish onto the ground.

"Whoa, nice catch." It was even bigger than the one he caught in the Savage River.

"Thanks," chuckled the man. He didn't seem that excited

despite what he had to go through to land the aquatic creature. He looked up toward Aaron, smoking away at his green cigarette. "You want it?"

"Huh?" asked a surprised Aaron. "You're giving it away?"

"I don't eat catfish." Looked like Bobby wasn't lying about the dietary preferences of the man's demographics, figured Aaron.

"Uhm, well, thank you. But I just don't have anything to keep it with."

"I got a plastic bag. Just stop at a gas station or something, grab some ice, and you're good." Aaron nodded in deep appreciation of the man's generosity.

"Thank you, sir. My friend loves cats, so I'll be happy to take that off your hands."

"He'll definitely appreciate you if you bring this big boy to him, that's for sure." Aaron chuckled and put out his jay. He stepped over to the man's setup and got the catfish. He shook the man's hands and headed back to his car for the trip back to Cumberland.

CHAPTER 22

"I don't understand," said Chiedu. "I can't even know the address I'm being taken to?" It was mid-November, less than a month out from the date of what was projected to be the highest odds of a second attack happening on Attah's life. He was at his dining room table with his assistant, Sade, and POPCO executive Francine. Across from them were Yemi and Karen in Raptor-branded black polo shirts, the bird of prey emblem in the left chest area.

"It's to protect you, Mr. Attah," assured Karen. "We're not taking any chances after the incident with Ellis."

"She's right, Chiedu," Sade commented. "They're not saying you can't be trusted. But it's just a fact of the matter that the more people who have knowledge of your location, the more likely there is to be a leak." Chiedu sighed.

"And if Raptor requires any support, backup, anything," Francine said. "POPCO has a close relationship with Titus, who can provide assistance if needed at any point."

"We'll be fine," responded Yemi. He made direct eye contact with her. It was the first time the Uzunmas had personally met Francine, but Yemi and Francine were very familiar with each other. He was aware that she knew all about his previous contract at Titus, and he corresponded with Francine at the beginning of her career at POPCO during Yemi's participation in the Niger Delta oil-related operations. Yemi knew that underneath that offer for help was really just the corporate octopus trying to wrap its tentacles around his free entrepreneurial spirit. By that point, Raptor was Titus' main competitor despite the vast differences in their operating budgets. RexCorp still hadn't recovered fully from the Ryan Frost assassination, and no other executive protection contractors in the DC area had honed in on a Bazaar-specific campaign yet.

"Have you ever been out to West Virginia?" asked Karen to Chiedu, looking to steer the conversation away from the subtle antagonism between Francine and Yemi.

"Yes, I have." A slight hint of melancholy was in Chiedu's voice when he responded.

"Oh really? What brought you there?"

"Adamu was considering school out there." Karen realized she had inadvertently touched on another sensitive topic. She eyed Yemi, and he signaled through a slight nod for her to just let Chiedu finish talking. "He didn't like Marshall, but he did get into W-V-U. When my wife and I found out about it being a party school, we convinced him to stay home." Pupils started to get wet, reminiscing about his son as Chiedu looked up at a framed high school graduation photo of Adamu that sat on a shelf across from the table. "How silly of us to think we were keeping him safe by keeping him close."

"Chiedu," beckoned Sade as she rubbed his back. "Don't say that. We've talked about this." The room remained quiet as Chiedu gathered himself to continue with the meeting.

"Death continues to follow me in this country. Adamu, Isaiah, Obi...I just wanted what was best for my family, but I at least had one back home. Now I just sit in an empty castle all day with no prince to carry on my crown."

"You still have time to live a joyful and prosperous life, Chiedu," remarked Karen. "We're here to make sure of that." Chiedu sat slouched in his chair for a few more moments in silence. He then looked up toward Karen and Yemi.

"Do you believe what that woman on the news said about me?"

"Chiedu —," whispered Sade.

"I want to hear their answer." Chiedu rarely backtalked Sade. From Yemi's limited interactions with Chiedu, he took notice that she was usually the logical, solution-oriented brain on the grounds. Especially since Adamu's mother had left him, another addition to the darkness in Chiedu's life.

"Sir," started Yemi. "We don't let any outside opinion affect our ability to provide you with the best protection possible."

"That was a political answer," said Chiedu with his same blank stare. "Perhaps you and I should switch positions."

"Where is the gentleman who runs ALAMUT?" asked Sade, changing the subject. "Vash, I think his name is?"

"His sister's wedding is today," answered Karen. "Otherwise, he'd be right here next to us. He sends his blessings, though."

"I understand we all have family engagements, but him not being present for this is a bit concerning," uttered Francine.

"I've surveyed the property," declared Yemi. "Vigorously. Chiedu is in good hands." The former ambassador nodded in approval. He had always held Yemi in high esteem.

"S-S-S only selects the best," Chiedu said in reference to Yemi's employment origin.

"That's right, sir. I am very proud to have served my country before arriving in this one." Francine cleared her throat, signaling to Yemi that she wanted to direct attention to discussing violent conflict in the land that they were in, not the one they were from.

"Just to confirm. Chiedu is to not step out of the residence for the twenty-four-hour period, correct?" she asked.

"We won't even allow him to walk past a window," Yemi assured her.

"I'm glad to hear that," said Sade. She gripped Chiedu's hand on the table like a concerned wife. Karen tugged on Yemi to take notice of the ring on her finger.

"Oh, I didn't even know," Raptor's CFO stated with admiration at the jewel symbol of engagement. "Congratulations, you guys! That's amazing." Chiedu almost smirked with slight embarrassment from Karen's observation. Yemi had realized Chiedu hadn't been the best at hiding his depression, but the former ambassador would be blushing red if he had significantly less melanin.

"Thank you," Sade said as she rubbed the arm of her fiance with deep affection.

"When is the wedding?" asked Karen, fascinated by this romantic development in their client's life. Yemi knew some of her attitude was genuine joy for Chiedu, who now had a bright spot in his year of turmoil. But Yemi knew his sister well enough that the other part of the fascination was a helpless feeling of slight jealousy over Sade. Not that Chiedu was Karen's type by any means, but Yemi knew tying the knot with a DC political influencer was on her post-Wake Forest bucket list while running Raptor.

"Second weekend of March," Sade responded.

"The two of you are invited," insisted Chiedu. Yemi saw a slight twitch in Sade's face when her partner said that, almost as if they hadn't discussed welcoming the Raptor founders to their monumental life event. He wondered if Sade wanted to see how December first went and if her partner made it out of West Virginia healthy.

"We very much appreciate that Chiedu," Karen said. "We'll mark it on the calendar."

"An invitation will be sent to Raptor's offices," Chiedu projected. Both Karen and Yemi saw another twitch on Sade's face, solidifying their suspicion.

"So," Francine began. "I think we've covered everything in the planning stage. I have a Zoom call in about thirty, so I have to get going."

"Great," Karen said. "It was a pleasure to meet you, Miss Van Zandt." Francine nodded her head respectfully toward Karen. Her choice to not verbalize her response was noted by the siblings. It was obvious she wanted Titus to handle this matter, but neither Karen nor Yemi could care less. Resistance from the beltway bandits of DC who wanted their taxpayer bounties all to themselves was a reality from the day they decided to enter the industry.

Yemi and Karen stepped out from the mini-mansion onto the paved walkway, cutting through the center of Chiedu's front yard. A sight Yemi was already familiar with from the first Attah mission, while Karen took joy in looking at the gargoyles. He knew she was praying to herself that she would be living in a similar structure in a neighborhood with the same median income within their next five years at Raptor.

"Want to go for a walk around the block?" she asked her big brother. Yemi surveyed the street. The only eye candy was really the other houses, all valued in the low millions, but maybe there was a park down the way.

"Sure, come on." The siblings went left and passed one of the 4 Runners they drove to the meeting. They both continued to gander at the large homes surrounding them. During their time in Nigeria, their family had property of equitable size, albeit at a fraction of the cost. But when the Uzunmas came to America, a single family, one-level 5,000 square foot homestead was what their accountant father and high school teaching mother's combined salaries could get them. Neither of them complained much, though. The middle class in Montgomery County, regardless of the size of your house, was a monumental privilege compared to how some of their friends back home ended up getting evicted from the comfortable upper echelons of Nigerian society to being forced to live in a place like Makoko, the floating slum of Lagos. It was nicknamed the "Venice of Africa," however, the Italian city remained one of the crown jewels of its respected country while the waterways of dark sludge were far off the list of desirable destinations for the Nigerian Tourism Development Corporation. The government cleared much of it out to make room for the expansion of the posh financial district of Victoria Island.

"How do you think we would have turned out if we grew up in a neighborhood like this?" asked Karen. Yemi took a second before he responded.

"Maybe we weren't spoiled, but we grew up better than ninety percent of Black kids on the planet."

"This is true. Sadly."

"So it's hard for me to truthfully answer your question since I don't really think about things like that."

"Okay, sheesh. I get it. We had it good." Yemi chuckled a bit at his sister submitting to his point of view. "But doesn't mean we can't do better." Yemi sighed and shook his head.

"Have you ever seen a full smile on Chiedu's face?" asked Yemi. "Seems like money has only given him trouble in paradise." Karen grunted.

"Why can't I just dream, Yemi? Without you always trying to give me a reality check."

"Cause fantasy will ruin your reality if it's distracting you from what actually exists."

"So what, you're saying Chiedu should have stayed a broke activist in the Delta? What if his son ended up getting killed by one of his political enemies over there?"

"I'm not saying anyone should do anything, sis. I specialize in reacting to situations, not predicting them."

"Whatever." A house with a gray gothic-esque architecture caught her attention. "I like that one," she said while pointing at it. Yemi looked at it. Despite his annoyance with Karen's obsession with wealth, he nodded in slight agreement.

"Whoever built that has good taste. Can't lie."

"See? Tell me you wouldn't want to wake up in that every morning to the sounds of your kids playing downstairs."

"Okay, see, this is where the conversation needs to take a different direction," remarked Yemi.

"What? You don't want our parents to have some grandkids before they become octogenarians?"

"I'm pretty sure you're going to be the first one between us to give them that," he chuckled.

"Yemi. Come on, you want a family."

"According to who? Plus, I'm not even forty yet. I've got time to make that decision if it's even what I desire." Karen sighed again and kept looking at the house, even with more envy than Chiedu's, from what Yemi saw in her face.

"You'd be a terrible husband, but I can imagine you being a great father."

"Yeah, well, keep that as an imagination. Remember what I just said about fantasy and reality."

"Oh God, Yemi."

"Before we turn around, listen." Yemi's tone changed. He was getting a little serious. "Jasper says a new site that acts as a discussion board for bettors and potential assassins tied to the Bazaar is gaining popularity. That's where he found out the date from, but the conversations on there about Chiedu are concerning. Doesn't seem like anybody has leaked the location, but we need to be on guard."

"What's it called?"

"Hitter." A snort of a chuckle came out of Karen's nostrils.

"Is that a play-off of 'Twitter' or something?"

"That's my guess."

"Okay, well, I'll reinstall the Tor Browser on my laptop and keep track of it for the next few weeks leading up to the mission. Tell Jasper he can chill on surfing the dark web until then."

"Telling Jasper to chill on any kind of research is a lost cause." Yemi couldn't help but smirk, knowing his best friend and fellow detail agent was the only person he knew who read up on military strategy more than him. "The addition of Nick seems to have only heightened his study habits."

"I swear the two of you need girlfriends."

"We're married to the game," Yemi said, exaggerating his tone, sounding like he had just dropped off multiple kilos of white powder at Chiedu's. "Just like those rappers on your Spotify."

"I don't know what school was like for you back home, but there's no way your corny ass would have lasted four years at a public D-M-V institution." The two laughed together.

"Private school kids are just as ratchet, if not more," remarked Yemi, remembering his rich boarding school classmates who would rack up thousands in credit cards on their trips to Europe if they weren't buying up everything at the Ikeja City Mall, all on the dime of their parents connected to either the government, oil industry, or agriculture companies.

"I know. I saw firsthand at Wake Forest," Karen responded. "And from Chiedu's own mouth, it seems like Adamu was not quite a member of the honor society." Mentioning Adamu brought Yemi's focus back to the task at hand the following month.

"Let's head back now," he suggested. Karen nodded in agreement, and the two reversed their direction to head back toward the car. "Karen."

"Yeah?"

"I know your views on exposure, but we gotta keep this one off of CNN."

"I'm hip." She patted her big brother on the back as they headed to the 4Runner, both in agreement that their operations had made enough headlines at this point.

———

"I don't know how Al Noor read that opening line and rejected it," Jessica Reynolds said to Abdallah while having The Boukan front page up on her laptop. 'How an International Game of Murder and Money has Spilled Into the Streets of DC' was the headline all browsers saw when they arrived at TheBoukan.com. "But then again," Jessica said as she tapped her arm in reference to the skin complexion she shared with her new co-worker. "I do know why."

"Well, I guess that's no longer going to be an issue for my career," Abdallah said with a humble chuckle. Despite what he had just said, as a reader, Abdallah had read Al Noor since he had been in high school while he rarely had ever checked out an article from The Boukan unless it was irresistible clickbait like claiming to have leads on who could be the owner of a bag of cocaine found in the White House. But media standards nor race played a role in Abdallah leaving the Dubai-based news network for the startup named after the Afro-Haitian meaning for 'bonfire.' The Boukan offered Abdallah a $15,000 increase in annual salary and also actually encouraged him to pursue more stories tied to the Bazaar. He'd also get to continue attending White House press briefings, stepping in for Jessica whenever her other engagements would interrupt her workflow.

"This is the kind of writing that can really distinguish The Boukan from the Essences, Revolts, you know the deal." Jessica continued her flattery of the new employee. "It goes beyond just our culture while still being something that's tied to us, whether the bourgeoisie wants to admit it or not."

"Well, the bourgeoisie are the ones being targeted, so I guess I can understand their lack of excitement to read any more news about how their dead pools are rising in popularity."

"Look at this text from none other than Erick McKenzie." Jessica handed her new iPhone over to Abdallah. In the conversation with Eric Mckenzie, 'All it takes is a few lil bitcoins to get these haters out my life,' followed by several laughing emojis, was in the most recent white bubble. Jessica had texted back several crying emojis to her billionaire boss. "He thinks you're the missing link from his creative properties reaching this generation."

"Wow."

"I said those exact same words when I read your article, Mr. Kalfat. Did you want to take your lunch now before we discuss your next story?"

"Sure." Abdallah stood up. "Any spots around you could recommend?"

"Oh, there are so many places around this area. What are you in the mood for?"

"I don't know. You have a favorite?"

"I love The Masala Chicken Company downstairs. But I cook most of the time, so I haven't been there in a while."

"That's what I'll start doing," Abdallah said in reference to Jessica cooking while he headed to the door. "I thinking I'm going to get a cookbook later this month as a Christmas present to myself on how to make more than ramen and PB & Js."

"Oh, chile," Jessica said in reminiscence. "You taking me back. Grape jelly, blueberry, or strawberry?" Abdallah couldn't help but slightly laugh before he exited the room, but he kept his head in to reply.

"So I actually just sort of lied. I use honey, so there's no J."

"Oooo, I need to try that. Maybe even make it for my husband."

"It's better. And actually a little healthier."

"Really?"

"Yup. Let me know what you think."

"I will, Mr. Kalfat. See you in a bit."

Was she offended when he brought up the sandwich being healthier? Did she think he felt he was a superior human being because he almost fit in the underweight category of Body Mass Index? The overthinking and racing thoughts hit Abdallah every so often. He had cooled his anxiety issues during Al Noor with his daily ten milligrams of Lexapro, but being around a celebrity like Jessica Reynolds triggered it a bit near the end of their conversation, being forever grateful that it was her who suggested a break for lunch. He also was still shook up from the unexpected home invasion in his apartment by a possible federal agent.

He then remembered her recommendation of the Masala Chicken Company. He saw a $15 special plate of butter chicken advertised at the front of the restaurant, where it claimed sales would stop after their capacity of three hundred meals. The restaurant was already a change of pace from all the others in the area around the White House, not only given by the price point but also its emphasis on limited supply, meaning it was most likely fresh and had locally sourced ingredients, with the obvious exception being the seasoning.

Abdallah decided to give it a shot and stepped in. Within a few minutes, he had a tray full of the orange-yellow poultry dish on top of basmati rice. Upon a few bites, he realized the limited tastebuds of his idol colleague. Although Indian food was supposed to be spicy, there had clearly been an over-compensation on the red chili pepper for the lack of tenderness in the chicken or flavor in the sauce. He could only stomach a few more bites before he pushed it away. He was eager to accept a position that required him to be in the office during his shift, but now he missed the affordable and flavorful Ethnic cuisines in the suburbs. He whipped out his cell phone and sent a text to Nick.

Abdallah Kalfat: Yo. New job. www.theboukan.com
Nick Rice: thats dope fam, congrats
Abdallah Kalaft: bro did you peep the article?

A five-minute pause came over the conversation. Finally, Nick's chat bubble responded.

Nick Rice: yeah bro, good shit.

It's just texts, but Abdallah was expecting a response with a bit more celebration. He brushed it off and got to the better news.

Abdallah Khalfat: We'll be able to publish all the shit we've been working on through a major platform. Told ya I got us.

Another pause, this one was even longer. Finally, Nick replied.

Nick Rice: We gotta talk about that.

Abdallah was a bit confused.

Abdallah Kalfat: Why? You good?
Nick Rice: I'm good. But yeah, some changes are happening on my end.
Abdallah Kalfat: Uh okay. When you are free?
Nick Rice: After this weekend.
Abdallah Kalfat: Ight cool.

Nick was having second thoughts on the leaks? That was only going to add to Abdallah's hypomania, but he decided to keep his mind focused on the positivity of his first day of working at The Boukan and Jessica Reynolds. He packed the rest of the Masala Chicken and headed out the door. There was a nearby man in his mid-60s in torn, dirty jeans and a faded, stained YMCA shirt camped at a coffee shop's outdoor seating area, asking passersby for change. Abdallah stepped over to him.

"Got any spare change so I can grab a sandwich inside?" the man asked in a voice hardly distinguishable from a philosophy professor.

"I got this if you're hungry." He handed the homeless man his butter chicken carry-out box. The man smiled politely and nodded affirmatively upon receiving the food.

"Appreciate it, brother," the man said. "You got utensils?" Abdallah froze. He knew his senses were deceiving him, but he heard the voice of the anonymous man behind him, making him transfer files at gunpoint.

"You okay there, friend?" the man asked. Abdallah snapped out of his trance.

"Yeah, yeah," said Abdallah as he took out a five dollar bill along with a fork and gave them to the man. "You definitely going to need a drink, though," Abdallah said. The man delivered a loud, choppy laugh.

"I love Indian food," he said.

"So do I, but this is yours. Have a good day." Jessica Reynolds probably didn't actually like Indian food because you couldn't like or dislike what you clearly don't know, an overthinking Abdallah pondered as he looked for the nearest 7-11 to get the rest of his lunch. Just like she clearly didn't know that she had just entered the Bazaar's top 200 as Abdallah had just read that morning.

CHAPTER 23

The squad had to be at Chiedu's front doorstep no later than 4:30 PM. It was a two-hour drive to Rio, West Virginia, from Vienna, but Yemi wasn't going to take any chances on a hitman tailing them for an opportunity to cash in if they hit unexpected late-night traffic or potential car trouble that would push them into midnight giving the contract killer a green light. Sade was there at the house to send off her fiance. Terry watched them embrace and kiss before he headed to one of the 4Runners. Terry picked up a different vibe in their affection than Desmond Ellis and his wife, and it wasn't just the fact that Sade was two decades younger than Chiedu. While there was no doubt that Lisa was concerned for her husband's safety before sending him off to Rockville, her body language hinted that she was confident he was going to return. Between the intense hug to the ten-second-long kiss, it seemed to Terry that Sade figured this could be the last time she would ever see the love of her life. Sade couldn't take her eyes off of Chiedu his entire walk to Terry and Lyle's vehicle, where he would sit next to Nick just like the last time, except it wasn't in his Mercedes, and Obi was no longer with them. Witnessing such a raw display of love up against the homicidal consequences of monetary greed gave Terry more motivation to ensure that their client returned back to Vienna healthy the following day. Jasper revved up the front 4Runner and led the Raptor EPT convoy out of the driveway. They pulled onto Interstate 66 and began their road journey west.

"Where's your laptop?" asked Terry, noticing Nick's computer was not on his lap.

"I'll hop on it when we get to the site," responded Nick.

"Makes no sense to get on it until the drones get in the air."

"How has it been for you since last year?" asked Chiedu as they went above sixty-five miles per hour on the highway.

"Funny, I was going to ask you the same question." They both smirked, and Chiedu looked out the window before Nick could answer his question. "It's been good. Obviously, if you've seen the news, there's been some hurdles, but it seems like Yemi is finally taking me seriously."

"I'm glad to hear that," Chiedu stated as he kept his attention on the world outside, zipping past them. "I see great things in this company's future. I don't know your five or ten-year plan, but you'll go far if you stick with Raptor for some time."

"That's what I try to tell him, Mr. Attah," Terry chimed in from the front.

"Hop off his dick," muttered Lyle under his breath. Terry made a face of disapproval but otherwise ignored him.

"Too many kids his age jump from job to job," Terry continued. "But they don't understand that helping a firm grow expands your opportunities at your current situation or even beyond."

"I like Raptor," said Nick. "Don't think I'm going anywhere else anytime soon." Terry looked at Nick in the rearview mirror. The young man's words seemed genuine.

Other than a refuel of gas after they crossed the border into West Virginia, the EPT motorcade had no breaks in their drive to the safe house. They arrived well before eleven, with three to set up their perimeter. Terry and Lyle led Chiedu into the building as Nick got his drones out from the trunk of their vehicle. He opened up the app on his phone and got the team's eyes in the sky within five to ten minutes. Once they were four hundred feet in the air, he followed Yemi and Jasper into the cabin. Nick had a little station set up in the living room on a coffee table in front of a wooden chair with a leather cushioned seat. He switched out the controls from his Android to his laptop. He immediately switched the perspective to infrared and checked the vast surrounding forests for thermal activity.

"Other than some nocturnal critters," Nick said to his team. "The aerials are clear on the first scan.

Yemi had walked back into the room from the house, checked with Terry, and the two headed to their guard stations. Yemi's was next to one of the living room windows at the front of the house, while Terry's was on the river side of the structure.

"Okay, just keep me updated," Yemi said back to him.

"I'll send all of you a link to the feed. Check texts." Terry opened up his phone and read the latest message in his inbox sent from Nick Rice. He clicked the hyperlink, and he was forwarded to a page with two different aerial thermal cameras depicting a dark Appalachia in 4k.

"Great," Yemi said as he was looking at the same image as Terry. "Nine forty-five. More than two hours out, but let's be ready." Terry grabbed a nearby black tactical backpack with the Raptor insignia printed on the front. He took out a pair of night vision goggles with a head strap. Yemi assured him they were civilian-issue to avoid any legal issues and cost under $500, but Terry still looked reminiscent of one of his Navy brothers who killed Osama bin Laden when he secured the device to his head. He was able to see forty yards into the woods from the window, but he was still tucked in by its corner, keeping himself from being exposed behind the glass.

———

Chiedu looked at the office he'd be staying in for the next twenty-four hours. The walls were decorated with framed photos of the surrounding Shenandoah Valley and the Blue Ridge Mountains. There was also a desktop computer set up for him at a desk, but his primary focus was on the twin-sized bed on the left side of the room. He removed his clothes down to his undershirt and briefs before he sat on the edge of the mattress. After so many months of sadness and mourning, the only thing on his mind was Sade. The drinking had finally subsided a few months with her help, and planning the wedding kept his brain occupied with thoughts of a bright future instead of the recent dark past. He had never felt such a strong connection with another woman, even with his former wife of 20+ years. He knew some of his relatives would think Sade was little more than a young, attractive gold digger at his wedding, but their opinions mattered less and less as the years went on. It was their social pressure that pushed him into a career in public service instead of his passion for theater. He had given up his dreams of being a Nollywood star once his cousin was fired from his position as an oil refinery supervisor in the Delta and put all his energy into being a voice for his people instead of just pretending to be on a movie screen. But the past was set in stone, and he wanted to make sure he would actually make it to his wedding day. He knew he was forbidden from using his phone at this location, but he took out his cell device once he felt a vibration. He read a text in his inbox:

Sade: I miss you already.

Chiedu smiles and types back.

Chiedu: I miss you too. About to sleep.
Sade: Dream of me <3

Someone knocked on his door.
"Yes?" Chiedu called out.
"Everything looks okay, Mr. Attah?" From the voice, Chiedu couldn't tell which member of the squad it was.
"Yes, it's just fine."

"Good, good. May I come in to obtain your phone?" Chiedu texted back a smiley face before he answered.

"Yes, come on in." The one who was of East African origin entered the room, and Chiedu handed him his iPhone. In return, the man placed a radio on the desk.

"Thank you. Just let us know if you need anything else. In case of any kind of an emergency, use this, please," he said in reference to the walkie-talkie.

"I appreciate you, uhm—"

"Jasper Kidanu."

"Oh, you're Yemi's right-hand man, aren't you?" Jasper politely grinned.

"We go back all the way to Africa." Chiedu nodded.

"Guess we're both a long way from home," the client replied.

"I've always been someone on the move, so it makes little difference to me."

"How does that work?" asked Chiedu, looking to make conversation with a member of his detail that he hadn't interacted with. "You can't grow any roots if you don't find a place to plant your seed." Jasper shrugged his shoulders.

"I like where I'm at and what I do. That's all I can say, honestly." He knew Jasper was being brief but not rude.

"Then you're living the dream as far as I'm concerned."

"Just trying to get like you, Mr. Attah." Another polite laugh from Chiedu, hiding the fact that he couldn't imagine any fool who wanted to be like him at that moment. They shook hands, and Jasper left the ex-ambassador to himself in the space.

———

As expected, the rest of the night was quiet. Jasper and Victor were stationed on the top floor. Terry, Yemi, and Lyle were all positioned in different spots on the ground floor while Nick occupied the same coffee table in the living room. As usual, it was Karen and Nick who were primarily overseeing the drone footage. Unlike the previous two gigs, almost every EPT unit member had a medium to long automatic weapon in their grasp. Yemi, Jasper, Victor, and Terry were all strapped with camo-colored scoped MCX-Spear assault rifles. Lyle, on the other hand, was armed with a solid black Dakota Tactical D54 submachine gun as he patrolled the windows of the kitchen, also equipped with a scope. Nick was the lone squad member whose primary gun was still the Glock 22, not having done well enough to Yemi's standards at the gun range for him to have anything with more firepower or range. Everyone was outfitted with the same night vision goggles Terry had taken out of the bag, going between wearing them and functioning without it, depending on their focus at the moment.

Yemi watched the white outline of a buck through his goggles slowly waltz across the front of the cabin, two dozen yards ahead of his guarded window. Nick switched back to thermal mode and identified the same deer through the drone footage. He followed the body heat of the mammal as it headed deeper into the woods, away from their base.

"Did you make sure to get enough sleep yesterday?" Yemi asked Nick, who was only a few feet from him. Nick tensed up a bit, still getting used to Yemi going out of his way to finally talk to the rookie.

"Yeah," responded Nick. "Just put on the latest Marvel movie when I got in bed, and it made it easy." A slight grin from Yemi as he continued to look out the window.

"You think they'll ever stop making those?" Yemi responded.

"The only way to get a gravy train off the tracks is when there are no passengers to pick up." The detail leader nodded his head in affirmation to Nick's analogy.

"So, according to that theory, when do you think the

Bazaar demand will subside?" asked Yemi. Nick evidently had to think for a moment before he could respond. Terry entered the living room after patrolling the opposite side of the ground floor. Yemi realized he had been listening to most of the conversation.

"Well, if it does, won't that hurt our bottom line?" asked Nick.

"Crazy, isn't it?" rhetorically asked Terry. "I thought my life's duty was to protect others from harm. But if there is no one to put them in danger, I'm out of a job." Terry shook his head. Yemi knew Terry was reminiscing over his career.

"You just described the whole reason behind this country's defense budget," Yemi said while observing the exterior wooded surroundings.

"I don't know what you saw in uniform," Yemi said toward Terry. "But what I saw at Titus told me enough about how this economy operates. Protection only matters if there's a profit."

"Oh no," said Terry. "Now I don't want your opinion on 9/11."

"Trust me, you don't," laughed Yemi. Terry laughed along with him as he turned around to head back to his original guard station. As Terry left, Lyle popped his head in from the kitchen area.

"Isn't Vash supposed to be here?" asked the Jamaican.

"He'll be here at the break of dawn," answered Yemi. "He'll handle meals, time checks, getting whatever Chiedu needs, and all that."

"Doesn't that leave room for a security breach?" Lyle usually wasn't this inquisitive, Yemi noticed. But it was a fair question nonetheless.

"He won't be within three hundred yards without Nick or Karen spotting him. We'll be good," answered Yemi.

"Cool. As long as you approve," commented Lyle as he

headed back into the kitchen. "And I get paid, of course."

"When have I ever asked you to work for free, Lyle?" Yemi called out to him. No answer as there seemed to be a mutual unspoken agreement between the two to not take the statement seriously. For how much Lyle complained about Yemi to his squadmates, the two had rarely butt heads directly throughout his entire career at Raptor. Yemi was well aware of Lyle's vast knowledge of how American criminal elements operated, and he could sense Lyle was warming up to the fact that Yemi might actually have known what he was doing in the leadership position.

"Hey, Yemi," said Nick.

"What's up?" Nick took a second before he could verbalize his curiosity.

"Were you planning on forming the Executive Protection Team from the beginning when you and Karen started Raptor? Or did it just come up after Chiedu's son was killed?" Yemi meditated on Nick's question for a few moments while looking out into the woods.

"I first found out about the Bazaar through Jasper. He sent me a link, how to access it with the Tor browser, et cetera." Yemi cleared his throat and took off his night vision goggles to rub his eyes for a brief period. "We went down the list and saw that a significant fraction of the individuals in the top two hundred were either in D.C. or the surrounding suburbs. A week later, Karen filed an L-L-C for Raptor. But for the first year, we just focused on contracts for property security while we got the executive protection thing mapped out."

"Did you expect to make headline news in your first year?" Yemi took another second before he could give a response that satisfied him.

"One thing that sports teach you is to thrive in chaos. Doesn't really matter what's going on the outside as long our team accomplishes our task, which we have been doing. And we will continue to do."

"You sound like my cross-country coach."

"Good," said Yemi as he placed his night vision goggles back on to look through the window. "Maybe he was onto something. Let's focus until the sun rises."

No action happened the following several hours leading up to daylight. The deer that walked past the house was the last live being that they were aware of, and only the occasional heat sensors of a mammal would appear on Nick or Karen's infrared footage. That changed once the clock hit 6:45 AM. A recent model BMW 4 series entered his aerial view from the drone.

"A vehicle is turning onto the mountain," said Nick into his radio. He read the thermals. "Approximately five hundred yards from our immediate perimeter. One occupant."

"I see it," responded Karen over the communication system. "It's Vash. Just confirmed over text."

"Copy." The luxury car sped up the road, cutting through the forest that was fifty-plus miles from civilization.

"Lyle," called out Yemi. "You and I escort Vash in. Nick, make sure nobody is following him. Everybody else, cover us while we're outside."

"Copy."

"Roger that."

"You got it."

Lyle entered the living room with his SMG pointed to the ceiling in one hand. A few minutes passed, and Yemi looked toward Nick. Nick checked the footage.

"He's pulling up, sir." Yemi nodded to Lyle, and the two filed out the front of the house and got in tactical stationary positions on the patio as the cream-colored BMW kicked up dirt on its way up the tree-scattered hill. Despite some of the debris beneath it being a slight on the eyes, Vash managed to park it pretty smoothly before the cabin. Yemi and Lyle briskly flanked the BMW as Vash pushed open his door and lifted himself out of the driver's side with his trademark smile.

"Good morning, gentlemen! Gotta grab some things from the trunk."

"We can help—"

"No, we can't," Yemi interrupted Lyle to correct him. Yemi always knew he was usually reluctant to show subversion, but he still nodded to acknowledge Yemi was right. Because he was, they absolutely could not have their hands preoccupied with anything other than their armaments for the remaining seventeen or so hours.

"Totally fine!" assured Vash. "I can get it all, trust me." Vash made his way to the back of the car and popped open its trunk. Within seconds, his arms were full of Tupperware containers, napkins, utensils, plates, and coffee grounds, all stacked on top of each other. He balanced all the food items and waddled between Yemi and Lyle as they escorted him into the cabin.

"Good morning, everyone!" Vash announced to the house as he entered. He made an immediate pivot to the kitchen, and Lyle sidestepped to allow him to drop everything on the counter. Yemi didn't bother to follow them, but he could hear every word from his position. "I got bagels, bananas, baguettes, with your choice of peanut butter, cream cheese, lox, you name it. Also picked up some citrus fruits. Gotta get our vitamins!"

"Thank God, I'm starving," said Nick as he headed to the kitchen. "Only had some ramen last night and forgot to pack any protein bars."

"You're not in college anymore, Rice," said Terry as he trailed behind the rest in the hallway. "Dried noodle blocks can't cut it as a diet anymore."

"Any coffee?" asked Lyle.

"I was about to ask the same thing," said Nick.

"Yes, of course." Vash removed a small package of coffee grounds from the pile he set on the tabletop. It had green, yellow, and red coloring with a male lion logo. "Straight from the Kaffa region of West Ethiopia. Just from that name alone, you should know the people who made this coffee take it seriously."

"Whatever happened to just Folgers or Maxwell House?" joked an unimpressed Lyle. Terry came through the kitchen entry along with Yemi. Vash reached for the coffee pot and set it on the stove, which sat at the center of the room, encircled by windows.

"What's the brand name?" asked Nick. "I wonder if Jasper had heard of it."

"Oh wow," said Vash as he got the kettle to boil. Yemi headed back to the living room, realizing he could wait for any nourishment and would rather not be in a crowded room. "I just had it in my hand, and the name is totally slippin—" Yemi heard the sound of glass shattering from a window in the kitchen.

"VASH IS DOWN!" Terry's voice tore through the radio. There was no time to make rational sense of how Vash was sniped. The three in the room quickly got their guns ready to engage, and they took tactical positions across the front floor.

Terry briskly strafed across the living room, ducking low to avoid detection by whoever had them in their crosshairs from God-knows-how-far-a-distance. He got back in his original spot to cover his range by the house. With his Glock 22 in hand, Nick stayed low as he lept to his laptop to look at the aerial view.

"Karen!" yelled Yemi into his radio as he kept his MCX-Spear aimed into the forest. "Are you or Nick able to tell us anything?" Yemi knew she was fighting back the involuntary urge to break down upon learning about the almost certain death of her friend Vash Ahmadabadi.

"I got thermals on, and I'm not seeing anything within three hundred yards," she barked through the radio. They were at the beginning of chaos, but Yemi was proud of her composure.

"Yeah, I'm not picking up anything either," stated Nick.

Yemi knew that on the top floor, both Jasper and Victor were probably taking similar tactical angles by their respective windows as the rest of their teammates.

"They're out of our range," Jasper said via the radio. "Definitely high-level snipers."

".50 cal bullets, too," Terry communicated to this team. "Going off the impact on Vash."

"Nick," commanded Yemi. "Just stay away from any windows and keep your attention on the drone. Soon as anything enters your field of view, say something."

"Yes, sir."

"Yemi!" yelled Karen into her radio. "They spotted one of our drones."

"Lost the feed," announced Nick to his boss across from him. They both sighed, but Yemi kept his guard up.

"Gonna switch to infrared, sir." Nick flicked on the infrared of the other drone in his control. Yemi studied the woods as he waited for Nick to update him on anything.

"Okay, I got something," said Nick. "I'm seeing some bodies about fifteen hundred meters out, north side."

"Good work," responded Yemi. "Now, get it back here before they spot you."

"Copy." A moment passed, and he heard Nick loudly hiss his teeth.

"Shit," said Nick out loud. "Second drone is taking fire."

"Keep trying to fly it out of there," said Yemi. The detail leader would never panic, but losing all aerial perspective would force the squad into an even trickier situation. The sharpshooters far away on another mountain took away their elevated advantage. Nonetheless, Yemi didn't have drones in gun battles on the Delta, so he'd figure out a way to succeed here.

Within a few moments, Yemi watched from his angle of the window and saw the device fall from the sky, smacking some bare trees on its way down.

"Rice," said Yemi. "Back up Terry to make sure nobody sneaks up on us from the back."

"Copy." Nick sighed in frustration from his main tools for his job being destroyed. He got his Glock ready, ducked down, and scurried across the living room to get around the corner to where Terry was stationed.

Yemi knew it was going to be a long waiting game. There was nowhere anyone on the squad could shift their muscle into view of the window, or they risked being taken off the roster in a single shot. If there was going to be an assault on the house, it was coming soon. A professional hit squad was not going to wait around for badges to thwart their assassination.

"Yemi," Karen stated over the radio. "Do you want me to get state police on the line?" Yemi peeked around the corner to study yards of trees in front of the window, waiting for something to appear. He was usually very quick at making decisions, but he couldn't find an immediate answer for Karen. "Yemi?!"

"No. Hold off." It was probably not the answer Karen wanted, but it was the one she was going to have to deal with because Yemi was adamant about no more headlines. And a police presence, even in the boonies, would attract the media like gnats to a lightbulb.

"You sure, Yemi?" asked Terry through the radio. Yemi liked Terry but always knew that his bias for law enforcement would show up at times.

"Yes!" Yemi barked back.

"Getting a visual of what's beyond us," Jasper said into the radio. "Hold tight." Yemi knew that Jasper had a periscope device that he could attach to his phone to zoom in through the trees, scanning around them for any movement.

"Potential hostiles arriving about four hundred yards out in vehicles," Jasper reported to his crew."They're stopping." Yemi looked down his scope, but he knew his field of range couldn't match his right hand man's.

"We got at least ten tangos now on foot heading our way," Jasper said over the radio. "Heavily armed with long guns." Yemi knew almost every squad member wanted to curse out loud over the radio, but they all resisted and stayed focused, knowing that showing any visible frustration would just chip away at the morale of their fellow team member. They would have to allow the assailants to get within medium close range of the cabin before they could fire back to avoid getting caught by a sniper.

"Two hundred yards out." Several more minutes pass. Finally, Yemi could see them on foot.

"Hold on," said Jasper over the radio. "Some of them have stopped about a hundred and fifty yards away."

Yemi observed one of the men remove a megaphone that was attached to his side. The man had an American flag bandana wrapped around the bottom half of his face and a camouflage hat on top of his head.

"Attention, occupants!" the man announced through the horn in his hand. "You know who we are here for. We also both know that you will face certain death if you choose to battle with us. I can assure you that you are vastly outnumbered, and as you saw from the fate of your friend in the kitchen, you are also outgunned. Send Chiedu Attah out within the next two minutes, or we will be forced to descend on a not-so-safe house. The choice is yours."

―――――

Aaron stayed covered behind one of the trees with his 3D-printed AR pointed in the air. Although everyone was masked up, he knew Doug and Bobby Z were the ones flanking him, staying protected behind their own respective trees. The man on the megaphone was Mason from the initial meeting in Southern Maryland a couple of months back. Aaron had started a timer on his phone once Mason had delivered the two-minute warning. Only forty-five seconds were left, and still no sign of Chiedu or any surrender from his executive protection team.

"Get ready, everyone," said Mason to all the men at his sides after checking his own timer.

"Aaron," called Doug from his right. Aaron turned in his direction. "Remember, we're going to hit the back entrance, so follow Bobby and I." Aaron nodded in agreement. Suddenly, a gunshot rang out. One of the men on the other side of Mason collapsed to the ground.

"Open fire!" yelled Mason. Every rifle blasted away at the cabin, breaking windows and splintering its wooden exterior. Gunsmoke from the strikes on the house made it look like the structure was breathing out the cold air. Aaron broke from shooting for a brief moment to look toward the first victim of the shootout. He noticed the long hair sticking out from the hat and realized that it was none other than the one who brought them into the mission.

"Scottie's down," Aaron told Doug as the trio pushed toward the left side of the cabin, making sure they were covered by trees.

"Shit," said Bobby as he tactically moved forward with his SKS rifle between the trees. "Fuck 'em, we'll take his split." They were careful as they shuffled between the structures of oak, making sure nobody from the kitchen or second floor spotted them like they did Scottie. Suddenly, tree bark splintered near Doug's face.

"Get down!" he yelled to his partners behind him with a bloody gash on his cheek. Aaron spun around a tree and quickly got an angle toward the window of the kitchen. He let off a few rounds, shattering the glass remnants from the earlier hit on

Vash. He then quickly raised his rifle toward the second-floor window and did the same until his clip went out.

"Reloading!" Aaron called to Bobby and Doug as he spun back behind the tree to stay covered. He changed magazines on his rifle as Bobby and Doug exchanged gunfire with members of Chiedu's protection team. When Aaron finished getting his rifle ready, he didn't yet get into his previous shooting position. Instead, he went into his tactical backpack and removed a new homemade tear gas grenade he prepared a week prior.

"Cover me!" Aaron yelled to his peers. On cue, Bobby and Doug made sure the two floors were lit up with bullets as Aaron dove before the tree and tossed the grenade as quickly as he could through the kitchen window. He was able to safely make it back behind the tree as it successfully passed the window sill and touchdown on the kitchen floor.

———

The tear gas made with the best organic peppers found in Western Maryland in December suffocated the entire kitchen in burning clouds within seconds. Lyle dove away from the kitchen and took cover in the living room near Yemi's position. The clouds spread from the kitchen. Lyle, Yemi, and Nick all reached into their packs and took out special safety goggles. They were not going to let a repeat of Veterans Plaza stifle their protection of Attah again.

"Tear gas has entered the kitchen," said Lyle into the radio.

"Yemi." Karen's voice over the radio was on the borderline of panic, but Yemi could tell she was still holding it together. "Please let me call backup now." Yemi quickly spotted another one of Mason's crew stepping from around a tree to throw another explosive projectile into the safe house. Within a hair of a second, Yemi delivered a succession of two shots into the man's body, piercing the plates on his vests. The man flopped to the dirt, and his grenade smacked the ground, sending wild smoke into the trees behind his corpse. The tear gas greatly irritated two gunmen in the immediate surrounding area, forcing them to retreat a few feet back.

"Do it," Yemi responded to his sister. The safe house continued to get riddled with bullets from the hit squad.

"Victor's down!" Jasper yelled into the radio.

"Shot hit me in the knee," the Venezuelan said right after his comrade saw him fall. "But I'm still in the fight."

———

Cooped up in his room and surrounded by the sound of a full-out firefight, Chiedu got off his bed and knelt before it. He never quite understood why so many of his countrymen worshipped a religion that was only brought to Nigeria through colonialism, but he bowed his head and prayed with every ounce of energy in his body to the Holy Spirit. It was the first time. Even when his son was killed, he wallowed in depression without seeking any spiritual help from a higher power. That changed that day, for if there was any force, whether physical or supernatural, that would bring him back to Sade, he was willing to test it out.

———

Yemi spotted three gunmen strafing through the trees toward the right side of the safe house. They went out of his range, but he knew Terry would fire toward the one in the front. Terry's side of the cabin was lit with a hail of bullets. Yemi could hear the glass shatter and shells penetrate the right section of the safe house.

"Just took one to the shoulder," Terry communicated to his fellow team. "Still covering right side."

Yemi realized that their castle was on the verge of being raided. While they were having some success keeping the gunmen at bay, their opposition's increasing desperation would only turn to more drastic measures to penetrate Raptor's defenses. Yemi heard an engine loudly rev in the distance. He didn't want to get put in the crosshairs of their sniper, so he took out a handheld mirror to get a view of the hundreds of yards directly in front of the safe house. He realized that one of their desperate measures was underway as a pickup truck was going full speed down the dirt road toward the cabin.

"Rice!" yelled Yemi to his rookie across from him. "Duck back and take cover! They're going to ram the place!" Yemi and Nick crouched down and ran into the parallel hallways of the cabin.

"Took out the driver," said Jasper into the radio. "But truck is still in full motion!" Within a second, the kamikaze F-150 crashed through the front of the cabin, obliterating the entrance and scattering debris throughout the living room.

With a much larger opening visible, the gunfire exchanged between the two sides grew even more violent. Yemi managed to share a hallway with Lyle. Both got a decent amount of cover as they fired upon their invaders from opposing angles. Yemi was holding off Mason and a few of his followers.

"Got three subjects attempting to ambush us from the back," said Lyle into the radio. "I'll keep 'em at bay."

Amid the chaos, Yemi hoped Nick found similar success in establishing a position in the other hallway along with Terry.

"Rice, you good?" he asked through the radio in between shots.

"Yeah, backing up Terry." Even with death knocking on their door, Yemi breathed a sigh of slight relief.

"Copy. Karen, make sure the cops know that they have snipers." They had taken out at least three members of their opposing squad, and Raptor's only loss so far in the battle was Vash, a non-combatant. Yemi felt that they were handling the raid pretty well despite the circumstances, yet knew law enforcement involvement at this point was a necessity.

"I still can't get through to them," said Karen over the radio. Huh? Yemi wasn't even aware she was having issues.

"What do you mean?"

"The number goes straight to dial tone. Like our number is blocked or something."

"That makes no sense," said Yemi as he fired off the last round of his mag. He immediately dug into his vest for another one.

"It doesn't, but that's the situation." Yemi sighed.

"If you have to get on your cell phone and dial 9-1-1, then do it, dammit!"

"Roger that." He knew Karen wouldn't take his tone personally, and she would do as she was told. Yemi realized that there might not be any backup from the boys in blue in the ordeal. Their ammunition was limited, probably far less than what their assailants had stocked up. Nonetheless, he knew they were having some success and could still pull off a victory.

"We're going to need them," Lyle said in the radio. "I'm outnumbered here."

"We all are," Yemi responded. "But we're winning." No matter how skilled Lyle was, Yemi never expected too much optimism from Lyle. But he would have never hired him if he really felt that the SMG-wielding field agent would betray their mission to cash in on the eight figure golden egg upstairs.

"One down," Lyle said. That response assured Yemi he made the right decision in the selection process.

Doug and Aaron watched their comrade crumble to the ground. His body gyrated as one of Chiedu's protection detail nailed Bobby Z with a succession of another three shots.

"Bobby!" screamed Doug. He spotted the mercenary's D54 barrel sticking out from the corner of the doorway and nearly emptied the clip in that direction, sending the Raptor field agent retreating. Doug strafed to his left as Aaron provided him with cover fire, and Doug dragged Bobby back behind a set of trees that blocked their opposition's aim range. Aaron continued to fire upon Chiedu's protection detail as Doug tended to their fallen fellow patriot.

"Keep breathing, bro," Doug said as he unstrapped Bobby Z's tactical vest to release pressure on his body. "Do you remember where you were hit?" Doug followed the blotches of crimson to pinpoint Bobby's entry wounds.

"I-uhh." Blood started to fill up Bobby Z's mouth, and it started to overflow onto his pale face like a pot bubbling on the stove.

"Never mind, just relax," Doug said. As Aaron returned fire at their adversary, he realized how dire the circumstances were for his partners in crime. As Doug's hands felt multiple bloody craters in Bobby's flesh, Aaron knew it was starting to hit Doug that it was the moment he had been fearing since the two boys from Cumberland robbed a Cash N Go in their local downtown not even a year out of high school. Doug told Aaron that they had taken notes from both their real idols, like Pretty Boy Floyd, and fictional heroes, like the various masked gun-wielding bank robbers from mid-90s American cinema. The two had been professional, clean, and anonymous, a far cry from their car-window-shattering meth-head counterparts who would be in and out of incarceration.

But on the first mission, that tight-knit crew opened their ranks up to join forces with others outside their circle. This was the result. Aaron backpedaled to Doug's position. Taking a tactical angle behind a tree, he glanced back at Doug kneeling over their fellow soldier. Bobby Z's breathing started to slow, and Doug noticed.

"Come on, bro, stay with me." For their whole time of knowing each other, Doug's presence always felt like someone who spoke with the authority and cadence of someone way beyond their years. But Aaron heard the voice of a child whimpering at his best friend moving away for good. Except they were two grown men, and one was heading off into the afterlife, not just another neighborhood.

Doug's tears dripped down his face, and Aaron knew that they were freezing cold with the December air, but it didn't seem like Doug cared. Aaron eyed him, feeling for Bobby's heartbeat.

"He's gone." Doug dropped his head at the realization that his friend had permanently checked out and tried to gather himself. Aaron ceased firing and also took some time to mourn someone he was starting to call a friend. There were parallels between Aaron and Bobby's relationship with him and Qasim.

"What do you want to do?" asked Aaron. He understood it was a difficult situation for Doug to accept, but the process of decision making couldn't be slowed any further. After a few seconds, Doug looked up from the body toward the safe house. The emotionally hurt boy was gone, and the man on a mission returned.

"Get fucking paid." Aaron knew immediately what that meant. Both he and Doug opened their packs and took out gas masks. Aaron loaded a new mag into his Ultramaker-produced assault rifle. He first aimed toward the second floor of the safe house to see if they had been spotted. He saw movement in one of the windows and immediately delivered rapid gunfire shots to the mounted glass on the second floor. He then focused his attention on the doorway the small machine gun had been shooting at them from. He fired some around the doorway to keep the mercenary back if he was starting to creep. He waved for Doug to join him in storming the cabin. They sprinted to the exterior of the rear of the safe house and took parallel positions outside an entrance. Doug knew he was the only one with a tear gas grenade left, so he took it out, checked to make sure Aaron was ready, and tossed it through the doorway. Even if the Raptor agents had face protection from the gas, the smoke would at least provide some temporary cover. Aaron cut through the entrance, spraying every corner as he arrived at the end of the hallway. He dashed into a small bathroom on the right and angled himself around whatever corner he could fit behind. He kept a close eye on the room across from him, knowing that was most likely where Bobby's killer had run to. Not even five seconds later, Mason was taking cover behind the rammed truck with four fellow members of his squad as they started their descent to the front entrance of the safe house. They took far heavier fire, though, than Aaron and Doug at that moment. Doug quickly hustled into the hallway and parked himself on the right side of the room entrance across from Aaron.

Mason and his crew preoccupying Yemi, Nick, and Terry had made this spot less of a target temporarily. Doug did a 180-degree pivot to prepare to storm the room next to him. He shifted his head to signal Aaron to begin the process. They were on opposing corners of the room doorway and spun into it, lighting every inch of it for what they assumed may be a waiting opposing field agent. After a few seconds of gunfire, they realized the room had no occupants, and the only victims of their 5.56mm shells were paperback romance novels, self-help books, a flower pot, and the shelves holding everything together. However, they also hit another door that led in the direction of the kitchen. Doug started to take a position by the door, but almost immediately, rapid machine gunfire pierced the fiberglass. Aaron and Doug took cover on opposing ends of the room, avoiding getting hit.

"Listen, man!" Doug called out to the shooter from their side of the doorway. "It's not too late to surrender. We just want the ambassador, and you can still get out of here alive!" There were a few beats of silence between the three of them. Doug and Aaron wondered if it meant their enemy was actually weighing in on Doug's suggestion as an option. But within seconds, a few 9mm bullets penetrated through the walls on Doug and Aaron's side. They returned the favor, blindly lighting up the knotty pine dividers to try to hit their adversary in the kitchen. Doug shifted himself to an angle by the doorway, rapidly scanning for the enemy's position. Aaron and Doug continued to trade fire with the Raptor squad member through the walls. Aaron then quickly side-shuffled across the back of the room in the best attempt he could to get to the original doorway as safely as possible. He managed to pull it off without getting hit by any shells, and he pivoted down the first hallway. He saw Mason and a few of his crew had advanced inside the living room, pushing Chiedu's detail into a corner in the parallel hallway. So, even though Doug may have been pinned, it was clear that it was Bobby's killer who was the one who would end up being immobile. Two of Mason's men diverted their attention to the kitchen from the living room area, set up firing positions, and traded gunfire with Aaron's target, who now had two different sides he had to worry about. Aaron snuck down the hall. He made sure Mason's people spotted him, and they saluted one another.

Aaron arrived at the end of the hall and was careful to go any further in the chance he arrived in their opposition's target range. However, before he could even get himself in the right position, two pepper spray hand grenades were thrown into the living room from opposite ends like it was coordinated by the Raptor squad. The fog sprayed out of the canisters as they spun 360 degrees. Two of Mason's men took Capsaicin to the face and were immediately rendered helpless as they pulled back. Mason managed to dodge the wrath, but the same couldn't be said of his comrade nearby him. He lost his sense of direction, and an opposing field agent used his sudden exposure to deliver assault rifle bullets that ripped through his abdomen and gave him an early grave.

Although Raptor seemingly had the upper hand, the gas mask-wearing Aaron took advantage of Bobby's shooter switching to another cover. Aaron figured he must have assumed most of the raid team was disabled. Aaron was able to catch him right in the crosshairs as he shifted to near the stove island. Aaron pulled the trigger and caught the dreadlocked man right in the lower abdomen and upper thigh. It forced him to fall onto the kitchen floor.

"Doug!" yelled Aaron to the other room. "Don't kill him. Hold on a sec." Aaron made sure nobody from the opposition was pressing forward on Mason. It seemed Mason was still holding his ground, so Aaron hugged the corner and turned into the kitchen like a cat. Doug joined him, and they descended onto the field agent they had been going after.

"Don't fucking move, or you're dead!" yelled Doug to the wounded bodyguard. Once they got before him, Aaron kicked away the submachine gun, and they both put him at gunpoint while he gripped his lesion. "Aaron, stand him up." Aaron paused on Doug's order. He wasn't sure what made him freeze.

"I got an idea," Doug followed up. "Just get him up." If it wasn't for the firearm in Aaron's possession, he wouldn't know any way of having to force the heavily muscled man to do anything. But given that the means of warfare had evolved from hand-to-hand combat to the automatic cannon in Aaron's hands, the Raptor employee obeyed his commands to stand himself up despite the damage he had taken.

"Bring him this way," said Doug as he tactically moved from the kitchen doorway to the living room and took a firing position from the side of the crashed truck toward the other hallway where the other executive protection agents on the first floor were. Mason continued to exchange fire with them from the opposite side.

"Mason!" called out Doug. "Hold fire for a second."

"Are you serious?" The ex-marine seemed to be in disbelief that his new fellow fighter wanted to pause the gunfight, but then he saw their captured hostage behind Doug and nodded in approval.

"Yemi Uzunma!" Doug yelled out so they could hear from the hallway. He didn't get an answer as expected and continued. "I have a proposition you may want to consider." Another few beats passed, and still nothing. "We have one of yours right now still alive." He turned to his hostage. "Say something." Yemi's subordinate didn't budge, so Aaron stuck the barrel under his chin.

"I'm good, Yemi," the man said. "Fuck what these assholes talking about. Send 'em to hell." Aaron shoved the butt of the gun into their hostage's ribcage, which brought him to his knees.

"Lyle!" A slightly African accented voice called out from the hallway. "You okay?"

"Yeah."

"He won't be in a few seconds if you don't cooperate," said Doug. "I know you may think you're lucky having killed off a few of us, but you all are still vastly outnumbered. We're going to get what we came for, whether you like it or not. But here's a chance to save your team and start over another day. Alive. Now answer my question. Is Chiedu Attah upstairs?" Silence for several beats as Aaron watched Mason and his other remaining comrades tense up like there was an aroma of anxiety in the room.

"I'm going to step forward," the voice finally announced. "Can we have an agreement of a cease-fire during that time?" Doug exchanged looks with Mason, Aaron, and the others. Everyone nodded affirmatively.

"You got a deal, Mr. Uzunma." The executive protection detail leader emerged at the living room end of the far hallway, still tucked in the corridor to give him the opportunity to fall back if need be. With his gas mask now removed, Aaron caught Yemi's attention.

"I've seen you before," Yemi called out to him. Aaron

made eye contact with the man he had battled with twice now. "You improved your tear gas recipe." Aaron couldn't help but smirk at Yemi's reminiscence of their shared history.

"Call him down, Mr. Uzunma," Doug said as he pointed his gun at Lyle's chin. "Let's not waste any more of our time here."

"Are you the one behind New Patriots?" asked Yemi. Doug returned a confused laugh in reaction to Yemi's casual tone amidst the stakes at hand.

"Bro," Doug said. "That shit isn't what it looks like, alright? Where's Chiedu?"

"The man you're holding at gunpoint helped put together a whole report on your group's activity." Doug raised his eyebrow in a 'the fuck?' manner.

"That's a lot of time on your hands," Doug said toward Lyle.

"He gets help from the guy upstairs."

———

"Upstairs? With the —" The New Patriot founder was repeatedly riddled with armor-piercing rounds through the floor above him. Yemi was keeping tabs on his position the whole time and relaying it back to Jasper. Yemi ducked back in the hallway as Mason's whole neck-to-head was shredded by Terry's rifle after he had shifted himself into the firing position.

"Lyle!" Yemi called while he took cover. There was no answer, so he couldn't be sure of his squad member's fate.

They took out a few in the living room, but another four entered the cabin.

"Yemi," Terry said to his commander as he reloaded. "I'm about to be on my last mag." Some shots from outside penetrate the walls of their current hallway.

"That's fine. Let's draw them in a bit. Choose shots carefully." By then, they all knew it was either protect Chiedu or die. Any negotiation on Attah's life for theirs was now clearly off the table. Another wave of bullets struck the hallway from the forest. A loud wince of pain emitted from Nick's position. Yemi and Terry saw that he had been hit in the outer area of the bicep.

"Fuck!" he yelled as he grabbed his fresh wound.

"Victor's down again!" Jasper communicated over the radio. "Checking on him in a second."

"Hang tight, Rice!" called out Terry. Terry quickly pivoted around the corner and managed to take down another one of the gunmen who were assaulting their side of the cabin. He then grabbed his nearby backpack and spun over to where Nick leaned against the wall. He whipped out the first aid kit and slammed it on Nick's chest. "Take out the gauze and apply as much pressure as possible. More than you think it needs. Step over here." Terry placed Nick in a relatively safe corner of the hallway to let him tend to himself. He then straddled his rifle and got back to his original station.

"He's alive," Jasper said over the radio. "But he's out of commission, Yemi. I'm running low on ammo as well. What are you thinking?"

"Whatever you do, do not allow anyone to get close to Chiedu's room. No matter the cost."

"You got it, my brother. Let's go to work." A member of the raiding opposition got bold and dipped from near the car to take cover by a couch closer to Yemi's hallway. The Raptor detail leader caught him in his crosshairs during his shuffle, and the large bearded man took multiple shots to his chest. He immediately succumbed to his injuries once his big body thudded to the hardwood floor. The man's nearby partner angrily cocked a semi-automatic rifle and unloaded back at the hallway.

No matter how low on ammo Yemi was, Aaron knew the firefight was taking far too much time. He had knocked Lyle unconscious with the butt of his gun and ran over his body into the kitchen to see if he could come across anything flammable. He stepped over Vash's corpse to grab a vase tucked on the window sill, and he quickly dumped out the plants with water. He scurried across the tiles and was able to pick up cooking oil, acetone, baking soda, as well as dish soap. He snatched a thin washcloth hanging near the fridge on a magnet. He turned the stove on before he shoved the rag into the vase, preparing a Molotov cocktail.

He eyed the front of the truck in the living room.

"Craig!" called out Aaron. "Pop open the hood a little more if you can."

"The truck?" yelled back Craig, another one of the men from the meeting in Southern Maryland. The sound of his voice hinted that he was bewildered at Aaron's request.

"Yes. Quickly!" Craig fired off a few shots toward Yemi and then backpedaled around the truck to get to the opposite side safely. The front had already taken damage, but Craig managed to crack open the rest of it. Almost like a football game, Craig flung the hood up like the center hiking the ball as Aaron ran past it to quarterback the cocktail into the engine. Everyone on their side immediately dipped out of the cabin as Lyle woke up and pushed himself up to stand.

———

"Yemi!" Lyle yelled out to his squad leader and into the radio. "Get back! The truck is gonna explode!" Lyle dove into the kitchen and took cover behind the walls as he glued himself to the tile floor. The fire encroached on the oil tank and battery.

BOOM! A burst of flames emitted from the Ford, launching the vehicle several inches in the air and causing even more destruction to the first floor of the cabin. Pieces of the wall in the kitchen fell on top of Lyle as debris was launched into the hallway with Yemi and the other EPT members. Splinters of wood and shrapnel stabbed Yemi and Terry throughout their bodies, causing them to temporarily drop to the floor. Nick didn't take any damage, but he was still tending to his original wound. A hail of bullets from outside followed the explosion, and the Raptor EPT felt truly overwhelmed without much ability to fire back. Clouds of smoke now began to fill the safe house from embers in the living room caused by the explosion. Their plan for victory had been changed into a game of survival.

"Jasper," Yemi said over the radio. "Help Victor up and prepare Cheidu for a rooftop evacuation."

"What about the snipers?" asked his right-hand man.

"They might not be able to get the south side of the roof in their scope. Either way, it's the only option at this point. He's a dead man if he steps outside until the rest of us secure the perimeter. When the South side of the forest is clear, help him down to us."

"Roger."

"Terry," Yemi called over to him. "You good?" The ex-cop ripped a piece of glass from his shoulder and got his rifle back in his grasp.

"Let's get the fuck up outta here."

"I hear you on you that." Yemi and Terry returned fire to their opposition besieging them. The heat from the flames only a dozen or so feet away from them was causing them to swelter in addition to the inhalation issues that the smoke threat was creating. Yemi could hear the sound of Lyle's SMG firing back and realized his comrade was able to arm himself again.

"Yemi," Lyle said through his blood-soaked radio receiver. "I'm going to exit through the back. It's too hot by the truck, obviously."

"Just stay alive, Lyle," said Yemi. "That's all I can ask for now." Yemi, Terry, and Nick were forced to the crawling position on the floor in the hallway. "Head toward the back," Yemi said to his immediate team.

Nick started as the lead as they crawled beneath the view of the hallway window, and shells penetrated the walls above their heads. At the end of their hallway, it turned right with two doors at the corner. Once Nick arrived at the wall's edge along the right side, he went to a crouch position and allowed Terry to peek around to see if any intruders had entered the safe house from the south side yet.

"Clear!" Terry said in an almost-rushed manner, given they were racing against the safe house burning down. All three got in the same stance as Nick as they headed down the new, smaller hall. Suddenly, a door to the left at the end of the new hall was kicked in. After the door fell down, the muzzle of an AK-47 turned the corner and blindly shot in their direction. The three responded with their weapons as they took cover at the opposite end of the hall, but Yemi felt a sharp pain at the right side of his head after he dove into a nearby small bathroom. The impact dizzied him for a moment, but the blur in his eyes sharpened and called out to his team.

"Blackwell, Rice. You good?"

"Yes, sir!"

"No injuries!"

"I got hit in my ear, but let's keep moving," Yemi said as he looked in a nearby cracked mirror above the sink that revealed that a gunshot had turned his ear into Evander Holyfield's during the second Tyson fight. "Blackwell!"

"Yes?"

"You got a pepper bomb left?"

"I don't, sir," responded Terry. Nick ripped a cylinder object from his utility belt.

"I do, though!" called Nick.

"Throw it. Now!" Yemi picked the perfect time to give the command. The AK-47's user returned to the spot and entered the hallway, but right at his foot level, he met a perfectly targeted toss of the pepper canister from Rice. The irritant mist hit the footsoldier right in the face, and Yemi annihilated his existence, his corpse collapsing to the outside. Nick stepped over and kicked the pepper bomb into the backyard in an attempt to push back any others trying to follow the same path. Terry took a tactical position by the door.

"Yemi! A few have arrived in the back."

"Jasper," Yemi spoke into the radio. "Hold off on getting to the roof if you can."

"Not much time, brother. My feet are getting warm from downstairs."

"Shit," Yemi muttered to himself as he took point behind Terry. They had to clear the backyard of any threats, but it was turning out to be one hell of a challenge given their limited ammo and the fury taking place in the living room that was spreading throughout the rest of the residence at a rapid pace. "Cover me," he said to Terry.

Taking a major but necessary risk, Yemi sprinted to the tree closest to the South side entrance. He was able to temporarily get to cover safely as Terry effectively sent back potential killers coming out of the woodwork with a few shots that hit bark and dirt. It became Yemi's turn to provide cover, and he took an angle at the corner of the tree toward a few hostiles that had joined from the front of the house. One exchanged shots with Yemi, and neither were able to really hit each other.

"Go!" yelled Yemi to Terry. Terry ran to another tree closer to the East side of the house and managed to dodge shots fired by the house raiders. Once Terry got in position, he took aim at their opposition, arriving at the other end of the backyard, and pulled the trigger. Yemi realized it wasn't safe for Nick to join them yet, as there were about five gunmen on the West side of the backyard. Tree bark around them went flying as automatic, and semiautomatic gunfire tried to take them out. Smoke rose from the cabin, seeping out the various windows.

"Yemi!" Nick panicked through the radio. "The fire has reached the hallway."

The EPT leader emptied his clip in the direction of their enemies. He managed to hit one of his adversaries in the right shoulder, temporarily disabling him. Yemi tossed his empty rifle and armed himself with his Glock.

"Go, go!" Nick bolted for Terry's portion of the forest. When he got within twelve feet, a shot went off, and Rice fell to the ground, wincing in pain, having just been hit in the thigh. Terry and Yemi returned fire to try and push back the attack on their young recruit. Nick let out an agonizing scream, and Yemi saw a bloody hole now present on Nick's tan boots. Terry ran forward while blasting away at the opposite end of the backyard.

"I got you!" Terry said as he ducked down and harnessed Nick around his shoulder. With one arm, Terry emptied the rest of his magazine toward the New Patriot alliance as he dragged Nick to safety behind the tree. Like Yemi, Terry ditched his empty rifle and switched to his handgun. He spun 180 degrees to check the east side of the cabin. He spotted two gunmen attempting to flank them, shifting through the trees. Terry fired his pistol in their direction, and now the shootout had expanded to both sides of the backyard, the EPT getting encroached by both angles.

"Yemi!" called Karen over the radio. "What's your status?" He sighed loudly as he took shots toward the black kid he remembered from Silver Spring. None of the shots hit their intended target, the pistol not having nearly the same accuracy as his Spear.

"Taking heavy fire. Terry and I are down to our sidearms. Rice is down, but he's breathing." A shell hit the tree only inches away from Yemi's face, and the bark splintered onto his face. When he flinched from the shot, a bullet nailed Yemi in the upper right arm. Yemi cursed to himself as he ducked lower behind the tree to cover himself from more gunfire. However, the raid party continued to push into the backyard, further decreasing the likelihood that Chiedu was going to have a clear landing for his evacuation.

"Boss," Jasper said over the radio. "We gotta make a move."

"Hold, Jasper!" Yemi fired off his Glock, and he finally managed to hit a member of the raid party in the chest area, and it sent the gunman to the ground.

"Craig!" yelled the voice of the creator of the tear gas grenades to their downed comrade. Yemi couldn't pinpoint his position.

"Terry!" Yemi called out to his fellow field agent.

"Yeah?" Terry said as he also managed to take out another gunman, leaving him 1-on-1 with an armed militant on the west side of the backyard.

"Your side secure?"

"Secure as it's gonna be."

"I'll help him," Lyle said over the radio. SMG bullets started to hit Terry's adversary from the side of the house. Yemi figured Lyle must have found a way safely out of the kitchen.

"Okay. Jasper. Get the ambassador out of there!"

"Copy." Just as Yemi raised his pistol again, a hole was blasted through his palm. The Glock fell to the ground. He fought through the pain of severed nerves going wild, but the teargas engineer ran over to kick away the pistol. The kid smacked Yemi in the face with the butt of his rifle and then grabbed the receiver on his chest.

"Your commander is down," the young man said into the radio. "Either bring Chiedu out now or burn with the house." The rest of the EPT squad, including Karen, were completely speechless. Out of range from any support from Terry, Yemi and the kid made eye contact.

"What's your name?" There was a pause.

"Aaron."

"How old are you, Aaron?" asked Yemi, getting a good look at the youth who had been his primary adversary since his first executive protection mission.

"Nineteen." Yemi grinned and shook his head.

"You could be my illegitimate son. Sheesh." Aaron went silent again. It was hitting Yemi that they were on opposing forces, yet they were both fighting for a bounty.

"I killed one of your friends in Silver Spring, didn't I?" asked Yemi. Bringing up history didn't seem to emit any different emotion out of Aaron.

"You know what's crazy?" said Aaron. Yemi was in slight disbelief that they were carrying on a conversation. It seemed Aaron felt the same way.

"If I finished high school and avoided that bullshit last year, I might have applied to work for you," Aaron said. Yemi smirked, and he looked past Aaron toward the roof. A hatch popped open, and Yemi assumed that it was Jasper beginning the evacuation process. Cheidu was going to land right in the middle of multiple guns pointed in his direction, but there were no other alternative scenarios at that point of the house fire.

"We're still hiring if you're interested." Aaron chuckled at the job offer as fellow members of his raid party joined him in the backyard.

"I'll keep my options open." Aaron raised his rifle and put Yemi's forehead in his crosshair.

"Shit!" yelled one of the gunmen in the background. Aaron turned to see another one of his comrades was a bleeding corpse on the ground. A mystery shot took out another gunman as he fell like a building demolition. Aaron leapt to a nearby tree to take cover from wherever this new assault was coming from. The sound of a helicopter came from a distance over the nearby river. Yemi watched a piece of pine splinter off near Aaron's face.

"Yemi!" Karen verbalized over the radio. "What's going on?"

"I don't know yet, but I think we have reinforcements." With his healthy hand, Yemi dug out his cell phone to use as a form of long-distance binoculars. When he zoomed in hundreds of yards into the forest from their position, he spotted heavily armed masked men in blue combat fatigues approaching their position.

———

Aaron and the last remaining New Patriot on that side of the house saw the incoming threat. He spun 180 degrees and could even see that there was another troop of combatants approaching from the South side of the forest. The two fired off in both directions, but within a few moments, Aaron's brother-in-arms had his head blasted open from a sniper shot. Aaron realized whoever this was that was crashing the raid had probably already discovered their own sharpshooters, taking away any long-range advantage the New Patriots may have had. He looked to his left to spot two of Chiedu's bodyguards arriving on the roof. Despite being injured, one of them helped Chiedu up the ladder as the other scanned the entire backyard for hostiles. He fired in Aaron's direction. Aaron couldn't get a solid shot off with all the different risks that now surrounded him. As the blue fatigues got closer, he realized he was going to have to make the same dreaded decision he did at Veterans Plaza.

Aaron threw his 3D-printed rifle to the side and sprinted down the hill toward the river. Gunshots hit the trees behind him as he ran past them, but nothing made contact with his body. All the events of the previous year flashed in his head as he made the run for his life. Losing Qasim, Doug, Bobby Z, and then seeing his friend Danny behind bars. A fate he would find himself in if he couldn't get across the cold North River waters fast enough.

When he got right to the shore and dove into the freezing stream, two boats whipped around the turn of the waterway and went straight for Aaron's destination. He tried to paddle back to the shore.

"Police! Don't move!" commanded an officer over a megahorn. The two olive-colored boats pulled up by him. An emblem for West Virginia Natural Resources Police branded its side. Aaron realizes he didn't have much of a choice then but to obey the commands. He stopped paddling and waded in the river. The boats' motors shut off, and half a dozen officers between the two seacrafts had Aaron blocked from all angles. The face of Danny rising out of that chair across from him during the last conjugal visit was burned into his head. He wondered if his fate would be the same when he would go into custody. But Aaron reminded himself even in this situation, it's about who thinks in the next five minutes versus the next five years. An opportunity would present itself to get him back to freedom. He would just have to keep his eye open.

———

With multiple wounds but no more hostiles in his immediate area, Yemi laid back against the tree to inhale and exhale for as long as he could.

"My side is clear," said Terry through the radio.

"I think we got it done, boys," Jasper communicated.

"Yemi," Karen stated. "Are you alright?" Yemi had closed his eyes, almost getting ready for a nap, but his sister woke him up.

"When medevac arrives, have them get me last. Get Rice and Evans checked first."

"How many times were you hit?" asked his sister.

"Enough to where I'm not moving. Jasper, get Chiedu down, and everybody else, just hold your position until whoever just saved our ass gets here." The blue fatigues reached the perimeter of the safe house. Yemi's eyelids started to flutter, darkness fading in and out of his consciousness.

"Yemi!" a familiar voice called out to him from the side of the burning house. Detail Leader Uzunma looked up, and he made eye contact with a fully armed and outfitted Kirk Fitzgerald. The letters 'DMRT' were stitched to the top of his hat, as well as a patch on the front of his tactical vest. Kirk slung his modified M4 assault rifle to the side, and he went to scoop Yemi to help stand him up. "The calvary is here, my friend."

"T-t-t..." The blood loss was having an effect on his speech. "Titus?"

"We'll explain everything later." As he got shouldered by Kirk, Yemi caught a glimpse of other DMRT operators assisting Jasper and Victor in securing Chiedu on the ground. "The ambassador is safe now. Let's get you out of this hell hole."

In the span of thirty minutes, the Digital Market Reaction Team secured every point of the burning cabin as they waved down for the helicopter to land in the backyard.

"It's just you guys?" Yemi managed to ask.

"State Police's tactical unit is patrolling the perimeter a few hundred yards out," said Kirk. "Behind them are other state troopers, county police, and Natural Resources. Nobody's getting away, don't worry." Chiedu and the whole EPT boarded the helicopter while being escorted by Kirk and a couple of other DMRT members. Yemi leaned over to Kirk.

"Nobody federal?"

"Not on site, no."

"What about the Secret Service?" Yemi's perception was fractured, but he couldn't help but feel a bit confused at no mention or hint of Chris Towers. Kirk sighed and exhaled.

"Just rest up, Yemi."

CHAPTER 24

"Federal police! Search warrant!" the lead special agent yelled throughout the upscale Chevy Chase, Maryland, home as his Special Response Team unit burst through the door. A chocolate lab barked at the highest octave possible from the mid-20th century built dining room that was immediately to the left. A middle-aged Filipino woman with a toddler in one hand grabbed the canine with her free hand, stopping one of the agents from sending the dog to heaven.

"Where is he?" demanded the commanding officer. The petrified woman paused for a moment.

"M-m-my husband?"

"Yes!"

"Upstairs." She gulped as she eyed their vests that spelled out 'POLICE HOMELAND SECURITY INVESTIGATIONS' on the backs of the agents who were facing the opposite direction. "To the right."

"Go, go!" Four HSI agents quickly began to march up the stairwell that was right before the front entrance. They stacked up by the door to the right, as pointed out by the woman downstairs. The special agent in charge balled his fist and knocked on the fiberglass four hard times.

"Towers," the man said. "You know why we're here. Open up so we can end this peacefully." No immediate answer. He motioned for one of his officers to step forward. The fourth man took out an opti-wand camera device and snaked it underneath the doorframe.

"He's armed, sir."

"Put the gun down, Chris. You can still have a life and be

able to see your daughter if you cooperate." Just more silence. The lead agent waved again for the squad to take action. The agent with the opti-wand switched to a breaching shotgun that was strapped around his back. A loud bang and the four-man law enforcement crew barged in, and all gun barrels pointed directly at the face of Chris Towers. He was sober and looked up from the desk with a revolver in his hand toward his former fellow DHS officers. He stared past them into oblivion as they repeatedly barked orders at him to take his hand away from the pistol.

"When the journalists arrive and ask for my last word," says Chris.

"Towers, don't—"

"Tell them I said..." A semi smile with some dark undertones forms on Chris' face. "Pam."

"PAM?" asked the lead agent with Towers' cranium at the center of his iron sights.

"Yes, pam. P-A-M. That's who was giving me orders." The lead agent paused.

"Orders to do what, Towers?"

"To protect our country and its allies, of course." Towers jolted with the pistol to his head. The four M4 carbines pointed in his direction beat Towers' trigger finger, and the former Secret Service agent became a pinata for bullets.

———

Finally waking and laying there in the hospital bed, mummied in his left arm, foot, and lower body, Nick couldn't move much, but his mind was trying to recall the last time he had a medical emergency. He thought there may have been one after he overdosed on Adderall his freshman year after the Taneka revelation with the two football players. But, alas, he couldn't think of another. And he really just wanted to stop thinking, in general, to focus on getting some liquids in. He reached for the orange juice with his less-injured arm and snatched it up to gulp it down. A get-well card was next to it. While drinking his OJ, he opened it up to read that it was signed by his mother, father, and older sister. They must have stopped in while he was still incapacitated. He tried to occupy his mind with the daytime television revolving around paternity testing six different potential baby daddies. It seemed to work as laughing at the mother, unable to figure out which of her multiple sexual partners was the father of her child, distracted his mind from the PTSD from the firefight the previous day. A nurse popped her head in.

"Mr. Rice?"

"Yes?"

"You have a visitor." He wondered which of his family members had returned.

"Send them in." Within a few moments, the tall, lanky Abdallah walked in with a plain back hoodie and blue jeans, dressed in an outfit that fit his mold as the hacker-journalist hybrid.

"The hoodie fits you," Nick said. "Where'd you decide to put your dragon tattoo?" Abdallah laughed and shook his head.

"How you hanging in there, bro?" asked Abdallah as he leaned over to fist-bump Nick.

"Hanging on by a thread," Nick says. "But I'm alive. Life experiences have told me to appreciate these moments."

"Life experiences? Care to elaborate?"

"Another time, my friend." Nick sighed, trying to forget that dark period during his first year in college. It was a miracle none of those psychiatric evaluations prevented him from joining Morgan State University Police. "Another time."

"Understandable."

"How are things at that uh... That new place?"

"The Boukan? Well, that's one of the reasons I'm here."

"Oh, I thought it was because we were friends, and you

were worried about my health."

"Well, of course—"

"I'm just messing with you, Abdallah," laughed Nick as he straightened out his body on the cot. "Go on."

"The only thing from yesterday and today that has made the news is Chris Towers."

"Towers?" asked Nick. "Why does that name sound familiar?"

"Secret Service. He was in charge of the DC chapter of the Cyber Fraud Task Force."

"Was? What happened?" Abdallah took a breath.

"Apparently, he was relaying intel back to the Anat Network since the inception of the Bazaar. And he got paid pretty damn well for it."

"The fuck?!"

"Right? They're already calling it one of the biggest internal scandals in the history of homeland security."

"So the attack in West Virginia was orchestrated by him?"

"Orchestrated? Don't think that was his role," said Abdallah. "No news outlet knows anything about the shootout yet anyways, but as an inside source." Abdallah leaned in to speak lower. "I'll just say that he was the overseer to make sure it went smoothly. And I'm sorry to reveal this to you, but it was me he got the intel from." Nick was speechless for a moment.

"Abdallah, multiple people were killed, not to mention I almost fucking died myself."

"You think I gave it to him willingly? He broke into my place and held me at gunpoint. I had no choice. But I went anon and notified his superiors as soon as I could." Nick sighed loudly and looked straight up to the ceiling. "But look. I came here with a silver lining. I proposed doing a whole profile on you for The Boukan, and they love the idea."

"Wait, what?"

"Yeah, man. This isn't like Al Noor at all. They're giving me free reign and eating anything I dish out. I pitched you as a young, black security professional on the frontline of the Bazaar phenomenon, and Eric Money in the Bank McKenzie himself said he may want a series if he likes the first article. He's even willing to hire a full production crew to follow you around for a day at the Raptor offices." The options swirled around in Nick's head for a moment.

"Could Towers be pinned back to me?"

"No." The joy of delivering the news slightly faded from Abdallah's face, but Nick knew he understood his concern. "Your name or anything is not attached to any of the files. Trust me, you're good." Nick breathed a sigh of relief, even though his suspicions wouldn't be over until he got confirmation. But either way, he had to make a decision on Abdallah's offer.

"Let me think about it. I also have to ask Yemi or Karen, and I think they may have a lot on their plate over the next few weeks."

"Cool, cool." Abdallah picked up Nick's phone from the ground beneath the bed and placed it on the small table next to Nick. "I guess this fell down."

"Thanks, man."

"You need anything from the cafeteria or whatever?"

"Uh." Nick paused for a moment. "You know what, could you see if they have pop-tarts?" Abdallah laughed and nodded.

"You don't want some toast or eggs? You know, something that was actually cooked, not re-heated after being processed?"

"Man, leave me alone. I cook all the time."

"Oh, that reminds me," Abdallah said as he stood by the doorway. "Before he was killed, Towers told the agents to tell the press that his last word was 'Pam.'"

"PAM? Like the cooking spray?"

"Yeah. Any idea what that could mean?" Even though

his upper body ached, Nick managed to tense his muscles up to generate a shrug.

"PAM... Oil... Popco? The Middle East?"

"What? You think he's the riddler or some shit?"

"I don't know! You asked me, acting like I'm a retired FBI profiler or something."

"You do give off Spencer from Criminal Minds vibes sometimes, not going to lie."

"Man, get your bitch ass out my room," laughed Nick.

"Alright, alright. Just focus on healing up, fam. We'll rendezvous a week or two or whenever you get healed up after your discharge. No rush on anything." The two dapped hands again.

"Peace, Abdallah." Kalfat headed out the door. Nick breathed in and out. He tapped on his phone to light the screen up but then decided to drop it back on the table before he read any messages. While he had an excuse to unplug from the world around him, he was going to take advantage of it.

———

Yemi didn't think he'd ever be back in the Titus building, let alone anywhere close to Tysons Corner again unless it involved a new potential client. But there he was, arm in a sling, walking through the newly added DMRT offices on the fourth floor with his old boss. Yemi looked at all the framed pictures of U.S. special operations members on various combat duties throughout the globe, with stills from Colombia, the Philippines, Niger, Libya, Iraq, Afghanistan, and others.

"Have you talked with Van Zandt yet?" asked Kirk. Yemi eyed a particular photo that depicted a youthful Kirk with a full head of hair flanked by four of his fellow Army Rangers in front of the tomb of Ahmad Shah Durrani in Kandahar.

"Francine? No. But, Chiedu informed us that it was her who had subcontracted you all without our knowledge."

"I know we're competitors now. But I don't want you to think I was trying to undermine you."

"Accusing the person who saved your life of trying to undermine seems pretty damn petty if you ask me." Kirk grinned and patted his former employee on the back.

"So look, I'm just going to jump straight to it. The Joint Terrorism Task Force bricked their pants after the Towers revelation. They don't want anybody from CFTF involved with the Bazaar, and they're even suspending the Secret Service from all meetings until the Towers trial runs its course. Instead, Homeland Security Investigations is taking over as the primary federal law enforcement agency tasked with all Bazaar-related crimes, and after the situation in West Virginia, they want to create a private-public partnership between the government and executive protection firms in the D.C. area. And they want me to lead that effort." Yemi nodded his head, seeing where Kirk was heading in this conversation. He wasn't particularly a fan of the direction. "If you don't wish to join me at Titus, I understand. But this may be an opportunity that can benefit everybody. I honestly don't even see any drawbacks."

"Any time there's a public and private partnership," Yemi said. "It usually ends up in a conspiracy against the public."

"Explain."

"Just read Wealth of Nations." The two walked for a few more beats as Kirk's impatience grew. "Adam Smith explains it better than I ever could."

"I'm lost here. What is your answer? You're not interested in Raptor joining the J-T-T-F?"

"Congratulations on your new position, Kirk," Yemi said as he shook the man's hands, dodging the question and failing to provide an answer.

"Come on, Yemi. Don't jerk me around. This is an opportunity that can define your whole legacy. We both know

RexCorp took a hit, but it's only a matter of time before they bounce back. It'll just be them and Titus getting the contracts as the Feds crack down on potential hits."

"Karen and Jasper are waiting at the food court at Galleria for me," he said, still refusing to give Kirk a straight 'yes' or 'no.' "It was great being back here. DMRT is going to change the game. I just know it." Kirk sighed, realizing he was defeated in trying to win over one of his favorite consultants.

"I hope you realize I'm always on your team," he stated as he shook Yemi's hand goodbye. "But until then, you and Karen keep on taking Raptor to new heights. I'll always be here to back you up when needed."

"We'll be fine, but it's appreciated, Mr. Fitzgerald." Yemi headed to the elevator.

———

He left the entrance of Titus HQ and walked down the pristine, clean streets toward Tyson Galleria, the far more upscale shopping center than Tysons Corner Center across from it. He didn't answer Kirk for a reason. Yemi's instinct always told him to be weary of state-bred bureaucracy, the exact type of relationship that the public-private partnership Kirk spoke of seemed to invite. But maybe Karen would convince him to join, and he wondered if it could expand their firm to another level. He looked at the skyscrapers of the Dulles Technology Corridor that were stories taller than any building in the nation's capital, and he started to imagine if Raptor could itself turn into one of the beltway dinosaurs fattening their profit margins from legislation guaranteeing their sales. But just like the ancient reptiles, some of those business models were due for extinction if the bubble couldn't be sustained. And Yemi had to make a decision on whether Raptor would evolve into a more efficient predator that would spread its wings to soar higher than Titus, RexCorp, or any of their so-called competition.

A lifelong fiction writer, Miles turned to penning novels after nearly a decade editing television in the D.C. area for platforms including NBC Sports Washington, theGrio, and the Federal Network. He has had an obsession with the effects technology has on society since being raised by a father who was a computer programmer and a mother in workforce development. He still pursues filmmaking in between books and finds that writing in the technothriller genre only enhances that passion even more. Miles is an active member of International Thriller Writers where his first book, Bazaar, was selected for their Debut Authors Program. He attends monthly meetings for the writers' group Novels in Progress DC.

Website: https://thebazaarverse.com/